Elizabet... heroines ...

... ts and a
... into the minds
... igations and onto
... age. Elizabeth graduated
... Michigan with a degree in English

... member of International Thriller
Dylid dych ... mance Writers of America. Visit Elizabeth
y d... ethneiter.com

**The item should be r...
by the last date...**

USA TODAY bestselling author **Barb Han** lives in north
Texas with her very own hero-worthy husband, three
beautiful children, a spunky golden retriever/standard
poodle mix and too many books in her to-read pile. In
her downtime, she plays video games and spends much
of her time on or around a basketball court. She loves
interacting with readers and is grateful for their support.
You can reach her at barbhan.com

Also by Elizabeth Heiter

Also by Barb Han

Discover more at millsandboon.co.uk

SNIFFING OUT DANGER

ELIZABETH HEITER

UNDERCOVER COUPLE

BARB HAN

MILLS & BOON

First Published in Great Britain 2022
by Mills & Boon, an imprint of HarperCollins*Publishers* Ltd
1 London Bridge Street, London, SE1 9GF

www.harpercollins.co.uk

HarperCollins*Publishers*
1st Floor, Watermarque Building,
Ringsend Road, Dublin 4, Ireland

Sniffing Out Danger © 2022 Harlequin Enterprises ULC
Undercover Couple © 2022 Barb Han

Special thanks and acknowledgement are given to Elizabeth Heiter for her contribution to the *K-9s on Patrol* series.

ISBN: 978-0-263-30337-7

0422

MIX
Paper from
responsible sources
FSC™ C007454

This book is produced from independently certified FSC™
paper to ensure responsible forest management.

For more information visit: www.harpercollins.co.uk/green

Printed and Bound in Spain using 100% Renewable electricity at
CPI Black Print, Barcelona

SNIFFING OUT DANGER

ELIZABETH HEITER

This book is for my niece and nephews, Kalan, Will and Miles, who are constant examples of what it means to be generous, kind and curious. They inspire me every single day as they create their own life stories.

Chapter One

She hadn't moved almost two thousand miles for *this*.

Ava Callan gritted her teeth as she climbed out of her modified patrol car and opened the door for her four-legged partner. Her gaze darted up, to the picturesque mountains in the distance, then back down, to the overgrown grass in front of her. Ahead was a line of concealing trees, and a little box house peeking through with its peeling paint and shuttered windows. The man who'd chosen to live on this big patch of land on the outskirts of Jasper, Idaho, wanted to be left alone by everyone. Especially the police.

Ava tapped her leg and Lacey, the two-year-old German shepherd she'd been paired with instead of a human partner, leaped to the ground.

Lacey's ears were perked, her nose in the air as she looked around, then up at Ava.

"Let's do this," Ava said, advancing slowly toward the house, her gaze on pivot as Lacey sniffed the ground.

Harold Bingsley, the man she'd been asked to do a wellness check on, had a history of methamphetamine use. Although Ava and Lacey had only recently finished training together, Lacey had already started her training as a drug detection K-9 before Ava even left Chicago for this thousand-times smaller town.

This police call was routine and low-risk, but five years

of working patrol and then narcotics in Chicago had taught her that no call was without the potential for danger. Letting her guard down was never an option. Not even here.

She'd parked on the street, mostly out of sight from the house, in case Harold was high, in case the sight of a police car gave him anxiety. According to his younger sister, who'd called from Oregon, he hadn't picked up his phone in a week. Maybe he was just angry with her for trying to convince him to move near family. *An endless argument*, she'd called it. But he didn't have any friends, and since he'd gotten clean, he had no one to visit. So, she didn't want to take the chance that he was hurt or sick and alone.

The slow trek along the dirt road toward the driveway was a far cry from Ava's last call out in Chicago. That had been a multi-agency raid on an illegal drug processing warehouse. She'd rushed in after SWAT had cleared it, enjoyed the congratulatory handshakes from a slew of federal agents on the work she'd done for the task force. Five months of her life had been dedicated to that bust. It had been her ticket to bigger and better things inside the Chicago PD. Instead of claiming them, she'd returned to the precinct and handed over her gun and badge.

There was a sudden tightness in the vicinity of her heart as she remembered her chief's frown, and the question he'd asked one more time. "Are you sure this is what you want?"

Shaking the memories loose, she focused on her surroundings. Beyond the couple of acres where Harold's house stood, the street was mostly commercial. Or at least, it had been at one time. Now, abandoned warehouses clogged the otherwise beautiful view, the exteriors slowly crumbling.

A beautiful May Saturday and Harold was presumably holed up inside instead of enjoying the cute little downtown. Not that there were a lot of entertainment options in Jasper, but he could have driven out to Salmon River, gone swimming or spread a picnic by the water now that it had finally started to warm up.

If she wasn't working, that's probably where Ava would have been. Pictures of the serene mountains and the river, so different from Chicago's constant hustle, had lured her here. That and the charming little downtown, framed by those towering mountains, had made her wire a security deposit for the house she'd rented, sight unseen.

She'd been determined to see the move as an adventure instead of a defeat. Three months later, that optimism was harder to come by, even if Jasper's natural beauty was better in person.

Skirting the rusted sedan and the motorcycle on its side on the long gravel driveway, Ava walked up to Harold's front door. She kept one hand near her holster as she watched Lacey.

The dog stopped beside her, staring up at her with intelligent brown eyes. But she didn't sit. Which meant that so far, she hadn't alerted on any drugs.

Nudging Lacey away from the door, Ava stood off to the side she keyed her radio and announced, "I've arrived at the Bingsley residence."

"Good luck," the cheerful voice of Jenny Dix, Jasper PD's only dispatch, came back.

Ava rolled her eyes. *Luck* would have been being sent to a real situation. Wellness checks ranked up there with parade duty. *Luck* would have been landing in a town where they appreciated her years of experience, where she actually fit in. Instead, she'd been given a K-9 and rookie duty. On the occasions when she tried to join the other officers after-hours at the local brewery, she'd always given up on feeling like part of something and gone home early.

Really, *luck* would have been not needing to leave Chicago in the first place. Her hand twitched toward the locket she wore under her uniform, with the photos of the family who had never supported her career choice. Family who was all lost to her now, for one reason or another.

Focus, Ava reminded herself. She'd made her choice. This was her fresh start and if she wanted it to work for her, she needed to work for it.

If that meant starting back at the beginning with everything—her career, her friendships, her sense of belonging—so be it.

Squaring her shoulders, she knocked on the door and infused her voice with friendly authority. "Mr. Bingsley? This is Officer Callan, Jasper Police. Your sister called us to make sure you were okay."

She listened carefully, ready to go for a weapon—lethal or otherwise—if he came out armed. He wasn't licensed to own a gun, but he'd been arrested with one in the past.

She heard nothing from inside, so she knocked again, a little louder this time. "Mr. Bingsley? I need to confirm you're okay or I'm going to come in to check on you."

Still nothing.

Holding in a sigh, and hoping she wasn't about to find forty-five-year-old Harold Bingsley dead, she positioned herself to kick in the door. A jolt of adrenaline hit, this simple forced entry the closest she'd come to the anticipation and anxiety of a drug raid since leaving Chicago.

The laugh stalled in her throat as the door ripped open and Harold lurched through it, his pale skin tinged gray and the pistol in his hand shaking violently.

Ava's gun was bracketed in her hands before she'd even consciously thought to reach for it. She slid in front of Lacey, who was trained to detect, not to attack and apprehend. Her heartbeat crescendoed, but she kept her voice steady and calm. "I'm here to help you. Put the gun down."

The gun in Harold's hand bounced rapidly up and down as he swiveled it toward her.

Her arms tensed, her finger tight against the trigger she didn't want to pull. "Harold, your sister thought you might be sick. That's it. You're not in trouble. Okay? Put the gun down."

His gaze darted around, not sticking on anything. His free hand reached up and started scratching at his face, leaving behind deep red gouges. The gun continued to bounce in his other hand, his finger inching closer to the trigger.

Ava held in a curse. He was definitely high. Which probably meant paranoid. It definitely meant dangerous.

She kept her voice calm and even, kept her feet planted solidly in front of Lacey, shielding her. "Harold, I need you to drop that gun before you hurt yourself, okay?"

His gaze skipped to the gun and he frowned, like he hadn't been aware he was holding it. He stared at it a long moment, his trigger finger jerking back and forth, almost nudging the trigger, then pulling away.

Ava locked her shoulders, kept her own trigger finger poised, ready to depress, wishing she was wearing a vest.

Harold yanked the gun up and Ava warned, "No!" as her finger started to tighten.

Then, he flung the gun aside into the long grass and darted away from the house, his gait uneven and clumsy.

Tucking her weapon into its holster, Ava ran after him. He was a good four inches taller than her 5'7", a solid fifty pounds heavier than her hundred and fortyish. But he was also seventeen years older and in much worse shape. Plus, she had training and momentum on her side as she pushed off and tackled him, landing hard on his back.

Before he could recover, she yanked his hands behind his

back and cuffed him, then patted him down for additional weapons as he muttered nonsense into the grass.

Keying her radio, Ava said, "I'm bringing Bingsley in. He pulled a weapon on me."

Jenny's response was lost under Ava's curse as Lacey went bounding past them, toward the abandoned warehouses.

"Lacey!"

The dog glanced back, barked once and kept going.

Yanking Harold to his feet, Ava pulled him along with her, following her K-9. Had Lacey scented on something? She hadn't at the house, but obviously Harold had had drugs to consume. Maybe he was keeping them in one of the abandoned buildings.

Ava picked up her pace to a slow jog as Harold stumbled along beside her and Lacey's lead increased.

At the entrance to the first warehouse—a massive building with cracked windows and some graffiti that reached a third of the way up the wall—Lacey sat. An alert that she'd found something.

Ava's heartbeat picked up again, anticipation at the slim possibility of getting a real case. Probably Lacey had just found Harold's extra stash. But maybe it was something bigger, a hiding spot for a distributor. "Good girl," she told the dog as she finally caught up.

Lacey glanced back at her, tail wagging, and Ava paused to pat her head.

This was the first time Lacey had alerted on something with Ava outside of practice, but unlike some K-9s who wanted treats or toys, Lacey's favored reward was a good ear scratch.

Checking her surroundings for any sign of people, any sign that this place wasn't actually abandoned, Ava keyed her radio again. Softly, she said, "Lacey alerted at the warehouse beside Bingsley's house. I'm going to check it out."

"Let me know if you need backup," Jenny's voice came back immediately.

"I'm good for now," Ava said, testing the door handle. It opened easily with a loud, high-pitched creak that made Ava cringe.

She spared a glance at Harold, who was using his shoulder to rub at his face where he'd scratched it earlier. "Is anyone in there?"

He just shrugged, but she wasn't sure if it was an answer or more scratching.

"Stay," she told Lacey as she peeked carefully inside.

Light streamed in through the damaged windows, illuminating layers of dust and abandoned machinery whose purpose Ava couldn't guess at. There were tracks in the dust in places, and a few abandoned beer bottles and other trash scattered on the floor, but the otherwise wide-open space looked clear and empty.

Easing the door open farther, Ava pushed Harold against the exterior wall and warned, "Don't move." Then she stepped slightly inside—not far enough that she couldn't chase after Harold if he took off, but enough to get a better look.

What she saw made her freeze, goose bumps rising across all of her exposed skin.

She backed out slowly, her hand already keying the radio, her breathing coming too fast.

Lacey hadn't alerted on drugs. She'd found a bomb.

Chapter Two

"Jasper PD just found a bomb. They need you on site now."

The Chief's words made Eli Thorne's pulse pick up. His hometown of McCall wasn't large. Even when tourists swelled it to more than double its population, he was more likely to get called to break up a bar fight than to defuse an explosive device. When he'd first gotten his certification from the FBI's Hazardous Devices School, his chief had thought he was wasting everyone's time.

That had changed quickly last year, during the packed tourist season, when someone had planted a bomb at Little Ski Hill and nearly destroyed one of their best winter attractions. Not to mention that there hadn't been enough time to evacuate everyone before Eli defused the bomb.

Eli stood at his desk, already planning the best route to get to Jasper, running through the steps he'd take when he arrived. "What do we know?"

"Not much. Just an address. Dispatch will get it to you when you're en route."

"On it!" He raced out to his police SUV, flipped on his lights and sirens and peeled out of the station.

Jasper, Idaho, was an hour north of McCall, but like most of the little towns peppering northern Idaho, they didn't have their own explosives expert. That meant Eli was on loan whenever someone uttered the word *explosive*.

Most of the time, the calls turned out to be false alarms; it was surprising the things people could mistake for a bomb. But if there was a real threat, an hour was a long time to wait. If the bomb was live, that time could mean the difference between life and death.

Eli punched down on the gas harder as he hooked around scenic Payette Lake, a lure for tourists and locals alike, and jumped onto US-95 North. He was ready for anything, with the back of his vehicle full of equipment he'd acquired slowly over the years after he'd gotten certified as an explosives expert. Equipment that had gotten a nice upgrade after his actions at the ski hill had helped him earn a promotion to captain.

At thirty-three, he was the youngest captain on the Mc-Call police force. He wasn't stopping there. He loved his job, loved his community and planned to stay on the force until his knees or his back went to hell and he had to retire.

Hopefully, he had more than thirty years to go.

With a grin, Eli whipped around a guy in a Corvette who was ignoring the speed limit. The guy did a double take as he spotted Eli's police vehicle and slowed down.

As Eli got out in front of all the other vehicles, he pushed his SUV a little harder, making it to Jasper in forty-two minutes. There, he slowed way down, maneuvering carefully around cars and people strolling and enjoying the small downtown. He headed to the far side of town, one of the few places in Jasper where the buildings were eyesores instead of oozing with old-fashioned charm.

A pair of police cruisers blocked the road, but one of them backed up to let him through before he could lean out the window and ask. More cruisers blocked off the far end of the street, with nothing but a dilapidated house and clearly abandoned warehouses in between.

Eli parked as close to the warehouse as he dared. Most

of the officers were keeping the perimeter clear, but one stood on the street across from the warehouse with a K-9 at her side.

She looked a few years younger than him with light brown skin, curly dark brown hair pulled into a high bun and a tight set to her mouth. The German shepherd beside her looked friendlier with a tail wag as soon as he hopped out of his vehicle.

"Eli Thorne?" the woman asked, her tone as serious as her expression with a little annoyance thrown in.

He was used to people being grateful when he arrived. Sparing her another quick glance, and wondering if it was him she had a problem with or just life, he hurried to the back of his vehicle and popped open the door. "That's me. What have you got?"

"I'm Officer Ava Callan," she said, peering into his open vehicle, curiosity on her face.

The dark tinted windows hid his expensive gear, allowing him to keep it ready to go at all times. As he pulled aside the tarp, there was an impressive array of equipment, including his bomb suit, tactical kit and his bomb-disposal robot with assorted attachments, controller and monitor.

"I had a prisoner with me when I spotted the device, so I didn't get close enough for a good look," Ava told him, her tone serious, her gaze skimming his equipment. "Lacey here alerted at the door."

The German shepherd wagged her tail at the mention of her name and Ava absently scratched the dog's ear.

"Technically, she's a drug-detection dog. Or at least that was my plan. More need than bomb detection. But she had some brief training with explosives before I started working with her. Good thing, too."

As she spoke, Eli carefully lifted his bomb-disposal robot and set it on the ground with a grunt. It was midsize, meaning that when the arm and claw weren't extended, it just barely fit inside his SUV. It was also heavy at a hundred and fifty pounds. The cost had been donated to the department and if he dropped the thing, they wouldn't be able to afford a new one. But it was worth every penny; a sophisticated machine that rolled on twin tracks and could climb stairs, open doors and lift up to seventy-five pounds.

He left his bomb suit in the vehicle for now. It was heavy and awkward, and hopefully wouldn't be needed. More often than not, bomb calls were false alarms. Last week, he'd suited up only to discover a series of toilet paper tubes wrapped in duct tape and wires and topped with a watch at the McCall high school.

Whenever possible, the robot was better than the suit, anyway. It was a luxury he'd only come by recently and as he set it up, Ava stared.

"From the doorway, what was in that warehouse sure looks like a bomb," Ava continued, more of that same tempered annoyance in her tone.

Directed at him for not arriving faster or not giving her more of his attention? Or because of the other officers, all keeping their distance securing the scene, no one volunteering to stand guard at the warehouse with her? Knowing the department as well as he did, Eli didn't think it was because of fear. For whatever reason, Ava didn't fit in here.

"I didn't want to go near it. My background is in narcotics."

He shot her a surprised glance as he turned on the controller and started maneuvering the robot toward the warehouse. He knew most of the officers in Jasper, but he'd definitely never met one with a narcotics background. And with or without the attitude, he would have remembered her.

If she ever smiled, he had a feeling she'd be a heartbreaker. In this job, maybe that was why she didn't.

"I don't have experience with explosives," Ava finished, sounding slightly embarrassed by that fact.

"That's why I'm here," he assured her as he worked the controls, the movements like muscle memory now that he'd been using the robot for a few months.

The robot glided toward the warehouse at three miles an hour, pushing open the door farther and moving into the wide-open space as Eli watched the screen he had propped open in the back of his SUV.

Ava moved closer, looking at the readout as he tried not to notice she smelled faintly of cocoa butter. "This is some serious equipment for middle-of-nowhere Idaho."

"It gets better," Eli mumbled, most of his attention on the inside of the warehouse the robot's fiber-optic camera was showing him. The rusted machinery, litter scattered across the floor, newspapers and a dingy blanket that suggested someone had once squatted here only held his attention for a moment. Then, it was entirely focused on the series of galvanized pipes and wires wrapped together.

His pulse picked up as the robot got closer to the scarred wooden table where the pipe bomb rested, giving him a better look. End caps were fashioned onto either end of the pipes. A simple kitchen timer was hooked to the pipe bomb. Crude, but effective.

"You were right to call me," Eli told Ava.

"Is it live?"

"That's what we're about to find out." The kitchen timer didn't appear to be counting down, but that didn't mean the bomb wasn't set. It might just have meant it hadn't gone off when intended. The wrong movement now could still detonate it—assuming it was hooked together properly.

Thumbing the controls, he eased the robot around the table to get a better look at the back of the bomb. The lead didn't appear to be attached to the timer, which probably explained why it hadn't detonated. But it still could.

He eased the robot into position to take a live X-ray, a cool feature he'd been amazed that his department had been willing to shell out for. But they'd had help from a series of large donations after the attempted attack on Little Ski Hill.

Switching to his other screen, Eli stared at the image, studying it closely. Then the tension in his neck and shoulders released and he set down the controller.

"What?" Ava asked, on his heels as he strode toward the warehouse.

"It's not live. There's a lead, but there's no fuse in there."

"Then what's the point?"

Eli spun toward her and she stopped short, close enough that he could see the fullness of her makeup-free lips, the wary intelligence in her gaze.

She took a step back as Lacey strode up beside her.

"Did you see anyone take off out the back when you came over?"

"No. But given the layout here, if he timed it right, I probably wouldn't." She gestured to the thick line of trees behind the warehouse.

"Well, we've got two options. Either you interrupted him before he could open the end caps back up and fit in the fuse. Or he was experimenting with bomb-making and he's got another target entirely in mind."

Ava stared back at him, worry in her gaze.

Whatever the case, Eli had a feeling this wasn't going to be the last time he got called out to Jasper for a bomb.

Chapter Three

Already back in Jasper.

Typically, Sunday was Eli's day off. Today, he'd returned to Jasper, with an SUV full of supplies and a suitcase, after his chief had agreed to lend him out to their police force temporarily. With a potential bomber on the loose, Jasper needed more than just officers on overtime. They needed an expert on explosives.

Settled in the station's large meeting room with a cup of coffee and homemade apple strudel baked by Theresa Norwood, Jasper PD's longtime secretary, Eli glanced around. The room was filling up with officers. Some he'd known for years, who waved or called "hello," and a few he'd never met. But he found himself searching for a woman with a hard set to her jaw and a direct, challenging gaze.

Ava was abrasive, and overconfident for someone who couldn't have been part of the Jasper PD for more than six months. But there was intelligence in that direct gaze, and a story behind her go-it-alone attitude. If her background was in narcotics, it meant she'd come from a bigger city. Maybe she was running from a mistake on the job. Or perhaps she'd figured she could rise up faster in a town with lower crime, fewer officers. Either way, she didn't seem like a team player. He couldn't help being curious what had led her to this tiny mountainous town most people had never heard of.

Ava slipped into the room when it was mostly full, leaning against the back wall with Lacey at her side. Another K-9, this one a Labrador retriever, sat across the room with her handler, Lieutenant Brady Nichols. Jasper PD's Chief of Police, Doug Walters, was a huge proponent of Daniels Canine Academy, a police and search and rescue dog training facility located in Jasper. He'd brought on a number of K-9s over the years, had even had a K-9 partner himself before becoming chief.

Despite the other dog, despite the empty seats, Ava stood apart. From the lack of greetings, he suspected she hadn't yet found a way to fit in with anyone on Jasper's friendly police force.

As the Chief stepped up to the podium, Eli forced his gaze away from Ava. Doug was in his early sixties, and he'd been appointed as chief six years ago, but he'd been part of the community forever. Eli had worked with him several times before and found him to be blunt, but fair.

"Roll call is going to be a little different today," the Chief said as all the conversations in the room quieted. "We've got a couple of standard notes first. With the tourist season coming up, we're going to start seeing an uptick in larceny and petty theft, so keep an eye out. Last night, officers responded to a fight outside of Millard's Diner. One of the instigators wasn't a local, but we have a description of the man and his vehicle. Lieutenant Hoover will pass that around."

The Chief took a deep breath, his pale skin looking sallow under the fluorescent lights. "Now, on to why we have Captain Thorne visiting from McCall. As you've probably heard, Officer Callan and Lacey found a bomb yesterday. We got lucky and it wasn't live, but it did contain explosive compounds and forensics has confirmed that if it had been armed, it could have caused significant damage."

Over the murmurs from officers, he continued, "We have to assume whoever was building it has access to more materials and might try again. We're going to form a team to focus on this until we have a better sense of the threat. Let's find this guy before he can try anything else."

Officers around the room nodded, a few of them shooting Eli quick glances, probably hoping to get picked for his team. Chasing down a bomber was the kind of assignment that came along rarely, if ever, in a town like Jasper. Eli knew his team would be small, probably three dedicated officers. He already had some in mind who he could count on to follow his lead, who would work together seamlessly.

"Before we get to that team," the Chief continued, "I have a bit of bad news. Officer Callan did some digging last night into the ownership of the warehouse where the bomb was found. Most of you probably remember JPG Lumber, which went out of business three years ago?" As many of the officers nodded, the Chief said, "Officer Callan confirmed that the owners moved out of state. There's no obvious target here. Given that the door was unchained and someone had clearly been squatting there at one point, there's probably not a direct connection to the company. We'll still look into who worked there, see who might have comfort or familiarity to use it as a staging spot if this was just a practice run."

"What about prints? Or a lead from whoever was squatting?" Jason Wright, the department's rookie, called out.

He was young—only six years out of high school—but eager. Once a foster to the owner of Daniels Canine Academy, he'd come to the force with a desire to prove himself, to give back, that had resonated with Eli since the moment he'd met the man. As soon as the Chief gave Eli a chance to announce the team he wanted, he planned to include Jason on that list.

The Chief let out a brief laugh that sounded less than amused as he ran a hand through his thinning hair. "We have tons of prints, most of them pretty degraded. But on the bomb materials? Absolutely nothing."

A chill ran through Eli. The lack of prints suggested the bomber had worn gloves. That told him Ava had probably interrupted the bomber before he could insert the fuse and activate it.

A deserted warehouse far from anyone except a single recluse was a strange target, but maybe the intent hadn't been to harm anyone. At least not yet. Maybe the first goal had been to create fear.

The bomb might not have been viable when Eli arrived, but that was only because of the missing fuse. As Eli had dismantled the bomb, he'd seen the attention to detail the bomber had used. If he wanted, Eli was certain he could create a bigger, more deadly bomb.

Whether this had been simple practice or an interrupted bombing attempt, using gloves implied the bomber wasn't taking any chances. This wasn't a one-and-done bombing where the bomber didn't care if people knew his name— or maybe even wanted them to. This was someone with a long game in mind.

That made him even more dangerous.

"Captain Thorne and his team will work to identify the squatter, see if that was recent, see if he knows anything. Right now, we don't have any reason to suspect that the person who was squatting is the one who built the bomb. But Captain Thorne will take the lead in making that assessment. Then, he and his team will run down any other leads. We'll have three of our officers focusing on this as their primary objective. Let's stop this guy before he can do any real damage. Captain Thorne?"

Eli nodded and stepped up to the podium. He'd been right; he'd get three officers to help him. A good number, and he knew exactly who he wanted.

He kept his expression serious, but a familiar thrill was building inside. The opportunity to take on someone who meant this community harm and bring them down.

"Thank you, Chief Walters. Most of you know me, but for those who don't, I want to assure you—I may be a Mc-Call PD captain, but my focus right now is fully on Jasper. We're all part of a bigger community and I'm glad to be able to help you stop this person. To that end, I'm happy to get the chance to work with a few of you on this."

He glanced at Brady Nichols, leaning back in his chair. The lieutenant with the olive-toned skin and close-cut beard had only come to Jasper two years earlier, but he and his tracking dog, Winnie, seemed like fixtures now. Eli had worked with him in the past and found him to be serious and focused. He was a bit of a hermit, but he still had the ability to project a calm confidence that put officers and civilians alike at ease.

"Lieutenant Nichols, I hope you'll be able to help out."

Brady nodded, sitting a little straighter in his chair as if he was already running through investigative avenues in his mind.

"We probably won't need Winnie on this, at least not to start."

The Labrador retriever dipped her nose and slid to the ground. Brady gave her a sympathetic smile and stroked her back.

"Don't worry. If we need to do any tracking, she's our girl."

The dog lifted her head again, tail thumping the ground.

Eli shifted his gaze toward Jason. The young Black man was sitting on the edge of his seat, tapping his fingers on the desk and looking hopeful. What he lacked in experience, he made up for with his tenacity.

"Officer Wright, I'd also like your help on the team."

As Jason flattened the smile that burst across his face, Eli glanced at the Chief, who nodded. The investigation would be good experience for the rookie.

Eli started to scan the room, looking for his final pick, when the Chief stepped closer.

"Officer Callan, we'd also like you and Lacey to be part of this team."

Eli felt a jolt of surprise. He tried to disguise it as his gaze darted from his team pick—Sergeant Dillon Diaz, full of charm and the needed ability to lighten the mood in the toughest times—to Ava. The new officer who couldn't seem to find a way to fit in, even in welcoming Jasper.

She was staring back at him, that same tightness to her jaw. This time, there was a mix of frustration and redemption in her gaze.

No doubt about it. She knew he hadn't planned to choose her. And she felt betrayed, probably since she'd been the one to locate the bomb in the first place.

He gave her a smile to show he was okay with the Chief's choice, even as his own frustration rose up. It was the Chief's territory, but it should have been his team to choose.

She didn't smile back, just stared at him as if he'd tossed her a challenge.

As the Chief dismissed the rest of the officers, Eli tried to rethink the strategy he'd had in mind for the team he'd assumed he'd get. Ava was a curveball he didn't need.

Not when there was a bomber on the loose, presumably anxious for another try.

Chapter Four

Eli Thorne didn't like her.

Ava ground her teeth as the idea rattled around in her mind. It shouldn't have mattered, not really. She wasn't here to be liked. She was here to do a job. But when you put your life on the line at work, forging strong bonds with people made a difference. What had come easily to her in Chicago felt like an uphill battle in Jasper.

The McCall police captain was an outsider, but even *he* seemed more at ease at the Jasper police station than she did. With his loose-limbed stride and easy grin, Eli had projected as much confidence inspecting the bomb as he had picking a team of officers to help.

She hadn't been on his list. Despite the fact that she'd found the bomb, despite the fact that she'd been the only one waiting outside the warehouse while everyone else stood at a distance.

He'd picked Jason Wright for his team, so obviously the white captain didn't have a problem with Black officers. Maybe it was because she was a woman? She'd faced that before—law enforcement was still predominantly male—but she hadn't gotten that vibe from him.

So, what was it?

From the back seat of her personal vehicle, Lacey whined. Twisting her head slightly to glance at the sweet-tempered dog, Ava reached back and stroked her head. "What's wrong, Lacey?"

The dog leaned into the front seat, pressing her head against Ava's shoulder, and Ava couldn't help her smile. It was almost as if the dog sensed her frustration and was trying to make her feel better.

"Don't worry, Lacey. We're going to take a break this morning and have some fun."

Against her shoulder, Ava felt Lacey's body shaking, knew her tail was wagging.

They were headed to Daniels Canine Academy for some extra training, but for Lacey—and even for her—it was more fun than work.

Training K-9s was serious, but it was treated like a game for the dogs, to help them enjoy the work when it really mattered. Lacey definitely enjoyed it, wagging her tail whenever they went to DCA.

Ava felt a similar happiness there. Of all the places in Jasper, DCA was where she'd felt the most comfortable, where she actually felt like she might fit in.

DCA was on the north side of Jasper, across town from her little rental, and a fifteen-minute drive from the station, which was in between. It was Ava's day off, but it was a good excuse to stop by on her way home and see if any progress had been made on the case. Missing out on the start of the investigation, on top of being the cop who was forced onto the team by the Chief, felt like one more hurdle to overcome.

Her hands tightened on the wheel and Ava took deep breaths, trying to relax as Eli's bright blue eyes and contagious smile filled her mind. A smile he seemed to flash at everyone, except with her it felt tempered, forced.

"Let it go," Ava told herself as she drove underneath the

large wooden sign with the silhouette of a German shepherd and the Daniels Canine Academy logo.

Still, Eli's easy smile, fading as the Chief announced he wanted Ava and Lacey on his team, then lifting again unconvincingly, didn't leave Ava's mind as she parked. Letting Lacey out of the car, Ava shaded her eyes from the early morning sun and stared out over the property. Behind her was the main house, but ahead the ranch was bustling. Emma Daniels's two rescue horses, a mellow brown American quarter horse and a more spirited black-and-white Appaloosa, were outside the barn, next to the kennel. On the outside agility course were a bloodhound and a Malinois training with their handlers.

As she headed toward the course, Emma strode over wearing jeans and a flannel, lifting a hand in greeting.

Ava couldn't help but smile.

The owner of Daniels Canine Academy was only a few years older than her, and was the person Ava had connected with most since coming to Jasper.

"Ava! Lacey!" As soon as she reached them, Emma bent down to pet Lacey, streaks of blond within her brown ponytail glinting in the sunlight. "Are you here for a refresher already?"

She grinned as she straightened again, and Ava felt the tension easing from her shoulders at Emma's friendly demeanor.

"Sort of." Ava stuck her hands in the pockets of her jeans as she debated how much to share. Emma was close to the Chief, who'd taken her under his wing after her adopted father, a K-9 officer, had been killed on duty. But that didn't mean he would share police business with her.

Deciding to leave out what they'd found in the warehouse, Ava said, "I know Lacey had some explosives detection training before I started working with her. I figured the two of us could practice that a bit."

Emma's eyes narrowed slightly. "Any particular reason? Not that a dog can't specialize in several things, but I thought you'd decided drug detection was going to be your focus."

"She can do both already, though. It just seems like a waste not to keep her fresh on both skill sets."

Lacey looked from her to Emma, as if she, too, was evaluating whether Emma was buying the lie.

"I can't argue with that," Emma agreed, but she was still studying Ava with a little too much focus, as if she didn't quite believe that was all there was to it. "Let me get something set up for you. Piper has our new trainees under control on the agility course."

Ava glanced at the course, where the redheaded Piper Lambert, Emma's right hand at DCA, was demonstrating how to get a tail-wagging bloodhound to go through a tunnel to a tall Latinx man Ava didn't know. Probably someone in search and rescue, the other focus of the Academy.

As Emma headed toward the kennel, where she also kept supplies, Ava started at her name being called out.

She turned toward the house and saw Jason Wright ambling toward her, his hand linked with Tashya Pratt. The young Black vet tech stayed with Emma and also worked at DCA. Apparently, she was dating Jasper PD's rookie.

Ava forced a smile. She liked Tashya, who was a little shy but had a way with even the most skittish dogs. While Jason was friendly enough, he was trying to fit in at the station, too. Not something best accomplished by hanging out with the outsider from Chicago who hadn't even rated a human partner.

"What are you doing here?" Jason asked, pausing to pat Lacey.

"A little explosives detection training. What about you? You're off today, too?"

Jason shook his head. "Nah, I'm on in an hour." He tugged Tashya's hand upward, dropping a kiss on her knuckles. "Figured I'd talk Tashya into grabbing a bite before my shift."

"Hey, Ava." Tashya gave her a smile, then told Jason, "I'm just going to let Emma know." Then she jogged toward the kennel where Emma was emerging with a handful of supplies.

"You hear anything else about the investigation?" Ava asked, wondering if the McCall captain had kept the rookie more in the loop than her.

Jason shuffled his feet, but kept his gaze locked on hers. "Not yet. You?"

Ava shook her head. The confirmation that she wasn't more out of the loop than anyone else was a small comfort, since the Chief hadn't approved her request to work on her day off. He'd warned her that an investigation like this, while time-sensitive, could also turn into a marathon. He didn't want her burning out at the start. While she could appreciate his logic, it still rankled.

"All set," Tashya called as she and Emma approached.

Jason nodded to her, then linked his hand with Tashya's and headed toward the drive.

"They're cute, aren't they?" Emma grinned. "I know they're adults now, but I fostered both of them and can't help feeling proud of how they're turning out."

Ava glanced back at the couple, surprised. She knew Emma fostered at-risk teens, but she was only seven years older than Jason. "Is it hard? Fostering?"

Emma gave a brief burst of laughter. "Hell, yes. Kind of like moving across the country to a town where you know no one and trying to find your place."

Ava must have looked surprised, because Emma gave her an understanding smile. "Don't worry. You'll get there. Now, give me a couple of minutes to set up and then let's put Lacey through the paces."

At the mention of her name, Lacey's tail wagged.

As Emma jogged toward the woods where she did some of the advanced training, Ava stroked Lacey's head. The motion was calming, easing the homesickness that had hit with surprising intensity.

Her colleagues at the Chicago PD hadn't wanted her to leave. Her friends had pushed her to stay, insisted that her brother just needed more time. That eventually he would forgive her.

But it had been five years since her parents died. Five years she'd spent reaching out to her brother, trying to make amends for something she never could have seen coming.

Blinking against the tears that rushed to her eyes, Ava took a fortifying breath. If Komi hadn't forgiven her by now, he never would. Since the only family she had left hated her, Chicago was her past.

She had to find a way to make Jasper her future.

Chapter Five

"Let's start with what we know," Eli said to his team, early Tuesday morning. Looking at Ava, who hadn't been on duty yesterday, he got her up to speed. "Yesterday, we dug deeper into JPG Lumber, the company that owned the warehouse."

Her lips tightened slightly, and she stood a little straighter.

Probably annoyed that he had retread ground she'd already tackled. But a cursory look at the status of the defunct company and the out-of-state owners wasn't the same as an in-depth check into grievances that might have outlived the company's demise, or easy access that could provide a starting point.

Right now, the only things they really knew about the bomber were that he could make a working bomb and he'd chosen to use the deserted warehouse. Since you could dig up a bomb recipe on the internet, the warehouse was their best lead.

"JPG Lumber, which manufactured lumber, was in business for seven years, but they were relatively small and just couldn't compete. According to the owners, who grew up around here, but moved to Oregon after their business failed, they never had any major problems with anyone. The bank took back the warehouse after the business failed, but like the other buildings on that street, there just hasn't been demand for them. It's been sitting empty since they left three years ago."

Ava's lips tightened even more, like she was holding something in, as Brady and Jason nodded from their respective chairs. But they'd both heard this yesterday.

"We've got a list of employees and we started going through them yesterday. Some left town when the company failed, but most are still here. No one pops as an obvious suspect, although we have a handful with something on their record, from domestic abuse to drug use to larceny. Today, I want to keep digging into that list and chat with the former owners of the other warehouses on that street, see if they have a different perspective. I also want to canvass the area, to see if we can figure out who was squatting, or if anyone else might have seen something."

"It's pretty deserted out there," Ava finally spoke up, her tone carefully modulated, but tension lay underneath.

"Yeah, it's a long shot," Eli agreed. "But right now, the only thing we know is that whoever made that bomb chose the warehouse. There has to be a reason."

"Could have been simple convenience," Brady spoke up, scratching his close-cut beard. "People who live here know it's empty. If someone wanted a practice location, it's a good choice. Unlikely anyone would notice, and with this kind of bomb inside a deserted warehouse, there probably wouldn't be any casualties." He shrugged. "Assuming this was practice for something bigger, which makes the most sense to me."

"I agree," Jason spoke up, his tone a little hesitant, but his gaze steady and sure. "Who does it really hurt to destroy a deserted warehouse? The bank? It's not even a local bank that owns it. Plus, it seems like they've cut their losses, since no one is actively trying to sell it."

"The target is odd," Eli agreed, "but the fact that this

guy wore gloves still bothers me. If he's that cautious, why leave the bomb pieces at all? Unless we interrupted him in the process of setting the bomb to blow."

"Or he wanted someone to find it," Ava contributed. "Put the town on edge. Generate fear."

Eli tried to keep his skepticism off his face. "You and Lacey found it totally by accident. What were the chances someone else would have gone in there?"

"Maybe he planned to call it in anonymously, or figured eventually the unlocked door would get noticed. Or that whoever was squatting would be back," Ava defended her theory, one hand stroking Lacey's head.

The German shepherd was calm, her eyes at half-mast, belying her incredible detection skills.

"It's definitely possible," Eli agreed, mostly because he didn't want to sound like he was shooting down her ideas. Still, his gut told him there was another reason, because it had been three days since Ava and Lacey had found the bomb and the press hadn't gotten a hold of it. If the bomber wanted to sow fear, he could have left another bomb by now. No, this guy had a specific target in mind.

"Brady and Jason, how do you feel about tackling more of the JPG Lumber employees today?" Eli suggested. "See if anyone harbors grudges, knows someone who does or knows of anyone using the empty warehouse for anything."

"Sounds good," Brady said, standing and stretching. He'd left Winnie at home today—apparently the Labrador retriever hadn't been too happy about it, but it made more sense to have a detection K-9 than a tracker right now.

"No problem," Jason agreed, the nerves in his eyes over-ridden by determination.

Eli glanced at Ava, whose own light brown eyes were filled with wariness. "How about you, me and Lacey do some canvassing?"

"Sure," she said, but he could tell she thought it was a waste of time, the kind of job handed off to a rookie.

Lacey looked more impressed, standing and spinning in a quick circle before staring up at him.

Eli laughed and gave her a pet. "Good girl." Then he looked at Ava. "Let's take my vehicle. I doubt we'll need it, but it can't hurt to have my detection gear with us."

She nodded silently.

He'd never had so much difficulty befriending a fellow officer before. Sure, there were officers he didn't like much, those he wouldn't hang out with outside of work. But on the job, he could usually get along with anyone.

Then again, he'd started off on the wrong foot with her by putting the Chief in a position where he'd needed to pick Ava for Eli's team. He wished he'd connected with the Chief first, known the Chief wanted Ava and Lacey on the team and announced it himself.

Holding in his frustration, and hoping he hadn't made a mistake pairing with her today, Eli led Ava and Lacey out to his SUV. As they hopped in, Eli asked, "So, what brought you to Jasper?"

He pulled out of the station as he waited for her response. The extra beats it took for her to answer told him he'd chosen the wrong topic.

"I wanted a change of scenery. I've always lived in a big city, so I thought a small town would be nice. A chance to relax, slow down a little."

It sounded like a practiced response, one that would keep him from digging more. But he hadn't been a police officer this long without sensing a lie.

Instead of calling her on it, he tried opening up to her. "I grew up in McCall—it's about an hour south of Jasper— and came back here after school. I loved the community, loved the way everyone knew each other and looked out for each other. When I was younger, I knew I wanted to be a police officer—my mom was on the force until I was a teenager and she decided to move into an administrative job. But I thought I'd want to join a department somewhere bigger, more exciting."

He grinned, remembering his days at college in Boise. He'd enjoyed having more options of things to do, but he'd missed the feeling that everywhere he went, he knew people. Missed the way people would smile and wave at each other, the way they'd help each other without needing to be asked. So, after finishing at the police academy, he'd applied back in his hometown. He'd never regretted it.

"It's definitely different than Chicago," Ava said.

From the way she said it, she wasn't sure if that was a good thing.

He could imagine her in Chicago, walking the busy streets in her uniform, exuding confidence. Could even imagine her after hours, dressed casually the way she'd been when she'd stopped by the station yesterday, in jeans and a flowy green tank top, her curly hair loose and wild. In Chicago, she'd probably spent her evenings hanging out late at restaurants or bars with friends. Here, her options would be a lot more limited and most places were shut down by nine o'clock.

He snuck another glance at her, staring straight ahead as they reached the street where they'd found the bomb, and wondered if she'd last in Jasper. Or if she'd miss the faster pace of a big city, decide that whatever she was running from wasn't so bad.

Despite the fact that everything he said seemed to rub her the wrong way, he hoped she stuck around. Maybe it was just that he enjoyed a good challenge, but he wanted time to connect, to convince her that he was a good team leader. And to find out why she'd really come to Jasper.

Eli parked at the end of Bingsley's drive. Harold would be talking to a judge later today, both about pulling a weapon on a police officer and having that unregistered gun in the first place. For now, his house was empty.

"Shall we take a walk?" Eli asked, jumping out of the vehicle.

Ava was beside him quickly, with Lacey next to her.

"No leash?" Eli asked, surprised. As he spoke, he realized she hadn't been wearing one that day at the warehouse. She hadn't worn one in the station, either.

Ava stroked the dog's head and Lacey's tongue lolled out a bit as she leaned into Ava's hand. "She doesn't need one. Not for this. I have a couple, in case we get into a dangerous search area and I want to keep her close. But most of the time, I don't use them."

Eli nodded, impressed as he stared down at her dog. "I know none of the other warehouses are occupied, but let's just take a look. See if there's easy access to any of them or if anyone is hanging around. It's a long shot," Eli added at Ava's reluctant nod, "but—"

"It makes sense," she agreed.

Her tone still told him she didn't like being the one to do it. He wanted to argue with her—this wasn't Chicago. They were a small team and he hadn't asked her to tackle this part of the investigation because she was new or as some kind of punishment. She should have known that simply because he'd come with her.

He darted a glance at her as they circled the warehouse beside the one where the bomb had been found, Lacey sniffing the air as they went. Maybe that had been another strike against him, a sign to her that not only did he think she deserved rookie duty, but that he didn't even trust her to do that alone.

He cringed at the idea, but wasn't sure she'd like the

truth much better. That he'd figured the chance to work together, just the two of them, would make her fall for his charms. Not in a romantic sense, but the way he could usually charm colleagues into seeing him as an ally.

Ava tugged on the back door of the warehouse, shaking her head. Her gaze shifted to a broken window twelve feet up. Her eyes narrowed. "It's an access point, and I've seen people scale some impressive things to get into a building. But usually the payoff would need to be something more than a deserted warehouse." She pointed at the uneven brick. "There are footholds big enough if you know what you're doing, but the glass is pretty jagged. Besides, even if someone went in that way, I think they would have still come out the door."

Eli nodded his agreement. People in small towns could get bored enough to do some outrageous things, but scaling the side of a building wasn't one that he'd encountered. Breaking a window closer to the ground to get in seemed more likely. "Let's check the next one."

As they walked, he noticed Ava's gaze on pivot, as though she were on a busy city street rather than between deserted warehouses and a beautiful forest. Birds chirped in the distance, and a hawk flew in a high lazy circle, but there was no sign of human life.

The trend continued as they walked the perimeter of the last warehouse on the street, which had once been owned by a company that made furniture. Along with the closed electronic manufacturing factory beside it, the company had moved to a bigger city. Most of the employees of both companies had gone with them, either commuting from Jasper every day or simply moving closer. Those moves had been a longer time ago, resulted in far fewer job losses than when JPG Lumber had closed.

Eli vaguely remembered that, because they had been

a big employer in Jasper. When they'd closed their doors, quite a few families had left Jasper in search of other work. A few had stayed but faced foreclosures. From what Eli remembered, neighbors had pitched in and helped them stay afloat, the way small towns often pulled together in times of crisis. So far, his research hadn't uncovered anyone who hadn't been able to move forward from the job loss.

"I don't think we're going to find anything here," Ava said, hands on hips as she stood at the end of the street, past the last warehouse, staring at the mountains in the distance.

In between was nothing but more forest, and a winding dirt road that eventually led to farms. Maybe someone had walked this way to use the warehouses, but certainly no one was close enough to have seen unusual activity here.

Lacey, who had stayed by Ava's side the whole way but hadn't alerted on anything, lay down and put her head on her feet as if she, too, was discouraged.

Eli sighed as he stopped beside her, petting Lacey. "We'll have to find another tactic."

He tried to keep his frustration out of his voice. Police investigations were often this way—a lot of tedious hard work before one small thing blew open a case.

He hoped Ava didn't hear his worry, either. Because whatever the bomber's goal, Eli was sure he wasn't finished.

They were on a ticking clock right now. They just didn't know the timeline.

Chapter Six

"I found the squatter," Brady announced as he set down his cell phone.

Ava's gaze jerked up from the paperwork she'd been staring at since returning from the warehouses with Eli. She glanced at Eli, whose bright blue eyes were intense, a hint of a grin on his lips as if he was looking forward to an interrogation—or the possibility that they'd just found their bomber.

"Who is it?" Jason jumped up from the far side of the conference table where he'd been working and hurried to Brady's computer.

Ava's head turned toward Brady, but her gaze still cut to Eli and that ghost of a smile. When she got a new lead on a case, she became serious and focused. She shouldn't have been surprised that Eli's reaction was excited anticipation. She'd known other cops like him, cops who enjoyed the job like it was a game.

She'd never quite understood it, though. She liked what she did, liked the satisfaction of putting criminals behind bars, the way it felt to help someone in need. But she didn't wake up itching for a good chase—even if she could appreciate the adrenaline rush of a takedown.

"His name is Ashton Newbury," Brady said, reading from

notes he'd jotted on his laptop. "Twenty-five years old. Lives at one of the farms a couple of miles from the warehouse."

"I recognize that name," Ava said, trying to place it.

"He's on our list of employees who once worked for JPG Lumber. It was his first job. He started there when he was eighteen and was out of work at twenty-two when they closed down. Since then, he's had a few short-lived jobs at fast-food places, but that's it. He's been living at his parents' farm, but according to one of his friends, who also worked for JPG, he's been known to sleep out at the old warehouse when he and his parents fight. Apparently, they have a contentious relationship."

"Should one of us go talk to him?" Jason asked.

"Why don't we all go?" Eli suggested. "It's probably overkill, but we can't rule out the possibility that the person who was squatting also made the bomb. What else do we know about Ashton?"

Brady's dark brown eyes narrowed as he hunched over and typed into his laptop. A minute later, he shook his head. "Not a lot. He doesn't have a record."

Ava's fingers raced over her keyboard, performing her own search. She skimmed through the results quickly, wanting to contribute. "Social media is pretty minimal. He has aired some grievances about JPG and the way they *betrayed their employees.* Those are his words."

"Recent?" Eli asked.

"Last year. Looks like he was fired from a fast-food job and was complaining about every place he'd worked. He seemed to hold the biggest grudge about JPG, probably because he worked there the longest."

"What about the parents?" Eli asked, looking at Jason.

The rookie darted back across the room, to his own laptop, and started typing.

Ten minutes later, as Ava was still scrolling through social media without finding anything else interesting, Jason said, "Parents have some history."

"What kind of history?" Eli asked.

"We've been out to their farm a handful of times, starting eleven years ago. Looks like the first time, Ashton called, saying his dad was threatening him. The next couple of times, the neighbor called. The farms are far apart, but each time, he was out working in his field and heard yelling."

"No arrests?" Ava asked, frowning.

"The incident reports say that when officers responded, everyone in the house claimed things were fine and promised to quiet down. No obvious signs of injuries, so nothing we could do. On that first call, Lieutenant Hoover—he was an officer back then—thought the kid, Ashton, who was fourteen at the time, was scared."

Eli nodded, his lips tight as lines appeared between his eyebrows. "So, we've got a kid who grew up with possible abuse, and hasn't been able to hold down a job since working at JPG. I haven't found anything that indicates he has explosives knowledge, but that doesn't really mean much these days. This kid grew up here. Does anyone know him?"

Ava shook her head, but Eli was looking from Brady to Jason, anyway.

"I've only lived here for two years," Brady said. "But I think I met the parents at a town event. I remember them being friendly enough, talking about their farm. I think they're known for their sweet corn."

"Yeah, that's probably them," Jason said. "Newbury Farms supplies vegetables to a lot of the restaurants here. Corn is their biggest crop. I'm familiar with the parents peripherally. They've got a big farm. Back in high school, kids used to go out into one of their back fields and drink."

The way he said it, Ava suspected he was one of those kids. "What about Ashton? He's close to your age, right?"

"He was in the class above me in school, but he used to skip all the time. I'd recognize him, but we never talked. It was a small school, but he was one of those kids who kept to himself. I do remember he was smart, though. Just didn't like school."

"Okay. Let's go talk to him," Eli said. "But let's tread carefully."

Brady stood and the rest of them followed him out the door.

Lacey trotted beside Ava, her steps high and excited, like she knew they were going to work.

Ava stroked her head as she hurried to keep up with Eli's long strides. He only had two inches on her five foot seven, but he moved like a runner.

She glanced at him from the corner of her eye, taking in that same hint of a smile. There was something compelling about his energy, something magnetic about the way his eyes widened when he grinned—which seemed to be often.

Maybe that was his trick for connecting with everyone so quickly. She'd try that, except a woman smiling at her colleagues a lot was often interpreted differently than a man doing it.

"Jason, why don't you and Brady take the lead, since Ashton might recognize you and feel more at ease?" Eli suggested as Ava tried to shake off her errant thoughts. "Ava and Lacey can check for any sign of explosives and I'll play backup."

The rookie nodded, a mix of nerves and excitement in his gaze as he glanced back at Eli.

"Your vehicle?" Brady called and Eli unlocked the doors with a loud *beep.*

Eli and Brady hopped into the front, while Ava and

Lacey squeezed into the back with Jason. During the ride, Jason pet Lacey, his hand moving quickly at first and then more slowly as her presence visibly calmed his nerves.

Ava hid her smile as she gave Lacey a quick pat. Besides being a great detection dog, she was also a sweet, sensitive girl who seemed to pick up on people's moods quickly.

"I don't want to overwhelm them," Eli said as he drove, his gaze never leaving the road. "So, Ava, let's stay off to the side. Lacey can detect from there, right?"

"Depends. If the explosives are nearby, then yes. If he's got them locked up in a basement or a barn or something, probably not. But it also depends on the compounds. Some have a bigger scent cone than others."

Eli pulled up to the farm—a massive swath of land that looked bare without the five-foot corn plants Ava knew would cover it in a few months.

Ava scanned the field, catching a hint of movement toward the back field. They were parked before she could tell whether it was human or perhaps deer. "Might be someone out back," she let the team know.

"Keep an eye out," Eli said as they hopped out of the vehicle.

Brady and Jason strode up the long drive, directly to the front door. Ava and Lacey took the field to the left and Eli took the one to the right. Someone watching out the windows would see them all, but if Ashton and his parents didn't know police were here until they knocked, the family would only see Brady and Jason. Hopefully that would make them more at ease.

Ava's gaze pivoted from Lacey to the door to the side of the house until they reached the front. Then she stood just a bit off to the side—not hiding, but not in direct line of sight from the door as Brady knocked.

After a minute wait, he was just lifting his fist to knock again when the door opened.

Then, everything seemed to happen at once.

Lacey moved toward the door quickly, sitting. An alert.

Goose bumps pricked the back of Ava's neck, and there was a blur of movement in her peripheral vision. She pulled her weapon, spinning around just as a man she assumed was Ashton's father darted from the side of the house, aiming a shotgun at her.

Chapter Seven

What he'd hoped would be a quiet interview went to hell fast.

His team reacted quickly, too. Eli hoped it would be fast enough.

As Brady yanked out his weapon and spun to back up Ava, Jason leveled his on Ashton, ordering him not to move.

Lacey's head pivoted, but without an order from Ava, she stayed planted where she'd alerted.

Eli, on the far side of the house, darted around the corner, hoping the man with the shotgun hadn't seen him. Or if he had, he'd be too focused on Ava and Brady to realize why Eli was slipping around the back of the house.

Had Mr. Newbury realized what Ashton had done, suspected the police were here to arrest him and planned to protect his only child? Did he think they were here for some other reason, maybe for more fighting he assumed had been overheard? Or was it something else entirely?

Eli had no way to know. But anyone who pulled a shotgun on police without provocation beyond a knock on their door was involved in something criminal.

They were also dangerous.

Pushing himself to move faster, Eli rounded the back of the house, scanning windows as he ran. Right now, no one knew where Mrs. Newbury was, or if she was also armed.

His heart thudded a little harder, imagining Ava facing a shotgun. He didn't know why she'd come to this tiny town from Chicago, whether there was an incident in her police record. Didn't know how she'd handle an armed civilian, whether she'd be quick on the trigger, too slow to react or good at talking someone down. He reminded himself that in the short time they'd worked together, she'd been professional and competent.

It didn't stop his anxiety.

Gun raised, Eli slowed at the back corner of the house, peering around it before moving slowly toward the front. Careful, silent steps as he approached.

Mr. Newbury was standing at the front corner, angled toward Ava. His finger was beneath the trigger guard and his arms were corded with tension.

The wrong movement and Newbury would see Eli in his peripheral vision too soon, might be spooked into firing.

Eli moved away from the house, farther from Newbury's line of sight.

Ava's voice reached him, calm and steady, infused with authority. "Mr. Newbury, we're here to talk. This doesn't solve anything. Put the gun down."

Eli could only see a sliver of Ava, her toned arm raised and bracketing her pistol, one long leg, her cheek and forehead. But he could picture her—all that smooth skin, the perfect cheekbones and serious eyes—lined up to a shotgun barrel. A twitch ran through him and he cursed his distraction. Seeing anyone in the line of fire was jarring, but he was too experienced to have it impact his ability to act.

Newbury shook his head, but his shotgun stayed steady.

Experienced shooter, Eli noted, a knot forming in his stomach.

A mix of anger and nerves rattled Newbury's deep voice. "Get off my property! You can't be sneaking around here."

"No one is sneaking around," Ava said, slow and easy. "We have a few questions for your son about his old workplace. That's it. You need to put the weapon down and let us do our jobs."

The shotgun lowered slightly, Newbury's biceps relaxing. "This is about Ashton's old work?" He sounded relieved, but also suspicious, like they were trying to trick him.

"Yes, sir. We need to ask him a few questions about something he might have seen. It shouldn't take too long."

There was a long pause, and Eli centered his weapon on the back of Newbury's head. His angle kept him out of Ava's line of fire and kept her out of his. If Newbury's finger moved against the trigger, the right head shot would prevent him from finishing that movement before he fell. It could save Ava's life.

Pressure built in his chest, an unfamiliar, heavier anxiety. McCall and Jasper were small towns, without high crime rates. He'd pulled his weapon before, even tackled someone who was holding a gun. But he'd never had to kill anyone on the job.

"Okay," Newbury said, lowering the shotgun to his side.

A breath left Eli in a whoosh and Newbury started to turn.

"Sir, I'm going to need you to put down the weapon," Ava said, drawing his attention back to her.

Eli could practically hear the man's scowl. But after another prolonged minute, he did it.

As Ava advised him what was going to happen, Brady rushed over and cuffed him, handing the shotgun to Ava. Sharing a relieved look with Eli, Brady walked him toward the vehicle as Eli settled his weapon back in his holster.

Ava did the same, looking a lot less rattled than he felt.

"Let's go talk to Ashton," she said, her tone serious and all business.

Eli followed her to the front of the house. He darted a glance at Brady, who gave a thumbs-up from beside the vehicle, where he was standing with Mr. Newbury.

Eli's SUV was set up to hold his bomb equipment, not to transport a prisoner, and he suddenly wished he'd thought to bring a second vehicle. But Newbury looked calm and somewhat chagrined as he nodded at whatever Brady was saying.

Ava and Eli stopped at a slight distance as Jason said to Ashton, "Can you step outside, please? We just have a few questions for you."

"What?" Ashton had his hands raised, his gaze darting from Eli and Ava to Jason to Brady and his father. His chin-length blond hair obscured his eyes and his jeans and T-shirt had a layer of dirt and dust on them. He chewed on his lip as he mumbled, "I didn't do anything."

Jason glanced at Eli as Ashton stepped outside, hands still up near his head.

Eli nodded back at him. He still wanted Jason to take the lead. Ashton was clearly nervous. Hopefully having someone he'd known as a peer talk to him would feel less threatening.

"Do you have any weapons on you?" Jason asked.

"No!" Ashton exclaimed as he lifted the bottom of his T-shirt to show his waistband, spinning in a slow circle. As he dropped the hem, he added under his breath, "I'm not my dad."

"Thanks, Ashton," Jason said. "Is your mom here?"

"No. She went to the store. Thank goodness," he added under his breath.

"Okay. We just have a couple of questions for you about JPG Lumber's old warehouse."

Ashton scowled, dragging his foot against the grass repeatedly. "This is about me sleeping there? Look, I've just got to get out of here sometimes. I can't afford my own place until I get a new job and I can't deal with flipping burgers all day. Who cares, anyway? No one has used it for years."

Jason glanced at Eli again, then over to Lacey, who was still sitting at attention.

"So, you just use it as a place to sleep?"

"Yeah. Look, the door has been unlocked for years. I never took anything, not like I could drag any of those machines out of there, anyway. And there's nothing else worth any money. Not that I would take it if there was."

"When were you there last?" Jason asked.

"Friday night," Ashton replied. "I came back Saturday morning and discovered my dad had a bonfire with my clothes. That's what I get for running out on an argument, he said." Ashton's frown deepened. "Asshole."

"Have you ever seen anyone else there?" Ava spoke up.

When Eli glanced at her, her expression was mildly curious, but the tension in her body gave her away.

"No." Ashton scowled again. "Why?"

"Do you have any experience with explosives?" Eli asked.

Ashton's gaze bounced to him, eyes widening. "No." He glanced from Eli to Jason. "What is this?"

"Are you sure you've never seen anyone else there, Ashton?" Jason asked. "Think carefully. This is important."

He shook his head. "Never. I wouldn't sleep there if someone else was using it as their getaway spot, too. I'd hit up a friend for the night."

"What about your dad?" Ava asked.

Ashton glanced at her, looking confused. "What about him?"

"Does he know where you go? Has he ever followed you there?"

"Hell, no. I don't tell him *or* my mom. With my luck, they'd drive over and yell at me some more."

Ava nodded, but her gaze was on Eli, not Ashton. She tipped her head to the side.

"Excuse us a minute," Eli said, following her cue and stepping out of earshot to speak with her. "What do you think?"

Her voice low, Ava replied, "I think he's telling the truth. I think Lacey alerted because of his clothes. From the look and smell of them, he's not lying about not having any other clothes. If he was last there on Saturday morning, it was probably before the bomber left the pipe bomb. But I bet the guy who made the bomb has been there more than once. I think Ashton has trace amounts of explosives on his clothes from being in proximity to where the guy was working."

Eli nodded. He'd been thinking the same thing. "Which means the warehouse *was* probably his practice spot and not a target. Maybe you were right about his plan. Maybe he'd seen Ashton there before—even if Ashton didn't see him—and he left that dead bomb intending for it to be found. But not by us. By someone who he figured would spread the word."

Ava nodded, looking troubled as she shifted the weight of the shotgun she still held. "I know it was my theory, and I stand by the idea of him trying to sow fear. But is the target the whole town? Does he want to make *everyone* afraid? Or do you think there's a deeper reason he picked the warehouse?"

"I wish I knew," Eli said. He glanced back at Ashton, who looked more afraid and confused than guilty. They'd have to watch him closely, in case he had them fooled. But in his gut, Eli knew he wasn't their bomber.

It had been three days since they'd found the bomb and

they were no closer to figuring out who had left it. How much time did they have until he set another one? And would the next one be live?

Chapter Eight

There was no place like Idaho.

Eli took a deep breath of cool, clean air and felt the tension he'd been carrying since that morning's jaunt to the Newbury farm fade. It was getting late, and he'd come to town to grab some dinner after leaving the station. Rather than heading to Millard's Diner like he'd planned, he'd found himself in the park in the middle of downtown.

Instead of feeling like an anomaly of green space surrounded by buildings, the park seemed like an extension of the rest of Jasper. With the mountains in the distance and the big trees everywhere, it was the businesses and homes that seemed as though they'd been dropped into the wilderness. Along with Jasper's small old-fashioned downtown, Eli sometimes felt as though he'd been transported back a hundred years.

There was a chill in the air as the sun cast streaks of pink and purple across the sky. Still, families were out in abundance, enjoying the fresh air after a particularly bitter snowy winter. Although Eli enjoyed having a bit *more* in McCall—more restaurants, more events, more family and friends—he could see himself retiring to a place like Jasper. Could imagine himself spending the day at the Salmon River, swimming or fishing. Could imagine sitting out on a raised deck overlooking the woods at night, his wife beside him. He hadn't found her yet, but he knew she'd be like him—someone who loved the peace and community of a place like Jasper.

"Eli, hi!"

There was surprise and wariness in the voice and Eli recognized it before he turned around. He pictured her face, calm and professional even after confronting a man with a shotgun.

"Hi, Ava. You taking the evening to relax, too?"

Apparently after leaving the station, she'd gone home and changed into a pair of curve-hugging jeans, a flowy white top that emphasized her smooth complexion and a small gold locket that didn't quite seem to match her personality. Her hair was loose from its bun, the curls wild to her shoulders, some of them hanging over her eyes.

An unexpected kick of attraction hit him.

Beside her, Lacey wagged her tail and Eli bent to pet her, and to keep himself from staring too long at her owner.

"It's a pretty night," Ava said. "And I'm not much of a cook."

"I love to cook," Eli admitted. "But I haven't had a chance to do much grocery shopping since I got here. And the only thing stocked in the place I rented was ice. You want to grab some dinner?"

She looked a little hesitant, like she wasn't sure if he was asking her out or just being friendly to a colleague, so he quickly added, "We can chat about the case some more?"

The lines that had appeared between her eyebrows disappeared and she nodded. "Sure. We'll need to ask for a table outside since I've got Lacey."

At her name, the dog's tail wagged and Ava grinned at her, patting her head.

"How about Rose Café?" he asked. Millard's Diner had the best coffee in town and burgers he'd been thinking about since finishing his shift. It was also a cop hangout and for reasons he didn't want to examine too closely, he wanted the chance to get to know Ava better without interruption or curious eyes. The small restaurant away from the center of downtown was a little pricier, more of a date-night spot. But it also had good, hearty food and got enough family business to be a safe suggestion.

Ava looked surprised, then relieved. "Sure. They have some great outdoor tables."

Apparently, she didn't want to be interrupted, either. Or maybe she figured Rose Café would be more accommodating of Lacey. Or she just didn't want her coworkers to see her alone with him.

Eli glanced at her as they walked away from the center of downtown. Lacey strode at her side, no leash as usual.

He thought back to the little bit she'd told him about herself when he'd first met her outside the warehouse. Somehow, it seemed like it had been more than three days ago. "So, you specialized in narcotics back in Chicago?"

Her eyebrows lifted, like she was surprised he'd remembered. There was something wistful in her tone as she replied, "Yes. It was something I'd been interested in since I first joined the force. I had to put in my time on patrol first, but when a spot opened, I jumped at the chance to work narcotics. It was a great team. I'd actually just finished working on a big task force before I came here." Her words, which had gained speed and excitement as she started talking, slowed down toward the end.

"I grew up in McCall," Eli said, keeping his tone light and hoping she'd open up more about why she'd come to Jasper, maybe even give him the real reason for her move. "I went to school in a city, and even though I enjoyed it, I couldn't wait to get back to small-town living."

He smiled at her as they reached the restaurant and the

hostess assured them it was fine to bring Lacey, then found them a table on the cozy terrace, next to a little fountain. The space was empty except for a couple and their two young children giggling and sharing dessert. The terrace was enclosed with a series of trellises, beginning to get overrun with green. In a month or so, flowers would fill them.

As Ava looked over the menu, Eli pretended to read his. He'd been here a handful of times and knew the menu well enough. Instead, he stared at her, trying to figure out the best way to connect with her. She was part of his team, whether he'd picked her or not.

Off duty, she looked more at ease, the tension in her jaw gone, even her posture more relaxed. It made her look more approachable, too.

As she set down her menu, he picked up where he'd left off on their walk, still holding out hope that if he opened up about himself, she'd do the same. "My whole family lives in McCall, my parents and my two younger brothers. Even my grandparents, who are all in their upper eighties now, live nearby. All of my aunts and uncles and most of my cousins live within a three-hour radius, too. My parents grew up down the street from each other. They met when they were twelve and the rest was history."

A wistful smile tipped the corners of Ava's lips. "That's really nice. My parents moved to Chicago from the Dominican Republic when I was a baby. All of my extended family is still there. I haven't seen most of them in years."

Her smile faded and Eli wanted to scoot his chair around the table, pull her in for a hug. Instead, he asked, "What about your parents? And siblings. Do you have any?"

Lacey whined and Ava turned to reassure the dog, but Eli saw the stark pain in her gaze before she turned away.

"It's okay," Ava told Lacey, even though Eli knew the dog was responding to Ava's hurt.

"Do you know what you want?" the waitress asked, appearing at their table with a clueless smile.

Ava gave her order quickly and Eli followed, waiting until she left to say, "I'm sorry if that's a sensitive subject."

"It's fine." She gave him an unconvincing smile. "I'm just not close to my family anymore. My career got in the way."

"Oh." Eli tried to read more from her face, but her expression was closed off, her gaze averted. His own family had been incredibly supportive. Of course, he'd been following in his mom's footsteps, so it would have been tough for them to dissuade him.

There was an awkward silence, but before Eli could figure out a way to fill it, she said, "To be honest, it's been a challenge coming here. Not really because I don't know anyone—well, I guess that's part of it—but it's just so *different* from what I'm used to." The wistfulness was back in her tone. "In Chicago, even when you're alone, you're still surrounded by people, all of them going about their own lives. Here, it's like everyone knows each other except for me." She shrugged, not quite meeting his eyes. "I haven't fully adjusted yet."

She missed Chicago, missed the life she'd led there. Part of her still wanted to return. That much was easy to see.

He still had no idea why she'd really come here. He didn't know why she hadn't yet found a way to fit in either, but he wondered more and more if it was simply because she was guarded, used to having a shield up that people didn't know how to breach. Still, she'd picked a great community. He could picture Ava truly at home in Jasper.

She'd worked seamlessly with the team today. Even not knowing why she'd left a big force like the Chicago PD for what must have felt like a downgrade in Jasper, he'd feel comfortable going into a dangerous situation with her. From the way Brady and Jason had responded at that farm, they felt the same.

So, maybe the issue was purely social, that shield of hers making people think she didn't *want* to truly be a part of the community, that she was happier as a loner.

Eli had known many of the people in Jasper for years, but even if he hadn't, befriending people had always come easily to him. He could find ways to bring her into the fold more, show her that she'd chosen the right place to make her future.

"Anyway," she said as he realized he'd let the silence drag on too long. "About the case. I was thinking that there's not an obvious place to park near the warehouse. The shared lot between JPG's old building and the one beside it isn't in great shape and anyone parking on the street should have been noticeable to Bingsley. Maybe the bomber parked at more of a distance and walked, but then a quick getaway would be tough."

Eli nodded, even as his mind was still partly on finding ways to help her fit into the community. If he could do that, maybe she'd stay in Jasper.

His pulse picked up at the idea, at being able to spend more time with her. He genuinely liked her, he realized. Behind the shield she put up—maybe instinct from years of being a Black female cop in a big city—was a really interesting person. Someone he wanted to know better. Someone he could imagine in a role other than colleague. A true friend. Or possibly even more.

"Well, what do you think?" Ava asked as Eli tried to wrap his mind around the idea that he was romantically interested in her.

When he didn't respond, she rushed on, "I checked before I left the station and Bingsley was released this evening. The judge gave him community service and he'll owe a fine for the unregistered gun. He was definitely high when I arrested him, but assuming he doesn't immediately get more drugs, I think he'd talk to me."

Eli nodded again. When she narrowed her eyes like she thought he wasn't really listening, he said, "Yeah, I think it's a good idea. Because I'm worried that we don't have many leads. It feels like we're just reacting, just waiting for the bomber's next move."

The words made his mind flip into work mode and he frowned. "We need to get in front of this, because whether the bomber meant for that inactivated bomb to be found or not, he probably knows we have it by now. If it was intended to scare the town, it didn't work."

Ava looked as worried as he felt. "Which means he'll probably try something more drastic next."

Chapter Nine

Ava zipped her hoodie up to her neck to ward against the early morning chill as she watched a couple of dogs in their runs beside the DCA kennel. She rubbed her hands together, trying to generate warmth and wishing she'd stopped for a cup of coffee on her way. But she only had an hour before her shift started and she wanted to get in as much explosives-detection training as possible with Lacey. If she and Eli were right, there would be another bomb somewhere in town soon.

Eli. The McCall captain had been so different last night than when she'd first met him outside the warehouse. Then, he'd been intensely focused on the task at hand, and she'd struggled to even talk shop with him. Yesterday, he'd been softer, easier to talk to.

"What are *you* thinking about?" There was amusement in Emma's voice, and when Ava spun around, it was on the woman's face, too. "Didn't you hear me calling your name?"

Embarrassment heated her. "No. Sorry. I guess my mind was wandering." Emma stared at her expectantly and Ava added, "Just thinking about how I don't quite fit in here."

It was partly true. Hearing Eli talk about how much he loved the area, how many friends and family surrounded him, she'd felt it even more acutely. She had no one.

Emma ducked her head as she pulled her hair up into a ponytail. "Jasper is a close-knit town. So many people have lived here their whole lives, going back generations. Everyone is friendly when you get to know them, but it can be tough when you're an outsider. Trust me, I know. I came here when I was eight, pulled out of a family that was…not good. But it was all I'd known."

Ava glanced around the ranch, surprised. She'd heard that Emma had inherited the ranch from her parents.

Emma smiled, apparently reading the direction of her thoughts. "Rick and Susan Daniels were my foster parents. Susan officially adopted me after Rick died, a few years before she followed." The smile faded, replaced by something bittersweet. "This place is their legacy."

"I'm so sorry." Her own loss was so much more recent and the words sat on her tongue, but Ava couldn't quite voice them.

"I still miss them, but I feel them with me when I train the dogs, when I foster like they did. Even with them gone, this place, the people here? They became my home. It wasn't always easy. I had times when I felt like I didn't belong at all. But when I was struggling the most, after my dad died, Chief Walters reached out to me, gave me the support I needed." She gave a self-conscious grin. "He kept me out of juvie, in fact."

Ava's surprise must have shown because Emma said, "It probably seems like I'm a fixture here, especially with all the work I do with your department. But it wasn't always that way. Everyone who comes here goes through that same transition, feeling like the one person in town who's missed some secret. It's just the way of small towns, when you're the one who doesn't know the people, doesn't know the history. It all happens, in time. You just need to let people in."

Emma stared at her, as if knowing there were things Ava

wanted to say. Anxiety cramped her stomach, the words still not coming. Because she was afraid to let anyone in, afraid they'd still reject her? Or because saying them out loud would make them true, would make her own loss something she had to face instead of running away from?

A weight settled on her heart, a mix of anger and grief that she hadn't been able to shake in five long years.

Lacey let out a low whine and leaned into her leg, knocking Ava slightly off balance.

Emma put her hand on Ava's upper arm and squeezed. There was understanding in her gaze as she said, "The dogs are sensitive. They know when you're hurting."

Surprised, Ava looked at Lacey again, into the gentle brown eyes staring up at her. She'd never worked with a K-9 before, didn't have much experience with dogs in general. Stroking her head with a hand that trembled, Ava told her, "It's okay, Lacey. Everyone is okay."

"You do have friends in Idaho," Emma said, her tone soft and sincere.

"Thank you." Ava's voice sounded a little watery and she coughed, trying to get a handle on emotions she usually had locked tight.

She didn't know Emma well, but the DCA owner had always been friendly, even inviting her a few times to stay for dinner after training.

Ava had always declined, feeling too much like an outsider as Emma had traded jokes with Tashya and the three teenage boys who worked at the ranch. Now, she wished she'd taken Emma up on her offer.

Emma tipped her head, giving a broader smile. "Come on. I know I'm not the *only* person here you've impressed. Don't tell me Chief Walters isn't happy with the work you and Lacey are doing?"

A smile trembled on Ava's face. "I think he is." The

smile stretched, thinking about her dinner with Eli. "And the team leader I've been working with on my new case seems to be getting over his initial dislike of me, which is a relief."

"Why didn't he like you?" Emma asked, her tone challenging, as if she didn't quite believe it.

Ava shrugged. "Maybe it wasn't dislike exactly, but he didn't want to work with me."

Emma waved a hand dismissively. "People stick with what's comfortable, that's all. Sometimes, you have to show them how to shake things up. Who's the team leader?"

"Captain Thorne. Eli. He's from McCall. You know him?" Ava found herself hoping Emma did, that she'd be able to share some insight.

Emma shook her head and Ava's shoulders slumped with disappointment.

Emma's eyes narrowed. Her voice was half teasing, half curious when she asked, "You're interested in this Captain Thorne, aren't you?"

Ava's face heated. "No." The denial came out too quickly, too forceful.

A brief laugh burst from Emma's lips, then she grinned. "If you say so."

"He's a coworker," Ava insisted. "I'm not even sure how well I like him." But as she said the words, she realized they weren't true. She hadn't liked him at first—or at least she'd been put off by the way he'd overlooked her for his team. Still, from the start, she'd been impressed by his skills in bomb detection and his confidence that bordered on arrogance. She'd envied his easy comradery with the other officers and wondered at his eagerness to head into potential danger.

They were nothing alike. Despite that, despite their rough start, something had changed last night, sitting on that terrace with him in the moonlight. She'd seen a glimpse of the man behind the uniform and she'd been more than intrigued. She'd been interested.

As she tried to process the realization, Emma waved a hand in front of her face. "All right, let's stop daydreaming and do some training."

Lacey gave a happy bark of agreement and Ava shoved back the mixture of bewilderment and nerves. She'd figure out what to do about her feelings later. Right now, it was time to get to work.

Chapter Ten

Eli didn't realize he'd been looking for Ava until she and Lacey jogged into the station's conference room.

They both looked energized, from Lacey's wagging tail and near-prancing steps to the upward tilt to Ava's head and the slight grin on her lips.

He felt a smile tug his in return. "Hey."

"Hi." She glanced around the room, probably expecting to see Jason and Brady there, but the other officers hadn't arrived yet.

She shuffled her feet, her smile becoming slightly self-conscious. "So, how long are you staying in Jasper?" Before he could answer, she rushed on, "I mean, is it a bad drive? Is that why you don't just commute? I've never been to McCall. I really haven't been anywhere in Idaho yet besides Jasper."

He studied her, trying to determine if it was his imagination or if something had changed since they'd sat together last night, gotten to know each other better. She seemed nervous, almost as if she'd felt the same spark he had at dinner.

He tried to hide a jolt of happiness. "It's an hour south of here. With a case like this, where I'm officially on loan to Jasper, I figured it made more sense to be here in case there was an issue when I was off duty. An hour is a long time if you've got an active bomb. McCall is great, though. You'd like it. It's a small resort town, survives on tourism just like Jasper, but it's bigger. Do you ski?"

"I've never tried it," Ava said, her gaze darting to the open doorway and then back to him. "But it looks like fun."

"We have some great skiing," Eli told her, hoping Brady and Jason took their time this morning and he got more time alone with Ava. They'd stayed until the restaurant had shut down last night, lingering over the dregs of their drinks long after they'd finished eating. He'd been surprised how natural it had felt to sit and talk to her after three days of awkwardness.

"I know Jasper has plenty of trails for hiking and they've got the Salmon River for kayaking, but you should try McCall's Payette Lake. There's also tons more shopping and dining, art festivals and live music. You should drive down when you have a free weekend. I'll show you around."

She nodded, dipping her head and stepping slightly away from him as Jason and Brady walked in, chatting about the log home Brady was building himself on a huge piece of property on the outskirts of Jasper.

Eli watched her from the corner of his eye, hoping he hadn't scared her off. He hadn't expected to feel an attraction last night, but now that he'd gotten to know her a little, he just wanted to know more. The best way to do that was to help her integrate into the community, show her around and let her see a real future for herself here.

"Sounds like the cabin is coming along," Eli said to Brady. To Ava he said, "Brady is building a house, all by himself."

Ava's eyebrows raised. "That's impressive."

Brady let out a brief laugh. "It'll be impressive if I ever get it finished. When I do, I'll invite you all over for a barbeque."

A hint of a smile pulled Ava's lips, and Eli felt one tug

his in return. All she needed was a little help connecting and everyone would like her as much as he did.

"So, what's the plan today?" Jason asked.

They'd only formed the team three days ago, but already Eli could see it building Jason's confidence. The rookie was a solid officer, and Eli sensed that he had a great future.

Eli turned toward Ava. "Ava had some thoughts about Bingsley and what he might have seen."

Ava stood straighter and told them where she thought the bomber would have needed to park in order to be close to the warehouse.

Brady and Jason both nodded and Eli said, "Ava arrested him four days ago, so Bingsley might not feel so favorable about talking to her. Why don't you two go and talk to him?"

Ava's smile turned downward, the brief sense he'd felt from her of being a real part of the team fading. She hid it quickly, telling them, "Watch for paranoia. He was high when I went to his house. He was also armed."

Brady nodded, his expression serious. "We don't want a repeat of the other day with the Newburys."

"What do we think about them?" Jason asked. "I mean, I doubt Ashton was lying. Still, I don't think we can completely rule that family out."

"Agreed," Eli said. "We'll keep an eye on them. But I think it's more likely that Ashton saw something and doesn't know it than him actually being the bomber."

Ava nodded, and he realized he'd been watching for her input. Any concerns he'd had a few days ago about some negative police incident sending her to Jasper had faded, replaced by a solid respect for her ability to recognize possible threats.

"What angle are you two going to chase while we talk to Bingsley?" Brady asked.

Eli glanced at Ava, who looked as uncertain as he felt. They could search for more connections to the warehouse, but that list could be long. The chance that it was someone who had no connection at all was high enough that Eli wasn't sure he wanted to waste the time.

"Right now, the only thing I can think of besides Bingsley is the warehouse."

The others nodded, all of them looking as discouraged as he felt.

Unless Bingsley could give them a lead, the case was feeling stalled. And they needed to make more progress *now*, before the bomber struck again.

AVA GLANCED DISCREETLY at the time on her phone. It had been over an hour since Brady and Jason had left to talk to Bingsley and there was still no word.

She glanced across the conference table at Eli, expecting to find him staring at his laptop with his forehead furrowed and his lips pursed. Instead, he was staring back at her, something pensive in his bright blue eyes that made her pulse skip.

Had he been asking her out earlier, when he'd offered to show her around McCall if she went down there for a weekend? Or was that just the way small-town neighbors treated each other?

She was usually pretty good at reading people, but she had no idea. She'd grown up in the city, with parents who'd pushed her to succeed, supported her in her goals until the moment they hadn't. People on the force had been similar to her family's attitude: say it like it is, good or bad. No ambiguity. No uncertainty over where someone stood or their motives.

Or maybe that was just her perception. Maybe she'd assigned motives and never second-guessed herself. Even when she met a man she was interested in, she didn't waver. She made a decision—move forward or don't—and stuck with it.

With Eli, she wasn't sure what to do, how to act. If he was just being friendly, she didn't want to embarrass herself by acting like it was something more. If it wasn't in her head—if it really *was* something more—she didn't want to give him the wrong idea, either.

They were colleagues. That was all they'd ever be.

Just as she realized she'd been staring at him too long, lost in her own thoughts, he gave her an amused grin that lifted one side of his lips and made her heart pound a little harder.

"How's the search?" she asked, infusing her voice with as much professional distance as possible.

His smile turned quizzical, but he shook his head. "Nothing. There are about sixty people who worked for JPG at the time they dissolved who still live here. No one stands out as a potential suspect. Some are unemployed and a handful have some kind of record, but nothing screams bomber. Nothing that suggests a grudge big enough to want to blow up the warehouse."

She nodded, not surprised. "I didn't come up with anything, either. The list of people the owners gave you who were let go from the company within the year before they dissolved is pretty short. Two of them moved away from Jasper and the other three have full-time work and no sign on social media of bad will. But the company is defunct, the owners are gone. I don't think this is about JPG."

Eli ran a hand through his hair, making her notice threads of red in the short brown. "Yeah, I agree. I'm not sure where that leaves us with leads."

Ava glanced at her side, where Lacey lay on the floor. At her look, Lacey's head lifted and her tail thumped the ground.

Ava smiled at the dog, who read nonverbal cues better than any human she'd ever met. "What if Lacey and I go out and explore some other abandoned areas?" She turned back to Eli. "If the bomber's test run was interrupted, maybe he'll try again somewhere else. If he sticks to pattern, that means he'll probably return to the same abandoned spot more than once. We might get lucky."

Eli stood, stretching his arms up and tipping his head back.

He was only two inches taller than her, the dark McCall uniform he wore each day despite working in Jasper emphasizing his pale skin and lean muscle.

He wasn't really her type. Not in looks or personality. But she couldn't stop staring, couldn't stop thinking about his words from earlier.

You should drive down when you have a free weekend. I'll show you around.

For the weekend. Not for the day, even though it was only an hour away. It sounded like an invitation to more than friendship, but Brady and Jason had walked in before she could figure out how to respond.

Not that she'd agree to such a thing, no matter how much she was starting to like him. Sure, he'd go back to McCall after the end of this case, but she got the impression that he worked with the Jasper police department—or at least coordinated with them—regularly. Not to mention that it was a small community, even several towns away.

She'd tried a workplace relationship once before. When things with DeVante had inevitably ended, it had been awkward even on Chicago's big force, despite not working the same shift and rarely seeing each other on the job. More than that, it had the potential to wreck the reputation she was trying to build here.

If she wanted to make Jasper her new home, she didn't

want rumors going around about her relationships with anyone on the job, not even a captain from another force.

"Well?" Eli was staring at her as though he was waiting for an answer.

"Sorry," Ava said. "What did you say?"

He gave her another of those perplexed looks, like he was trying to figure her out, then said, "Are you ready? I'll go with you. If Lacey alerts, I'll have my equipment."

Closing her laptop, Ava pushed back her chair and motioned for Lacey to follow, trying to hide her nerves. She could have used some time alone, to get her emotions lined up with her head.

Because as she followed Eli out the door, awareness of him—of his loose-limbed stride and easy confidence, of the faint scent of some kind of woodsy aftershave—filled her senses.

Somehow, in the span of a few days, she'd gone from not being sure she even liked him to far too interested. Still, she wasn't going to let a fleeting attraction—because they were too different for it to be anything more—distract her from creating a new life for herself in Jasper.

Chapter Eleven

There weren't a lot of abandoned or empty buildings in Jasper.

The three warehouses on the street with Bingsley's house were an anomaly. Although the town wasn't big in terms of population, tourism kept increasing each year—not just in Jasper, but in the whole area—and businesses were paying attention. The latest addition was a river tour and rafting company that was having their grand opening soon. They'd grabbed the building practically before the old hardware store had put up their For Sale sign and moved off Main Street and into a more affordable space.

Eli was seeing similar growth in McCall. He was used to his town swelling to double or even triple the people during the summer and holidays, but Jasper had always been farther off the grid. He hoped neither of them grew too fast, lost the small-town charm and connectedness that had brought him back here.

"Not much is empty in downtown," Eli told Ava as he headed down Main Street, away from the Jasper police station. "The city is growing faster than space can keep up with demand."

She let out a small laugh and he remembered she was used to Chicago standards of growth.

He shrugged. "I mean that if a building in downtown

opens up, it tends not to stay empty. The warehouses are different because most of the businesses here don't need that kind of space and it's not worth converting, especially since they're not near the main square."

"So, what have we got?" Ava asked, twisting in the passenger seat to face him.

He tossed her the notepad that he'd set on the seat between them, filled with the list of abandoned buildings he'd gotten from the Chief, who'd lived in Jasper all his life. Eli had known a few of them, places that had been empty since he was a kid. Others he wouldn't have found without someone who'd lived in Jasper a long time.

"None of these are even on the outskirts of the downtown." Ava sounded disappointed as she scanned the short list. "Seems less likely that our bomber would want something so out of the way if he's looking to create fear. Then again, he's probably nervous to return to where we found the first bomb. If there's nothing else around…"

"Like I said, the downtown is pretty small, but there's plenty of demand. Locals like the downtown, of course, but the draw is tourists. They come for the mountains and the river, hiking and rafting. Then they wander around the cute downtown for dinner or coffee. Or they come to Jasper as a day trip, for the homemade furniture. Those warehouses are mostly on the other side of town, and I doubt they'll ever go empty."

Ava nodded. "If I wasn't renting a place that was already furnished, that's the first stop I would have made after moving here."

"You're renting, huh?" There were plenty of rentals, mostly for tourist season, and since Ava had moved a few months ago, while demand was low, she'd probably gotten a good deal. But a rental was a lot less of a commitment than purchasing a home.

"I figured it made the most sense," she replied, not elaborating as she pulled up addresses from his list on her phone.

He glanced at her, trying to read on her face whether it made more sense because she wasn't sure she planned to stay, or just because she'd chosen a place over the internet. She was focused on the addresses, her lips pursed as she looked at the list that already had him discouraged.

Sure, a falling-down barn on twenty acres of land would be an easy place to sneak in and out of, and it was unlikely to have any casualties if the bomber wanted a practice run first. But it was also unlikely that a deactivated bomb would be found quickly and get people talking. And it was less likely to scare people in the same way that blowing one of the warehouses would have.

"Here's the first one," Eli said, parking on the gravel drive that led up to the barn. The land was vacant, the house long gone after an accidental fire had driven out the owners when Eli was a kid. Only the barn had survived. Faded red with a large hole in the roof, it was a known drinking and make-out spot for teenagers. Over the years, police had increased patrol here at night and cut down on all the activity. Now, it would be an easy spot for someone to leave a bomb with little fear of being seen.

Ava hopped out and Lacey followed, striding beside her owner as Ava took in the overgrown fields, which were high enough to block curious gazes from all directions. "It's kind of spooky."

Eli glanced around, seeing it as someone who was used to people, buildings and concrete everywhere might, as a place invisible to prying eyes, far from help. To him, it was serene, quiet except for birds chattering and deer bounding through the field in the distance.

"What does Lacey think?" Eli asked, keeping a close eye on the dog.

She didn't react to hearing her name, just moved forward with her nose in the air. Hyperfocused on the job.

"No alert yet," Ava replied as she scanned the fields and barn area as if they were in a densely populated city.

It was pretty unlikely anyone just happened to be hiding in the fields, but it couldn't be ruled out, and Eli listened closely for any sound out of place.

As they reached the barn door, which was standing wide open, Eli glanced at Lacey again.

The dog walked into the building at Ava's command, but showed no sign of having scented on anything.

Eli followed them in, squinting as he peered into darker corners, beyond the various panels that had once separated different animals. He stayed behind Ava and Lacey, letting them work.

The barn was dank, the scent of molding hay tickling his nostrils. Empty beer cans and a handful of cigarette butts were piled in one corner, but they didn't look recent. Above him, a pair of doves perched at the edge of the hole in the roof, singing their melancholy song.

"Anything?" he asked Ava as they reached the far end of the barn.

She shook her head, but he wasn't surprised. This was a long shot. If the goal was for someone to find the bomb and spread the news, it would have been left somewhere obvious that a pair of teens, focused on drinking or making out, would still have spotted it. If the goal was to blow up the barn, then why leave a bomb that wasn't ready and risk police finding it like they had at the warehouse? In that case, it would have been set off immediately.

Still, checking the deserted spots was the best lead they had, other than Bingsley. He glanced at his phone, hoping for news from Jason or Brady, but there was still nothing.

"Next spot?" she asked.

"Yep."

As he led her back toward the car, she said, "I might have to take Lacey back to DCA tonight, give her a chance to alert on something we set up for her to find, so she can get rewarded. I don't want her getting discouraged."

Eli glanced at her, smiling fondly as she pet the German shepherd.

"Maybe we'll get lucky." He tried to sound encouraging. Even though he didn't think they'd find anything, it had still been a good suggestion. It was also more fun than sitting at the station, digging through old records for the second time.

As they hit three more of the abandoned spots on the list—a dilapidated silo, a foreclosed home with the back wall missing and a massive old storage shed—it was hard to stay positive. All of them were empty, no signs of recent human visitors or bomb materials.

Ava and even Lacey were starting to look frustrated, too. Until his phone buzzed.

Eli glanced at it and saw Brady's name on the readout. "5454," he told her as he handed her the phone. "That's the code. Want to see how they fared?"

She looked surprised that he'd so easily share the code for his phone, but she didn't say anything as she entered it and pulled up his text messages. Then her shoulders slumped and she shook her head. "According to Brady, Bingsley didn't seem high or evasive, and he claims he never saw any unexpected cars or people on the street. He also says he never went into any of the warehouses, that he had no reason to. Of course, that doesn't mean no one was there. It might just mean Bingsley has been too high lately to notice."

Eli swore, then gave her what he hoped was an encouraging smile. "It was still a good idea to check. So was investigating empty buildings around Jasper."

"I just wish it had worked," she said.

"We still have three more spots," Eli reminded her, pulling up to the next one, an old mill near the river. It had been turned into a coffee shop and then an ice-cream parlor before ultimately being shut down for safety issues with the structure. It had sat empty ever since.

As they stepped outside, Eli heard the distant laughter of people traveling along the river. Maybe a group canoeing or kayaking. The water was slow today, tranquil, with geese preening at the shore.

The parking lot, with its broken concrete and warped wooden picnic tables between it and the river, was empty. The old mill—Eli always thought of it that way, from seeing it functional as a young kid when his family would come out here for a change of pace—looked like it was closed up tight. There was grime on the windows and a board across the door. The wood waterwheel was partially moss-covered, but still felt like a landmark to him along the river.

Eli paused a minute, remembering the last time he'd come out here with his family a few months ago. His mom and dad had been laughing as they'd paddled a tandem kayak, his younger brothers egging each other on as they swerved into each other's paths. He'd been paddling more leisurely at the back of the group, taking in the sunshine and imagining a future with the family expanding; his brother had started talking about his plans to propose to his girlfriend that afternoon.

He'd pictured both of his younger brothers married, with kids, and himself, too. While both of his brothers were in serious, long-term relationships, he was still single. He wasn't in a rush to get married, but that day he'd felt a pang of anxiety, thinking that part of his life wasn't moving fast enough.

Walking here with Ava, he could suddenly picture her in a kayak alongside him, her curls loose and her head thrown back with laughter.

The image caught him by surprise. He faltered even as she picked up speed, moving toward the mill with Lacey.

He needed to focus on the job, keep things professional. He couldn't be distracted by this new attraction, couldn't let his desire to help her fit into the community shift into flirting the way it had earlier. Maybe once this case was over, he could ask her out. But not now. As the image of Ava beside him on the water, of Ava across from him on a real date flashed through his mind, he tried to ignore it.

His eyes narrowed on her, a different type of anxiety building as the daydream of some kind of future with her faded into the background.

Lacey was running toward the mill, Ava right behind her.

Eli glanced at his SUV, wondering if he needed to grab his equipment, then took off after them.

Just as he caught up, rounding the corner to the side of the mill and seeing a slightly open door, Lacey sat.

"She found something," Ava said, peering through the doorway. Then she glanced back at him, her expressive brown eyes wide and worried. "I think there's another bomb."

Chapter Twelve

"Don't go in," Eli shouted.

Even though Lacey hadn't made a move, Ava grabbed her collar as she glanced back at Eli with alarm. "Do you see some kind of trigger or trip wire? Would walking through the door activate it?"

"No. I don't know." He pushed down the panic he'd felt hearing her words about a bomb while she was standing on the threshold. There was no reason to think the bomber had rigged this one. But police had found the last bomb, so if he'd been counting on them searching other abandoned buildings, Eli couldn't rule it out.

"Let me get my gear and take a look first," Eli said, even as he stepped closer and peered around her.

The inside of the mill was set up like an old ice-cream parlor, with a long counter that wound its way through the store. Stools had once been pushed up all along the counter, in a rainbow of colors. Now, there was just the counter and the old freezer, with the door removed. On top of the counter was a pile of wires and fuses. Clearly bomb-making materials, but nothing had been assembled.

He frowned, scanning the space for anything else. "Did you see an assembled bomb or just the parts?"

Ava stepped up beside him, her shoulder brushing his, the scent of cocoa butter as calming as it was distracting.

She pointed at the wires and fuses. "I guess not. I saw what's on the counter. Lacey alerted, so I assumed it was a bomb."

She turned toward him, her breath brushing against his chin, her lips with their exaggerated cupid's bow so close he could just sway and touch them.

"It's not?"

When he just stared, she backed up, bumping the door frame. "Eli, it's not a bomb?"

Focus. He swore at himself for getting distracted at a time like this. In the decade he'd been a police officer, no matter the distractions or emotions he'd faced, he'd never lost his focus before at a crime scene. How had Ava gotten under his skin so quickly, so deeply? It was exactly the reason he couldn't pursue her until this case was over.

"No. It's bomb materials, for sure. But it's not assembled."

He squinted into the space, holding his arm across the doorway as he searched for any sign that there were more materials somewhere, perhaps assembled. He couldn't rule it out. But he didn't see anything.

The bomber had obviously meant for this to be found. By a kayaker who stopped to explore? Someone who would call it in to the police, but maybe also tell all their friends or put a picture on social media? Or by the police, searching for the person who'd left it? If the plan was the latter, knowing that they hadn't shared it with the public before, what was the end game?

"Let's be careful," Eli said, his gut screaming that something about this wasn't right. "You and Lacey stay outside, but call it in. I'm going to put on my bomb suit and get closer."

When he turned back toward her, Ava still had her hand locked around Lacey's collar, even though he doubted the dog would move without her handler's command. "You're worried that this seems like a setup?"

"Aren't you?"

"Yeah."

She glanced around, and Eli's gaze followed, to the towering trees and overgrown field behind the mill, to the river flowing alongside it. Sure, someone could pull their boat out of the river here and decide to explore. But it wasn't like the barn, known for trespassers.

Eli knelt closer to the door, examining the lock. It had definitely been forced, probably with a crowbar. Probably by the bomber.

"Call it in," he said again, striding back toward his SUV. He heard her and Lacey following, heard her on the phone with her chief as he stepped into his heavy, stifling bomb suit. With the helmet on, all of his senses felt dulled. Only his hands were free to let him work. Except for his hands, the suit would protect him from most blasts that a bomb like the one they'd seen at the warehouse could create.

"Be careful." Ava's voice trailed him as he waddled toward the mill with his nylon bag full of tools.

He glanced back at her, one hand across her forehead like a visor against the sun, worry in her gaze, and nodded. Then he trudged forward, mentally reviewing each step.

At the doorway, he bent down, searching for a trip wire, for any kind of triggering device. Seeing nothing, he took a fortifying breath and stepped inside.

He didn't realize how hard his heart had started pounding until he moved inside and the world around him didn't explode.

The inside of the mill was covered in a layer of dust, but not quite enough to make footprints obvious. Eli knelt close to the ground, the movement more awkward in his full-body suit. There were a few lines across the ground, as if someone had dragged their feet, but only near the bomb materials.

Sweeping his gaze down low, he looked for any sign of another device. Then he did the same thing at waist-height and standing. The only thing he spotted were the wires and fuses centered on the counter, like a pile of presents. A lighter was beside them.

Eli knelt next to the counter, eyeing the bottom of the pile for materials that were attached. An active bomb that might explode if he moved the wires and fuses on top. There was nothing.

Frowning, he stood and stepped behind the counter, then moved into the back room. It was tiny, just space for a sink, a few cupboards and an open spot where there must have once been a dishwasher. Slowly, he eased open the cupboards, but there was nothing inside except an old can of whipped cream on its side.

He made another pass of the entire inside to be sure, then keyed his radio. "As far as I can tell, it's clear, Ava. Can you bring Lacey in to do a better check?" He was good, but he couldn't see inside walls. A detection dog like Lacey would be able to smell a bomb hidden there. She'd also be able to tell the difference between chemicals on the bomb materials set out on the counter and a bomb somewhere else.

"On our way," Ava said. "So is backup."

She took longer than expected, but when she finally entered, she told him, "Lacey and I did a pass outside first." Turning to Lacey, she said, "Find the bomb, Lacey."

The dog's tail wagged as she followed Ava's lead. Instead of moving toward the materials, Ava walked Lacey in a pattern around the room, pointing for the dog to sniff in certain areas. When they reached the counter, Lacey sat beside the stack of bomb materials.

Ava rubbed her ears. "Good girl, Lacey. Good girl."

The German shepherd's tail thumped the ground, then Ava commanded, "Find the bomb, Lacey," and led her into the back room.

When they emerged, Ava shook her head. "Nothing else."

Eli nodded. He wanted to lift off his helmet, but it was too awkward to hold at the same time as his tools. And he wanted a closer look at what they'd found.

Bending his knees, he put himself at eye level with the bomb materials. There were a variety of fuses, multiple options to create a bomb that made tension knot Eli's back. Whoever was doing this had either spent a hell of a lot of time online researching or had real experience with bomb-making.

"Eli." The blend of excitement and urgency in Ava's voice made him turn toward her.

She was bending next to him, but her gaze was locked on the shiny blue lighter beside the bombing materials. She pointed at it with a slightly shaky finger. "Is that…"

His breath caught as the light streaming in from the window hit it at just the right angle. "A fingerprint."

Their gazes caught and held.

"I think this case is about to break open," she said, excitement in her voice.

That meant very soon, he could ask her out.

Chapter Thirteen

As soon as they walked into the station, Lacey picked up on the frenzied excitement and started prancing around Ava.

Ava glanced around the open bullpen, searching for her team.

"Nice job, Callan," Sergeant Diaz said as he strode past.

She startled at the praise. "What happened?"

He paused, turning back toward her. "The print you found at the old mill had a match in the system."

Anticipation built in her chest and Ava picked up her pace, heading for the conference room. As she strode inside, Lacey pushed past her and sat at Eli's feet.

Eli laughed and gave the dog a pet on her head. Then his gaze locked on hers, excitement in his always-alert blue eyes. "We have a suspect."

"Who is it?"

Brady, who was seated at the head of the conference table, turned his laptop toward her. "Her name is Jennilyn Sanderson. She's got a history of violence, which is why we have her prints in the system."

Ava glanced around the room, from Eli to Brady and over to Jason, who was standing in the corner, his fingers tapping against his legs like he couldn't stay still. The anxiety transferred to her, a readiness to get Sanderson in a cell before she could detonate anything.

She wondered how long the rest of the team had been here before she'd arrived. She snuck a glance at the time on Brady's laptop, seeing that she was right on time. At the moment, it still felt late. "Are we getting a warrant for an arrest?"

"Not yet," Eli answered. "We need to proceed carefully."

"Why?"

From the way Brady and Jason both frowned slightly, they already knew the answer.

Frustration bubbled up, that somehow she'd missed so much this morning. It felt like a continuation of the problems she'd had since arriving a few months ago, always being the outsider.

Eli's eyes narrowed slightly, his lips pursing like he could tell what she was thinking. His gaze locked with hers and a spark of awareness shot through her. "This just came in. You didn't miss much. The evidence tech went over everything, all the wires and the fuses. The only item with any prints was the lighter."

"A good lawyer will get her cut loose, say the lighter isn't connected to the fuses or the wires," Brady said, even as he rolled his eyes. "Doesn't matter that it was *right beside* everything else, the only items in the place that didn't belong. To be sure we can make it stick, we need more. We don't want to spook her."

Ava nodded, trying to resist the urge to look at Eli again, to ignore the spark of attraction that just wouldn't go away. The pressure that should have decreased because they had a suspect ramped up instead. Things could get tricky when you didn't want to bring that suspect in right away. "She probably wore gloves when she left the wires and fuses—intending us to find them—but leaving the lighter was unintentional. Something that she was carrying but hadn't wiped down, because she didn't mean to drop it."

"Exactly," Eli said. "So, that's good luck and bad."

She nodded. Good because they had a name. Bad because it was too circumstantial. "We're still going to talk to her, right?"

"Definitely, but we need to dig into her history more first. You walked in about five minutes after we got the news on the prints, so we haven't done more than pull up her record."

Relief loosened her shoulders and Eli gave her a nod, like he knew why she'd been worried.

Tearing her gaze from his too-perceptive one, Ava peered at the image of Jennilyn Sanderson on Brady's laptop. In her mug shot, her lips were twisted upward into an angry snarl and her pale skin was flushed blotchy red. Her light brown shoulder-length hair was snarled, and her T-shirt was ripped along the arm, like she'd been in a fight. The expression in her light brown eyes said she'd won, but still wanted to go two more rounds.

"What was the arrest for?" Ava asked.

"Bar fight," Brady said. "Apparently it was a brawl, so multiple people were arrested that night. This was about five months ago. I wasn't on duty that night, but I remember hearing about it."

"I was there," Jason said, "but I wasn't inside. I was handling crowd control outside. The fight drew a pretty big crowd. It was around the holidays, so we had a lot of out-of-towners here for our winter festival. It's nothing like McCall's Winter Carnival—" he grinned at Eli "—but it's still a draw. That night, a lot of people had wandered into the bar after the festival."

"Bartwells?" she asked, surprised that a brawl would start at the cop hangout.

Jason shook his head. "No. Shaker Peak."

Shaker Peak was the spot for hard drinking and occasional dancing, whereas Bartwell Brewing was known more for their beers on tap and assortment of games, like pinball and dartboards. The cop hangout was clean and modern, whereas Shaker Peak was dark inside and looked like the kind of place that survived on day drinkers and out-of-towners looking to party.

"That makes sense," she said, remembering the one time she'd stepped inside, mistaking it for the "bar" that all the Jasper officers went to after work. She'd glanced around, seen only an old man in overalls with his head on the bar and a bored-looking bartender, and walked right out again. For days, she'd thought her colleagues had been playing a prank on her, until she realized she'd just misunderstood the location.

"Let's see what else we can learn about Sanderson," Eli said, settling into a seat, his gaze already locked on his laptop.

Lacey glanced from Ava to Eli, then followed him and laid down on his feet.

Eli laughed and paused to stroke her long fur. "You do deserve a break, girl. You've done a great job helping us on this case."

Her head lifted briefly as she peered up at him, her tail thumping the ground, before she laid her head on his feet again.

The jealousy that streaked through Ava surprised her. Lacey usually followed her everywhere, whether they were on or off duty. Ava had even moved Lacey's dog bed into her bedroom, since the German shepherd had taken to sticking close at night, too. She and Lacey had bonded well since the Chief had paired them up last month.

Before that, Ava had mostly worked with whomever was available. She'd been paired with Brady on a few calls, and once with Jason. It was different here than Chicago, the smaller department meaning that officers often worked alone. When the Chief had brought her one of Emma's trained dogs to be her partner, she'd been offended.

It was a slight that was surely a result of her inability to fit in at Jasper PD. Still, since they'd worked together, she'd come to see the value in a K-9 partner. She'd connected with Lacey more than with any of the people in Jasper. Seeing the dog get attached to Eli so quickly made her wonder if she was wrong about her and Lacey's bond.

"I've got an incident report," Brady said, snapping Ava out of her thoughts.

She hurried to join the team at the table.

"What was the incident?" Eli asked.

Brady frowned at the laptop. "Guy called saying Jennilyn had smashed up his car. We responded, but by the time we got there, she was gone. We tracked her down, but soon after the guy changed his tune, saying it was an accident. According to the report, it clearly wasn't and we still did some follow-up. But ultimately, no arrest was made."

"Do we know why?" Ava asked.

Brady shook his head. "Dillon responded to the incident, so he probably knows more."

"When was this?" Eli asked.

"Four months ago."

"So, not long after the bar incident. Anything more recent?" Eli asked.

"No. Nothing prior to the bar fight, either, although I don't recognize her name. I don't think she's lived here that long." Brady looked over at Jason.

"I think she's a bartender at Shaker Peak. She looks vaguely familiar," Jason said. "But you're right. I don't think she's a longtime Jasper resident."

"Anything else in our system?" Eli asked, even as his own fingers continued to move frantically on his keyboard, his gaze moving rapidly on the screen as if he were speed-reading.

"Nope," Brady replied.

"What about social media?"

"Nothing obvious," Jason said. "But she could be using a shortened version of Jennilyn and not listing her hometown as Jasper, which means a lot more accounts to dig through. That could take a while."

Eli nodded, leaning back in his chair, his gaze moving to Brady. "Who was the arresting officer for Sanderson in the bar fight?"

"Captain Rutledge."

Eli's eyes rolled upward briefly, then he nodded. "Ava, why don't you, me and Lacey talk to Dillon Diaz and Arthur Rutledge, then pay Sanderson a visit?"

Brady's and Jason's gazes cut to her simultaneously. Even though she and Eli had paired up a lot during this case while Brady and Jason did the same, she read a mix of resentment and surprise there and dipped her head.

She wanted this chance, wanted the opportunity to prove herself. It made sense to have a detection dog when talking to Sanderson. Still, she was the newbie getting chosen to participate in the best part of the case. She didn't want her colleagues to think she was getting special treatment, to have one more reason not to fit in.

Her gaze met Eli's as she headed for the door, and she saw that same spark of interest she'd noticed the other night at dinner. She quickly averted her gaze, wishing she could eliminate her own interest as easily. Because if she didn't already have enough reasons to keep things professional, she'd just found one more.

Chapter Fourteen

"Captain Rutledge, can you help us out?" Eli called as he caught up to the man heading into the parking lot.

Arthur Rutledge sighed, glancing at his watch as he turned to face Eli and Ava. When he spotted Lacey, his lips twisted downward and he took a small step back, reminding Eli that the captain didn't like dogs.

Eli and Arthur were both five foot nine, but every time he talked to the captain, Eli swore the man tried to stretch taller.

Brushing his dark brown hair away from his eyes as a gust of wind lifted it, Arthur said, "What is it? I was just running out to grab a coffee."

"You might have heard that we have a possible suspect in the bombing."

Looking more interested, Arthur nodded. "Who is it?"

"Her name is Jennilyn Sanderson. You arrested her about five months ago during a bar fight at Shaker Peak."

Arthur, who was in his early fifties, but tried to look younger by growing his hair shaggy, pursed his lips for a long moment, then shook his head. "You're talking about that big bar fight? I arrested a lot of people that night. Name doesn't ring a bell."

"I think she was a bartender at Shaker Peak. Ava, can you pull up the arrest report?"

Before she could open her laptop, Arthur was nodding.

"Yeah, okay, I remember her. Former Army, so she knew how to fight." Arthur rubbed his knuckles, like he was remembering a tough arrest.

"Army?" Ava gave Eli a meaningful look and he nodded back.

They'd need to see if they could dig up details about her service, especially whether she had any experience dealing with bombs.

"Yeah." Arthur crossed his arms over his chest. "Several people mentioned it when I was asking about the fight. I think she liked everyone to know she's former military, because I remember she was wearing an Army T-shirt. She wasn't that big, maybe five-five, but she had some serious muscle. A lot of the people we arrested that night bailed out the next day, but not her. She went to court and ended up with community service. She put a guy in the hospital."

Surprised, Eli asked, "She only got community service?"

Arthur frowned, as if he didn't like it. "It would have been more, except enough people said the guy threw the first punch and she was defending herself. You ask me, she could have defended herself without breaking some guy's arm, but what do I know?" He shrugged, but rolled his eyes. "I'm not a judge."

"What else do you remember about the incident?" Ava asked.

Arthur stared at her a minute, his expression vaguely unfriendly, and Eli wondered if there was a story there. Not necessarily why Arthur didn't get along with Ava—it could have been anything from the fact that she had a K-9 to simply her being new and relatively unproven—but maybe it was contributing to Ava's defensiveness. After all, Rutledge was second-in-command at Jasper PD. He wondered if there was a tactful way to tell her not to take anything Arthur did to heart.

"Like I said, it was a big fight. Most everyone who was working that night got called over to help break it up. All told, we probably arrested a dozen people. There were plenty more who stood on the sidelines watching the brawl."

"What started the fight?" Ava persisted, her jaw tense.

Arthur snorted. "Some guys who drank too much and were making offensive comments to a couple of women on the dance floor. Harmless stupidity, but the women yelled back and then people were throwing punches."

Instead of arguing about what constituted harmless, Eli asked, "Do you remember anything else about Sanderson?"

His brows came down, then finally he said, "Besides her being aggressive and coming *this close* to resisting arrest? I think she might have been there with someone. I remember she was working, but I have this feeling someone had come in to see her that night. Maybe a boyfriend? I don't know if he was one of the people arrested or he just sat on the sidelines, watching his girlfriend beat someone up."

"Thanks." Eli sent Brady a quick text to look into a possible boyfriend for Sanderson.

As Ava thanked the captain and Eli started to head toward his SUV, Arthur called after him, "You want my take? I think Sanderson has a bad temper. She was quick to jump into the fray, even if it had nothing to do with her. I could see her deciding to set off a bomb somewhere. She seems like the type to take things too personal, and to take them too far."

Eli nodded as Arthur slid a pair of sunglasses from his pocket and put them on, then headed to his own vehicle. The captain had always rubbed Eli the wrong way, but second-in-charge at the Jasper PD wasn't a position he'd come by easily, even in a small town. That meant his opinion on a suspect was probably solid.

"Let's go pay her a visit," Eli said.

"What about talking to Diaz?" Ava asked as Eli realized she hadn't followed him toward the SUV. "He handled that incident where Sanderson smashed up a car."

Eli was anxious to get moving, but the more information they had, the better prepared they'd be for the conversation. Especially since they didn't want to bring her in to the station quite yet. "Yeah, let's find—oh, here we go." He pointed to the large glass front doors, where Dillon was exiting the station. "Hey, Dillion, you have a second?"

The Hispanic/Irish sergeant nodded, heading over to them in a few long-limbed strides. "What's up?"

Eli told him about their suspect. Before he'd finished reminding him about the incident with the smashed car, Dillon was already nodding, his dark eyes troubled.

"Yeah, I remember her. I didn't like that call at all."

"Why not?" Ava asked as Dillon leaned down to pet Lacey, who had stepped over to the sergeant and was staring up at him expectantly.

The German shepherd's tail thumped the ground a few times as Dillon paused to grin at her.

"Well, the guy who called to report his car being smashed up did it from work. He's in sales at one of the furniture stores at the edge of town. Can't remember which one. Anyway, he was working late one night, came outside and found his Beemer all smashed up. It looked like someone had taken a baseball bat to the headlights and the sides of the car. Everything except the windshield, which was intact but had the word *asshole* scratched into it, probably with a key. It was a mess. Not the kind of dents you can easily fix, either. Whoever did it put some real muscle behind the hits. They were trying to make that car virtually unsalvageable."

"Your investigation led to Sanderson?"

"Well, the guy—Kellerman was his name, Kurt Kellerman—led us to Sanderson. He gave us her name right away, said she'd been threatening him. He said he hadn't seen it happen, but there was no way it was anyone else."

"What was their disagreement about?" Ava asked.

"He claimed he didn't know why she disliked him," Dillon said, "but it was clear he was lying. I couldn't get him to budge on what motive she might have. So, I went to talk to her at that bar where she works, Shaker Peak. She claimed she hadn't done it, but gave me a bunch of hypotheticals. What if some guy sexually assaulted a friend of hers? What if that friend had seen the process of reporting sexual assault to police back in college and watched as someone *she* knew got no justice? What if she thought going to the police was a waste of time? Didn't the guy who'd hurt her friend deserve *some* kind of punishment?"

Ava scowled. "So, you think Sanderson busted up Kellerman's car as revenge for him sexually assaulting a friend of hers?"

"Yeah. I'm pretty sure it was someone who worked at that bar, too, because Sanderson kept her voice down while we talked, kept glancing around. At first, I thought she just didn't want anyone to overhear what she'd been accused of doing, but then I realized she was looking for someone specific. And I realized it wasn't so much her actions she was trying to keep quiet, but the little bit she was sharing about the assault. I tried to convince her to have her friend talk to us, but no dice. Without more to go on, there wasn't much I could do about investigating the assault. When it came to destroying the car, Sanderson was pretty good at keeping her words in hypotheticals. She never actually admitted to anything."

"So, then what?" Eli asked. "You couldn't find enough to prove Sanderson had smashed the car?"

"Not exactly. I'll be honest, I felt like I was digging into the wrong person. But we had a report, so I pursued it. But when I talked to Kellerman the next day to get some more details, he'd completely changed his tune. The first day, he'd been ranting and cussing Sanderson out, saying she'd been after him for months and finally seen her chance. When I went back, he had this really calm anger about him. He said he'd thought it over and decided he was wrong, that Sanderson had nothing to do with it. Said he didn't want to press charges against anyone and he'd just deal with his insurance."

"Any idea what caused his change of heart?" Eli asked, already suspecting the answer.

"I think Sanderson paid him a visit. I think she scared him. Hell, maybe he figured he'd gotten lucky, just having his car destroyed, and he didn't want to push his luck and have the friend press charges for sexual assault."

Eli nodded. "What's your take on Sanderson? Can you see her as a bomber?"

Dillon's lips twisted upward. "I don't know. I didn't get the impression that she would go for something indiscriminate like a bomb. But she was clearly discouraged by authorities in general. She mentioned being former Army, but she definitely had no love lost for anyone in authority. Maybe it was because of what her friend told her, maybe something else, but she seemed to resent not just my investigation, but also me."

Before Eli could say anything, Dillon continued, "I get it. Still, I think there was more going on there, because despite her obvious pride in being former military—she was wearing an Army hat when I interviewed her—she talked about military leadership in a similar way."

Ava looked at Eli. "Maybe Brady and Jason should try to dig into her military background? See if she left under questionable circumstances?"

Eli nodded, sending another text to Brady.

"So, do I think Sanderson could be the bomber?" Dillon repeated, and Eli looked up. "Yeah, given the right circumstances, I could see her being motivated by some kind of avenging mission."

Ava shared a worried look with Eli as he wondered what else Sanderson might want to avenge.

"The thing is," Dillon said, his tone ominous, "if it *is* her, she's good. That furniture store has plenty of security cameras, and she took just one of them out before she smashed up the car—the one that would have shown her on it."

"How'd she take it out?" Ava asked, her tone suggesting she had her suspicions.

"BB gun," Dillon said. "Perfect shot. Just one and the camera was toast."

As Ava nodded like she wasn't surprised, Dillon continued, "She's careful and she's not afraid to get her hands dirty. I honestly struggle to see her setting off a bomb where innocent people would get hurt, but maybe something has angered her and she thinks there are multiple people—or even a town—to blame. I can't imagine what it might be, but if it *is* her, you'd better get her behind bars fast."

Chapter Fifteen

"What's our play here?" Ava asked, glancing at Eli from the driver's seat of her police vehicle, a standard black Charger that was minimally modified for Lacey in the back. Even though it was silly, being in the driver's seat this time gave her a needed boost of confidence after their chat with Captain Rutledge had left her feeling sour.

Every time she engaged with him, she felt it all over again: she was the outsider and everyone knew it. It was never anything overt, just the way he'd look at her, eyes narrowed and lips tight, like he was staring at a suspect. The kind of thing she couldn't even really come out and ask about or he'd probably just call her crazy.

Right now, Ava tried to shake it off and focus on the case. They were headed to Jennilyn Sanderson's house to talk to her. It would be a tricky line to walk—getting information that might incriminate her, without tipping her off that she was a suspect. Or at least not tipping her off that she was a *primary* suspect, and potentially triggering her to act sooner than she might otherwise by placing a live bomb this time.

From what they'd heard about Jennilyn from Sergeant Diaz and Captain Rutledge, Ava worried that line was way too thin.

"I don't want to mention the lighter at all," Eli said. "If she knows we have forensics, I think it will spook her."

"Yeah, I agree. Maybe we can lead with the mill? Act like we're investigating some damage or graffiti and say someone saw her near there? Play it like we think she might have information about who *else* was around, and see if she gives us something useful?"

"What if we try that, but about the warehouse instead? Maybe in an attempt to give a plausible reason why she'd be there, she'll give us a hint about what her grudge is? It seems more likely that she has a direct connection to the warehouse than the mill. That could help us figure out her next potential target, get ahead of her."

Ava nodded, liking the idea of knowing what they were up against. If they could identify a motive, it could help them prevent a live bomb, but it could also help them get a warrant when the time came. "The thing I'm worried about for both approaches is what if these spots were just conveniently deserted? What if they were meant to sow fear, but the place itself doesn't actually matter? What if she's saving the real target for later, once the town is already afraid? Then are we just tipping our hand?"

"Yeah, I'm worried about that, too," Eli said. "But I'm not sure how else to go about this, because what Brady said about an arrest is spot-on." He sighed. "I'm anxious to talk to her, but maybe we need to spend more time digging into her background first."

Ava eased the vehicle off the road, onto the edge of a cornfield, and Lacey pushed her head through the seats, giving a slight whine.

Twisting to pet her, Ava said, "We're not there yet, Lacey. Hold on. You'll get to work soon."

Although Lacey barely moved, just opened her mouth

and let her tongue hang out, Ava could have sworn the promise was making her smile.

Turning toward Eli, Ava said, "Maybe we should call Brady and Jason and brainstorm? The news about the print came in and we dove into everything so fast. Maybe we need a brief pause to strategize more. Plus, that will give us a chance to see if they've discovered anything else we can use."

He'd pulled his phone out of his pocket before she'd finished speaking. "Good idea." He called Brady and when the Lieutenant picked up, Eli put him on speaker and said, "Ava and I are close to Sanderson's house. We're hoping you've found something that will help us."

"Sorry," Brady answered, and Eli's shoulders slumped. "We haven't come up with the name of a boyfriend. We haven't found her on social media. And we don't have any information on why she left the Army. We've been searching, but the only thing we've discovered is that she bought her house in Jasper about six months ago. She hasn't been here long."

Eli nodded at Ava and she knew what he must have been thinking. That was something, at least. If she'd only lived here for six months, then either she'd come to Jasper with a preexisting grudge, or something had happened during that time. It definitely narrowed the search.

"We should focus on looking for any incidents since she moved here that could be triggering her," Ava suggested.

"Jason is already looking into that angle," Brady said. "Although based on what Eli texted earlier about Sanderson possibly thinking of herself as some kind of avenging force to help others, it might not be that easy to find what set her off."

"Worth a shot," Eli said.

"Oh, definitely," Brady agreed. "But I doubt we're going to have anything before you talk to Sanderson. Sorry."

"Well, that was only part of why we're calling," Eli said, giving her a rueful look. "We also want to strategize. I think I was a little hasty rushing out here without a plan."

Ava shook her head at him, not wanting him to think she'd been criticizing. She was more cautious by nature, but she admired the way he relied on his gut, the way he trusted himself. They needed to talk to Sanderson. Waiting too long could give her a chance to set up at her new target, and there was no guarantee they'd be in a better position to arrest her. One misstep could mean a literal explosion.

He gave her a quick grin in return, as if to say *we're good* and she felt the force of that smile all the way down to her toes. An unexpected flush heated her cheeks and chest.

His smile dropped off, replaced by a heat in his eyes as he held her stare.

She looked away first. She'd always been attracted to men who approached the world the same way she did, with caution and a long-term plan. Apparently, she wasn't just upending her entire life; she was also upending the way she evaluated others.

Maybe it was about time, after so long feeling guilty for who she was and the things she wanted, to give herself a little freedom. And maybe opposites really did attract.

Still, freedom didn't mean destroying the future she was building by pursuing another officer. Maybe it just meant not being too hard on herself for what she was feeling. A little fantasizing never hurt anyone. Because Eli Thorne might not be her normal type, but those bright blue eyes and that cocky grin were definitely fantasy-worthy.

She tried to keep the smile off her face, but she saw Eli's eyes narrow when she looked back at him, like he suspected what she was thinking.

Slowly, Brady's words penetrated, as if he were speaking way too quietly, and Ava tried to refocus.

"I think we should ask about the warehouse," he said as his words from earlier about Sanderson's avenging mission swirled in Ava's mind. "Ignore the mill entirely. The warehouse is the most likely place to be connected to motive."

"Yeah, we talked about saying someone saw her near the warehouse," Eli told Brady. "But if that was just an easy place to test a bomb…"

"We could end up with nothing," Brady agreed, even as excitement began to build in Ava's gut.

"What if we go about this another way entirely? We can still say someone saw her near the warehouse. If she gives us her connection to the place as a way to try to make it seem like she had a legitimate reason to be there, great. But what if we chat with her for a while, let her get comfortable and then level with her? Or at least, *pretend* to level with her?"

"What do you mean?" Eli asked.

"Well, maybe she'll claim she wasn't near there, or maybe she'll give up some other name, try and lead us in the wrong direction. Whatever she says, we can keep pushing her about who else she might have seen, or even if she saw evidence that someone else had been there. If we push in that direction long enough, hopefully she'll feel comfortable with the idea that we're not after *her*."

Eli nodded slowly. "It makes sense. No matter what, she's going to know she's on our radar. It's a good idea to keep the pressure low. Make her feel like we want her help, so she doesn't feel pushed to act sooner."

"Right. Remember what happened when Sergeant Diaz talked to her about the car?" Ava reminded them.

"She gave up her motive without admitting to anything," Brady said, a hint of admiration in his tone.

"Exactly. We ask enough questions about someone else she might have seen, then we act like we're reluctantly telling her it's because we found bombing materials. See if we can get her to theorize about why someone might want to set off a bomb."

There was a long pause, but she could tell from the hint of a grin that pulled at Eli's lips that he was on board with her plan.

Pride filled her, the sense that she could really do this—she could find a way to fit in here, with her colleagues and in this town long-term. She might not be able to regain all the things she'd lost, but she could still make a future for herself where she was happy.

She was *so* ready to feel happy again, to shake loose the guilt that intellectually she knew was unfair. To stop replaying the disappointment in her parents' faces, the fury in her brother's eyes. To truly start fresh. To finally feel like she belonged somewhere.

"It's a great idea," Brady finally said into the silence.

"It could definitely work," Eli agreed. "We'll let you know how it goes," he told Brady. Then he stared at her. "You ready to do this?"

"Let's get our suspect to tell us her motive," Ava agreed, pulling back onto the empty stretch of highway.

They made it to Sanderson's house in fifteen minutes. The two-story home with wood siding and cheerful blue shutters was fairly small. It seemed even smaller because of its surroundings. The bartender lived on a big patch of land, with mountains visible in the distance and woods all around.

Ava felt a chill rush over her skin as she parked on the street and stepped out of her vehicle. The grass here was clipped short, not overgrown like it had been around the abandoned barn, but it gave Ava the same anxious feeling, like she was being watched.

Her gaze swept across the open front yard and she focused on the windows of the home, trying to spot anyone inside.

"You ready?" Eli asked, joining her on her side of the vehicle.

Pushing back her nerves, which were probably more a result of not being used to policing in the country than any actual threat, Ava nodded and opened the back door for Lacey.

"Let's do this." Eli moved like he always did, with confidence and certainty, heading toward the house without a backward glance.

Not reckless, but with an assuredness Ava rarely had without first prepping a plan and then a backup plan.

Ava's feet stayed planted longer than she'd intended and then she hurried to catch up, as Lacey trotted by her side.

She was about ten feet behind him when Lacey started barking, a deep timbre to her voice that startled Ava.

Eli glanced back at them, then whipped forward again. He pointed off to the side and mostly behind the house, where the hint of something man-made was visible among the trees. A shed, Ava realized.

Eli lifted his hands, making the motion of someone running, then took off in a run himself, toward that shed.

Had he seen Sanderson? Had she spotted them and made a run for it? If so, did that mean she thought they'd come to arrest her?

The jumbled thoughts raced through Ava's head as she tried to process what was happening. She squinted at the tree line as she started to run after Eli, but she didn't see anyone.

Lacey kept barking, more frantically now.

Had *she* spotted Sanderson? Lacey almost never barked, especially on the job. She wasn't alerting, either, not sitting down to indicate she'd detected drugs or a bomb.

Dread hit Ava hard, slamming into her chest with the force of a suspect trying to knock her over. "Eli, *no*!" she screamed at him, even as Lacey overtook her, racing after Eli.

Her dog got out in front of Eli, barking at him and then running toward him, as if pushing him backward, as his confused gaze twisted toward Ava.

Then, the world around her exploded in a deafening blast of heat and fire.

Chapter Sixteen

The ringing in Ava's ears was overwhelming as she forced her eyes open, tried to get her bearings. Her lungs contracted painfully, refusing to give her enough breath, and the world spun. Hazy gray that passed to show sudden spots of blue, and little sparks dancing across all of it.

Ava tried to understand what she was seeing, tried to figure out what had happened. But her mind was as hazy as her surroundings. She blinked, bringing everything into sharper focus.

She was lying in the grass, on her back. Where there should have been sky above her was mostly gray smoke and small sudden sparks of fire, catching in the wind and then fluttering past.

A bomb has gone off.

The knowledge shot through her, tightening her lungs again, and Ava fought against the pain, pushing herself up on her elbows.

Where is Eli? Where is Lacey?

Panic hit next, a remembered fear that made her hands shake and tears rush to her eyes. *No, no, no. Not again.*

The fire that had engulfed her parents hadn't been from a bomb, but a car crash. She hadn't seen it, but since the moment she'd heard of it, she'd been unable to stop imagining. That night, after she'd come home from a truncated

Academy graduation, after she'd left the hospital being told they were gone before the ambulances even arrived, she'd seen the pictures on the news. A pileup, her parents in the middle of it. Her brother spared because he'd decided at the last minute to travel separately. In his mind, she was to blame.

Those flames, sinister orange and red shooting into the sky, still dominated her nightmares sometimes. Right now, they were directly in front of her.

The cute little house that had been standing moments ago was nothing more than stubborn blackened walls of brick and studs, fire consuming what was left in the middle. Pieces of the house, debris as small as the sparks lighting on the wind, and as large as a bent and battered claw-foot bathtub, were scattered around her. The scent of charred wood and plastic burned in her airways, made her eyes itch and tear.

What about Eli and Lacey?

Ava shoved to her feet, her balance as wavy as her vision. Or maybe it was the smoke and fire in the air creating the illusion that everything was still in motion.

Beyond a flaming piece of wall, thrown partially intact twenty feet from the home, were two figures, immobile in the grass.

"Nooooo!" The scream burst from her, terrified and anguished.

The force of it tore through her body, bent her in half. It left her gasping for breath, her tears blurring the rest of her vision, even as she stumbled awkwardly forward. A broken prayer repeated itself on her lips, a desperate hope that they were only knocked unconscious, that they were still alive.

She froze as Eli seemed to move, a twitch of his arm and then a partial roll.

Had she imagined it?

Squinting through the haze, she started moving again, faster now. It seemed to take forever to reach him, even though he hadn't been that far ahead of her. She dropped to the ground beside him as he groaned and rolled fully over.

A heavy breath of relief left her, and she swiped her arm across her face, trying to wipe away the moisture. She blinked at the sudden pain in her eyes, then noticed the layer of ashy soot on her arms, the smear of blood over her hand.

"Are you okay?" She could barely hear herself over her heartbeat pounding in her ears, the residual ringing making her want to shake her head hard.

"I'm okay," Eli assured her, even as she ran her gaze and her hands over him, searching for injuries.

He was covered in ash, too, lending a gray tone to his skin and flaking in his hair. There was a gash in the leg of his uniform and she ripped it farther, checking the skin beneath. The slash through his skin was ragged and oozed blood, but it was shallow.

He had other wounds, scratches across his forehead and blood and grass matted on his hands, probably from the force of his fall. But nothing looked too serious.

"I'm okay," he repeated, and she turned her hopeful gaze to Lacey, lying a few feet past him, closer to where the house had stood.

Her dog whimpered, her legs all twitching at once as she tried to roll to her feet. With another cry, she dropped back to the ground.

Ava shoved to her feet, spotting the blood, the short piece of wood piercing just above Lacey's hip. Tears rushed forward and she tried to blink them back, tried to be strong for her dog.

"Lacey, stay there, girl." She ran to the German shepherd, whose tail thumped once at her arrival. Her head lifted slightly, her pleading gaze locked on Ava's.

"Good girl, Lacey. Good girl." Ava heard the terrified waver in her voice as she stroked the dog gently, trying to see how bad the injury was.

The short blackened piece of wood—Ava had no idea what it was from—was embedded deep enough to have stained Lacey's fur and the ground partially red. It didn't seem deep enough to have hit an organ. But what did she know? Dogs were built differently than people.

She had some basic training in trauma response as a police officer, but she wasn't a vet. She didn't know whether to leave the wood in or to pull it out. She didn't know if Lacey would be okay.

"We need to get her to a vet," Eli said, suddenly beside them.

Ava nodded up at him, hoping he would have answers she lacked. When she'd trained to get a K-9 partner, she'd learned about basic care for Lacey in an emergency. But there'd been no guidance on what to do if a bomb exploded shrapnel into her.

"I'll carry her to the car and we can call it in on the drive," Eli said.

Ava continued to stroke Lacey's fur, the feel of blood on her hands making the tears well up again. "Should we be moving her?"

"We need to get her to a vet," Eli repeated. He glanced around, then ran for a flat piece of wood—maybe part of a long table—in the grass a few feet away. He reached for it, then lunged away, swearing. "It's too hot."

"The shed." Ava pointed at the shed he'd been running for when the bomb went off. It was a small green metal structure mostly hidden in the woods, but resting up against one side was a stack of wood boards in various sizes. It looked like pieces of a garden bed that someone had taken apart.

While Ava stayed with Lacey, whispering to the dog that

she'd be okay, Eli raced for the shed. Somehow, after having just been unconscious, he looked steadier on his feet than she felt. His hand hovered near his holster and Ava remembered he'd thought he'd seen someone near the shed right before the explosion.

Ava's gaze swept the area, taking in the shed door, still closed. Empty? Or a convenient hiding place? Taking in the woods, dense enough for someone to be standing nearby, watching.

Had Jennilyn seen them coming? Had she rigged her own home to blow as a final exit after she'd set up more bombs somewhere in town? When they'd arrived, maybe it had changed her plans. Maybe she'd decided to slip out the back and blow it early, take them with it.

Was she still out there, potentially armed?

Ava's free hand darted to her holster as her gaze swept back and forth across the woods, looking for a color out of place, for any movement.

She saw nothing except Eli, his strides fast and sure. He grabbed the biggest board and then he was back at her side, giving her calm directions to lift Lacey with him.

The dog let out a small whimper when they lifted her onto the board, but she let them move her without any other complaint.

She and Eli strode to the car, holding either end of the board as they wove around debris that had blown out from the house.

They loaded Lacey into the back and Ava climbed in beside her, holding Lacey in place as Eli leaped into the driver's seat and put on the siren.

Then they were racing for the vet, and Ava's mind was on repeat, saying a prayer for Lacey.

Chapter Seventeen

The acrid scent of burnt materials—plastic and wood and metal—seared the inside of his mouth and nose. Even an hour later, it hadn't dissipated, just sent a new reminder rattling his lungs with every breath.

Eli and Ava had been sitting in the vet's office for forty-five minutes, waiting for word on Lacey. She'd been rushed in for surgery while Eli had called in the bomb to Jasper PD and told them about the figure he thought he'd seen running for the shed. His imagination? Or Jennilyn, spooked enough to blow up her own home if it meant taking him and Ava with it?

Whatever the case, this had been no pipe bomb. It had been something much bigger, much more powerful.

During the multiple calls with Jasper officers, notifying them about what had happened and then fielding follow-ups, he'd held Ava's hand.

She'd sat mutely beside him, staring at the wall, not seeming to notice anything happening around her. In shock.

Only now did she turn toward him, her gaze still slightly unfocused, her voice hoarse as she said, "I should go back. I should help at the scene."

He shifted toward her, taking in the smears of soot across her face and uniform, the grass and dirt streaking the sides of her arm and leg. There was more dirt smudged high on her cheek, the skin below abraded and slightly swollen. Deep scratches ran across the tops of both her hands, the blood dried and caked onto her skin.

Still, it was her eyes that worried him, that thousand-yard stare that said she was reliving the trauma over and over.

It had been her voice that had brought him back to consciousness, lying in the grass outside of Sanderson's house. The pain and panic he'd heard that made him fight to open his eyes and move.

"Your department has the scene covered. You don't need to worry about that right now." Eli squeezed her hand gently. "Lacey's going to be okay. Marie is a really good vet. She said she thought Lacey would make it through the surgery fine."

Ava's head jerked up and down, an imitation of a nod, like she was only partially hearing him.

"Ava." He took her other hand, tugged until she was twisting on the chair toward him.

She blinked a few times and finally seemed to focus on him. Then her pretty brown eyes welled over, tears spilling down her face.

Tugging a hand free, she wiped the tears away and ducked her head. "I'm sorry I'm losing it. I should be more professional. My job—"

"This is traumatic," he reassured her.

"She's just a dog," Ava said, her voice breaking at the end.

Eli stared at her a minute, surprised, then he asked softly, "You've never had a pet, have you?"

She shook her head, some of the curls that had been barely hanging onto her bun finally coming loose. They fell around the sides of her face and Eli tucked them behind her ears so he could see her expression.

Fear. Guilt. Embarrassment.

"Once you get to know an animal, you develop a special bond with them. If you've never had a pet, maybe you don't expect it. But they're all unique and special. They all have emotions and the capacity to love, just like us. You shouldn't feel guilty or embarrassed for loving her. She's a great dog."

Ava's forehead creased. "I don't feel guilty for that. I just—" She sighed. "Some K-9 handlers talk about their dogs like they're just a different type of law enforcement tool. That's what I expected when I started working with her. I didn't think..." She shook her head, then stared past him again.

"It's hard not to love them once you get to know them," he agreed. "I grew up with dogs and cats and a bunny, so I know how terrifying it is when an animal you love is hurt or sick."

Her gaze shifted back to his face, but he sensed she was only partially paying attention.

"You don't have pets now?"

"I do, actually. He's with my parents while I'm in Jasper. I didn't know what my hours would be like, but I have a Newfoundland. His name is Bear, because when I first brought him home, the little boys—three-year-old twins—who live next door yelled to their mom that I had gotten a pet bear."

Her eyebrows lifted. "A big dog."

He laughed. "Tell *him* that. He thinks he's a lapdog." His amusement settled and he squeezed her hand, making her glance at it. "He'd get along with Lacey."

As he said it, he realized he wanted to introduce them, wanted to see Ava and Lacey in his backyard, in his house. Wanted to get to know her better.

He'd felt it when they'd been at dinner together. Maybe

before then, if he were being truly honest with himself. With every moment they spent together, that feeling was growing. The desire to see her outside of work, to get to know her more as not just an officer, but a person.

Her gaze rose from their hands and she seemed perplexed, like she hadn't realized he'd been holding her hand for the past hour. She gently tugged it free, then made a show of tucking her hair back into its bun.

"Ava?"

The soft voice made Ava leap out of her seat, and Eli followed her to where Marie Beaumont, Jasper's primary veterinarian, stood.

The vet had always struck him as cautiously friendly with everyone, but generous with her affection for animals.

Right now, Marie tucked her short brown hair behind one ear and put a hand on Ava's upper arm. "She came through the surgery just fine."

Ava's whole body seemed to relax, and Eli felt the same relief.

"Can I see her?" Ava asked.

"You can come back for a minute, but she's not awake yet. We're going to want to keep her under observation here for a few days, so we can closely watch her stitches because of the location. But I expect she'll make a full recovery."

Ava let out a heavy sigh, squeezing her eyes closed briefly. Then she whispered, "Thank you."

"It will be a few weeks before she can return to her normal activity and her K-9 duties, but she's strong. The wood was more shredded than I would have liked, but it didn't pierce any organs." The vet, a few inches shorter than Ava with a more compact build, gave Ava a gentle smile. "Come on. I'll show you."

Ava glanced back at him, a request in her gaze.

He didn't wait for her to ask, just said, "I'll come, too, if that's okay. Lacey saved my life."

A grateful smile lifted the corners of Ava's lips as Marie nodded and led them toward the back.

Before they reached the room where Lacey was recovering, a young Black woman who looked vaguely familiar hurried over and gave Ava a tight hug.

Ava looked surprised, then awkwardly hugged her back. "Tashya, I didn't know you were working today."

"Tashya helped out," Marie said, giving the younger woman an encouraging smile.

"Thank you," Ava breathed, hugging her a bit tighter before letting go and stepping into the recovery room behind Marie.

Ava made a slight sound of distress when she saw Lacey, bandaged and asleep on the table.

"She's doing great," Marie reassured her as Eli slipped his hand into Ava's again.

This time, Ava squeezed back, tightly.

"I know it looks scary, but I promise she's okay. She should wake up within the next hour. She'll be groggy for a bit after that, but before you know it, she'll be up for a real visit. It's just going to take some time." Marie put a hand on her arm again, stepping in Ava's path so she was forced to look at her. "Why don't you go home, get some rest? You can come back tomorrow and Lacey will be awake and starting to feel a little better. By the end of the week, trust me, you'll have a hard time limiting her running."

Ava nodded rapidly, like she was trying to believe it.

Eli tugged on her hand slightly. "Why don't we go and let Lacey rest?"

Her head swiveled toward him, her eyes wide. She nodded, but instead of moving toward the door, she stepped around Marie to Lacey. Carefully, barely making contact, she stroked the top of Lacey's head. Then she leaned close and, in a whisper she probably thought no one could hear, said, "I'm so sorry, Lacey. You'll be okay, girl. You'll be okay."

Then she backed slowly toward the door, not taking her gaze off the German shepherd until she was out of the room.

"I have to go see another patient," Marie said. "But I'll call you if anything changes. And you can call the office to check on her, okay? You know our hours, but I also live right upstairs, so I always peek in during the night to check on patients who are in recovery."

Ava smiled at the vet. She still looked shell-shocked, but there was gratitude all over her face. "Thank you."

"Go take care of yourself now." Marie looked at him and said, "Make sure she does, okay?"

"Yes, ma'am," Eli told the woman, who was only a few years older than him.

Then he led Ava outside and opened the passenger door for her. She looked briefly surprised; it was her car. Luckily, she'd parked on the street at Jennilyn's place, so it hadn't been damaged, except for a big dent in the hood from a nearly intact toaster oven that had been catapulted in the blast.

When he climbed into the driver's seat, Eli felt the adrenaline that had been carrying him since he'd woken up on the grass, his ears ringing and his body aching, fade in a sudden rush. It left him so exhausted that he wondered if he should drive. But Ava was in no shape to do it, so he took a couple of deep breaths until he felt a little better. Then he started the engine and asked, "What's your address?"

She sat a little straighter, making a valiant effort to appear normal. It didn't reach her eyes, which were still wide with shock. "Shouldn't we go to the station? I'm sure there are things to do. I want to see how everything is going at Sanderson's house and—"

"Brady and Jason will keep updating us," Eli said. "They've been texting while we were at the vet's. So far, we don't know a lot, other than no one was spotted by the shed or in the woods. The shed was locked. We don't know yet if there were any casualties in the house."

"Don't you think—"

"We're no good to anyone right now," Eli insisted. "I'm exhausted. You're exhausted. We need to get cleaned up, get some rest and come back fresh tomorrow. There will still be plenty to do. If Sanderson is in the wind, hopefully it will slow her down with whatever her ultimate target is."

There was a long pause and he was readying his next argument when she sighed and gave him an address.

Thankfully, she didn't live too far from Marie's vet office downtown. Still, by the time he'd reached the short drive in front of her rental, a cute two-story with a wrap-around porch and a great view of the mountains, he wasn't sure he could have driven much farther.

He'd been through stressful calls before, but he hadn't felt this level of exhaustion since he'd defused that bomb at Little Ski Hill.

He turned off the engine and glanced at Ava, who had stared mutely through the windshield the entire drive. "I don't think I can make it back. Can I come in?"

Surprise flashed across her face, followed by uncertainty. Before he could say he'd get a ride, she nodded. Her voice barely above a whisper, she said, "I'd like that."

Chapter Eighteen

She'd lived in Jasper for months and this was the first time she'd invited anyone inside her house.

Ava glanced at Eli from the corner of her eyes, watching him take in the open-concept space. The front hall flowed right into the kitchen, which flowed right into a great room with expansive windows. And that view of the mountains, the one that had made her sign a rental agreement from across the country.

A dream of a new life wrapped up in a simple, serene view. She'd held tight to it ever since, but with each day she tried and failed to fit in, the dream had seemed further away.

Trying not to think about all the things that seemed out of reach right now, she followed Eli into the great room. The furnishings had come with the rental, a mix of raw-edge wood she loved and plaid she could have done without. She hadn't added any of her own touches yet, had put most of her belongings in storage back in Chicago.

At the time, she'd called it convenience. Why did she need to pay to bring her furniture across the country when the house already had plenty? She'd intended to have them brought over once she moved out of a rental and into a home she bought. But she'd been here for several months now and hadn't even considered looking at homes for sale. Suddenly she wondered if it had been her way of not fully committing.

As much as she wanted this fresh start, she'd left a part of herself in Chicago. The part that still hoped there was a chance to mend things with her brother. The part that wished she could go back in time and not pressure her parents to come to her Academy graduation. If she hadn't pushed, maybe they'd still be alive.

The idea pinched her heart, an ache that was never far from her thoughts.

"What a gorgeous view."

It took a minute for Eli's words to penetrate, and Ava tried to smile. It felt forced and shaky and she gave up on it. Instead, she nodded and said, "It's why I chose this place."

"The house? Or Jasper?"

"Both."

He nodded, staring at her as if that answer told him a lot, but that he still wanted to know more.

The idea made her shiver. She wanted friends, wanted to forge bonds here that would take Jasper from the place she lived to truly being her home. But reaching out hadn't been easy.

In Chicago, she'd been more fearless about making friends. She was cautious at work, of course, especially after that failed relationship with DeVante. It had put a strain on colleagues' faces that always made her wonder, what had they heard?

Still, it was much more than just her relationship with DeVante souring too publicly. It was the years of trying to rebuild one of the most important relationships in her life—with her brother—and ultimately failing. No matter what spin she tried to put on it, coming to Jasper was her admitting that failure.

"Why did you come here, Ava?"

Eli's words were soft, empathetic, like he already knew the answer held some kind of tragedy.

When she focused on him, she realized he was no longer standing at her big window, but right beside her. The scent of his woodsy aftershave blended with the scent of smoke that she didn't think even a dozen washes could take out of her uniform or her hair.

His nearness made her pulse pick up, made her breathing shallow. It seemed like the more she tried to ignore this attraction, the more it grew. It wasn't just physical desire. She wanted to be honest with him, wanted him to really know her. And she wanted to know him in return.

She took a deep breath, her nose itching at the smoke. All connections, whether they were friendships or something more, took a leap of faith. Maybe it was time to leap again.

She pulled the locket out from underneath her uniform, happy to see it hadn't been damaged when the blast had thrown her to the ground. Opening it with hands that shook, she held it slightly away from her body to show Eli.

He leaned in, that woodsy scent intoxicating even with smoke over top of it.

"My brother, Komi, and my parents." Her voice broke as she watched him stare at the pictures, and then his gaze rose to hers, his eyebrows lowered and worry in his eyes.

She closed the locket and took a step back, away from his concern and caring. Moving to the couch, she sat in the corner and stared out the window at the looming mountains, serene in the distance.

Eli sat at the opposite end of the couch, on the edge, his body angled toward her, all of his attention on her.

He waited, not pushing as she tried to figure out how to share the story. She'd never talked about it with anyone who didn't already know at least some of the details. It had caught the fancy of local news stations and no matter how many *no comment*s she threw at them, they still wrote about it. A personal interest story that was such a mix of triumph and tragedy.

Her fingers rubbed the locket as she said, "My parents didn't support my desire to become a police officer. Not just because they thought it was too dangerous and not just because they thought a woman didn't belong in law enforcement, both of which they did. But mostly because of the history of law enforcement and our community. Both of my parents had been pulled over more than once for DWB. You know, Driving While Black. I wanted to be an officer because I wanted to help people, especially after I saw how police could make a difference for someone in trouble. But I also wanted to be part of the solution, part of the change. They thought I was being a traitor."

She sighed, staring at her lap, all the embittered words she and her parents had tossed back and forth, all the tension between them, rushing back. A familiar anger and frustration followed, but it was swallowed up by the grief. All that lost time, being angry at one another. She'd run out of time to change their minds. And that wasn't the worst of it.

"When I told them about my graduation from the police academy, they refused to come. I fought them on it, day after day, trying to wear them down. Trying to get them to support me, even if they didn't understand, even if they didn't agree. To put their love for me above their hatred of the system." A sob worked its way up her throat as she said, "It worked. I convinced them. Because they loved me."

Eli scooted closer, moving into the center of the couch. He put his hand on top of her hand that rested on the seat beside her. He didn't squeeze or fit his fingers between hers, just let it sit there, a silent show of support at a level she could handle right now.

She looked up from her lap, focused her gaze on his face, full of concern and sympathy.

Her voice shifted into a monotone, her gaze moving to those mountains, her favorite source of calm. "There was a pileup on the freeway that day. Eighteen cars, and everyone in the first seven vehicles was killed by either the crash or the flammable materials the truck was carrying that ignited. Firefighters didn't get there in time. My parents were in the seventh car." *So* close to the dividing line between who had lived and who had died that day. "They died on their way to my graduation for something they didn't believe in, that I'd *made* them come to."

"Oh, Ava," Eli breathed. "I'm so sorry."

Her lips twisted, a familiar bitterness welling up. "I spent five years on the force in Chicago, trying to prove that I'd chosen a worthwhile profession, that their deaths hadn't been for nothing." Something else those damn reporters had picked up on, tried to turn into a way for them to make money. "Five years trying to convince Komi that I wasn't to blame."

The hand over hers squeezed slightly, and then his fingers did interlock with hers, but instead of feeling like too much, it felt like the anchor she needed. She squeezed back, holding tight.

"Five months ago, I tried calling Komi again. I'd called him every couple of months ever since the accident, left him messages. He rarely answered, and when he did, it was more of the same: he couldn't forgive me." Her voice broke again. "He didn't know if he ever would."

She took a couple of shaky breaths, trying to calm the grief rising up in her chest, tightening her lungs and making the backs of her eyes sting. "This time, he told me to stop calling. Said it was enough, that it was time for both of us to stop trying, to stop pretending. He said that I wasn't his sister anymore."

"You know none of that is your fault," Eli said, his thumb stroking the side of her palm.

She shifted to face him, her lips lifting in an ironic smile. "Intellectually, sure. I didn't cause the ice storm that day. I wasn't driving the truck that slid on the ice that started the pileup. The truck that was carrying flammable materials that ignited when the first car behind it tried to stop and couldn't, slamming into the truck just like sixteen more after that. But that doesn't stop me from feeling guilty every day. And honestly? I'm angry, too."

She'd never admitted that part to anyone before, hadn't even wanted to admit it to herself. Right now, saying it out loud felt freeing. "I'm angry that my brother blames me, when we should have been grieving together."

She took another deep breath, the tension around her heart loosening slightly. "My extended family is all far away. I love them, but I don't see them all that often. My brother is only a year younger than me. We've always been close. We should have supported each other through this time, not had it separate us, too."

"Grief makes people act in irrational ways," Eli said. "Hopefully, someday he'll realize that."

"I hope so," Ava said, her free hand squeezing tight around the locket. "Because in so many ways, it feels like I lost him that day, too."

Eli sat silently for a long moment, maybe sensing that she needed to sit with the impact of her words, with the complexity of her feelings.

Then, he said softly, "I'm sorry you had to go through all of that. You and I don't know each other well yet, but I'm your friend. I want to support you, however you need."

She felt her lips twist a little at the word *friend* and she wondered if he'd seen it, because he shifted a little closer. Words started to form on his lips that she wasn't sure she was ready to hear.

She cut him off, admitted in another confessional rush, "I came here for a fresh start. A way to clear the slate, to not have to see that freeway where my parents died or the reporters on TV who hounded me for months afterward, looking for a story. I thought it would be easier. But I just don't fit in."

Not with anyone besides Lacey, who'd been hurt today because she hadn't realized what Lacey was trying to tell her soon enough. She didn't say those words out loud, because she knew it was more irrational guilt. Even if she owned a part of the blame, she didn't own all of it. She hadn't set the bomb.

"It takes time," Eli said. "Small towns are great in many ways. The sense of community, the way people look out for each other, is unlike anything you'll find elsewhere. But people in small towns can be insular, too. It takes a little time to go from outsider to part of the community."

Ava nodded, appreciating that perspective but knowing part of the problem was her. Her fear of facing more rejection. Her wariness of letting anyone else in who she might lose.

Frustration built inside her that she felt this way, that she feared what she needed most. Connections.

"You were right. I love Lacey. I feel closer to her than anyone. But it's hard to form connections at work when you're not just the outsider, but the one that the Chief thinks could only get along with a dog."

Surprise flitted across Eli's face, followed by a slight smile. "Ava. The Chief is the biggest supporter of a K-9 program that I know. He has been for his entire career. Before he was chief, he was a K-9 handler himself. Pairing you with Lacey wasn't a punishment. It was an honor. It was his way of saying he believes in you."

As Ava let those words roll around in her mind, surprising and powerful and buoying, Eli added, "It takes a really special person to be a K-9 handler."

She stared at him, seeing the intensity on his face, the strength of his belief in those words. The frustration and guilt she'd been feeling faded, replaced by something new. Something scary, but exciting. Something she'd been waiting for, but had been afraid to reach out and grab.

Before she could lose her courage, Ava leaned across the seat, closing the distance between them. She slid her hand out from underneath his and locked both of her hands around his neck.

She read the flash of surprise on his face, followed by an intense wanting that made desire flutter in her belly.

Then her lips were on his, softly at first, fitting them to his, learning the feel and taste of them. Then harder, encouraging him to meet her tongue at the seam of his lips.

He didn't hesitate, sucking her tongue into his mouth with a passion that made all her nerve endings fire to life, every inch of her skin suddenly oversensitized.

She slid one hand into his hair, holding his head tight against hers, while the other traveled downward, over the bunching muscles in his back. Her tongue kept dueling with his, as she moved closer, the angle on the couch awkward, too much space between them and too many clothes.

His hands bracketed her ribs, then slid downward, over her waist, then digging in at her hips. His lips and tongue kept moving with hers, quickening the pace, the taste of smoke with something sweet underneath.

A moan emerged from her mouth, something desperate and passionate. It surprised her and she lifted her lips from his, pulling back slightly to stare at him.

He gazed back at her, his blue eyes wide and dilated, his lips damp and his pale skin slightly flushed. His breathing was as hard as hers, a mix of desire and surprise still stamped in his gaze.

A fresh wave of emotions flooded her. A desire to throw herself back into his arms, let him sweep her away into an hour or two where nothing mattered but them. A blend of fear and excitement that suddenly she knew exactly what she wanted.

The certainty that this was the wrong move. The wrong time.

She let out a shaky breath and stood. "I shouldn't have done that. We're coworkers. I—we need to keep this professional."

Eli stood more slowly, never taking that smoldering gaze off hers. "We're only truly coworkers until we find that bomber. Once we do, I'm going to pursue you with everything I've got." Then he gave her a wide confident grin.

Even as he stepped away from her, she felt herself swaying toward him. Felt herself falling toward something that seemed inevitable.

Chapter Nineteen

When they stepped out of her dented Charger in the police station's parking lot on Friday morning, Ava glanced around and then her shoulders slumped with obvious relief.

No one was there to see them arriving at the station together, first thing in the morning.

Eli knew he should feel the same way. He didn't want rumors starting and he didn't want Ava to feel uncomfortable, especially after everything she'd shared with him yesterday. Still, he wished she hadn't looked quite so relieved.

He also wished she hadn't been quite so embarrassed after she'd kissed him, or quite so shy the rest of the evening. Not that they'd spent a lot of time together. She'd pointed him to the guest bathroom and he'd showered the smoke off as best he could. He'd tossed his uniform in her washing machine, even though ultimately it would go in the trash. But he'd had nothing else to wear. He'd waited out the washer and dryer time wrapped in a towel and trying to pretend he didn't notice all her furtive glances while they devoured a hastily-warmed frozen pizza together.

Then he'd climbed back up the stairs to her guest bedroom, where he'd passed out until this morning. He'd had her swing by his hotel so he could get a change of clothes, but his vehicle was still in the Jasper PD parking lot.

The drive in to work had been full of slightly awkward

small talk. Whenever their gazes locked, she'd start fidget-ing. The only time she'd seemed unconcerned about being alone with him was when they'd swung by the vet's office to check on Lacey. For those moments, Ava had been too focused on the dog to look nervous.

They'd found Lacey groggy and clearly in some pain. But she was moving around, walking gingerly and her tail had wagged like mad when she'd seen Ava.

He and Ava had both pet Lacey and praised her until Marie had finally given them an understanding smile and told them Lacey needed a chance to rest some more. Then they'd climbed into Ava's vehicle and she'd slid back into that anxious silence.

Now, she glanced around the empty parking lot one more time and then hurried inside, not giving him a chance to take advantage of the fact that they were alone.

Not that he would have said or done anything in the po-lice station parking lot. No, he'd already told her his plan last night. He understood her desire to press pause on what-ever was happening between them while they were work-ing together. But he wasn't giving up.

As soon as he followed her inside, they were surrounded by other members of the department, officers slapping them on the back or checking that they were okay.

Eli nodded, giving praise where it was due: to Lacey for warning them, for physically putting herself in front of him when he hadn't realized what she was saying. He'd thought she'd seen the same figure he had, running for the woods or the shed. In retrospect, had he actually seen a person? Or could it have been an animal, a deer or even a caribou or moose? He wasn't sure.

It had all happened too fast, just a flash of movement and color where it didn't belong. Then, the world around him had exploded. He'd been flying through the air, too quickly to try and protect his face or brace himself for the fall. Then there'd been nothing until Ava's tortured scream woke him, a scream he'd heard in his nightmares last night.

All he knew was that if Lacey hadn't gotten in front of him, making him stop, he would have been running full force toward the shed behind the house when the explosion hit. He probably would have died in Sanderson's yard.

He glanced at Ava, looking flustered by all the attention, and he was overwhelmed by relief. Not just that he hadn't died yesterday, but that he hadn't put her through losing someone else in a fiery blast.

He didn't know her as well as he wanted to yet, but he could tell she blamed herself—at least partially—for not having recognized Lacey's warning sooner. If something had happened to him, he knew she would have done the same second-guessing, especially since she'd encouraged him to stop and think over a plan before arriving. She'd wonder if they should have spent more time planning, more time researching.

The guilt she carried now was unfair, and he ached for her. She'd faced so many losses in such a short time, and all connected to the dream she'd had for herself of being a police officer. What must it be like for her going to work every day with that connection, even if logically she knew she wasn't to blame?

"Hey, Eli, Ava," Jason said as he slid past the group of officers slowly moving back to their own work. "Are you okay?" He put a hand on Ava's arm before they could answer. "I'm so glad Lacey is going to be all right. I talked to Tashya ten minutes ago and she said that Lacey was standing and having some food. She and Marie will take great care of her while she heals."

Ava nodded, her smile genuine, even though she still looked slightly uncomfortable with the attention. "I got to see Lacey this morning before we—before I came in. I'm so relieved."

"You two are okay?" Jason persisted, his gaze going from the bandage on Eli's forehead to the angry red abrasion on Ava's cheek. "Because Brady and I can hold down the fort if you need more time to heal."

"No, we're okay," Ava insisted, tucking her hands, which had large bandages across the tops of them, into her pockets. "Just some cuts and scratches."

It was mostly true. He barely felt the various cuts over his body, besides the deeper one on his thigh, which was a constant dull ache.

She hadn't mentioned the fact that he'd been unconscious briefly, that he was fairly sure she had been as well. Neither of them had gotten checked out, which was probably a mistake. But neither of them had shown any symptoms of a concussion, either, and it had been almost twenty hours since the explosion.

Eli nodded his agreement. "We're ready to dive back into the investigation." He followed Jason and Ava toward the conference room. "What do we know so far?"

"Brady and I headed there as soon as you called it in, but there wasn't a lot we could do besides search the woods and open the shed. Firefighters had to come and put out the blaze before anyone could go near that house. We were on the scene for about eight hours and then Lieutenant Hoover and Sergeant Diaz took over."

When they followed Jason into the conference room, Brady leaped to his feet and hurried over, studying them both as if looking for injuries. "Are you okay? I can't believe Sanderson blew her own house."

Ava nodded as Eli assured Brady, "We're fine. Thanks to Lacey."

"I heard." Brady gave Ava an impressed look. "She's a hero."

"She is," Ava agreed. "Hopefully she'll be back at work in a few weeks."

"There's been no sign of Sanderson since her house exploded?" Eli asked, wondering if there was a chance it hadn't been her but someone else who'd blown the place. Maybe an accomplice who was worried Sanderson was messing things up.

"Nope," Brady said. "She didn't show up for her job last night and her boss said it's strange that she didn't even call in. Apparently, she's his most reliable bartender. He heard about the explosion, assumed it was a gas problem and feared she'd been inside. Cal Hoover was just in here confirming that there was no body in the rubble."

Ava glanced at him, looking unsurprised but troubled.

Sanderson blowing up her own house felt like an end game, or desperation. Had she just overreacted, thinking they had more evidence than they actually did? Or had she spotted them and panicked?

In either case, would she forget her grudge and run far from Jasper? Or hide somewhere and set off another bomb soon?

"I think we'd better start talking to her family and friends," Eli said.

"Did you find anything interesting in the shed?" Ava asked at the same time.

"Just standard garden tools," Jason said.

"Do we have any more on her time in the military?" Eli asked.

Brady shook his head. "I'm waiting for someone to call me back. But you know how it goes with red tape. All they would confirm so far is that she was honorably discharged."

"Well, that's something," Ava said. "But not particularly useful right now."

"Did we learn anything else at the scene?" Eli asked. "What do we know about the bomb?"

"It was a big IED," Brady said. "Nothing like what you found at the warehouse or the sawmill. As you could probably tell, it contained a lot of explosive material. Still, it wouldn't have caused that much damage except it had been placed beside the house's gas boiler in the basement. Looks like the gas line snapped during the explosion and fueled a much bigger explosion. The bomb had both a timer and a remote way to set it off."

Eli frowned. "I don't suppose we know if the timer was set?"

Brady shook his head. "We assume it was detonated remotely, and that the timer hadn't been set yet, but Sanderson must have had iron nerves to live on top of that thing. Or supreme confidence in her bomb-building skills. Because what if something had set it off by accident before she was ready?"

Eli nodded. "Depending what she was using for her remote detonation, that's a definite possibility. Not to mention that it's pretty extreme to put a bomb under your own house. But who knows? Maybe once she set the bomb or bombs in town, she planned to come back to her house and take herself out rather than wait for us to figure out it was her and arrest her."

Ava gave an exaggerated shiver at the idea. "Do we have any thoughts on who might take her in, hide her?"

Brady and Jason shook their heads in unison. "She doesn't have any family here that we could find," Jason said. "Her parents are back in Kansas. I was planning to give them a call today, see if they've heard from her, if they can tell us why she moved to Jasper or if she holds any grudges."

Eli nodded. "Great. Why don't you and Jason do that? Contact her family, and follow up with the Army? If you learn about any friends she's got in the area, maybe pay them a visit. Ava and I can go to Shaker Peak, talk to her boss in person and talk to the other bartenders and servers."

Jason and Brady were nodding in agreement with his plan before he'd even finished sharing it. Ava gave a forced smile and a nod of her own and Eli tried not to react.

It made sense for them to continue pairing together, and let Brady and Jason stay grouped as well. Besides, he wanted to make sure she was okay after what had happened to Lacey. Clearly, she didn't like the idea.

Maybe she just felt awkward, didn't want him to bring up that kiss—that mind-blowing, eye-opening kiss. Or maybe she was worried the two of them working closely together would mean someone seeing there was more happening between them.

Whatever the case, he wasn't about to change his plan now.

He gestured for her to go first, then followed her out of the conference room. As they wove their way back through the bullpen, several other officers stopped them to express their happiness that he and Ava were okay.

He snuck a glance at her as she thanked them, seeing the smile lifting the edges of her lips. Maybe she was finally beginning to realize that she *was* liked here, that this community could easily become *her* community.

He'd planned to help her fit in before, but his determination to keep her in Jasper doubled. He had a long way to go to get past her defenses, even after they'd stopped working together. He may have only known her less than a week, but one thing he knew for sure.

Ava Callan was worth pursuing.

Chapter Twenty

Shaker Peak was as dismal as Ava remembered. From the dim lighting—probably meant to disguise the fact that the counters could have been cleaner—to the chairs that creaked when they moved and the peeling paint on the walls, the whole place seemed depressing. Maybe that was the point. You came in wanting to drink and the atmosphere made you want more.

Glancing around, Ava took in the only patrons there at 9:30 a.m. on a Friday. A middle-aged white man with a thick mustache wearing a suit with his tie askance and staring forlornly into his whiskey at the bar. A Latinx woman in a black dress that looked more appropriate for an evening at a club, scowling in a cracked corner booth. Her stilettos were on the table beside her beer and peanuts.

Behind the bar, a tall, thin Black woman with a series of tattoos on both arms eyed them as she wiped down the counter. "Can I help you?"

Eli stepped forward and Ava couldn't help but notice how assured he looked, no matter whether he was sending a robot into a warehouse to check out a bomb or talking to people in the course of an investigation.

Or when he was telling a woman he planned to pursue her with everything he had. The memory rose Ava's temperature, and she blinked it away, focusing on the here and now.

Eli gave the bartender a friendly smile, lowering his voice as he asked, "Do you know Jennilyn Sanderson?"

Her eyes narrowed, and she glanced from him to Ava. "Why do the cops want to know about Jenny?"

"Your boss didn't say anything to you?" Eli pressed.

Her forehead crinkled, and her expression went from hostile to worried. "He said there'd been an explosion at her house. Some kind of gas leak?" Her hand fisted around the rag, moving rapidly across the counter. "She wasn't home, was she? I haven't heard from her."

"She wasn't home," Ava said.

The bartender let out an audible sigh. "I'm so glad. Do you know why she didn't come in for her shift? I mean, even considering that her house blew up and there are probably things she has to deal with, it's weird that she didn't call. She's shown up to a shift so sick she could barely stand."

"Can we step outside and chat?" Eli asked.

The bartender glanced at the patron at the counter, who was leaning noticeably toward them, trying to eavesdrop. Scowling, she swatted her rag at him. "Mind your own business, John." Then she called into the back, "Pete, I'm taking a cigarette break!"

"Again?" he called back. "Hurry up!"

"Come on." She didn't wait for Pete to take over at the bar, just strode for the entrance, squinting as she moved from the dark bar into the bright sunshine.

"Let's start over," Eli said. "I'm Captain Eli Thorne and this is Officer Ava Callan."

"Sasha," the bartender introduced herself.

"So, Sasha, we need to ask you some questions about Jennilyn. Hopefully your answers will help us find her."

The bartender frowned, glancing between them again. "She's missing?" There was a long pause, then finally she sighed and pulled out a cigarette, lighting up.

"She is," Ava said, resisting the urge to wave a hand in front of her face to dispel the smoke. "We're trying to figure out why. How well do you know her?"

"Well, she started working here about six months ago, when she moved to Jasper. Shaker Peak doesn't really need more than one bartender at a time except on weekends, but Jenny and I always saw each other switching shifts. And we worked together a lot on the weekends." She shrugged, but her movements were jerky, her drags on her cigarette long. "We got to be good friends. I can't believe she's missing. You think something happened to her? Is this connected to the gas leak?"

"We're not sure yet," Eli answered. "What can you tell us about her? Has anything been bothering her lately? Anyone or anything she expressed anger toward?"

"I mean, what do you want to know? Jenny is Jenny. She is opinionated and kind of a badass, if you want to know the truth. No one messes with her. No one messed with me when she was around, either. Because you know, mostly the clientele here aren't interested in anything except drinking, but like every bar, we get the ones who are looking to start a fight. Or the alcohol loosens them up and they decide it's a good idea to harass a woman."

"So, they all knew Jennilyn wouldn't stand for it?" Ava asked. "She was like a bouncer?"

Sasha laughed, an anemic sound that didn't match her much deeper voice. "I guess. I mean, she definitely threw a few guys out on their asses."

"Anyone in particular?" Eli asked.

"Not really. Just whoever needed it. But you know, she used to be in the Army, so she had skills."

Ava shared a discreet glance with Eli. "What kind of skills?"

"She is strong. I mean, she isn't all that big." Looking Ava over, she said, "A few inches shorter than you. But her muscles are killer. Those biceps?" She laughed again. "I don't know how she did that." Sasha flexed her own slender arm, and the muscle barely showed. "Jenny said she didn't even go to a gym. I guess she had lots of weights at home." Her amusement faded at the word *home* and she took another series of drags from her cigarette, shaking the ash onto the street.

"Do you know what she did for the Army?" Eli asked.

Sasha shrugged. "I don't know. What does anyone *do* for the Army? Fight, I guess."

"What about explosives?" Eli persisted. "Did she have any experience with those in the military?"

"Explosives?" Sasha glanced between them, perplexed. Then she shook her head rapidly. "Oh, no. No way. You think Jenny blew up *her own house*? Why the hell would she do that?"

"We're not sure," Ava said carefully. "But there's some evidence that she might have. Whether or not it was her, it's really important that we talk to her."

Sasha's lips formed a thin line, her cigarette burning low in her hand. Just when Ava thought she was going to have to give more incentive, Sasha said, "Look, I know Jenny has a temper, but this makes no sense. She wouldn't blow anything up, especially her own house! I mean, yeah, she was kind of underwater on the mortgage since she couldn't rely on half the cost from that jerk of an ex. But good riddance. She dumped him, so she knew she was better off owing money than dealing with him, no matter how much he begged. She certainly wasn't so torn up over it that she'd blow the place up to get rid of the memories."

Ava felt Eli's gaze on her as she asked, "What's the ex's name?"

"Dennis something. Dennis… Ryon! That's it. Listen, if you go talking to him, don't believe anything he says about—ow!" Swearing, Sasha dropped her cigarette, which had burned ash down to her fingertips, then stomped it out. Sucking on her fingers, she mumbled, "There's bad blood between him and Jenny."

Tension built inside Ava, an anxiousness to get moving and talk to Dennis Ryon. Maybe he could tell them where Jennilyn might be hiding. Or maybe he was a potential target they needed to warn.

She glanced at Eli, who asked, "One more thing, Sasha. Do you know where Jennilyn might go if she needed a place to hide out?"

"Nah." Sasha scowled as she blew on her fingers. "Look, she was a good friend, but we were mostly work friends, you know? I've never been to her house. We didn't really hang out outside of the bar." She glanced at it, the windows dark with grime, and turned away from them. Over her shoulder she said, "When you find her—and you realize she *didn't* blow up her own house—do me a favor and ask her to call us, okay?"

She didn't wait for an answer, just disappeared back inside.

Chapter Twenty-One

Tracking down Dennis Ryon wasn't easy.

Three hours after they'd left Shaker Peak, Eli pulled his SUV into the parking lot of Salmon Creek Motel, a cheap but clean motel that had sat on the outskirts of Jasper for as long as Eli could remember. Despite the fact that the tourist spot was Salmon River and the motel was nowhere near it, they did a steady business. They rented to the tourists who flocked to the area in the summers and winters, needing a place to stay as they drove from one small town to the next, skiing or swimming. They also rented longer-term, especially in the off-season.

At first, Eli had thought Dennis had left town when he and Jennilyn broke up. Eli and Ava had called Brady and Jason to update them, and have them ask Jennilyn's family about Dennis. Brady had called back twenty minutes later and said that the family had never met Dennis, but it hadn't stopped them from disliking him.

They said Jennilyn had met him during her time in the Army and the two of them got out at the same time. When her family had expected her to finally come back to Kansas and settle down there, she'd announced she and Dennis were moving in together. They wanted to have an adventure, find someplace neither of them had ever been and buy a home. Their only requirements were that the spot be quiet and small. And apparently, somewhere *not* in Kansas.

Dennis and Jennilyn had bought the house together, but because of Dennis's bad credit, hers was the only name on the mortgage. When he left last month—they didn't know what had caused the split—she'd been left with a house she couldn't afford. Still, she wouldn't come home, they'd lamented.

"What impression did you get of the family?" Ava had asked while Eli stared at her.

The bright early morning sun streaming through the windshield had highlighted the way her light brown eyes got a little darker around the edges. It put a glow on her smooth, soft skin, and showed him the slight highlights in her hair, making him want to pull those curls out of the bun, the way they'd been at dinner three nights ago.

She must have sensed him staring, because her gaze had shifted to his, held briefly—just long enough to send a jolt of desire through him—then focused resolutely out the windshield.

"I wasn't impressed with the family," Brady had said. "They didn't come right out and say they wanted her back so she could help them out. But they kept talking about how the Army paid good money and how her loyalty should have been to the people who raised her."

"They didn't seem all that concerned when we said she was missing, either," Jason had added. "They were just angry, like they thought she'd simply left Jasper without telling them where she was going next."

"So, she's probably not in contact with them," Ava had sighed.

"I doubt it." Brady had sounded discouraged as he added, "All they could tell us about where Dennis might be was that they thought he'd gone to stay at a motel. They thought he was biding his time, hoping Jennilyn would take him back. Apparently, the breakup was her decision."

"Did they think she would take him back?" Eli asked.

"Not sure."

After he'd hung up with Brady and Jason, he and Ava had driven around town, working their way outward, checking each of the hotels and motels, and even the camping grounds. The town was small, but since tourism was one of its biggest industries, there was no shortage of places to stay.

After the fifth spot, they'd started making calls instead, trying to get the managers to tell them over the phone if Dennis Ryon was a guest. Some had refused to answer, and he'd marked them down as places to visit in person. Others had just heard *police* and dug through their records. They'd finally gotten lucky with Salmon Creek Motel.

"How do you want to play this?" Eli asked, knowing from the time they'd spent working together that she liked to go in with a plan. Whereas with interviews like this, he'd often play it by ear, let the tone of the conversation lead him to the right tactic.

But he wasn't inflexible. And he wanted her to feel like she had as much say in this investigation as he did.

She twisted toward him, and Eli couldn't stop his gaze from dropping to her lips. She'd shocked the hell out of him when she'd kissed him, but ever since he'd been having trouble focusing on much besides strategizing how to get a repeat.

"Sasha made it sound like Dennis wanted Jennilyn back," Ava said, her tone all-business, so much so that he thought she could read the train of his thoughts.

He gave her a quick grin and her words stalled before she rushed on, "I think we need to be careful not to make it seem like something he tells us could get her in trouble and wreck his chances. But he might have good insight into who she'd hate enough to target with a bomb."

"Agreed. So, the you're-helping-us-help-her angle?"

Ava nodded, reaching for the door. "Yep. Let's do this."

Surprised, he jogged to catch up as she walked toward Room 113. Like all of the rooms, it was accessible from an exterior door. Maybe he was rubbing off on her if she thought that sufficed as their plan. Just like she was rubbing off on him, having him suggest one in the first place.

They made a good team. The thought didn't surprise him, exactly, but it did make his steps slow as he stared at her, striding purposefully toward the motel.

He'd always had a vision of himself, far into the future, sitting on a wraparound porch like the one at Ava's rental, lounging on a glider while a wife—someone whose features were hazy—chatted from a rocking chair beside him. Right now, he could picture Ava on that rocker, Lacey by her side while Bear laid at his feet.

Shaking the image clear—it was *way* too soon for that kind of daydream—he hurried after her again as she knocked forcefully on the door of Room 113.

The man who answered looked about her age. His blondish-brown hair was sheared short, like he was still in the Army, and his biceps—displayed beneath a sleeveless T-shirt—were well-developed. Only the slight paunch at his waistline suggested he'd fallen off the Army routine.

He frowned from Ava to Eli, slight nerves underneath the confusion, a common reaction to a police visit. "Can I help you?"

Eli stepped up beside Ava. "Dennis Ryon?" When he nodded, Eli said, "We wanted to chat with you about Jennilyn Sanderson."

The frown deepened, but there was something in his hazel eyes—a hint of glee, like he was happy to have any reason to talk about her. "She get in another bar fight and want me to bail her out?"

"Not exactly," Ava said. "Have you spoken to her friends or family recently?"

Dennis's frown shifted into a scowl. "No. Jenny and I broke up a month ago." He shrugged, but it was forced, angry. "She'll change her mind. She always does. But she didn't get along with her family, so I never really talked to them. And I haven't talked to her *friends*."

He spit the last word out in a way that made Eli want to dig deeper, but Ava pressed forward. "I hate to be the one to tell you, but her house exploded earlier today. She's fine," Ava rushed on, "but we have reason to believe Jennilyn is the one who blew it."

Dennis's eyes widened and he glanced back and forth between them with surprise, but his lips trembled.

Suppressed amusement? Fear? Eli wasn't sure.

He studied the six-foot tall white man more closely, trying to read him. Dennis definitely had conflicting emotions when it came to Jennilyn—love and anger and frustration all blended together. Would it be enough to make him help them, either out of revenge or in order to try and help his ex? Or would it go the other way, make Dennis close off?

When Dennis finally spoke, his tone was careful, modulated. "Why would Jenny blow up her house? I mean, I know she was mad about the cost after we broke up, but what was I going to do, keep paying when I wasn't living there? Besides, she loved that place. We checked out a lot of little towns before we landed here. Jasper was *her* idea. I would have kept looking. I mean, no offense, but this place could have a *few* more job opportunities, right?"

When neither of them answered, he sighed. "Look, I don't know why you think Jenny would blow up the house. But no way."

His words were confident, but the way he glanced back and forth between them, like he was trying to convince them, wasn't.

"She had bomb-making knowledge from the Army, though, right?" Eli guessed.

"Well, yeah." Dennis shoved his hands into the pockets of his loose jeans. "So what? And look, I know she's got…anger issues, but that doesn't mean she'd *blow something up!*"

"What kind of anger issues?" Ava asked.

His eyebrows lifted. "I thought you knew about the bar fight. And the time she smashed up that guy's car with a fricking baseball bat. But she's never used a bomb." He glanced back and forth between them again, like he hoped they were buying it.

"Who else is she angry with, Dennis?" Ava asked softly.

"No. No, I don't… I'm not helping you get her in trouble."

"Maybe you're helping her stay out of it," Eli said.

He stared at the ground a moment, and Eli nodded at Ava, telling her silently to wait him out.

Finally, he looked up, his jaw tight, but with that same suppressed happiness in his gaze, like he believed this could be his ticket back into Jennilyn's life. "Maybe the owner of the bar? She always said he was spineless, that he wouldn't stand up to anyone who was causing trouble at the bar. That she had to take care of the lowlifes herself."

Eli nodded, catching Ava's concern from the corner of his eye. "Who else?"

"I don't know. Maybe the bank? She was pissed that they used my credit score as an excuse to try and give us a high interest rate. She didn't want to go on the mortgage alone. I didn't want that, either," Dennis said quickly. "But she was really mad about it. She used to complain about the loan officer all the time."

"What bank?" Eli asked. "Do you know the loan officer's name?"

"Jasper Financial was the bank. You know, the one out by all those furniture stores? I don't remember the guy's name, but he wore these ridiculous plaid suits every time we met with him. You can't miss him if you go in there."

Ava nodded. "Is there anyone else you can think of?"

When he shook his head, Eli asked, "What about somewhere Jennilyn might be staying? A friend's house or maybe a hotel under a different name? Or squatting or camping somewhere?"

Dennis frowned, shook his head tightly. "I don't know."

"Are you sure?" Ava pressed. "Because if we can find her, maybe we can stop her from doing something she can't undo."

The words hung in the air a long time, but when Dennis's gaze locked on first Ava, then Eli, it was hard. "I'm sure."

Chapter Twenty-Two

"You think Dennis knows where Jennilyn is staying?" Eli asked, glancing at Ava in the passenger seat.

They'd called Brady and Jason, who were headed to the bank now. He and Ava were taking the bar, which in his mind was the more likely target. Normally, he'd ask the other team members to take the closer spot, but since he had the most bomb experience, this plan seemed best.

"I don't know." Her brow was furrowed, her fingers tapping a rapid beat against the display in his center console. "He acted different when we asked where she was. Angry, almost. Like he knew she was at a friend's house when she could have come stayed with him? When he talked about her friends was the only other time he seemed *mad.*"

"You noticed that, too, huh?"

"Yeah. I didn't want to get distracted with his hang-ups. Given the way Sasha talked about Dennis, it seems like that was a mutual feeling. I doubt his dislike of her friends will tell us anything about her next target."

"If Sasha is such a good friend, you think Jennilyn would actually target the bar? Risk killing her?"

It had been bothering Eli ever since they'd gotten back in the SUV. Captain Rutledge's description of Jennilyn during the bar fight, combined with the way Sasha and Dennis had talked about how she jumped into action there, made the grudge against the bar owner seem the strongest. If the bombing was a planned escalation of the violence she'd shown before—against men harassing women in the bar and a man who'd assaulted her friend—someone who sat back and let that kind of behavior happen, in a *place* that was also a likely spot for trouble, seemed a good potential target. Still, he wasn't sure Jennilyn would risk hurting a friend in the process.

"She might know Sasha's schedule," Ava suggested. "Or she could have set a bomb to blow after the place was closed. Take out the owner's livelihood without actually planning to endanger anyone?"

"Maybe," Eli mused, hoping Ava was right. "She *did* smash up that guy's car instead of taking the baseball bat to his head. And even though she put someone in the hospital during the bar fight, it was a broken leg. Not a broken neck."

Ava nodded, catching his eye as he glanced at her. "True. She probably has the training to have done worse."

"Why graduate to bombs?" Eli wondered. "Why try to scare the town if her targets are specific?"

"I don't know," Ava said as he pulled up to the bar, which had a few more cars parked in the lot now that it was lunchtime. "Maybe we were wrong about that. Maybe it was just where she was practicing with the materials."

"Then why leave them behind where someone could find them? I mean, it's not like she was nervous having them nearby if she'd set her own home to blow."

Ava gave him a worried look as they both hopped out of the SUV. "We're definitely missing something."

"Why don't you talk to the owner while I start checking the place out?" Eli suggested.

"Let's do this," Ava agreed, her stride purposeful.

As she walked through the back door, holding it open

for him to grab behind her, Eli glanced around, searching for any sign of Jennilyn lurking.

The skin on the back of his neck prickled, his shoulders coming up as an image of the house exploding formed. The gash on his leg ached with the memory, and his breathing came faster, thinking of the movement he'd seen in the trees.

It wasn't just his life on the line, but Ava's, too. He'd been the one running for the trees, running for whoever might have been hiding there. Like he always was, decisive when he chose a course of action. Relying on his instincts.

In the close to a decade he'd been a police officer, those instincts had never steered him wrong. The officers he worked with trusted his gut as much as he did. But Ava had been behind him yesterday. Too close behind him.

Had Jennilyn blown the house when she knew they'd be injured but would be unlikely to be killed? A warning to back off? Or had she misjudged, meant to end his and Ava's investigation for good? Could she be trying to track them now, looking for another chance?

He saw no one on the street besides a young woman pushing a stroller. Ignoring the anxiety churning in his gut, he followed Ava inside.

Blinking to adjust to the dim lighting, he paused at the doorway, glancing around, looking for possible hiding spots for a bomb, while Ava strode right for the bar counter.

The woman behind the bar—a reed-thin white woman with bright red hair—watched her approach, frowned as Ava asked for the owner, then waved her behind the bar and into the back room.

In the main part of the bar, the patron who'd been there that morning was still at the counter. Now, his elbows were perched on the wood, his shoulders stooped downward, his chin almost resting on his collection of empty glasses in a variety of sizes. The woman who'd been in the corner booth was gone, but a group of men sat in the center of the room, their conversation loud and obnoxious, a mix of beer bottles and shot glasses on their table.

"You wanna join us, cop?" one of them called to him as his buddies laughed.

Ignoring them, Eli circled the edges of the room first, peering under tables and behind the old pinball machine that looked like it hadn't worked in a decade. Spots that would be easy to slide a bomb underneath while walking through a room. Jennilyn could have carried it in her purse, then tacked it to the underside of a table when she sat down for a break. Or she could have put it somewhere harder to access, less likely to be spotted even if someone fell down—not an unlikely occurrence in a place like this. Perhaps she'd set it while the bar was empty and she was the only worker.

The group of men watched him for less than a minute, calling out questions about what he was looking for, then voicing pseudo-whispered insults about what it might be. Finally, they gave up on getting his attention and went back to drinking.

Only the bartender continued to track his movements with narrowed eyes. When he reached the bar, she asked, "What are you looking for?" From the nervous way she scrubbed at the counter with a rag, he suspected Sasha might have told her about the bomb.

"Us being here is just a precaution," Eli said, meeting her gaze with a confident, relaxed expression. There was no reason to panic anyone. Especially since, so far, there was no sign of a bomb.

"Your partner is in the back," she said as Eli moved behind the bar, checking the shelves beneath the counter, between bottles.

His partner. For now, it was true. He wanted to find the bomb, find Jennilyn and end this case soon, so he could ask Ava out. But he also enjoyed the day-to-day with Ava, working beside her. She was a good officer, a good K-9 handler. She was insightful and thorough, and although he loved the thrill of jumping into a new day, not knowing what challenge would be thrown at him, he also appreciated her more cautious, methodical approach. He even liked the simple, companionable silence of riding with her to a scene. He was going to miss everything about partnering with her when he returned to McCall.

He glanced toward the double swinging doors that led into the back room, then refocused on the shelves full of bottles. He peered inside each one, making sure Jennilyn hadn't emptied one out and slid a compact pipe bomb inside. It was tedious, and dust rose up from many of the bottles, making his nose itch. Each one gave the telltale slosh of liquid as he investigated.

His shoulders came down with each inch he searched that revealed nothing. The right-sized bomb could easily be hidden, and in a workplace where others could stumble upon it and destroy her plan, Eli was sure Jennilyn would have picked a good spot.

As he reached the end of the bar, Eli glanced around once more, making sure he hadn't missed anything. He was about to move into the back room when Ava pushed open the swinging door, almost knocking him down with it.

"Sorry," she said, her eyes wide as she spotted him right on the other side. Then she shook her head. "Nothing there."

"You sure?"

"Oh, yeah. I checked everything, not that there's a whole lot. They don't serve food here beyond peanuts and chips, so there are basically storage cupboards and a desk in the corner stacked with papers. It's much tinier than you'd think, but I also looked in the closet where you can access electrical. Nothing."

Eli frowned. "What about the owner? Did you tell him we wanted to check out the exterior of his house?"

Ava nodded. "Yeah. He has no interest in coming with us, but says to knock ourselves out. I suggested he change the locks at the bar, but he doesn't want to waste the money."

Eli sighed. Noticing that the bartender was listening in, he nodded toward the back door. The group of men in the center of the room had plenty to say as Ava passed and she shook her head at him as she strode right on by, ignoring them all.

His jaw clenched and he gave them his most aggressive warning look as he followed her outside.

Before he had a chance to ask how she didn't look furious at the filth they'd spewed at her, she said, "If this is her target, she still has access. She could slip in at night and leave a bomb. Maybe we'll get lucky at his house—she does seem like the kind of person who'd want to be specific about her target—but I'm worried, Eli."

"Me too," he agreed, thinking of all of Jennilyn's potential targets. All the different types of bombs she could have encountered working for the Army. Not to mention all of the knowledge she would have gained about how to ambush someone when they least expected it. "I think we need to stop chasing where she could have *been* and find a way to track where she is *now*."

Chapter Twenty-Three

"No sign of a bomb anywhere," Eli said as he hung up the phone with Brady.

Ava frowned as she slid into the passenger seat of his SUV, exhausted and filthy from searching the exterior of the bar owner's house—including under the deck. Mosquito bites itched on the back of her neck and, inexplicably, on her legs covered by her uniform.

Eli looked worse than she felt, his light skin caked in a layer of dirt, his hair sticking up. His uniform, black just like the Jasper PD uniforms, was so dust-covered that even the dark color couldn't disguise it.

All for nothing. If Jennilyn was targeting the owner of Shaker Peak, she was biding her time.

"Brady and Jason checked the bank *and* the loan officer's house?"

"Yep," Eli confirmed. "His car, too."

Ava nodded, remembering how Eli had circled the bar owner's car in the lot, looking underneath with a retractable mirror. Finding nothing there, either.

Day had slid into evening as they'd searched, getting nowhere and losing time. Time for Jennilyn to hunker down deeper wherever she was hiding. Time for her to come up with a new plan or set a bomb somewhere they hadn't considered.

Ava sighed, glancing at Eli from the corner of her eye as he put the SUV in gear, at the lean muscles in forearms revealed by the rolled sleeves of his uniform. Even covered in dirt, there was something compelling about him, something that made her gaze want to linger.

He looked at her, giving her a slow grin that crinkled the corners of his eyes, before returning his attention to the road.

He'd glanced at her while they'd worked quietly at the bar owner's house, too. Quick, probing glances like he was trying to go deeper than she'd already let him in, sharing the most painful parts of her past with him as if she'd known him for years instead of just a week.

Seven days. It seemed impossible that she hadn't known him longer. The proximity, the pressure of the investigation, was making everything intensified. But it was more than that. Almost like pieces of her lined up just right with pieces of him, a mix of similar and opposite that felt like they belonged together.

Inevitable. It was what she'd felt after she'd kissed him, after she'd stepped back and he'd let her press pause, hadn't pressured her for more. After he'd promised to give her time, but not to give up.

A shiver of anticipation slid through her as she darted one more glance at him. She wanted this investigation over *now,* wanted to experience the thrill of whatever it meant to be pursued by everything Eli Thorne had.

Too soon, she reminded herself. Even if it wasn't, she wasn't making the same mistakes twice. Wasn't going to risk alienating colleagues she'd barely started to connect with for the *possibility* of a relationship.

Maybe what she really needed was for this investigation to drag on and on, give her a chance to get to know him better. Maybe then she'd realize it was attraction without enough common ground, something that would sizzle out as fast as it had ignited.

But as she felt his gaze on her again, as she forced her own gaze to remain steady out the window, she knew that was just the fear talking. The worry that she'd fall too hard and he'd walk away. That he'd be one more person who left her all alone.

The buzzing of her phone startled her, tickling her leg. She pulled it out of her pocket, her pulse jumping when she saw Emma Daniels's name. "Emma," she answered in a rush. "Have you heard something about Lacey?"

The German shepherd had looked fine when they'd stopped by that morning, but Ava knew how quickly medical prognoses could change. When her parents died, she'd known she should avoid the news coverage. She'd tried, but she hadn't been able to deny herself the agony of knowing what they'd experienced, in their final attempt to support her. She'd heard about the couple in the car behind her parents, admitted to the hospital but expected to be fine. A few days in the hospital, though, and instead of being released, the woman had a setback. She'd lived but a closed head injury meant she'd never be the same.

She shivered at the memory, at how hard she'd tried to convince everyone she was fine. While the reporters had hounded her at home, she'd insisted she was able to start work as a police officer. The job she'd known she wanted since she was fifteen and an officer had talked a friend of hers down from the ledge of a building they'd snuck inside together. Her, having no idea of her friend's true intention. The officer, so calm and steady, taking an hour of his life to make sure her friend kept his. The job she'd still chosen to pursue, even with her parents' disapproval, even after their deaths.

Eli's hand closed around hers, jolting her back to the

present, and she realized Emma had been talking. "Is Lacey okay?" she repeated, because she hadn't heard whatever Emma had been saying.

There was a brief pause and then Emma said quickly, "She's fine, Ava. I talked to Marie a couple of hours ago and she was doing great."

A huge relieved breath escaped and Ava nodded at Eli, who squeezed her hand. She blinked back the tears that had been gathering and tried to focus on Emma while her fingers twitched, still linked with Eli's.

"If anything happened, Marie would call you first," Emma assured her. "I was just calling to see how *you* were doing."

Warmth speared Ava's chest, the feeling that she'd forged more bonds here than she'd realized. "Thank you. I'm doing okay. Just a little stressed. It's weird not to have Lacey with me on calls."

As she said it, she realized how true it was. She'd had a human partner back in Chicago. She and Shaun had gotten along fine, and she'd trusted him to have her back, but they hadn't been friends. Their bond had been one of necessity. If he was out for a day and she had a different partner, she'd never felt as if she were missing anything.

Now, as much as she enjoyed working with Eli—far more than she'd expected, and not just because she was attracted to him—she constantly found herself glancing down by her side, expecting Lacey to be there. Feeling a pang of disappointment when she wasn't.

"She'll be back before you know it," Emma predicted. "In the meantime…are you still working with that handsome captain?"

A flush of heat speared up Ava's face and she darted a quick glance at Eli, hoping he couldn't hear her conversation. He was staring out the windshield, seemingly oblivious. But the hand still locked with hers squeezed when she looked his way.

Redirecting her gaze, Ava kept her tone neutral as she said, "Yes, we're working now, actually."

"Ohhh." Emma's voice was teasing as she said, "I'll let you get back to that, then. Say hi to the captain for me."

"Nope," Ava said, refusing to rise to the bait.

Emma laughed and when Ava hung up, Eli asked, "Lacey's okay?"

"Yes. It was just Emma, checking on me."

"That was nice," Eli said as he pulled into the police station parking lot.

Ava glanced around, spotting Captain Rutledge striding through the lot with a take-out cup from Millard's Diner, and the Chief grinning at something Theresa Norwood was saying to him by the entrance.

Ava was suddenly hyperaware of the hand still entwined with Eli's, and discomfort wormed through her. Still, when he slid his hand free, she immediately missed it.

Stepping out of the car, she lifted her hand to wave at Arthur, but he slipped into the station as if he hadn't noticed.

The Chief glanced up when they stepped out of the vehicle, his eyebrows raised.

Ava belatedly brushed her hands over her uniform, dislodging a cloud of dust that made her cough but probably didn't do much for her appearance.

"How'd it go today?" he asked as Theresa nodded hello to them, then headed inside.

Ava shook her head. "No luck."

The Chief glanced from her to Eli and back again. "Can I have a word, Officer Callan?"

"I'll meet you inside," Eli told her, giving her an encouraging smile as nerves tensed Ava's stomach. "Sure, Chief. What is it?"

"Well, first off, how is Lacey?"

The nerves eased up a little. "She'll be okay. Thank goodness."

"Good. I called Marie myself to check on her, but a handler knows their dog best. You and Lacey make a good team."

The compliment made her smile and she remembered Eli's words about it being a show of confidence that the Chief had partnered her with Lacey. "Thank you for pairing me with her."

He nodded, something knowing in his gaze. "I actually wanted to chat with you about something else. I know you haven't had a chance to go on a call with Captain Rutledge yet, but you've worked with him some since you've come to Jasper. How has that gone?"

"Oh." The question felt disconnected with everything in her life right now, and Ava tried to come up with a response that would be honest without being rude. "He seems to know the town well. He's really smart about police procedure."

The Chief's lips turned downward a little, his eyes narrowing. "He is, at that. But what about his personal skills? Working with officers, with the public? This is between us," he added.

"Well, I haven't been here that long," Ava hedged. "I'm sure keeping some distance can help with retaining authority in a small town."

A hint of a smile quivered on the Chief's lips. "I appreciate your diplomacy, Ava. And I get it. Thanks for your insights."

He turned and headed for his personal vehicle before she could ask why he'd wanted her insight in the first place. Over his shoulder, he called, "No overtime, Officer Callan. I want you rested. This investigation could last a while and I need you fresh tomorrow and the next day, too. Not just working yourself into exhaustion tonight in hope of a break."

"Yes, sir," she answered, glancing at the time on her phone as she hurried into the station. Technically, her shift was already over.

"Everything okay?" Eli asked when she jogged into the conference room.

She nodded as she glanced around, finding the room empty except for the two of them.

"We just missed Brady and Jason. The Chief sent them home." He smiled sheepishly. "According to Captain Rutledge, who just passed through here, the Chief wants us to call it a night, too."

"Yeah, he told me." She shrugged. "I get it, and I could definitely use a shower, but I'm anxious. I don't like feeling that we're a step behind. We have to be missing a target."

"We're probably not going to come up with it tonight, though," Eli said, sounding more agreeable to the idea of calling it a night than she felt.

Maybe some of it was simply that she wasn't ready to say goodnight to Eli yet, to go home to her quiet, empty house.

"You want to get some food? I bet Millard's Diner would let us sit on their patio, even covered in dirt."

Even though she'd just been thinking that she wanted to spend more time with him, Ava couldn't stop herself from glancing out the open door of the conference room, hoping no one had overheard.

Eli gave her a half smile that didn't quite meet his eyes. "I'd have invited the whole team if they were still here."

"Oh." She shuffled her feet. "Yeah, of course." She fought an internal battle—wanting all the time with him she could get, but not wanting the rumors that were bound to start if the two of them showed up together at the cop hangout.

Then, she pushed down her anxiety. Yes, her workplace romance with DeVante had fallen apart more publicly than she would have liked. But if she truly wanted a new start, she needed to stop letting the past hinder her from making connections.

She nodded, that quick movement feeling like a big step in the right direction. "Let's go."

Eli grinned, this time a real smile that made creases appear in the dirt alongside his eyes.

She couldn't stop her own smile in return, her pulse picking up. Somehow, in the week she'd known Eli, he'd helped her form a totally different vision of what her future in Jasper could be. With every moment that passed, she sensed he was going to be a big part of it.

Chapter Twenty-Four

Millard's Diner was quieter than usual for a Friday night at the end of a shift. Normally, there would be a group of cops grabbing their last coffee of the day or stopping for a burger before they headed home. Today, there was only a group of teenage girls in a big booth, who stopped giggling long enough to gawk at Ava and Eli as they walked inside, still covered in dirt.

Relief loosened Ava's shoulders, but she realized it wasn't because there were no colleagues to see her out alone with Eli. It was because they wouldn't feel pressured to invite anyone to join them. She'd get Eli to herself a little longer.

She looked at him, a couple of inches taller than her, his arms loose at his sides in that stance that made him seem relaxed no matter the situation. He'd told her about his dog, about feeling connected to his community so much that he'd known he was going to spend his life there. She wanted to know *more*.

She wanted to know if he was close to his family, what he did with his friends. She wanted to know about his hobbies and how he had gotten into bomb detection. She wanted to know *everything*.

When he glanced at her, seeming to sense her gaze, she gave him a slight smile, suddenly overwhelmed by the intensity of her feelings. Then, she turned back to the owner, standing behind the bright blue counter in the retro diner, waiting for their order.

Millard Jr. looked them over with raised eyebrows. "You look like you had a long day. Coffee?" he asked as his wife, Vera, scowled at them from the corner.

"And a couple of burgers," Ava said, glancing at Eli for confirmation. He nodded and she added, "We'll eat them at a table outside."

Vera's scowl eased, but she kept watching them as they turned for the door. Ava glanced back before she stepped outside, and tried not to laugh at Vera's intent stare. She'd overheard some of the younger cops joking that they liked to place bets on whether anyone could get her to smile.

Settling into a small two-person table right outside of Millard's, almost on the sidewalk, Ava stared at Eli. She could tell he was tired by the way he leaned back in his chair with a sigh, but his bright blue eyes always seemed alert and focused. Right now, they were completely focused on her.

Even though they were filthy, sitting outside of a cop hangout, tonight suddenly felt more like a date than even their dinner on the romantic terrace at Rose Café. Maybe it was because she knew him better now, or because she'd kissed him, or because he'd stated his intent to pursue her. He'd promised to wait, but right now, she didn't want to wait for anything.

The idea made her feel lighter, almost giddy, but she ducked her head so he wouldn't get an idea of what she was thinking. Wanting something didn't mean she should act on it. Then again, once he was back in McCall, maybe it was far enough away that no one would care. Was it really so important to put up artificial boundaries while they were on this case? Or was now the perfect time to push the boundaries, to see what this attraction could turn into, while he was right here in front of her?

"Here you go."

Ava started at Millard Jr.'s voice, then nodded her thanks as he set two cups of coffee on a tray with sugar and creamers in the center of the table.

"Burgers will be up shortly," he called over his shoulder as he ambled back inside.

Then, Ava met Eli's gaze, saw the surprise there at what she must have been telegraphing. "Tell me more about yourself, Eli."

He sat straighter, keeping his gaze locked on hers in a way that made anticipation tighten her belly. "Feels like a first date. I wish I'd cleaned up better."

His tone was joking, giving her an out, but she nodded. "Yeah, me, too. But maybe this is better. Share it all now, the good and the ugly, and see where it takes us."

He gave her one of those slow grins that was somehow sexy even with the dirt ground into his face. "Where should I start?"

She leaned forward, settling her chin on her fist. "Tell me more about your family." Somehow, she knew he was close to them. She could only imagine him as part of a tight-knit family, not one that argued as much as hers had.

"Well, I told you that my parents have been together since they were kids. The whole family lives in or around McCall. I've got two younger brothers, Benjamin and David. Ben just got engaged a couple of weeks ago. I'm hoping I'll be back in McCall before their engagement party at the end of the month."

She nodded, although the idea of him leaving, even a few weeks from now at the end of May, put a hollow feeling in her stomach. "Are your brothers in law enforcement, too?"

"No. But my mom was, until I was a teenager. It's the

reason I wanted to do it. Ben and David stuck close to the system, too. Ben is a social worker and David is finishing his law degree."

"Wow." Ava tried to imagine a world where most of her family had jobs that intertwined. A stab of jealousy hit at the easy comradery he seemed to have with his family, but she pushed it aside, glad that Eli had those strong bonds. It was probably part of what made him the way he was, so generous and friendly.

"What about your dad?"

"He's a carpenter," Eli said. "It's funny, because even though my brothers and I gravitated toward careers connected to what my mom did, we all do some woodworking in our spare time."

"Really?" An image of Eli working with his hands, sanding down an old table, covered in sweat and sawdust, filled her mind. She glanced at those hands, with their long nimble fingers that had been so sure working the controls of his bomb-disposal robot. The remembered feel of those fingers digging into her hips while she'd kissed him made her skin tingle.

His head tilted slightly, the hint of a grin playing on his lips, like he could read the direction of her thoughts.

"Why bomb detection?" she blurted, trying to focus on getting to know him better and not her daydreams.

He laughed. "Total fluke. I heard about this program the FBI put on—teaching law enforcement officers around the country some of the most cutting-edge techniques—and I thought it sounded fun." He shrugged. "It was."

Before she could ask more, he said, "What about you? What made you want to become a cop?"

"When I was fifteen, I had this one friend. I'd always get into trouble with him. Stupid stuff, trespassing and things like that. I was just testing boundaries, trying to express my independence." She shrugged, remembering the thrill of sneaking out, of getting in somewhere she wasn't supposed to be. Looking back on it, it all seemed silly and potentially dangerous. Then, it had felt like a slice of freedom from a house with too many rules.

"My friend was trying to escape. I knew his home life was bad, but I didn't realize quite how bad until we snuck into this building downtown. He went out the window, and when I thought we were going to sit out there together and look out over the city, he told me to go home. I realized he was going to jump."

Eli cursed under his breath.

"I went outside, anyway. I've never been afraid of heights, but knowing what he planned to do..." She'd been terrified. "I knew he'd never jump with me watching. He was too good a friend. And he didn't. I called the police while he cried and begged me to leave. They came and one of them spent an hour talking to him, promising to help."

"Wow," Eli said softly.

"Yeah. Back then, I didn't know how tough it was to intervene in domestic violence situations, how hard it is to make that stick in any meaningful way. Back then, both of us just believed him. Somehow, he got it done. Showed up at my friend's house and before I knew it, my friend was moving in with an aunt across the country. I missed him, but he'd write me and I could tell what a better place he was in. Anyway, that day, I decided that I was going to become a police officer."

"It's one of the things I like best about being in law enforcement—helping the community. That invisible thread that ties us all together, if we let ourselves be bound to it."

Ava smiled. "I never quite thought about it like that." To her, being a cop was about helping people, but even in Chicago, where she'd felt like part of a team, she'd never had that bigger connection. She'd never felt like the whole city was in something together. Especially with her parents seeing anyone in blue as the enemy—and it was a perspective she understood, even if she didn't share it. Maybe in a smaller town like Jasper, where there was a real possibility of her eventually knowing most of the people who lived here personally, she'd have that feeling someday.

"What—"

The ringing of Ava's phone cut Eli off. She pulled it out to silence it as Vera silently dropped the burgers off at their table, but then she saw the caller. "Komi," she whispered, unable to believe it.

Her heart started thundering in her ears. Had something happened to someone in their extended family? After everything Komi had said five months ago, she couldn't imagine him calling for any other reason.

Saying a silent prayer, Ava answered. She heard the fear in her own voice as she said, "Komi? What happened?"

Eli's hand reached across the table and she put her free hand in his, taking the support and holding on. In the back of her mind, it registered how natural and easy it felt to rely on him.

"Ava," her brother said, his voice soft and serious.

When the pause dragged on, Ava insisted, "What happened? What's wrong?"

"Wrong? Nothing." Komi sighed. "Look, Ava, I know after everything I said…"

Her pulse slowed a little at the realization that no one was hurt, then took off again. Was it possible he was calling to forgive her?

"I know…" He let out a low laugh, so unlike her decisive brother, and her heart ached just hearing his voice again. "I know I've been unfair to you. I know it's not really your fault that Mom and Dad died." Another pause, then he rushed on, "And it's not right of me to blame you for it. I just—I can't help it. I still don't know if I can get over it, if we can ever go back to where we were. But…"

"But what?" she pressed when he went quiet again, as hope burst inside of her, almost painful in its intensity.

"I miss you, Ava. I really miss you."

"I miss you, too," she said as tears blurred her vision and Eli squeezed her hand, his smile the only thing she could see.

"That's it," he said with a laugh. Then, more serious, he added, "It's all I've got right now, Ava. But when you left Chicago, I realized that for all the time I'd spent pushing you away, I still expected you to *be there*, to be nearby in Chicago, even if we weren't talking. Even if we never talked again."

The idea made her heart pinch, even though she'd resigned herself to it when she'd moved to Jasper.

"I know how unfair everything I'm saying is, Ava. I'm truly sorry that I can't just snap my fingers and feel differently, no matter how badly I wish I could. No matter how much I know, logically, that you've been grieving as much as I have."

Maybe even more, Ava thought but didn't say. Komi was her little brother. He might have been only a year younger, but she'd always felt responsible for looking after him, for keeping him safe.

When her parents had died, she hadn't just wanted to be the strong big sister for him— she'd also needed that role for herself. Without it, all she'd had was her grief.

"I wanted to hear your voice," Komi said. "I wanted to see if there was a path for us to start fresh. For us to *try*. I still need some space," he added before she could agree. "But I wanted you to know that I do miss you. I miss us together, as a family. I love you, Ava."

"I love you, too," she whispered, closing her eyes at the joy of it.

She'd given up on Komi when she'd moved to Jasper. Given up on ever having that sibling bond back. Given up on the life she'd built for herself in Chicago, so she could avoid the constant, painful reminders of losing her entire family—one way or another—all at once.

This was a small step, but it was so much more than she'd expected, five years after her parents had died. Five months after Komi had completely given up trying, given up the false starts and the angry undercurrents that had plagued every conversation they'd had since their parents' deaths.

Now, suddenly, returning to the life she'd left behind felt like a possibility again.

Chapter Twenty-Five

"There's something about this situation with Jennilyn Sanderson that's bothering me," Ava spoke into the silence.

Eli nodded, in full agreement, even though this wasn't what he wanted to discuss. He wanted to talk about the drastic change in mood that had happened as soon as Ava's brother had called.

He was happy for her. From the way she'd teared up and the excited disbelief that had flashed across her face, he'd known even before she'd told him what her brother had said. He'd also realized what she hadn't said: if Komi could forgive her, she would probably be moving back to Chicago.

He'd never see her again. There was no sense pursuing something when they lived in different states. Not when he couldn't ever imagine leaving the community he had in McCall. Not when her ties to Chicago were pulling on her so strongly. He couldn't imagine a future where either of them would be happy living away from the places they wanted to call home.

So, where did that leave them? To get to spend any time with her would probably be worth the heartache. But damn, he didn't *want* the heartache, didn't want to start something he knew he'd regret when it ended.

Judging by the way she'd shifted from flirtatious and

inquisitive to pensive and work-minded after ending the call with her brother, she felt the same way.

At least he knew *now*, instead of after he and Ava had let things get any further. Because there was no doubt in his mind, if he let Ava Callan in, he'd never want to let her go.

But it was hard to feel relieved when all he wanted to do was pull her into his arms and try to convince her to stay.

"I'm just not sure what it is," Ava said, and Eli tried to focus.

It took him a minute to remember what she was talking about. "Right. Jennilyn Sanderson. Something does feel off. I'm not sure what it is, either."

"I know we're supposed to be off duty." Ava scrunched her lips as she admitted, "The Chief insisted that we not have any overtime. But I've got this itchy feeling like we're missing something important. I don't want to leave it until tomorrow."

Handing some cash to Vera, Eli waved Ava off when she tried to pay for hers. "We could swing by the bar," Eli suggested. "It's a relatively short walk from here. Ask about the friend who she smashed up that guy's car for. It was someone who worked with her, right?"

"Yeah." Ava swore. "You don't think it was the woman who was bartending when we were there earlier, do you? I was so focused on searching for a bomb that it didn't occur to me to talk to her. I was just trying to avoid her listening in and spreading rumors, spreading panic."

"Yeah," Eli agreed. "That was an oversight on both our parts. But at the time, getting to the bar owner's house was more important."

"Let's remedy that now," Ava replied, jumping up and striding in the direction of the bar.

Eli followed more slowly, watching the determination in her steps, the curls that had started to slip loose at the back of her bun. He tried to match her purposeful energy, but there was a weight on his chest he couldn't shake, the knowledge that something amazing had slipped away from him before he'd even fully grabbed hold.

Normally, he'd fight. Continue to find ways to integrate her into the community. Find ways to make her want to stay.

But he knew how much her relationship with her brother meant to her, how much she missed him. Eli couldn't begrudge her the chance to get that back, no matter what it cost him.

"Shake it off," Eli muttered to himself, then picked up his pace to catch up.

As he stepped up alongside her, Ava asked, "What did you say?"

"Let's shake things up," Eli said.

She narrowed her eyes, like she didn't think that was what she'd heard, but let it go. "Hopefully this will give us something new. I'm not even sure what I'm looking for."

"I'm not, either," Eli agreed. "But my gut agrees with yours. We missed something."

Her strides increased, and Eli kept pace, impressed with her speed. When they strode into the bar, the same bartender was there from earlier in the afternoon.

She frowned at the sight of them, but no one else in the bar—a pair of twenty-something guys deep in conversation and a woman in the corner who was staring vacantly at the wall—seemed to notice the filthy cops.

When they reached the counter, Ava leaned toward her, keeping her voice low. "I'm not sure if you know why we were in here earlier?"

"Looking for something to tell you where Jenny is hiding?" she guessed.

"Not exactly," Eli replied, surprised. He'd assumed she'd

known about the bomb. "Do you know what happened with Jennilyn?"

She shrugged, picking at her faded nail polish. "The owner said something about a gas leak at her place? He was definitely lying, but Sasha took off before I could ask her about it."

"Is Jennilyn a friend of yours?" Ava asked.

"Yeah, kinda. I don't know her all that well really, but she sticks up for you if you need it."

"She stuck up for you before?" Eli asked, hoping this was the woman Jennilyn had helped by smashing a car.

Her gaze met his. Her eyes were slightly bloodshot, her eyelids drooping, but there was defiance there, too. "Yeah, she did. So whatever you're here for, whatever you think she did wrong, I'm not helping you."

Eli glanced at Ava, trying to silently communicate that she should take the lead. Hopefully the bartender would respond better to a woman.

"We're trying to help Jennilyn," Ava said, and the woman huffed.

"Really, we are," Ava said. "We're all part of the same community here. We need to look after each other."

Eli shot her a sideways glance, not wanting to distract her when her words were having an effect. The bartender's defensive posture was loosening, her angry gaze calming.

If only Ava's words were true. If only she planned to remain part of this community.

"What's your name?" Ava asked in the same soft, easy-going tone.

"Amber."

"Okay, Amber. So, I know Jennilyn went after some guy's car because he did something terrible to a friend of hers."

From the way Amber jerked at Ava's words, Eli didn't

need to ask. Amber was the friend who'd been assaulted, who Jennilyn had tried to help.

"It's not the only time Jenny has tried to help out, right?" As Amber nodded slowly, Ava said, "I know she jumped into a bar fight, too, standing up for some women who were being harassed."

"She's always willing to put herself between other people and danger," Amber said softly. "I wish I were that brave."

Ava nodded. "Here's the thing, Amber. It's one thing to punch someone, to break a leg or smash a car. People recover from that. A bomb is something else, something that could destroy *Jennilyn's* future."

Amber jerked, dropping her hands to her sides as she glanced wide-eyed from Ava to Eli and back again. "What bomb?"

"It wasn't a gas leak at her house," Ava said.

Amber's eyes got even wider and she jerked a hand up to her chest. "Someone *blew up* her house? Why? Because of what she did for me?"

"No, Amber. She blew up *her own* house," Ava said.

Amber was shaking her head before Ava finished. "No way."

"I know it seems strange, but it was her way of getting out of here. She set it off earlier than she planned," Eli said.

Amber looked like she was going to argue again, but Ava jumped in. "We were here earlier to see if she'd set a bomb at the bar, because we heard from her ex that she held a grudge against the owner. Because he didn't stand up against some of the wrongs Jennilyn had seen. Because she was tired of doing it herself."

Amber kept shaking her head, her overdyed red hair swishing across her face. "Her ex said that?" she scoffed. "Look, this place might not be Jenny's dream job." She waved a hand expansively, vaguely, at the room. "I mean, it's not exactly any of our dream jobs, right? But it pays okay. And she had *friends* here. Unlike Dennis, who nobody liked so he was always just hanging on to her friends. I mean, hell, he couldn't even hang on to a job. Even the Army kicked him out."

Eli felt a kick in his gut. "The Army kicked him out? I thought he and Jennilyn voluntarily left together? To start a new life in a small town?"

"Well, *she* left voluntarily. If he hadn't been kicked out, she probably would have re-upped." Amber shrugged. "At least that's what she told me."

"Do you know where Jennilyn might be?" Ava asked, tension in her voice now, as she probably picked up on the same thing he was feeling.

Amber shrugged. "No. But she's not just tough. She's also smart. If her place was bombed, it wasn't Jenny blowing up her own house. It was someone else, maybe someone she beat up who couldn't take the humiliation. If it was that guy who attacked me…"

Amber swallowed hard enough for Eli to hear, then rushed on, "She's not hiding from the cops. She's hiding because someone is trying to kill her."

Eli held in a million curses, suddenly certain what had been nagging Ava that they'd missed.

It wasn't Jennilyn they needed to find. It was Dennis, who had completely played them.

Chapter Twenty-Six

"His name is Dennis Ryon?" Brady's voice echoed on speaker in the car.

They'd called him at home, after notifying the Chief. Brady had sounded tired when he picked up, but Ava had been impressed at how he'd instantly shifted into work mode when they updated him about what they'd learned.

"That's right," Eli confirmed. "We spoke to him about six hours ago at the Salmon Creek Motel. We're heading back there now. In the meantime, we're hoping you and Jason can dig up as much as possible."

"I'll give Jason a call and head into the station as soon as we get off the phone," Brady agreed.

"According to the bartender at Shaker Peak, Dennis was dishonorably discharged from the Army. That might be a place to start," Ava put in.

She gazed at Eli out of the corner of her eye as she spoke. His attention was fully on the road, both hands on the wheel, his expression intense. Fully focused on work again.

Another pang of regret struck and she tried to push it back, reminded herself she was doing the right thing. She liked Eli too much to leap into something that had an expiration date.

Earlier tonight, she'd felt her first real stirrings of excitement about building a future in Jasper. In the past few days, things had finally started turning around. She was making progress with her coworkers. She'd accepted the strength and importance of her bond with Lacey, who was doing better each time Ava texted Marie or Tashya to check on her progress. And the possibility of a relationship with Eli had felt so *right*.

But Komi was her family. For five years, she'd done everything she could to mend that bond. If he was finally willing to repair it, she didn't want to be eighteen hundred miles away. She needed to be right there, needed him to see she was just as committed to being a family.

She missed Chicago. Missed her friends there, missed the buzz of the city and the easy comradery of her fellow officers in narcotics.

She would miss Jasper when she left, too. But she'd only been here for a few months. She couldn't trade the people she'd known all her life for what she'd barely started to build here.

Still, that ache in her chest didn't subside as she stared at Eli's profile. It had become so familiar in just a week. The idea of leaving him, of leaving the possibilities she felt when she looked at him, felt wrong, too.

"Ava. Ava, your phone is ringing."

She jerked, realizing she'd been so caught up in her own thoughts that Brady had already hung up.

"It might be Amber," Eli added, and she scrambled to pull the phone out of her pocket.

Before they'd left the bar, they'd tried to convince Amber to tell them where Jennilyn might be staying. She'd hesitated long enough that Ava suspected she knew, or at least had an idea. She'd steadfastly refused to give it up, only reluctantly agreeing to try and get a message to her.

"Hello?" Ava answered just before her phone would have gone to voice mail.

"Is this Officer Callan?"

The voice wasn't familiar and Ava's enthusiasm dimmed. "Speaking."

"This is Jennilyn Sanderson."

Eyes widening, Ava put her on speaker. "Jennilyn, thanks for contacting us."

Eli glanced at her, surprise on his face. But he stayed quiet.

"Yeah, well, Amber said you thought I blew up my own house."

"If you didn't do it, then who did?" Ava asked, keeping her tone even.

"Are you kidding me?" she snapped, then muttered, "And people wonder why I don't trust the cops to get things done."

"We came to your house because of something of yours we found near bomb materials," Ava told her, hoping she wasn't making a mistake. Since they'd spoken to Amber, that itchy feeling she'd had that something about their investigation was off track had disappeared. She was pretty sure she knew exactly who they were looking for, but she didn't want to lead Jennilyn. She wanted the woman to say it herself.

"That asshole," Jennilyn spat. "It figures. I dumped him and it's not enough to try and kill me. He also wants to frame me for my own death."

Eli's gaze darted to hers again and Ava nodded, knowing what he was thinking. Dennis hadn't been trying to frame Jennilyn for her own death—or at least, that hadn't been his primary objective. There had to be another target.

"You're talking about your ex, Dennis Ryon?" Ava asked, still in the same calm, neutral tone.

"Yeah, I'm talking about Dennis," Jennilyn snapped, then she blew out a loud breath. "Look, he's just… He's gotten scary. He's not the guy I thought I knew."

"Tell me what happened," Ava encouraged, hoping Jennilyn could give them insight into not just why Dennis was setting bombs, but who he might be targeting. Maybe she could even give them enough to get an arrest warrant. "How has he changed?"

"When I met him in the Army, he was so full of purpose. Then they accused him of misconduct. I don't know all of the details, but they claimed when he was overseas, he knocked down some civilians with his gun, kicked them, spat on them. He was pissed, said he was being railroaded because people didn't like him. He claimed the incident was blown out of proportion, that the civilians had posed a real threat and he'd only asked them to leave the area. He said some of his unit didn't like how he'd always be out in front, like he wanted the limelight, so when the civilians made the bogus charges, a couple of guys in the unit backed it. Which made sense to me. I always thought he was just confident, but yeah, it sometimes bordered on cocky. He didn't have tons of friends."

She sighed heavily. "Anyway, when the Army kicked him out, he asked me to go with him. We'd only been dating for a few months then, but I saw a future with him. I mean, I just *knew*, in this way I've never felt before, that we were supposed to be together."

Ava's gaze darted to Eli before she could stop herself. His gaze was locked on hers, projecting the same kind of understanding she felt. A bone-deep knowledge that she and Eli could have something special, the kind of gut feeling that almost never failed her in an investigation.

But gut feelings could be wrong. Jennilyn was proof of that, in more ways than one.

Eli broke eye contact first, his attention returning to the road as they traveled back the way they'd come early this afternoon, toward the motel where Dennis was staying. Hopefully, before they got there, either Jennilyn or their team would give them the ammunition they needed to bring him in.

"I understand," Ava said softly, this time keeping her gaze firmly on the phone as she felt Eli look her way again.

"I was wrong," Jennilyn said. "It took me a while to realize it, but after I agreed to go with him, we decided to move somewhere brand new. We checked all these places out, and from his perspective, none of them were good enough. Finally, I put my foot down in Jasper. This was it. I thought all we needed was a chance, a fresh start together, and we could make it work."

"What happened?" Ava pressed when she went silent.

"What *didn't* happen?" Bitterness underlaid each word. "He was getting into fights at Handall's Furniture, where he worked delivery. With his coworkers, with his boss. He hated the friends I was making here, thought they were bad-mouthing him and wanted me to stop hanging out with them—even though most of my friends I met at work. Plus, he was still *really* bitter about what had happened in the military, constantly talked about how it wasn't just a few bad apples who'd lied about him. It was the whole system out to screw him. He thought he should have still been in the Army, still working a job he actually loved. He started taking it out on me. I tried to be understanding, but it just kept getting worse, until finally I realized it wasn't everyone else making the problems. It was Dennis."

"So, you broke up with him," Ava said.

"Yeah. And he didn't take it well. He started screaming about how I was just like everyone else. Even put his fist through the wall. I'd never seen that side of him before."

"You were scared of him?"

"Hell, yes. Look, I'm no pushover. Dennis might be half a foot bigger than me and he might outweigh me by eighty pounds, but I got the same training he did. I don't show fear easily. Still, there was something in his eyes when I told him to move out…"

Ava started to ask about Dennis's training, but Jennilyn was talking again, faster now, the frustration and fear seeping further into her voice.

"I changed the locks, but he still found a way to get in. He ripped up some of my clothes, smashed my computer."

"Did you contact the police?" Ava asked. They hadn't seen anything when they'd dug into Jennilyn's history, but they'd been focused on her as a suspect, not a target.

"No. I just—I didn't want to enrage him further. One of my friends has a camper, so I borrowed it, started staying out—well, somewhere Dennis wouldn't think to look. I figured it would blow over. Then I heard he got fired from his new job, too, and I knew that would set him off all over again. I started to think I was going to have to leave Jasper completely if I ever wanted to be free of him."

Ava felt Eli's gaze on her again, but she didn't need to glance over to know what he was thinking. A series of rejections over the past year, from the military to his girlfriend to multiple jobs. A pattern like that was always worrisome, especially when the person had a history of violence.

Although they hadn't checked if Dennis had a police record, given what Jennilyn was saying, Ava suspected the Army hadn't gotten it wrong when they'd kicked him out.

"Jennilyn, does Dennis have bomb training from the Army?"

There was a pause, and then Jennilyn admitted, "We

both do. It's where I first met him, in bomb detection and disposal training."

Before Ava could ask for more details, Jennilyn rushed on, "But I swear, I've never *set* a bomb. Honestly, I never even had a chance to detect or defuse one before Dennis got kicked out and I decided to go with him."

"What about Dennis?"

"I'm not sure. Look, I've been out of my place for a couple of weeks, ever since Dennis got in there and destroyed my things. I haven't been home since. I was still going to work, even though I knew it was a way for him to find me. I figured he'd show up there eventually. Stupidly, I thought he wouldn't want to make a scene in front of other people."

"He came to the bar?" Ava asked.

"No. I got a call from my neighbor saying my house blew up. I was on my way to work when he called and I turned right back around. Didn't call in or anything because I was so freaked out. I knew immediately it was Dennis. Right now, I'm just hiding, but he'll find me eventually if I stick around. So, I'm getting out of here before he figures out where I am."

"We can help you—" Ava started.

"No. I called because Amber said you thought *I* set that bomb. I'm not letting him destroy my reputation along with everything else. But if you think I'm trusting you to keep me safe, you haven't been listening. I know how this kind of thing always goes when men harass women."

"Blowing up a house is a lot more serious than harassment," Ava said.

"Yeah, well, maybe if you'd done something when he was harassing his coworkers, I wouldn't be in this position now!" There was a brief pause, then Jennilyn said, more calmly, "You want to deal with Dennis, great. Just don't expect me to do your work for you."

She hung up before Ava could ask anything else.

"I don't think Dennis wanted us to find those bomb materials at the JPG warehouse," Eli said.

It took Ava a minute to realize where he was going. "You think he was practicing, that he needed a place to keep the materials since he's been staying in a motel where a cleaning crew might come in. He wore gloves out of caution, not because he was expecting anyone to discover them. So, when we found the materials, he was worried it would lead us to him."

"Yeah. I think that's when he decided to hand us Jennilyn with the next set of materials. When he broke into her house, he didn't just destroy things. He also took her lighter. Something that would have her prints on it. It's why everything else was clean. Because this time, we *were* supposed to find it."

"We got lucky finding that," Ava disagreed.

"We did. I think we messed up his plan. I think he set it up, then planned to set off a bomb somewhere in town first and then call in a tip about the old sawmill."

Ava nodded slowly, the pieces falling into place. "Direct our investigation to Jennilyn and then blow her house when we went to talk to her. He was planning to make it look like she panicked after setting the bomb and took herself out."

"Right. Except we found the lighter too soon. He probably followed us to Jennilyn's house. Or maybe we arrived not long after he set the bomb there. Either way, *he* panicked when I saw him in the woods."

"Are you sure it was him?" Ava asked.

Eli laughed. "No. But it's my theory."

"It makes sense. You figure the original plan is that while we were digging through the evidence at the house, he'd be tracking down Jennilyn and killing her, then skipping town? Or maybe that he'd kill her first, leave her in the house so we'd find a body in the rubble?"

"It lines up with what she was saying about his escalating aggression," Eli said as he pulled off the road across the street from the motel, out of the line of sight from the rooms.

"It does," Ava said, troubled. "He could be going after everyone who he thinks did him wrong. It sounds like that's a long list. His colleagues, the military, Jennilyn's friends who didn't approve of him. If she's telling us the truth— and I think she is—he's a prime example of someone who blames others for his own failures, and is willing to take it out on everyone around him."

Eli glanced at his phone, silent in the console between them. "Brady said he'd text us as soon as he had anything, but I don't think we should wait."

"Yeah, I agree. If he's keeping tabs on things, he may know we were at the bar today talking to Jennilyn's friends. I'm sure he knows it was only a matter of time before his name came up. I want to get ahead of it. Maybe talk to him on the same pretense as before, more questions that are supposedly about Jennilyn, see if we can trip him up?"

"And hope that meanwhile Brady and Jason can get us enough for an arrest warrant?" Eli nodded. "Yeah. If we don't get that, at least we can keep tabs on him, make sure he's not out planting any bombs."

"You ready?" Ava asked, reaching for the door handle.

"Let's do this," Eli said.

She followed him outside, across the street and as he carefully maneuvered around the bushes that had blocked their view from the rooms.

He took off running before she'd rounded the bushes, but she followed immediately, her pulse jumping and her hand hovering over her weapon.

Then she saw why he'd moved so quickly.

Dennis's room door was ajar, a man in a cleaning uniform standing outside of it.

He looked startled as they raced up to him, putting his hands in the air as Eli peered into the room and swore.

"Where is he?" Ava asked.

The man shook his head. "Don't know. He checked out an hour ago."

Chapter Twenty-Seven

Dennis Ryon was gone.

Ava and Eli had called it in immediately and every officer out on patrol was watching for him. Meanwhile, they'd returned to the police station to search for leads, and hopefully to get enough for an arrest warrant when they found him.

Ava stared at herself in the mirror in the ladies room, where she'd run to clean up as soon as they reached the station. Despite having rubbed her face and hands vigorously with paper towels to get off the dirt, her skin still had a strange grayish cast to it. There were dark circles under her eyes and a slump to her shoulders. She felt as exhausted as she looked, and it wasn't just from already having worked a full shift.

It was everything. A week ago, she'd been trying—and failing—to fit in with her colleagues, with her neighbors in Jasper. She'd felt lost, and lonely. Since then, Lacey had almost died and that moment had made her realize just how much she relied on her K-9 partner, at work and in her life. She'd made the first small step toward reconnecting with her brother. She'd finally started bonding with her coworkers. She'd met Eli.

An hour ago, when Komi had called, she'd been ready to toss everything she'd started building here, to run back

to Chicago. As she stared at the locket around her neck—
the one she'd worn for five years as a remembrance, a
penance—she wondered if Chicago was really where she
belonged.

She'd loved her career in the Chicago PD, loved working narcotics. But this week, she'd finally been finding her
groove. The thrill of *this* job had started to fill her, the possibility of being a true community officer, the way she'd
dreamed back when she was fifteen years old. The idea of
leaving Lacey behind made panic build in her chest. Lacey
wasn't just her partner—wasn't just the best partner she'd
ever had—the dog was also her family.

She'd lost so much family already. She didn't want to
do it again. If she left, would Lacey even understand that
Ava couldn't bring her, that the K-9 technically belonged
to the Jasper PD? Or would she feel as betrayed and devas-
tated as Ava had felt when Komi had cut her out of his life?

Then, there was Eli. She'd only just met him, but he
was more than a passing interest who would fade from her
memory if she left Jasper and never came back. If she gave
it time, she knew he would become someone important in
her life. Would she find anyone like him in Chicago?

No, a voice whispered in her head. There was no one
like Eli.

Still, how could she pass up a chance to make things
right with Komi, the little brother who had felt like her
shadow for most of her life? The little brother she'd missed
so desperately for the past five years?

Scrubbing a hand across her eyes, Ava stared harder at
her reflection, as if the answer were there in her gaze. All
she saw was someone who looked slightly panicked, someone with no answers. Not for her life and not in this case.

"Get it together," she whispered. Now wasn't the time

to make big life decisions. Right now, she needed to do her job and stop Dennis Ryon from setting a bomb.

Tossing the dirty paper towel in the trash and squaring her shoulders, she headed back to the conference room.

While she'd been cleaning up, Brady and Jason had arrived. Both officers looked tired. Brady's always closely groomed beard seemed like it had grown in the past few hours, and Jason kept rubbing the back of his hand over his eyes.

Eli had taken the time to clean up, too. He'd done a better job of it than she had, somehow getting not only his skin clean, but also his uniform. He even looked energized, his bright blue eyes intense as his gaze met and held hers just long enough to feel intimate, but not long enough to draw attention.

Ava flushed, too many visions of Eli flashing through her mind. When she'd first met him, ultra-focused on his bomb-detection robot. On the case together, scouting out behind the warehouses. At Rose Café, all his attention on her, as if she were the most important thing in the world. At Jennilyn's house, in those seconds before the house blew and she knew he was in danger. Earlier tonight, disappointed understanding flashing on his face when she shifted from date mode into all work.

As Eli gave Brady and Jason the longer version of what he'd told them over the phone about Dennis, Ava let herself imagine him in the future. His hands brushing hers quickly while they were on the job, a shared, secret glance. Melding her lips to his again, feeling that same sense of inevitability. Even further, into territory she'd never daydreamed about with anyone else: meeting his family, looking for a house with him. Something permanent, somewhere between Jasper and McCall.

She blinked the images away before they could continue, focusing on Eli's words.

"Let's split up the work. Since Dennis doesn't have a police record, Ava and I will focus on digging into his history. We'll see if we can contact Jennilyn again, check out his social media. Try to figure out who else he's close to or where he might be hiding. Brady and Jason, I want you two to focus on his next target. If we can't find him first, we need to get in front of a bomb."

"Sounds good," Jason said.

"Yeah, I'm worried that he took off," Brady added. "Either he did it as a precaution because you found him to ask about Jennilyn or he knows you're on to him. Whatever the case, right now, we've got three options. He's gone to ground somewhere to plan. He's skipped town already and given up on revenge for now. Or he's moved up his time-table, whatever it was, and we probably don't have long before there's another bomb."

"Agreed," Eli said. "I doubt he skipped town. I'm hoping he's gone to ground, found himself another hiding place, maybe with a friend we don't know about or at a campsite. Otherwise, we probably have a day or even hours until he sets off another bomb."

ELI SQUEEZED A hand around the back of his neck, trying to ease the tension from too many hours on a laptop. So far, what he'd found was unsurprising and unhelpful.

Dennis Ryon was a loner. His social media presence was almost nonexistent. He had an account with no profile picture. A few people had tagged him over the years, from Army buddies to coworkers. Even in those photos, he was on the edges, slightly separated from everyone, the look in his eyes disinterested.

Eli and Ava had reached out to Jennilyn again, but she'd

had little to say on the friend front. They'd slowly faded away, she'd told them, until she couldn't really say if he'd stayed in touch with any friends.

Targets were the opposite. There were too many to check out individually, too much wasted time. Colleagues from the military—two of whom actually lived on the outskirts of Jasper—or from the job he'd had at Handall's Furniture just inside the Jasper town limits, or from Blaze's River Tours and Rafting, where he'd told Jennilyn he was finally going to start fresh. His attempt to prove to her that he was going to change. He'd been fired even before they opened, not long after she'd broken up with him. Then there were Jennilyn's friends at the bar, people he thought had a hand in convincing Jennilyn to instigate the breakup.

They'd kept the small department updated anyway, made sure officers out on the streets drove by potential targets in case anything looked suspicious. Or they got lucky and spotted Dennis. So far, that hadn't yielded any results, either.

"It's six a.m.," Brady announced.

Eli blinked at him, refocusing. Had they really been in this conference room all night?

"I've got to get some coffee, something to eat," Brady added. "Or I'm going to crash soon."

"Millard's Diner opens at six," Jason put in. "I'll go over with you and grab some food." He glanced at Eli and Ava. "You two want anything?"

"Coffee," they said in unison, drawing Eli's attention back to her.

She looked tired, but there was a determination in her light brown eyes. Curls had slid free from her bun hours ago and she'd been tucking them absently behind her ears ever since. Two of them had bounced loose again and Eli longed to pull the rest of her hair free.

Shaking off the thought, he added, "Food would be great, too. Anything with protein. I think I've exhausted the information we can find from the station. We need to get out on the streets soon."

"Same for me on the food," Ava said. "Thanks," she added as Jason and Brady hurried out of the room.

When she stood and dialed a number on her cell phone, Eli stood, too. Instead of stretching like he'd planned, he found his feet moving toward her until he was standing close enough to run his hand through the curls dangling across her cheek.

"Hi, Marie? I was just calling to check… She will?" A smile burst on her face and her gaze lifted to his, happiness overriding the exhaustion. "Okay… Okay. Thank you!"

When she hung up, she told him, "Lacey is doing great. I'll be able to take her home tomorrow afternoon."

"That's great," he said, imagining how happy the German shepherd would be to see Ava, and vice versa.

Leaning backward, he peered into the bullpen through the part of the conference room that was glassed in. The bullpen was empty, most of the other officers out on the street, watching for anything of concern or any sign of Dennis.

Refocusing his attention on Ava, he said softly, "Whatever you decide to do after this case is finished, I'll support you."

Surprise flashed in her gaze, followed by an uncertainty that told him he still had a chance.

Trying to taper the hope that flared, he stepped slightly closer and added, "But I have to at least make sure you know how much I want you to stay."

She blinked, and this close, he could see the desire overtaking her uncertainty.

Before she could regain her equilibrium, he reached up

and tucked that curl behind her ear, letting his hand slide over her soft skin. Her eyes dilated and she swayed toward him just slightly.

It was a bad idea to kiss her in a police station. But his mind couldn't override his emotions as he leaned in and pressed his lips against hers. Softly, enjoying the plumpness of her lips, the way her eyes slid shut and her palms planted against his chest like she needed him to support her.

His thumb stroked the edge of her cheek as his fingers twitched in her hair, anxious to pull the rest of it free. His lips moved gently over hers, enjoying, savoring, memorizing.

She sighed, her lips parting, and he couldn't resist slipping his tongue into her mouth, using his free hand to pull her tight against him.

Her hands spasmed against his chest, then fisted there, like she wasn't sure if she wanted to push him away or yank him closer still.

A noise in the bullpen made her pull back, her gaze unfocused.

He glanced behind him, but there was no one. He breathed her in once more—the faint, intoxicating scent of cocoa butter he'd started to crave whenever she wasn't around. Then he forced himself to step away from her, not to tarnish her reputation in the station where he wanted her to remain.

Ava, stay, clogged in his throat, and he forced himself not to say it, not to pressure her when he knew how badly she missed Chicago, missed her brother.

"I…" Ava laughed, high and nervous, her hands tucking curls back into that bun. "I shouldn't have done that. We need to focus on work."

He smiled at her, remembering the last time she'd kissed him and then told him they needed to keep things professional. Remembering the promise he'd made to pursue her as soon as this case was over.

"I think this time, the blame is on me," he teased her. "But anytime you feel like instigating something, I'll be good with it."

He grinned, and she blinked at him a few times, then her own grin emerged.

The grin slowly faded, her gaze turning pensive. But there was something in her eyes that made his heart leap. "I think—"

Her words were cut off as Brady and Jason rushed into the room, no take-out bags in sight.

"There was a line at Millard's Diner today," Jason said, breathless. "People who'd driven into town early for events."

"There's a military veterans event scheduled to start in a few hours at Bartwell Brewing Company. Today is also the grand opening of Blaze's River Tours and Rafting."

As Ava swore softly, Eli said, "This is it. It's got to be one of those events. We just found Dennis's target."

Chapter Twenty-Eight

"Which one is it?" Jason asked, glancing from Eli to Brady to Ava and back again. "Bartwell Brewing Company or Blaze's River Tours and Rafting? The military that started Dennis's downward trajectory or the company that fired him most recently, ruining his shot to turn things around?"

Eli's pulse picked up, anxiety spiking at the idea of searching the wrong place. "Jennilyn said the military was his dream job. This veterans event isn't specifically connected to anyone who he thinks turned him in and got him kicked out, but he blames the whole military now. Blaze's was a much newer job, not as prized, but the specific person who fired him will probably be at the event." Eli shrugged. "I could see Dennis picking either one."

"When do the events start?" Ava asked.

Eli glanced at her, trying not to think about what she might have been getting ready to say before Jason and Brady burst into the room. She'd looked so serious, but not like she was about to shoot him down. Instead, she'd seemed as though she might have been ready to give him hope, to say that her mind wasn't made up about returning to Chicago. If that were the case, would he be so wrong to do his best to convince her to stay?

He shook the thoughts free, focusing on what mattered right now, as Ava continued speaking.

"If he's targeting an event, especially now when he's truly gone into hiding, he's probably not just aiming at a few specific people who did him wrong. He's looking to make a statement, either to the military or to this town."

The grim prediction made the room go silent briefly, then Jason spoke up.

"The military event starts at nine, but according to a couple of Army guys who were picking up coffee, there's already a line. Blaze's grand opening starts at eight, but it sounds like there's a line there, too, because they're giving away gift certificates for rafting adventures. The first fifty people get extra raffle tickets."

Ava glanced at her phone. "It's six twenty now. Not a lot of time to do a thorough search of each of those buildings, plus any outdoor setups."

"Not to mention defuse anything we find," Eli said. "Especially since we can't rule out that Dennis might have picked *both* events. If there are two bombs, it's not like I can be in two places at once."

Brady swore. "Divide and conquer? Jason and I can search Bartwell Brewing, since the military event starts a little later. You and Ava go to Blaze's. If we find something at Bartwell before you're finished searching, we can get someone to take over for you. We can ask the Chief to put everyone on standby to evacuate either place if we find anything. If we're not finished searching, I think we should just clear out both spots at seven thirty."

Eli nodded, waving frantically at the Chief, who chose that moment to walk by the conference room.

He did a quick turn, rushing inside, his craggy face serious, his hazel eyes intense. "What's happening?"

"We think we know what Dennis is going to target," Eli said. He told the Chief their plan.

The Chief glanced at Ava. "I wish we had Lacey right now."

"Me, too," Ava said. "But she's not cleared—"

"No," the Chief cut her off. "I'm not suggesting you bring her in while she's still healing. She's an officer, too. I'm not risking the rest of her career for one investigation, no matter how important. Besides, if she's not fully healed, she might not be up for the job. The plan we have is good. I trust you all to do what needs to be done." He glanced at his watch. "But you have one hour. Then we're evacuating those buildings, plus anything nearby. If a bomb goes off downtown, especially something like the one at Sanderson's house…"

"There could be a lot of casualties," Eli said, feeling the pressure build. On a Saturday morning, even people who had no interest in either of the big events would be downtown, enjoying the warming weather.

"I'll be in command mode," Chief Walters said. "Radio if you need anything."

As they hurried for the door, the Chief called after them, "Good luck."

Eli raced for his SUV, the adrenaline rush chasing away the last of his fatigue. Mentally, he catalogued all of the gear in the back of his vehicle, deciding he'd go in with just his standard kit of bomb disposal tools, plus his portable X-ray scanner. Easy to carry and he'd maneuver a lot faster than the robot, especially with a lot of people around. He didn't want to panic anyone.

He waved to Brady and Jason as the pair got into Brady's police vehicle and headed to Bartwell's, lights and sirens off to keep everyone calm. It wasn't a long drive to the brewery, located in an alley off Third Street.

Blaze's was even closer, on Main Street just like the station. With Ava right behind him, Eli hopped into his SUV and turned out of the station, onto the street.

He couldn't help but notice how many people were already out, walking their dogs or pushing strollers and laughing, carefree. Enjoying the first weekend of the year that was supposed to reach almost seventy degrees.

"Why couldn't we have gotten lucky with some thunderstorms," Eli muttered.

"We'll get there in time," Ava said, her voice confident. "He's not going to blow this bomb until the event is underway. Whatever he's targeting, he wants to be remembered for this explosion."

Eli nodded, but he couldn't help but picture the blast of heat and sound that had lifted him off his feet at Jennilyn's house. An explosion triggered by Dennis at their arrival.

"We need to act normal, pretend we're not in a rush," Eli said as he parked across the street from Blaze's, which was bursting with people.

The line was already snaking down the street, people laughing and chatting, kids snacking on bags of popcorn the company was handing out. Employees milled around, handing out flyers and pointing to a fancy kayak on display in front of the store. A grand prize for one lucky raffle winner, according to the sign.

Eli texted Brady the same thing as he told Ava, "Try not to draw attention. Maybe even ask a few people about Jennilyn when we arrive."

Ava's brown eyes were wary as she stared back at him. "You're worried that if he spots us—"

"He could set the bomb off early."

Chapter Twenty-Nine

Eli pasted a smile on his face as he slung his plain black nylon bag over his shoulder. It could pass as a laptop case, but it actually contained bomb disposal tools. Everything from a hook-and-line kit to a multi-tool with knives and plyers to carabiners, mirrors and a compass. All the things he'd need to defuse a bomb if they found a live one. Just not a bomb suit to keep himself safe, because right now, it was more important not to incite panic or cause Dennis to set the bomb off early.

He glanced at Ava, who'd looked worried when he'd told her he was leaving his suit and the robot in the vehicle. He gave her a confident nod, hoping she couldn't tell that he was nervous.

Usually, he arrived at the site of a potential bomb with cautious anxiety, trusting his training and his equipment. Usually, beneath the worry over what he might find was an undercurrent of excitement. The knowledge that he could defuse and dismantle whatever he came across. The pride in taking care of his community.

Today, that excitement was totally missing, replaced by a churning in his gut. His instincts, telling him they were going to run into trouble? Or concern for Ava, who would be going into a building right alongside him that might be set to blow?

It was a little bit of both, he realized, as she gave him a similar nod in return, like she was also trying to put on a brave front for him.

Striding through the crowds, Eli scanned the outside area for anywhere a bomb might be hidden. The kayak on display was the most obvious option. As Ava chatted with a few people in line, asking with casual interest if they knew Jennilyn Sanderson and if anyone had seen her recently, Eli pretended to tie his shoe next to the kayak.

As he bent down, he peered beneath the kayak and along the metal display holding it up, looking for any sign of a bomb. There was nothing. With a quick tug to the knot on his shoe, he stood and said to Ava in a tone meant to be overheard, "Let's step inside and see if anyone there has seen Jennilyn."

She nodded, thanking the people she'd been chatting with, and followed him as he asked the employee holding the door to let them inside.

The minute he stepped inside, a weight pressed on Eli's chest. The store was probably a thousand square feet. It was packed with rafting and camping gear, each shelf a potential hiding spot for a bomb. That wasn't including the office or storage areas Eli couldn't see. There was no way to inspect it all in less than an hour.

There were no customers allowed inside yet, but half a dozen employees hurried through the room, straightening merchandise and setting out flyers advertising the company's Salmon River tours on every available surface.

Eli glanced around the room, trying to decide what would be Dennis's best bet if he wanted a bomb to remain unseen during a busy opening. Dropping to the ground, he pulled a mirror from his kit and started peering underneath shelves and counters.

"What's he doing?" one of the employees asked.

"Safety check. We're making sure nothing is unstable," Ava told her loudly, then asked Eli, "How can I help?"

A couple of other employees gave them perplexed looks, but continued working.

Eli handed her a mirror. "Help me search."

Half an hour later, his body aching from jumping up and down, he hurried over to Ava. "Find anything?"

She shook her head.

Swearing under his breath, Eli snagged one of the closest employees and asked, "Where's the owner?"

The frazzled-looking woman pointed vaguely toward the front of the store, where a man had just entered. Then she pulled free, continuing to set out flyers.

Eli followed Ava, not bothering to act so casual now that they were inside, out of sight from prying eyes. Wherever Dennis was, it wasn't in the store.

"Are you the owner?" Ava asked when they reached a tall stocky white man with prematurely gray hair and an infectious smile.

"That's me," he replied, his smile fading in the face of their serious expressions. "Blaze Peterson. What can I do for you? If this is about the crowds, we'll be keeping a count on how many people enter at once. We know the fire code."

"That's not it," Eli said, keeping his voice low. "Have you seen Dennis Ryon recently?"

"Dennis?" Blaze scowled. "I had to fire him a few weeks ago. I thought he was going to be great with stocking inventory, considering what a strong-looking guy he is, and being former Army and all. But he was always picking fights with my other employees, acting like he was in charge when he wasn't."

"Is there any chance he still has access to your store?" Eli pressed.

Blaze scowled. "I'd like to say no. I never gave him a

key. He wasn't senior enough for that. But I overheard him bragging to one of our other employees that his work in the Army had taught him to get in anywhere and that our locks were a joke."

"Do you have any reason to think he's been in the store recently?" Ava asked.

Blaze shifted his weight, starting to look nervous. "Why?"

"We think he may be targeting someone for what he considers revenge. We're just not sure who that might be."

Blaze's meaty hands formed fists. "Well, I can tell you that he threatened to destroy me when I fired him. The look on his face when he said it made me nervous, I have to admit. Do you think he's planning to ruin our grand opening?"

"It's our goal to stop that," Ava said. "What area would Dennis be most familiar with? Is there somewhere he spent a lot of time working or during breaks?"

Eli nodded at her, liking the way she was thinking. There was no way to search the entire store before their seven-thirty deadline. Most likely, they'd need to call the Chief and evacuate, which meant a potential risk that Dennis could set off a bomb during that evacuation. By starting somewhere Dennis felt comfortable, maybe they'd get lucky.

"Yeah, sure," Blaze said. "He was going to be a tour guide once we opened. He was a strong kayaker and we were working to get him familiar with the script and the river. Until then, he was helping us with stock. It's not the best layout for big stock, but we wanted as much space as possible for the actual store. So, we kept our stock in the basement."

Blaze pointed to a door marked Employees Only and Eli hurried toward it, Ava on his heels. If you wanted to cause structural damage to take down a whole building, a basement was a good location to set a bomb. Not to mention that he'd chosen that spot when he'd blown up Jennilyn's house.

"There's an outside entrance, too," Blaze called after them, and the sudden urgency in his voice made Eli glance back. "A service elevator that goes to the back. In case we want to haul boats out that way. I know I locked it when I closed up last night, but I found it unlocked this morning when I showed up at six."

Sharing a worried glance with Ava, Eli pulled open the door to the basement and his pulse ratcheted up more. The stairs were dimly lit and his footsteps echoed as he raced down the extra-wide staircase. At the bottom, he found another light switch and flipped it.

Hopeful anxiety shifted into defeat as he took in the space, which looked as large as the store's footprint above. Big metal shelves took up a lot of the space. Huge boxes labeled with pictures of kayaks and canoes were stacked on the bigger bottom shelves and smaller boxes with other camping gear was up higher. Open stock—or maybe employee kayaks and oars for the tours—were lined up to the right of the staircase. Excess streamers and a Grand Opening sign half the size of the one out front were stacked on top of the boats.

Eli cursed, staring into the cavernous space. It would be easy to place a bomb anywhere down here. It would take forever to clear.

He looked at Ava, ready to split up the space and start working, get as far as possible, when a scurrying sound toward the back of the basement made him freeze.

Just an animal? Or the shuffle of someone's shoe as they tried to hide?

Dropping his hand to his weapon, Eli gestured for Ava

to move down the aisle in front of them while he went down the next one.

Eli moved quickly, cursing the way Blaze had built the shelving, so each of the aisles had a break partway down them. New aisles started up again in a staggered design, so he could only see halfway to the back of the basement.

Hurrying down the section he could see, hearing Ava's lighter tread in the aisle beside him, Eli pulled up short in the open space that bisected the aisles. He glanced in both directions, seeing no one, and was about to shift into the aisle to his right that would take him to the back of the space, when he spotted a plain black box the size of a suitcase that didn't look like anything around it.

Awareness from all of his training screamed at him.

Pivoting back, he knelt down and peered between two boxes. His heart gave an extra thump as he looked closer. The plastic container had no labels. It definitely didn't belong.

Setting down his tool kit, he checked for any obvious trip wires on the outside of the case. When he saw none, he pulled out his handheld X-ray machine.

"Is that what I think it is?" Ava asked in a whisper, nerves in her voice as she settled on her heels beside him.

"We're about to find out." He turned on the machine and swore at what it revealed. "It's a bomb." He peered closer, inspecting it for any sign that opening the case would set it off. When he was sure it wouldn't, he slowly opened the lid, double-checking with his mirror to be sure there wasn't a trigger he'd missed.

With the lid open, Ava gasped. "This is no pipe bomb."

"No." It was an IED packed with enough explosives to potentially take down the building. "This is probably what he used at Jennilyn's house." Eli glanced around the basement, searching for an obvious ignition source, but saw none. Maybe Dennis leaving the bomb next to a boiler at Jennilyn's had been unintentional. Just an easy spot to hide it.

That didn't mean a bomb of this size, placed below the building, couldn't cause enough structural damage to bring it down. It probably would. But it was unlikely to cause quite the fireball they'd seen at Jennilyn's.

A small hint of relief filled him and it grew when he looked closer at the bomb. "There's a timer, but it's not activated. We'll get the robot in here and get it contained."

He checked it over more carefully, making sure he wasn't missing anything, as he told Ava, "Check in with Brady and Jason, will you? Make sure we're only dealing with one bomb. Then let's try to get the robot down here discreetly, maybe from the back entrance. If Dennis is watching, he could activate this remotely. Normally, I'd evacuate now, but I think that will set him off, especially if this is the only bomb. Makes it more likely he's nearby, watching."

"On it," she replied, pulling out her phone and tapping away.

Almost immediately, she was tucking her phone back into her pocket. "They're pretty sure Bartwell's is clear. They're going to double-check everything, but one of the veterans had actually worked in bomb disposal for the military for more than a decade. He helped them check it."

"That's lucky," Eli said, his tension slipping down another notch. But the fact that there was only one bomb made it even more important not to let Dennis know they'd found this one. "Now, let's radio in to the Chief what we found. Ideally, I'll get this disarmed quietly and no one outside the department will even know there was a threat. Still, I want the team on standby to evacuate in case I run into trouble."

Ava nodded, giving him a reassuring smile. "You've got this."

He smiled back, knowing she was right. No bomb dismantling was a guarantee, but he knew he could do this safely.

Picking up his mirror again, he was leaning toward the bomb when a gunshot rang out, hitting a box one shelf over. The side of the box popped open and a waterfall of colorful folding knives spilled to the floor beside them.

Eli spun toward the back of the basement, where the shot had come from, and swore as a figure darted out of sight. Then another gunshot rang out.

This one hit closer, and Eli tackled Ava, pushing her into the aisle she'd walked down. As a third gunshot bounced off the metal shelf above the bomb, Eli cringed.

Then, a sound even worse reached his ears. A set of beeps from where he'd just been working.

They were pinned down. And the bomb had just been activated.

Chapter Thirty

Eli was squashing her beneath him, pressing her against
the shelving as he tried to shield her from the gunshots.

When a series of beeps sounded beside her and Ava
spotted a red light from between the shelves, she swore.
"Is that what I think it was?"

Eli's voice, calm and confident even in the most stressful situations, was tense. "He activated the bomb."

"Can you defuse it from here?" Ava shifted beneath
Eli, trying to pull him with her closer to the shelving unit,
closer to the bomb. Away from the bullets.

He was more solid than he looked, and even though he
let her move them against the shelf, he wouldn't let her slip
out from underneath him.

She couldn't tell where Dennis was, but judging by
where the gunshots had hit, he could probably still see
them. The fact that he hadn't hit them didn't mean he was
a bad shot. It meant he was a sadistic bastard who wanted
to pin them down, make them watch the countdown.

Since he knew exactly when it was set to blow, he could
keep them pinned long enough to prevent them from de-
fusing the bomb. He could give himself just enough time
to get out, and watch them get buried in the rubble.

"Can you defuse it?" Ava asked again, when Eli didn't
respond. She twisted beneath him, trying to get a better

look at what was happening. They were facing the wrong direction and it was awkward.

"No. I can probably reach it from here, but I'd have to move it toward me to work on it, and I don't know if that would set it off. I didn't have enough time to inspect it for anti-handling devices. Plus, my tools are out in the aisle and I can't get to those. Dammit!" he swore as another gunshot blasted, sending a waterfall of ropes on top of them.

"Do you see him?"

"No." Eli shoved some of the rope off them. Then he twisted, managing to keep himself on top of her while turning to face the direction where Dennis had to be hiding. "I think he's hiding on one of the bottom shelves. They're a little emptier on the back half of the shelves, from what I can tell. But I think he's close. He's using a kayak box as cover and peering over it to shoot. It puts him slightly above us, gives him some cover."

"Is he trying to shoot the bomb?"

"No. He's trying to stop us from disarming it."

"If you move a little, I can help aim at him," Ava whispered, hesitant to squirm out from underneath him while he was aiming his weapon in Dennis's direction. She didn't want to throw him off if he got a shot.

"We have to be careful. If we just injure him, he'll be able to use his remote detonator. If we get a shot, it has to be a kill shot. I'll keep my weapon on him. You call it in to the Chief," Eli insisted. "We need to get officers in from the other direction. They can enter through that other doorway. Blaze must not have realized Dennis was still here when he found it unlocked."

"If we trap him, he won't have anything to lose. He'll just set off the bomb!"

"What choice do we have? We need to evacuate as many people as we can."

He didn't say it, but she knew what he was thinking from the hard set to his voice. He thought she should be one of those people. He thought he could keep Dennis from shooting her while she ran back the way they'd come. Leaving him behind to die in the rubble with Dennis.

Panic fluttered in her chest, even though she'd never leave Eli alone. There had to be a better plan, a way to get to Dennis without him detonating the bomb.

Ava maneuvered awkwardly, digging her phone out of her pocket. Not wanting her voice to carry, she texted the Chief instead, giving him an update but warning him not to breach. Not yet.

She glanced at the time on her phone and her pulse skipped. Ten minutes until they'd originally planned to evacuate. It would probably be far less before police arrived and started clearing people from the store and the sidewalk above them.

The police would try to do it as calmly and quietly as possible, but with that many people, it wouldn't be silent. Dennis would probably hear the evacuation, especially once they started clearing everyone from inside the store.

Once that happened, it didn't matter what the countdown on the timer read. Dennis would just use his remote detonator and blow up as many people as he could.

The Chief responded to her text immediately, exactly how she expected. He was sending all available officers to evacuate the store and the surrounding area and he'd put help on standby. Ava set the phone on the floor beside her and squeezed her eyes shut, saying a silent prayer. The station was only a few minutes away. She needed to move fast.

Squirming quickly out from underneath Eli, Ava pivoted. Instead of pushing herself up beside him, she slid in the other direction.

"What are you doing?" Eli whispered.

"I'm going to need you to distract him in a minute."

"Ava, *no*."

"This is our other choice, Eli. I'm not letting you sacrifice yourself for the rest of us." Checking to be sure she wouldn't accidently knock anything into the bomb, Ava slid a box labeled Flashlights into the aisle.

It was heavier than she'd expected and made a soft *thump* as it landed on the floor.

Silently, she swore, but Eli shoved one of the thicker, heavier ropes against the shelf across the aisle, making more noise. Then he fired a single bullet.

The shot echoed as it hit metal and Ava hoped the noise would cover the sound of her sliding onto the shelf where the box had been. She pulled herself across it with her arms, trying to be as silent as possible. A sharp edge of the metal shelf snagged her pant leg, piercing the skin beneath, and she clamped down on her jaw to keep from shrieking at the sudden, surprising pain.

Reaching back, she freed the material. Blood slicked her hand, more than she'd expected, and she swiped it against her pant leg. There was no time to worry about whether she'd hurt herself badly. Not when she needed all of her focus to find and sneak up on Dennis.

Her heart thundered in her ears as she slid out onto the aisle on the other side. Pulling herself into a crouch, Ava took her pistol out of its holster, trying to stay as small as possible against the shelf.

Since the aisles were staggered, even if Dennis peered out through the aisle on the other side, he shouldn't be able to see her. Not yet. Hopefully he'd just assume she'd slid backward in the same aisle as Eli, out of sight. But once she moved into the bisecting aisle, she'd be out in the open. A target for Dennis, but also a warning to him of what she planned. A chance for him to set off the bomb with a single press of his finger.

She should have taken more time to formulate a plan, to decide on a signal with Eli. Instead, she'd acted on instinct, knowing time was limited.

Staying close to the shelving, Ava stood slowly and moved on soft feet toward the front of the aisle. She wanted to look down at the bomb, to see how much time they had left, but she forced her gaze to stay focused. It didn't matter what the timer read.

Painfully slowly, she eased her head forward just enough to peer around the shelf. Her heart thumped hard when she spotted the kayak box on the bottom shelf across the aisle and over one. The spiky tops of Dennis's blondish-brown hair were just visible above the box.

He was only eight feet away from her. But eight feet was too far when it meant sprinting toward him and tackling him in a way that didn't allow him to detonate the bomb. Especially when she had no idea whether the device he was using to control it was buried in his pocket or clutched in his free hand.

There had to be a way. Ava glanced around, moving only her eyes, not wanting to make any movements that Dennis might spot.

Her breath stuttered in her throat as his hand—holding a cell phone—appeared at the edge of the box, clutching it as if for stability. Then the top of his head and his gun popped up quickly above the box and he fired a single shot toward Eli.

Ava's hand jerked, instinct wanting to take over. Wanting to fire back and protect her partner.

Except Dennis wasn't trying to hit Eli. He just wanted to keep him pinned. Since no bullets had been fired at her, he hadn't realized she'd moved.

She could do this.

One of Dennis's hands was holding his gun. The other was still clutching the edge of the box. His phone was pressed between his hand and the box. It had to be how he was controlling the bomb.

Ava squeezed her eyes shut, focusing on evening out her breathing. She was a good shot. But it wasn't a big target. And she'd only get one chance.

Opening her eyes, Ava glanced down, making sure her leg wasn't dripping enough blood to make her slip. She cringed at the small puddle at her feet, then moved that leg slightly forward, away from it. There was no room for error.

Lifting her weapon slowly, Ava eased it past the edge of the shelf, lining her eye up with it. She took one last breath, then exhaled as she pulled the trigger.

A scream echoed with the gunshot, but Ava didn't wait to see if she'd hit her target. She just shoved her gun back in its holster and launched herself away from the aisle.

Before she reached the shelving where Dennis was hiding, three more gunshots rang out from behind her. Eli, knowing exactly what distraction she needed.

Pushing off when she was halfway into the aisle, Ava crashed into Dennis, slamming both of them through the shelving and into the aisle on the other side.

Her head and back skimmed the top of the shelf above them. Pain erupted all over her body, but Ava ignored it, her gaze going to Dennis's hand that had held the cell phone. It was covered in blood. And it was empty. She'd hit her target.

Her relief was short-lived as he flipped beneath her, powerful enough to send her to the ground. He smashed a huge fist into her bicep and she slid across the floor, back into the shelving. A box fell from above, slamming into her and stealing her breath.

He scrambled the other way, toward the gun he'd dropped.

Then another gunshot rang out, making Dennis scurry backward as Eli raced toward them, his gun centered on Dennis. "Don't move!"

Ava shoved the box off her, trying to catch her breath. Pulling her weapon from her holster with a hand that trembled, she aimed it at Dennis.

He was crouched on the ground, his gaze darting to her left.

Ava's gaze followed, landing on his cell phone just as he made a leap for it.

She wasn't sure who fired first, her or Eli.

Dennis dropped instantly. She didn't need to check to know he was dead.

Head and leg throbbing, lungs aching with each breath, her gaze rose to Eli. She tried to shut out the pain, to ignore the relief that he was okay and focus on what mattered most right now. "How much time do we have?"

Eli holstered his weapon and spun back toward the bomb.

His curse reached her just as she raced up next to him. "He wasn't waiting for the grand opening to start."

She stared at the bright red numbers on the bomb.

They had less than a minute until it exploded.

Chapter Thirty-One

"Get out of here *now*," Eli said, dropping to the ground next to the bomb.

If only he had his robot. With its disruption tools that could separate a bomb from its trigger without setting it off. Or his bomb suit, to protect himself in case anything went wrong.

Of course, even a bomb suit, while it could protect him from bomb fragments, could only do so much when it came to the overwhelming force of an IED like this. It didn't matter how protected he was from the initial blast if it brought the building crashing down on top of him.

Right now, he'd even settle for his containment chamber. With an IED of this size, with this type of explosives, it wouldn't contain the whole blast. But it would be blunted enough that it wouldn't take down the building. Most likely, it would blunt it enough to save the lives of everyone here, especially if he could set the bomb inside the chamber and run.

There were so many options for dismantling a bomb like this. Far, far at the bottom of that list was what he was doing now, tackling it with his most basic tools, no protection and barely any time.

One wrong move and it wouldn't just be his own life gone. It would be everyone in the immediate vicinity. Beyond that, there would be amputations from the blast and flying debris, contusions and overpressure injuries that ended up being fatal after someone thought they'd survived the worst of it.

But he had no other option. The timer was already down to forty-nine seconds.

When Ava didn't move, he wasted precious seconds to look up at her, to take in the panicked expression in her eyes. Vowing to get through this, to have a chance to fight for her, he snapped, "Go now, Ava. Help them evacuate."

Instead, she dropped to her knees beside him. Her voice was calm and sure. "Tell me how to help."

Swearing, he stared at the bomb, assessing as fast as he could, thinking back to the pieces of devices they'd found at the warehouse and the sawmill. To the very limited information forensics had gathered so far from the bomb set in Jennilyn's basement. Clues to Dennis's methods? Or a way to lead them off track?

All the materials they'd found intact at the warehouse and sawmill had been pieces of pipe bombs. They'd been nothing like the higher explosive load at Jennilyn's house, a bomb they only had small pieces of to analyze. Nothing like the more sophisticated IED staring back at him now. Enough explosive material to take down a building, and the potential for hidden anti-tampering devices that would set it off if he attempted the wrong approach.

He started to tell Ava to radio the Chief, but she was already doing it, advising him to evacuate now, to do it loudly and quickly.

Almost instantly, he heard Arthur Rutledge's voice booming over a loudspeaker, asking everyone to leave the area as quickly as possible.

Eli tuned out the details he knew would follow: leaving behind possessions. Leaving in an orderly fashion. Helping anyone who needed assistance, but moving fast. *Moving fast.*

If there was any chance that they could all evacuate far enough, he would have grabbed Ava and run, too. Left the area and let the building blow. Prioritizing life over property. But he only had thirty-six seconds left.

The people outside in line had a chance to get clear of the explosive range if they ran. With a bomb this size, ideally they would get at least fifty feet away from the bomb. That would probably save their lives from the initial blast. Getting them eighteen hundred and fifty feet away—the outdoor evacuation distance to protect them from flying debris from a bomb of this size—would be impossible.

Many of them would follow police orders and move far enough, fast enough. Those people would at least survive. The people in the store probably didn't have enough time to truly get clear, if the bomb worked as intended. At least some of them, plus the police officers helping people evacuate, would surely be killed.

Hand entry, manually rendering a bomb safe, was something he'd done in practice. It was even something he'd done out in the field, wearing his bomb suit. But it was dangerous in the best of conditions. With no time to fully evaluate the bomb before he made decisions, this was far from the best of conditions.

He trusted his gut, trusted his training. But this was the worst scenario, the one he'd never dreamed he'd face when he'd volunteered—no, *fought*—to become a bomb technician.

With an IED, it was all about interfering with the detonation or triggering system. But there were so many possible configurations, so many possible ways to detonate it during that process. Assessing the bomb was one of the most important steps. It determined everything else, from whether you tried to move it to how exactly you attempted to render it safe. Right now, that assessment would be cursory at best.

He tried to close everything from his mind except the bomb itself, all of the little clues about what might trigger it or disarm it. He could still hear Ava's voice, calm and focused, continuing to advise the Chief about the size and type of bomb, where she'd seen civilians, the closest exits and entrances.

His heart thundering in his ears, Eli evaluated how to access and disrupt the triggering system. Dennis had been smart, making it tricky to reach, tricky to tell for sure if there was a secondary trigger on it.

Twenty-seven seconds.

The world around him dimmed, even Ava's voice fading into nothing, as Eli fell back on his training. Those six weeks at the FBI's Hazardous Devices School, where he learned to use his robot, how to do a contained explosion and right now, most importantly, where he'd practiced disabling bombs in place. In practice, he'd worn a bomb suit. In practice, he'd had more than twenty-seven seconds.

Sliding his mirror along the inside of the black case, Eli searched for any sign of a second trigger tucked among the explosives. He didn't see one.

Twenty-two seconds.

His heart thundered, the loudest sound he could hear, as he selected a precision cutting tool from his case. It was an awkward fit, slipping his hand in sideways between the explosives and the case, to get to where the triggering device was positioned.

He slowed his breathing, relaxed his grip and slid the tool farther into the case, using his inspection mirror to guide him.

Seventeen seconds.

"Ava," he said, and immediately she was leaning closer. "Hold the mirror right here."

When she took it, he grabbed his spudger, a precision tool that let him separate small, sensitive components. He slid it in beside the cutting tool and used it to slide the wire he wanted away from the explosives slowly, to confirm the connection to the triggering device.

Nine seconds.

Easing the cutting tool up behind the trigger, he said a silent prayer and snipped.

Afterward, his heart continued to thunder in his ears, his gaze laser-focused on the triggering device.

Then, Ava's voice reached his ears, amazed and relived. "You did it. The timer turned off."

Letting out a breath, Eli slid his tools carefully away from the bomb. "Let's get the containment chamber down here to transport it safely."

He stood, and Ava squeezed his hand as she radioed up to the team, "It's safe. Eli disarmed the bomb."

She grinned at him as cheering filled the radio, and then individual voices started chiming in. First the Chief's, then Brady's and Jason's, then other members of the team. Congratulating him and Ava.

Her smile grew, the happiness in her eyes overshadowing the dirt and blood smeared across her uniform and her face, the snarled mess of her hair.

He could see it on her face. She finally, *finally* felt like part of the team.

But would it be enough to make her stay?

Epilogue

"Lacey!" A grin broke on Ava's face, far bigger than she could ever hope to contain, as the German shepherd came striding out of the back of the vet's office.

She wasn't moving with her usual speed or grace, but her tail was wagging.

Ava knelt in front of her and buried her head in the dog's long soft fur. Relief enveloped her. "I'm so glad you're okay, Lacey."

The dog nuzzled her head closer and Ava laughed. She didn't move until she heard Marie's voice.

"As you can tell, she's doing great."

Giving her dog one last pet, Ava stood. "Thank you for taking such good care of her."

"Of course. I'm happy she gets to go home today."

From the way Lacey's tail loudly thumped the ground, Ava thought she agreed.

"I'm glad you didn't need her yesterday," Marie continued. "I read in the paper this morning about the bomb that was disabled at the grand opening of Blaze's. I couldn't believe it. You were there?"

Ava nodded, thinking of those final moments beside Eli, watching him work. Choosing to stand beside him, knowing he could save them all.

She'd been right. And it hadn't just been Eli who'd gotten a hero's reception when they climbed up from the basement. Her team had slapped her on the back, Jason kneeling to bandage her leg before an EMT could get through the crowd. Even Captain Rutledge had given her a genuine-looking smile, his tone heartfelt when he said, "Great job today, Officer Callan."

Somehow, she'd been pushed through the crowd of officers and civilians and put into an ambulance. They'd insisted she get checked out at the hospital. As the ambulance doors had closed, she'd seen Eli from a distance, heading back into the building with his bomb containment chamber. When her cuts and abrasions had been stitched up and debrided, and she'd finally been cleared by the doctor hours later, the Chief had told her to go home. He'd said Eli had already headed back to McCall.

Her heart pinched remembering it. Eli had left without even saying goodbye. Because he didn't want to bother her in case she'd gone home to sleep off the day, hell, the whole week? Or because he thought there was nothing left to say?

She'd been the one to change the tone at Millard's after her brother called. Maybe this was Eli trying to honor her wishes. But what had happened to pursuing her with all he had?

Shaking off the heavy disappointment weighing in her chest, Ava tried to smile as she told Marie, "I was there. I'm glad it's all over." She tried to mean it.

"Well, the department already paid for Lacey's care, so you're all set there. Here's her medicine." Marie handed her a small paper bag. "Call me if you have any questions or if Lacey doesn't continue to improve."

Ava must have looked worried, because Marie patted her arm. "Don't worry. She's doing great and I don't expect any setbacks. I wasn't kidding when I told you soon you'll be frustrated trying to limit her movements. She'll be back to a hundred percent before you know it."

"Thanks, Marie." On a whim, Ava leaned in and gave the vet a hug.

As Marie hugged her back, Ava thought about the call she'd missed that morning from Emma Daniels. The energetic K-9 ranch owner had left a long jumbled rush of a voice mail. How glad she was that Ava was okay, how she was looking forward to helping Lacey with any training she needed to get back up to speed, how one of these days Ava needed to stay for dinner with her and Tashya and whoever else was at the ranch.

She was making friends here. It wasn't the easy new start she'd expected and hoped for, but it was beginning to feel like home.

As she thanked Marie and headed for the door, Lacey at her side, Ava tried not to think about what was missing.

"Eli."

His name burst from her lips as soon as she stepped outside into the brilliant sunshine. She glanced at his side, taking in the enormous black dog beside him, tail wagging. Then her gaze rose back to his. "I thought you went home to McCall?"

"I did." He strode closer, his dog keeping pace, until he was right in front of her, those intense blue eyes she'd already missed in the past twenty-four hours focused solely on her.

Nervous excitement rose in her belly as she stared at him. From the corner of her eye, she watched Lacey stepping closer to the Newfoundland and the two dogs sniffing each other.

"Don't worry," Eli said, taking her hand.

She closed her hand around his tightly, hanging on, as he continued, "Bear is a gentle giant. He and Lacey will get along famously. That's why I went home. I needed to get some rest and wanted you two to meet Bear."

He grinned at her then and she couldn't help but smile back. Couldn't help but notice the nerves underneath his confident posture.

"I'm glad I made it back in time. I asked Marie when you were supposed to pick Lacey up, but you're a little bit early."

"You did?"

"Yeah." His thumb stroked the tops of her knuckles, making her nerve endings fire to life and her breathing become more shallow.

"I was hoping to bring you and Lacey back to my place for dinner. Or, if it's too far for Lacey to be in a car right now, maybe I can cook at your place?"

"You want to make me dinner?" Surprise and happiness burst inside of her and put some flirtation into her tone. "Is this step one of your plan to pursue me with everything you have?"

His grin grew wider. "You've got that right." It faded into something more serious as he added, "That is, if you're planning to stay in Jasper?"

Her smile turned tender at the fear and hope in his voice. "I do want to repair my relationship with my brother. I think it's going to happen, but it will take time. And I'm going to do it long distance, because Chicago just isn't where I belong anymore. Even though coming here wasn't quite as simple as I expected, there are things worth staying for." She touched her palm to his cheek, her voice dropping to a near-whisper. "There are *people* worth staying for."

Eli was worth staying for. It was early still, but he was special. Their connection was special.

She wasn't in a rush, but staring up at him now, just like when she'd first kissed him, she had that same certain feeling. Building a relationship with Eli wasn't just right; it was inevitable. And it was exactly what she wanted.

Woof!

A burst of laughter escaped as Ava glanced at Lacey, who had turned her head back toward her. She stroked Lacey's head gently, adding, "And there are dogs worth staying for, too, Lacey."

Appeased, Lacey turned back toward Bear, whose tail was wagging.

"I think you were right about them getting along," Ava said, her attention returning to Eli.

His expression was serious, intense, the grin nowhere in sight. "And you're worth pursuing with everything I've got, Ava Callen. So, get ready for some serious courtship."

Then, that grin reappeared just long enough to make her heart flutter, before he dipped his head and kissed her.

* * * * *

UNDERCOVER COUPLE

BARB HAN

All my love to Brandon, Jacob and Tori,
the three great loves of my life.

To Babe, my hero, for being my best friend,
my greatest love and my place to call home.

I love you all with everything that I am.

Chapter One

Emmaline Ree Sheppard, aka Ree, squinted into the blaring south central Texas sun on what was turning out to be another scorching hot July morning. A wooden sign on the side of the road read Welcome to Cricket Creek, Home of the Annual Cricket Toss Festival. Ree involuntarily shivered as she connected a call with her brother. She would have to take a pass on that festival.

"Hey. What's up?" Shane asked.

"I pulled a marriage assignment. Newlyweds. I couldn't call you before now. Got any last-minute advice about what questions I need to ask my 'spouse' when I arrive? I won't have much time with him and you know I can't explain why," Ree said. Shane had been married the longest and she figured he would be the best go-to person in this situation. Pulling an assignment to work with a legendary agent like Quinton Casey strung her nerves tight and she wanted to be as ready as possible.

"How much time do you have before you get to your assignment? Can you tell me that?" Shane asked.

"According to GPS—" she checked the screen "—less than five minutes."

"Wait…what?" Shane's surprise was laced with a familiar sound. All four of her brothers had warned her of the dangers of following in their father's footsteps, and that worry came across in their tone at times. Her mother still hadn't forgiven Ree for her career choice. At least Shane had been the only brother who hadn't tried to talk her out of working for a government agency in law enforcement. Still, his concern slipped in despite his attempt to cover with a cough.

"No time to explain and you know I wouldn't be at liberty to discuss a case anyway." She lifted her hand to shield her eyes from the now-blinding sun. "I have some ideas but need to know if I'm on the right track. What basics would a wife know about her husband?"

Shane took in a deep breath. "Okay, here goes. Off the top of my head, you should probably know favorite food, color, and what kind of drink he'd order at the bar."

"Right." Ree made a mental note. The drink question was golden as she would be interviewing for a waitressing job and her "husband" was likely to come in since they'd be living across the parking lot from the establishment. She gripped the steering wheel a little tighter as another minute ticked by. Four left. "What else?"

"Know the basics about his family, like how many brothers and sisters he has and what their names are. If he has parents, grandparents and whether they are living," Shane continued, his voice hitching on the last word. He often joked they all stuffed their feelings down like any good Irish Catholic family. They never talked about their father.

Another minute passed, reminding Ree she didn't have a second to spare.

"Got it." The little things could trip up an undercover operation, especially since she'd be flying straight out of the gate. She'd just completed her second year as an undercover agent for Alcohol, Tobacco and Firearms. This was her first "married" assignment. "Anything else?"

"I'm sure you'll discuss basics with your partner." Shane was right and she already knew pretty much everything he'd just said. Hearing her brother's voice calmed her nerves.

"He's a big deal in the department, from what I hear," she admitted.

"Then go in knowing your ground rules," Shane stated.

GPS let her know the location was coming up on her right. Two minutes had gone by in a blur.

"Got it," she said before pausing. "Thanks for the tips."

Ree stopped her sedan in front of the one-room cabin with a motorcycle parked in front. She hesitated, unable to bring herself to end the call.

"Even if he outranks you, don't let him intimidate you," Shane insisted.

"I grew up with four brothers," Ree said. "Since when have I ever let that happen?"

Shane laughed and the sound brought her nerves down a notch. She'd debated making the call but was glad she had. Her brothers could be overprotective at times. The word *overbearing* came to mind. She'd worked her whole life to prove she could stick up for herself. And yet, at times like these, she still needed her family.

"Valid point," Shane conceded.

"I hear this agent can be a real hothead," she said.

"Since when have you not been?" Shane teased, echoing her words. "Mom accuses your temper of coming from the Irish side of the family."

"I have the red hair to prove the Irish part," she

quipped, thinking it had been too long since she'd seen her family.

"Speaking of Irish, Preston asked about you the other day," Shane said.

"And you're bringing this up to me right now?" she asked, not bothering to hide her frustration. Preston had been the closest she'd come to going all in with a boyfriend. He also happened to be her older brother's best friend.

"Right. Bad form. Forget I even said anything," Shane said along with an apology.

"Already done." She did her best to keep the hurt out of her voice at the memory of her ex. Preston was the only one she'd second-guessed walking away from. She had her reasons for ending the fling. But then, her brother pointed out she had her running shoes parked at the door every time she started to get serious in a relationship. Whether he was right or wrong, Ree had realized she needed to draw the line at having her brothers involved in her romantic life.

"Hey, sis. Be careful," Shane warned as she heard her three-year-old nephew Liam wail in the background.

"You know it." She pulled in beside the Ducati Diavel motorcycle, about to meet her "husband" for the next few days, possibly weeks. "Kiss Liam for me."

"Come home and kiss him for yourself," Shane quipped and then seemed to realize she didn't stay away so much because of her nephew. "Or you could FaceTime."

"I can take a day off when this assignment is over. I'll be sure to stop by or call him then," she promised. "Give Evelyn a hug for me and kiss baby Cara in the meantime."

"Will do. And I'll hold you to the visit," Shane said as Liam's howling got even louder.

"I knew you would," she said before bidding good-bye and ending the call.

Ree had no idea when that might be. The assignment to see if the bar owner was involved in arms dealing was on its own timeline. Working with a reputed agent—one she was about to meet for the first time—when she'd just celebrated her second year on the job after a promotion had her nerves on edge. She could do this, she reminded herself. Shane's advice to go in strong was probably right. Someone with Quinton Casey's background would want a confident partner.

A couple of deep breaths for fortitude and Ree cut off the engine before grabbing her purse. The hot late-morning air slammed into her as she stepped out of the junkpile she'd been issued for the assignment. The run-down teal green Ford Fiesta's door groaned as she banged it shut.

A wall of humidity hit with the force of a rogue wave and had a similar impact as she stood in the sweltering heat. She plucked at her white button-down blouse, regretting the high but fashionable collar, trying not to soak herself with sweat before she met the man inside the cabin. Her high-waisted forest green pants fit well enough to show off long legs that she'd worked hard to tone at the gym. The cuffs struck just above her ankles. Her auburn hair was styled in a low side pony. Black, spiked heels rounded out the interview outfit.

As she balled her hand into a fist and then raised it to knock, a wave of panic gripped her and a knot formed in her stomach. There was no other way to get through this first meeting than face it head-on. Agent Quinton Casey had a reputation for coming on like a bull. She steadied herself, getting ready for the charge that was sure to come at her.

Besides, stand in the sun any longer and she might actually melt. Before she lost her nerve, she knocked. Of course, then she realized she should have used the key. It was a simple mistake. Anyone could have made it. And yet, humiliation burned at the misstep. This assignment wasn't off to a good start and she prayed it wasn't a bad omen.

"Door's open," came the masculine voice—a voice that was like whiskey over ice.

She opened it and stepped inside, immediately shutting the door behind her.

Agent Casey practically sneered at her as she stared at the hulk of a man standing on the other side of the one-room cabin. His muscled torso formed an improbable V at the waist, and even with day-old stubble on his chin the man would be considered hot by most standards. Seeing him in person, she wished someone had prepared her for his sheer size. He had to be six feet three inches, with the kind of body most athletic recruiters would kill for if he was college age. It wouldn't surprise her at all to learn he'd played ball in his youth. He had the whole "chiseled jawline, strong, hawklike nose and piercing eyes" bit down pat. Her pulse kicked up a few notches just looking at the man. She couldn't afford to be distracted or intimidated.

Her brother's voice rang in her head. *Go in knowing your ground rules.*

The famous Agent Casey stood there like he was issuing a challenge, as expected. She'd heard the rumors he'd become difficult to work with, and knew she would get one shot to make a first impression. She needed to be strong. More of her brother's words came to mind. *Don't let him intimidate you.*

Summoning all her courage, she started right in. "Okay, so this is how it's going to go."

"Do tell," he said, his voice a study in calm but his gaze practically boring a hole through her.

She could admit her nerves had her coming on a little stronger than intended. Taking another deep breath, she resolved to soften her tone.

"We don't have long before I have to be next door for my interview," she said. "So, just to make sure we're on the same page, my favorite color is blue, and my second favorite color is green. Now you go."

He didn't respond or seem amused. Instead, he gripped the counter's edge until his knuckles turned white.

Her bravado faltered. She checked her watch, needing to head next door sooner than she'd like. She didn't want to be late to her interview and she needed to have a few basics down to sell the lie in case the conversation turned casual and her future employer asked questions about her spouse.

"Green like a garden hose or like a leprechaun?" he finally asked, crossing his feet at the ankles and then folding his arms across his chest. There was a slight smirk on his face as he leaned his hip against the counter.

"We don't have a whole lot of time to lay the groundwork before I have to head next door and land a job, or this assignment is over before it started. So maybe you want to take this a little more seriously?" She tapped the toe of her shoe on the dated wood flooring. The man was being annoying. He wasn't the only one who could fold his arms over his chest. She mimicked his stance and that seemed to further amuse him.

No response came. His eyes belied his casual demeanor. Even from across the room she could see a storm brewed in those sapphire blues.

"What's your favorite beer?" she asked, refusing to be intimidated. If he was testing her, she intended to pass with flying colors. In fact, she excelled at taking tests. So this guy needed more than a smirk to throw her off.

Not only did he not respond, but he yawned. Okay, he must be trying to get under her skin. See how far he could push? Test her? She needed to regroup. Come at this from a different angle.

"Fine. Let me tell you my ground rules before this whole—" she waved her arms in the air "—newlywed thing gets started."

He dropped his head. His boot suddenly became real interesting to him. This way, she couldn't read his reactions and she had no idea if this was part of the test or not. His first move was to throw her off her game. His point there. She definitely felt on edge. His reputation had her playing defense when she should be playing offense. She was starting to second-guess herself and to wonder whether or not she was the right person for this assignment.

Nerves were good, she reminded herself. Being afraid would keep her mind sharp. She'd been on several dozen undercover assignments so far. This one would be no different. Of course, she would have a few more nerves working with Agent Casey. This assignment was serious, a possible career maker. The agency wouldn't partner her with the A-team if this was a no-brainer.

There was no reason to be unnerved by Agent Casey

despite how quickly her pulse climbed with him in the room. He was a man just like every other, despite being disquietingly good-looking. He might be a few steps ahead of her professionally, but she was a quick study.

Some of her bravado was shrinking but she wasn't going to let that stop her. Shane was right. Go in strong. *Be brave.*

Ree cleared her throat and continued, "Holding hands is fine, so is incidental touching. In fact, the more the better because we're supposed to be newlyweds." All she could remember from her brother's first year of marriage was how lovey-dovey he and his new wife, Evelyn, had been. The thought of physical contact with Casey caused her stomach to free-fall. "So feel free to touch me but watch it. I don't want to have to file any conduct reports when this is all done."

Casey didn't immediately speak. The longer the silence stretched on, the higher her nerves climbed, until they were strung so tight she thought they might snap.

When she was just about to tell him he needed to start cooperating, he looked up at her. Those intensely blue eyes of his locked onto her as he closed the distance between them in a few quick strides. Despite her heart galloping and all her warning signals flaring, she stood rooted to the spot, strangely transfixed. By this point, her heart was beating wildly in her chest and her instincts said *run*. But she didn't get to be *who* she was or *where* she was by giving in to fear, so she challenged him with her gaze, daring him to keep going. That worked right up until he took the final threatening step toward her that had her automatically stepping back until the wall trapped her.

He brought his hands up to cup her cheeks, tilting her face toward his. And then he brought his lips down on hers, hard and unyielding. All Ree could do was surrender to the heat flowing inside her, and the pressure building. There was so much passion and promise in the kiss that her brain was swimming in a fog. She couldn't remember the last time she'd been so thoroughly swept off her feet, but his lips moving against hers were pure heaven.

They were gone almost as quickly, leaving cold air between his face and hers. She slowly opened her eyes to meet the most intense stare she'd encountered in her life. Her breath caught and she had to swallow to ease the sudden dryness in her mouth.

"Let me tell you my rules," he practically ground out. "Nothing is more important than catching the bad guy. So, if that means kissing on the lips, so be it. You don't have to enjoy it and neither do I, but be clear on this one point—my only responsibility is to make sure a slimeball ends up behind bars when this is all said and done."

Ree met his gaze head-on and with bravado she didn't feel said, "Fine. Can we get to work now?"

"Fine," he parroted, obviously a little thrown off she hadn't crumbled or ripped into him. "Where would you like to start?"

"Names," she said. "What do we call each other in public?"

"It's probably easier if we stick to our actual first names, so I went ahead and had documents made up. You can call me Quint or *honey*," he said before retrieving a pair of wedding bands. He handed one over to her and then slipped the other on his finger. "Just please don't call me *babe*. It's fingernails on a chalkboard."

"Got it," she said, figuring there was a story there somewhere. "I'm Ree. And ditto on the *babe*. Not my cup of tea, either. What's our last name?"

"Matthews," he supplied before walking over to a duffel bag and taking a knee. A couple of seconds later, he produced a wallet. "There are credit cards in there and a DL in your new identity."

Ree took the offering, ignoring the frisson of electricity when their fingers grazed. She traded out her wallet and handed the old one over to be locked in the tackle box he retrieved next. "The job next door was advertised so I'm guessing that means the owner—"

She stopped midsentence, reaching for the name.

"Charley Davies," Casey… *Quint* supplied.

She nodded and flashed a smile. "Right. I need to remember that, considering I'll be meeting with him soon."

"His name is on the ad, so that's a good idea," he agreed. Then he added, "My story is that I was part owner in a moving company and had a career-ending accident." He pointed to a boot. "We're moving here to save money while I go to online school for computer programming certification."

The timer dinged on her phone. She glanced over at Quint and nodded. "Time to go meet Mr. Davies."

QUINT DIDN'T EXPECT to feel the stab of guilt at hurting Ree's feelings earlier. She'd bucked up and held her ground, but a split second of hurt had darkened her eyes, and he'd felt two inches tall. Both were skilled at covering their emotions. He'd read her jacket. She was a solid agent with an impressive track record.

He cursed himself again for the way he'd treated her. She'd come on too strong and he'd reacted. His reaction caught him off guard. He had half a mind to text his boss and tell her what a bad idea it was to force him to work with a partner, *any* partner. Quint did his best work alone. But he'd convinced a psychiatrist and his boss that he didn't have any hang-ups after Tessa's death. If he went back now and said he couldn't work with another female partner they'd know he was struggling. He'd gone to great lengths to stay on the job because that was his only tether to sanity. Besides, what would he tell his boss? Life was hard? Quint hadn't gotten over the past?

Nope. There was only living with it and trying to get through this case so he could move on to the next, then a few more until he got his rhythm back. Stay on the horse another day and then another, until saddling up felt like the most normal thing again.

The sexual current running between him and Ree had unnerved him. The kiss had been meant to prove a point. It wasn't supposed to rattle Quint like it had. It was the only reason he could be affected by Ree. No big deal. He would get over it and get on with his job.

Quint started pacing in the one-room cabin. The place had everything the two of them needed to survive this case: a kitchenette, a bathroom, a living room and bedroom combined. The hall closet held a stackable washer and dryer. Definitely a bonus. The sofa was a pullout. He could sleep on the lounger and give her the bed over to one corner. It was the least he could do after being a jerk.

Ree had been something to look at in her blouse, pants and heels. The white fabric had hugged ample breasts. The green of her pants highlighted her eyes— eyes that were shielded by the thickest, blackest lashes he'd ever seen. The way those eyes had sparkled with something that looked a helluva lot like need when he'd kissed her had sent his pulse skyrocketing.

He chided himself on the bad form. Those green

eyes, her stubborn chin, had thrown him completely off his game when she'd challenged him. At least he'd pulled it together. The conversation had gotten back on track. A very large part of him wanted to march next door so he could spy on what was going down. The setup was that Ree was supposed to be trying to get a job as a waitress. When she got on the inside, he would come over as her husband, a guy who was trying to better his life by going back to online school for computer programming.

Once they established a relationship with the owner, Quint would "volunteer" to help with computer needs either as a thank-you for hiring his wife or a thank-you for the occasional free lunch. Quint would have to feel Charley Davies out to see which tactic would work best.

He stabbed his fingers through his hair, wishing he was the one next door selling their cover. This was the hardest part of working with a new partner.

Ree was a professional; she could do this. If not, he would figure out a way to salvage their cover story and infiltrate the establishment that was part bar and part restaurant for foodies.

Ideally, Quint and Ree would have had more time together before she had to go in. An icy chill ran down his back at the thought something might happen to her. No, Quint. This was Ree, not Tessa.

He managed to keep at bay the flashbacks of his former partner's fatal injury while on an assignment together, practically wearing a hole in the wood floor from pacing in a circle, wishing the hell that the door would open and Ree would come back with a job secured.

The clock said she'd only been gone twenty minutes, but it felt like an eternity. Going next door might make him seem too eager. It might raise a few red flags. Quint issued a sharp sigh.

A half hour later, with still no sign of Ree, he decided he couldn't afford to sit around and wait for her to return. Charley Davies might have seen right through her. She might have given herself away. She could be locked in a closet, or worse. A half dozen scenarios ran through his mind, none of them good. More flashbacks stamped his thoughts. Tessa in the hospital. The beeping sound of the machine temporarily keeping her alive. The utter and complete silence when the doctor flipped the switch to off. Anger shot through Quint. White-hot fury boiled inside his veins. He couldn't afford to spiral down that dark, familiar path.

There was no way he could stay here without knowing if his new partner was in trouble.

Chapter Two

The best way to disarm someone was to gain their sympathy. Part of Quint's cover involved wearing a walking boot that made it seem like he was recovering from an injury. His physical size could put the bar owner on the defensive, so the boot was meant to convey weakness and vulnerability. He slid his left foot inside and pulled the straps tight. Then he double-checked his ankle holster where his SIG Sauer was secured. Everything was good to go there.

Quint made the trek next door to the combo restaurant and bar. Dark images edged into his thoughts. He stopped them right there, gave himself a mental slap and shook his fear off. Getting inside his head would be bad for him and his partner. Let the past creep up, and he might as well hand over their cover. He needed to keep his head in the game.

He and Ree needed to go over the list of employees when he got her home. There was still a whole lot to discuss.

Surveying the lot, he took note of six cars, three trucks, four motorcycles and three parked RVs. He skimmed the license plates as he walked past, memorizing as many as he could and observing that several were from out of state. This wasn't the time to rebuke himself for not thinking to capture a few of the license plates with his cell phone while he was still inside the cabin a few moments ago.

There was very little in the way of surveillance equipment in the parking lot. Small towns were known for being safe and for residents having each other's backs. An illegal operation could have multiple people involved, including the county sheriff. Ree hadn't been brought up to speed on the fact the bar owner and sheriff were second cousins. Even if they weren't in league, the bar owner would know the sheriff's blind spots. Family could be a huge blind spot. The single mother who'd raised him was nothing short of an angel in his eyes. After some of his stunts, she probably deserved sainthood. And he would do anything for her if she was still alive. Families usually could be counted on to cover for each other.

As Quint reached for the door handle, a big, burly biker-looking guy with one of those handlebar mustaches pushed it open from the inside and took a couple of steps before holding it for Quint. "Here you go, man."

He wore black from head to toe and sported a leather vest with the Harley Davidson logo on the left-hand side. At least his T-shirt was short-sleeved in this heat. Quint assumed the man owned one of the motorcycles in the parking lot.

"Appreciate it," Quint said with a nod.

Once inside, he immediately skimmed the restaurant, taking it all in. His gaze stopped at the bar area on the left-hand side of the room, back corner. The darkened bar wasn't open for the lunch crowd. Otherwise the place was brightly lit, with open seating, cafeteria style. There were at least a dozen tables scattered around the main section.

In the center of the back wall, there was a pair of stainless steel doors leading into what must be the kitchen. They had twin windows that looked more like portals on a cruise ship. One of the doors was marked In, and the other, Out.

The restaurant buzzed with conversation. It had a little bit of a retro diner feel to it, with glossy, red vinyl booths lining the perimeter. The tables were small four-tops with stainless steel chairs that had cushions in the same material as the booths. The setup was reminiscent of a 1950s soda fountain, and the smells coming out of the kitchen made his mouth water. This was the kind of place that he could easily see ending up on one of those diners-and-dives shows on TV. There was original art hanging on the walls with handwritten price tags. Locals?

Quint's blood pressure started to climb when he didn't immediately see Ree. If he was the owner and the restaurant was this busy, he would park someone he was interviewing in the bar area. The fact she wasn't there or anywhere else in view kicked up his racing pulse a few more notches.

He studied the faces of the people at the tables. They were some families, some locals as well as foodie types on the road who were making a pit stop on their way somewhere else. Then there was the biker club. Several sat in a corner booth, hunkered over their plates and barely mumbling a word to each other as they ate. He would keep an eye on them.

The restroom sign to the right caught his eye. He took a couple of steps toward it and saw a long hallway. There was a counter and stools over there. Looked like the place had counter service for single diners.

A college-age waitress in a blouse that was unbuttoned down practically to her belly button and tied off underneath her breasts bounded toward him. She had on leather bike shorts and white boots.

"Just one today?" She smiled at him. Her cheeriness seemed forced and her cheeks flushed as she picked up a menu.

"That's right," he confirmed.

"Booth, counter or table?" She practically beamed at him, her gaze sliding down his body, stopping at his boot. He could have sworn she frowned.

"Counter." He figured that area would afford the best visuals to the kitchen. The spot would block most of his view of the restaurant and he wouldn't see any of the bar area, but a sacrifice had to be made.

Quint needed to know where Ree was, and he needed to know now.

"Right this way." The waitress's name tag read Zoey.

Quint focused on the tile floor and its black-and-white checkered pattern as he followed Zoey to his stool. The area looked straight into the kitchen. The waitress stopped and faced the kitchen, leaving very little room between her and the stool. Rather than risk touching her, he walked around to the other side instead. Was flirting part of the job? She looked young enough to be his daughter, so the move did little more than cause his stomach to churn.

A frown brought the corners of her mouth down and creased her forehead. It was more than a frown…a pout? Even if Quint wasn't "married" on this assignment, Zoey was far too young for his liking. When he dated, he went for someone closer to his age, someone who liked the same era of music and was more than a pretty face. He liked someone he could have a real conversation with. Someone who set her phone down when she spoke to him. Call him low-tech, but he preferred to talk to someone who looked at him during a conversation and not at a screen. Then again, flirting might be part of the job.

Zoey made a humph noise before asking, "Can I get you anything to drink?"

"Coffee and water," he stated as he scanned the kitchen staff.

His gaze stopped on Ree. She stood at the order counter across from the kitchen staff, balancing a tray in one hand while taking plates off the counter with the other. Her coordination skills were on point: he'd give her that. Relief washed over him that she wasn't tied up somewhere, bound and gagged.

She wore the same outfit as Zoey. The shirt showed off way too much of her ample cleavage and those shorts hugged her body like…

Never mind. Suffice it to say the company uniform didn't get two thumbs-up from her "husband."

As she turned, their eyes caught, and a look of panic crossed her features. Quint cleared his throat and looked down at the menu, figuring he'd caught her off guard and thrown her out of her comfort zone.

Again, he kicked himself.

If he could read her, then so could a seasoned criminal. There was no way Quint could protect her without being by her side 24/7. Now that she'd met the owner, maybe they could come up with an excuse for her to disappear. Something sudden could have happened in the family, like her mother falling ill. It would be for Ree's own good.

Quint stopped himself right there, the dark hole threatening to drag him under. He put his face in his hands and then rubbed the scruff on his chin. This assignment was nothing like the one that had killed Tessa.

"WHAT ARE YOU doing here?" Ree forced a smile as her new coworker joined them, bringing coffee and water to Quint. Her gaze dropped to his lips—lips she'd been trying to forget since leaving the cabin more than an hour ago.

"Came to look at my beautiful wife," he said, shooting her a look that threatened to melt all her carefully constructed defenses. This man was good. A little too good if anyone asked her.

"I'm working right now, honey," she said as her cheeks flushed. A look passed behind those serious blue eyes of his. She'd scored a direct hit on something. No idea what it meant, though. She made a mental note to figure it out later when they were alone. The thought of being holed up in a one-room cabin with a man who caused her pulse to skyrocket every time she looked at him didn't do good things to her blood pressure.

Ree took in a deep breath. Rather than panic, she could use her nerves to her advantage. They made her bold. She set her tray down, leaned over the counter and drew on her most seductive smile. "But I'll see you at home later."

Quint's gaze momentarily dipped and her cheeks warmed. She realized the move had given him a bird's-eye view of her cleavage.

He cleared his throat like he couldn't find his voice.

"Is that a promise?" His voice was a low, throaty growl.

Ree smirked. She couldn't help it. Throwing Quint off his game even for a second was satisfying. Besides, the whole exchange would only sell the fact they were newlyweds.

Zoey took the hint, dropping off the drinks without so much as a word and beating feet so fast it looked like she was training for a track meet.

The sapphire color of Quint's eyes darkened with something that looked a whole lot like need when he locked gazes with Ree. She shouldn't gloat but, damn, it felt good to know she wasn't the only one who'd been affected by that kiss. Seemed like it might have been a two-way street and the ever-cool, ever-in-charge, living legend Quinton Casey had a moment, too.

"I gotta serve my customers." Ree picked up the tray and walked away, sashaying her hips.

Her ego had her taking a look back a moment before she walked away. Big mistake. Head down, Quint was studying his cup of coffee like it was a midterm and he was one failing grade away from being booted out of school.

After delivering food to her table, she didn't get much chance to look at Quint again considering the next hour was nonstop. The restaurant was bustling, which was good for tips and a great way to prove herself to Charley Davies. Her interview with the man had lasted all of three minutes when he'd gone to a locker in the backroom, tossed her a uniform—if it could be called that—and then asked if she could start immediately. Business was picking up.

She'd nodded, smiled and gone into the restroom to try on the getup. It fit. Charley had a good eye for sizing, but she also figured he only hired one size, and could easily be classified as a chauvinist. The way he'd eyed her up and down when they'd first met had her wanting to take a shower. He'd stopped short of apologizing when he casually mentioned his customers were picky about who served them.

Letting the comment go went against her nature. Her brothers might pick on her but they never treated her like she was breakable or couldn't handle their teasing. In many ways, she was just like one of them and they were equal opportunity pranksters. Stuffing down her feelings wouldn't be easy, but this was her job and she reminded herself of the greater good she was doing.

Besides, her immediate reaction to Charley was that he was guilty of something. It was her job to figure out what it was, because last she checked, being a restaurant/bar owner who only hired a certain type wasn't technically against the law.

Three hours after her interview, the lunch crowd waned. At some point, Quint had gone home. And the waitresses were down to filling ketchup bottles to prep for the dinner crowd that—she checked her watch— would start in roughly an hour. All she wanted to do was go home and put her feet up. Being on the go for literally three hours straight without so much as a restroom break took a toll. Her dogs were barking.

"Great job today." Charley's voice right behind her caught her off guard.

She gasped, and then spun around.

"Thanks," she managed to say.

"Looks like you'll be a good addition to the family," he said. Charley was tall, with a runner's build. He had sandy blond hair and gray eyes. Some might consider him good-looking. He had a small scar above his right cheek and straight white teeth. Ree couldn't quite pinpoint what it was about him—the air of a creep or criminal, or both— that made her want to be as far away as possible, but it was her job to find out.

"The people seem nice and the tips were better than I've ever made," she said.

Charley took a step back and smiled. "Good. See you in an hour for a double shift."

An hour? She couldn't imagine turning around and doing this again with a longer shift. Then again, it gave her an excuse to spend more time here.

"One of my waitresses called in sick," he explained. "Do you mind coming back?"

"Sure," she said before he walked back to the kitchen.

Ree topped off the last ketchup bottle and checked out. Sweat practically dripped off her as she made the walk next door, a wad of cash in her pocket. The money was good at Greenlight Bar and Restaurant. If she'd made this kind of cash in three hours at lunch, she could only imagine how much she could make at dinner. None of it was hers to keep, though.

As she approached the cabin, the door swung open. Her nerves tingled at seeing Quint again, but she told herself it was only because of the kiss earlier. And since she always faced her fears, she walked straight up to him before he could say a word and planted the steamiest kiss smack on the man's lips.

Her breath quickened, her heart raced and her body hummed with electricity. There was one question on her mind. Had she gone too far?

Chapter Three

The feel of Ree's lips pressed to Quint's reminded him of just how long it had been since he'd been with a woman. Not good. His last relationship hadn't ended well when he'd been accused of being in love with his former partner. Former dead partner now.

Ree brought her hands up to his shoulders as her tongue probed the inside of his mouth. Her touch was the equivalent of a bomb detonating inside his chest. Again, not good.

Quint let Ree have her moment. At least, that was the lie he told himself. Admitting she'd knocked him off balance meant he was so far off his game there was no coming back.

Pulling on all the willpower he had, Quint peeled her fingers off his shoulders and broke contact. They both heaved for air as though they'd just sprinted two blocks in the Texas heat.

Realizing the door was wide-open, he sidestepped Ree and closed it. And then the reason for the kiss dawned on him.

"You proved your point," he conceded.

She whirled around and poked her index finger in his chest. "Don't ever doubt whether or not I'm capable of doing my job again."

Her eyes were still glittery and he took some solace in the fact the kiss had shaken her as much as it had him, at least on the surface. He put his hands in the air in the surrender position, palms out. "I needed to know you were capable of going the distance if the case called for it."

"Yeah? How did I do?" she asked, issuing a challenge with those incredible green eyes of hers.

"I think we both know the answer to that question." He motioned toward one of the chairs at the two-top table in the kitchen area. "This might be a good time to get better acquainted."

"Sorry." She toed off a high heel, and then the second. A little mewl escaped when her feet were finally free. He'd heard the same sound when their lips had first touched. Twice kissed and they hadn't even gotten through their first day. It had to be a department record. "But I have to be back there in—" she checked her watch "—fifty-five minutes."

"What? Why?" He didn't bother to hide his shock.

"To work the dinner shift," she said, walking over to the couch instead of where he'd instructed.

"There has to be a law against overworking employees." He joined her in the living space, taking the chair across from her. The cabin's decor could best be described as simple. The sofa lined one wall and there were two chairs and a coffee table to create a sitting area. A rug defined the perimeter. Creaky, original wood flooring ran the entire open-concept room. A queen-size bed was tucked in another corner, affording very little privacy.

"Charley was already down one waitress and someone called in sick," she said.

"What was your impression of him?" Quint asked.

"He's a sexist jerk, for one." The fact she didn't hesitate meant there'd been some kind of run-in. Then again, he'd seen the tight-fitting uniforms. Quint fisted his hands thinking about a guy like Davies making a move on Ree. She seemed to realize how little clothing she had on at the mention of the guy, buttoning up her blouse and untying the bottom so she could wear it like a real shirt instead of a glorified swimsuit.

"Did he try anything with you?" Quint managed to ask through clenched teeth. The fact his protective instincts flared only served to remind him that he hadn't been able to distance himself from the memory of Tessa.

"Nothing like that," she said. "Just trying to get a feel for the guy."

"You must be tired after that shift. There's Coke in the fridge. Or I can put on a pot of coffee," he offered.

"Coke would be nice. Thanks." She started to get up, but he stopped her with a hand up, waving her off.

"This one's on me," he said as he stood. He retrieved two bottles, popped the caps and then set them down on the glass coffee table.

"Where'd you get these?" She picked hers up. Her forehead wrinkled with the question and it was about the sweetest thing he'd ever seen. It wouldn't be difficult to fake an attraction to someone like her: bold, intelligent and naturally beautiful.

"Corner store." This wasn't the time to get caught up in all things Ree Sheppard. Memorizing her quirks would help him down the line when he needed to know what she was thinking. Besides, those were the little things couples knew about each other. Those oddities that made up a person. Like the way she twisted a strand of hair in between her finger and thumb when she was thinking. Or the little concern line that scored her forehead when she was afraid she'd made a mistake.

Yes, he'd sat at the restaurant long enough to watch her when she was too busy to notice. And then, he'd exited before he could be identified. During the lunch rush, it had been easy to get in and out while staying under the radar. But Charley would have made note if Quint had stuck around. The bar owner might have already, which would say a whole lot about him and his character. Someone who constantly sized others up probably had something to hide. There was no doubt weapons were going through the back door at Greenlight. But who was involved?

"The other waitresses seem intimidated by him," Ree finally said after taking a few drinks from her Coke. She tucked a stray hair behind her ear, which he'd noticed meant it was time to get serious.

"It's possible he runs a tight ship. It's one way to keep his staff minding their own business," he said. Again, his hands fisted at the uncertainty of it all. They were going to have to work with another agency on this case most likely at some point. The realization brought all the flashbacks to mind. His blood boiled as he thought about the mistakes made on the night he'd lost his best friend, and remembered that she'd asked him to be the godfather of her kid. He still couldn't figure out how she'd talked him into holding off on telling their boss about the pregnancy. She'd asked for time to deliver the news on her own terms. And Quint would spend the rest of his life regretting giving in to her request. Because she and her baby would be alive right now if he'd stood his ground the first time. Tessa would have been assigned to desk duty and he would have gone into the bust alone.

"Everything okay?" Ree's voice broke through the memory.

"Yes. Fine. Never better." Quint shook it off. "What did you say before?"

She shot a look, and her forehead wrinkled.

"I stood up to him," she admitted. "I'm not sure he's used to getting that reaction from his waitresses."

"It could make him watch you closer." Quint didn't normally have an issue with keeping his temper under control. But right now, regrets about that other assignment sent his blood pressure soaring and gave him an intense need to put his fist through a wall. Better yet, find a boxing ring and go a couple of rounds with a willing participant.

Quint released a sharp sigh. Keeping his thoughts out of the past was proving more difficult than he'd imagined it would be.

He reminded himself this case was no different than the dozens of others he'd been on, and he could handle whatever came his way. Questioning himself on the fact would only lead to second-guessing himself in a critical moment. Ree deserved a partner with open eyes and a clear head.

"I SHOULD FEED you before you have to get back," Quint said and, for the first time, looked more concerned than angry at her.

"The food next door is amazing based on what I've seen and smelled. I get a dinner break, so I should be fine until then." Ree tucked her feet underneath her bottom as she finished the last of the Coke. It was exactly what she needed. That, and a few minutes to refresh her makeup before she headed back into the lion's den. The same nervous excitement struck every time she was about to go deep undercover.

"What have you done so far?" Quint reclaimed his seat.

"In terms of…?"

"Work assignments?" he asked.

"I'd rather talk about *this* one first, if you don't mind." Those last few words came out defensive, so she took in a slow breath to calm her nerves. Partnering with someone like Quint, with his formidable reputation, had a way of ramping up her nervous system. She had to remind herself she'd been assigned because she was ready for a case with the legend. She was going to make mistakes. Period. In life. In this job. Mistakes were inevitable. Granddad had once told her it wasn't the fact that she'd made a mistake that was important. It was the way she recovered that mattered.

Recovery was everything.

"That's fair," Quint said. "I was trying to get a gauge on whether or not you'd dealt with any weapons cases to see if we could find any links."

"None recently," she said.

"We both had access to the same file, so I know the basics about you," he continued.

Why did her stomach flip-flop at the thought Quinton Casey knew *anything* about her personal life? Or was it the lack of one that had her wishing she could sweep the whole topic under the rug?

"Ditto," she said.

"As far as this case goes, we know what we're looking for," he said.

"Any signs of weapons being run through the restaurant or via Charley, an employee or his suppliers," she said.

"The question isn't whether or not it's happening. We know that part is true after busting Lionel Turner," he continued after nodding his approval.

"Too bad he didn't give us names," she said.

"That would make this a little too simple for me," he countered.

She nodded. Right. The department wouldn't send someone like him for such easy pickings. Or her, for that matter.

He pulled a document up on his cell phone. "Greenlight has a total of five kitchen crew—a cook, two assistants, an expeditor and a dishwasher."

She nodded.

"Did you get any names?" he asked.

"One goes by Chef. The two assistants are Pele and Craig. The expeditor goes by Fender, and the dishwasher is Eddie."

He nodded as she rattled off names. "Chef must be Lorenzo Rocco, according to IRS payroll." He cocked an eyebrow. "Fender must be Alec Feeny."

"No idea what the real names are," she admitted.

"Waitresses are harder to identify since he only shows two on payroll," Quint stated.

A moment of silence passed. His forehead wrinkled.

"My favorite color is orange," he said, circling back to their earlier conversation. "Not like a pumpkin but like the burnt orange of a perfect sunset. When it feels like you're looking straight into a fire and are mesmerized by the orange glow."

"Burnt orange sunset. I got it." In fact, after the way he described it, she didn't think she'd ever forget it. She also liked that he was telling her something about himself that most people wouldn't know or be able to guess. Her heart gave a little squeeze in what felt like a strangely intimate moment happening between them.

"Pizza any day over a burger and my favorite beer is whatever is on tap," he continued. "I like those pizzas where the chef throws together ingredients that maybe shouldn't work together but somehow do."

"There's a place on Third Street in Austin that has the best craft pizza. Ronnie always comes out to the table when the special is ordered," she said.

"I know Ronnie." He quirked a brow. "You know Ronnie?"

"Not exactly *know* him. But I do know his pizzas and they are hands down the best in the state," she said, unable to contain the excitement in her voice.

"That's where I took you on our first date, then," he said with a glimmer in his eyes that caused her stomach to free-fall.

"It was a perfect night," she said, continuing on with the cover.

"I knew the minute you ordered the special you were different," he said. His eyes lit up. His expression softened. The way he spoke about their fake date almost like it was real was incredibly sexy. "I never believed in love at first sight but I sensed you were going to be important in my life."

Well, now she really was transfixed.

"The same was true for me," she said. "There was something about sharing that first slice that made my whole future flash before my eyes. Us. Kids. A house."

Quint cleared his throat, as if it had suddenly dried up. He took a swig of his Coke before setting the bottle down on the coffee table and glancing at the clock on the wall. "You have to head out in ten minutes. I think we've got enough for now."

"Yeah. Right." Ree forced her gaze away from him. She pushed up to standing and oriented herself toward the bathroom. Something was missing. It didn't take long to figure out what it was. "Right. What was I thinking? My suitcase is in the trunk. I'll just go—"

"I got it." He waved her off.

"Not so fast." She rounded the coffee table in time to grab him by the arm. He whirled around a little too fast and the heat of his stare caused her breath to catch. She swallowed to ease some of the dryness in her throat.

The look he gave her could have melted an iceberg.

"Your ankle," she managed to get out. "How will it look if you bring in my suitcases when you're supposed to be hurt."

He stared at her, boldly, unapologetically. He had to know she was right and yet he didn't seem ready to accept it. Someone like him, young and strong, would have a hard time leaving her to her own devices. Turned out chivalry wasn't dead. She'd witnessed it too many times in her home state where men opened doors for women. Not because a woman couldn't do it for herself, but because he followed a code that said, ladies first.

"All right," he finally grunted out. "But I'm helping because if I don't and Charley's watching he won't buy into the newlywed angle."

"Sounds good," she said. "I'll make a show of forcing you to let me take my own suitcase."

"That'll help." His face still looked pinched at the prospect of leaving her to it.

"And the story is still that you are studying to get certification in the computer field after being hurt on a job with your moving company, right?" she asked.

"The injury is the last straw since I'm not twenty anymore," he said with a nod. "At forty-two, I realized that I needed a desk job."

"And I'm going to be the one working and supporting you while you finish your studies," she confirmed.

"That's right. We're also looking to pare down expenses now and are ready for a change from big-city life," he said with an approving smile. One that shouldn't send her heart fluttering.

It dawned on Ree that she could use her body's reaction to sell the newlywed bit. Her cheeks flushed unintentionally when Quint put his full attention on her. She could use it to her benefit rather than constantly fight against her biology.

There was no use belaboring the point about who carried the bag inside. They were making progress on the rules-of-engagement front, on the getting-to-know-the-little-things front and on the working-together front. She would take the progress as she excused herself. She walked out to her car, if it could be called that considering how bad a shape it was in, and popped open the trunk.

Quint lifted the suitcase out as she insisted on helping. Thankfully, it was on rollers despite the gravel parking lot. She threw her arms around his neck, and quickly realized how much the move caused her breasts to press against the wall of his muscled chest.

For the second time her breath caught, her heart hammered her ribs, and an urge to kiss him overwhelmed her senses. She could do this assignment without getting personally attached…right?

Chapter Four

"Why did you show up at work, by the way?" Ree asked, following Quint inside.

Honesty was probably the best policy, so he didn't hide the truth. "I was concerned about you when you didn't return."

Her eyebrow shot up as she kneeled and then opened her suitcase. She located a small floral bag with a zipper, and then walked to the bathroom. "You didn't trust me?"

"I didn't trust him." He nodded toward the restaurant as he followed. "I didn't know you."

Both statements were true. Neither covered his real motivation. Guilt stabbed him for the way he'd treated her and he was doing his level best to shake off his mistakes with the Tessa case.

"Fair enough," she finally said.

"I owe you an apology," he continued. "You can write me up for the kiss if you'd like. I promise that I do know how to respect boundaries even if it means—"

"We're newlyweds," she said, putting a hand up to stop him. "And they kiss all the time. Believe me, I've seen it with my brother. You were right to remind me of the fact. Besides, I could have walked away at any time. You need to know that you can trust me to do what is necessary and I didn't back away in order to prove to you that I can. You weren't wrong. I was."

"I'll do my best to minimize physical contact," he offered.

"You better not. Go watch any newly married couple. We might blow our cover," she said, fixing her gaze on the mirror as she freshened up her makeup. As far as he was concerned, she looked perfect.

He couldn't tear his gaze away as she pulled out a small round metal tin. After unscrewing the top, she dabbed her pinkie finger into the container and then dotted her lips with a light pink gloss.

Quint swallowed to ease the sudden dryness in his throat. The surge of attraction was a normal reaction to being in close proximity to an intelligent, beautiful woman. Nothing more. This was proof Quint wasn't off his game even if it was misguided. Where was a reset button when he needed one?

Ree squirted her hair with something that made it look even more silky, and a stab of jealousy knifed him in the chest that she was making herself more beautiful to walk next door. How was that for keeping his cool?

"Do you have any brothers or sisters?" she asked out of the blue.

"None that I know of," he said. "My dad didn't exactly keep in touch when he left me and my mom to our own devices."

"Oh." She immediately reached over and touched his hand, a simple gesture that meant a lot to him. "I'm really sorry."

"We survived all right without him." He heard the defensiveness in his own voice. "Which is to say she worked two jobs to support us and I was a total jerk until I found my way."

"That must have been hard on you," she said. The compassion in her voice touched him in a place long forgotten.

Ree checked the time and gasped.

"I'm sorry. I have to go." Her eyes pleaded forgiveness.

"I'll walk you over," he said, shaking off the moment happening between them. "It'll give me a chance to check out the vehicles in the parking lot again. Plus, it won't hurt if Charley sees you with your husband. We need to find a way to work me into the conversation and possibly figure out how to get me on his computer."

In part, Quint wanted to make a statement to the man that she was off-limits, and he also needed to make himself known to her boss. Charley would be seeing Quint around, and it was time to lay the groundwork.

"Okay," she said before turning and wrapping her arms around his neck. When her green eyes met his, he took another hit square in the chest.

He peeled her arms off him.

"What was that for?" he asked, hearing the huskiness in his own voice.

"Practice," she said, almost beaming.

"Right." He coughed, thinking there were a few other marital things he'd like to be doing right now with Ree. Since those thoughts were as productive as digging in dry Texas dirt with a hand trowel, he shelved them.

Quint gave himself a mental slap and forced a smile. "Ready?"

"As much as I'll ever be," she admitted with wide, beautiful eyes. He could see the same mix of excitement and fear he experienced on a new case. Now he got more of the adrenaline rush—some might even call him an adrenaline junkie—but not so much of the excitement, since Tessa. This career was it for him, though. It was the job he'd trained for. The job he'd expected to still be doing and loving for years down the line. And the one he planned to get a pension from.

In short, it was all he knew how to do.

The pair walked across the parking lot, hand in hand. He discreetly checked license plates. Quint stopped at the glass doors where it would be easy for anyone to see him from inside the place. "This is where I make my exit."

There weren't a whole lot of cars yet. It was probably too early for the dinner crowd. A truck pulled up as Ree repeated the same move from the bathroom earlier, throwing her arms around his neck. He didn't want to notice how right she felt pressed against his body or how firm her breasts were when they were flush against him.

Instead of overthinking his physical reaction, he looped his arms around her waist, dipped his head and kissed her.

"See you at home tonight," she said, slowly opening eyes that glittered with something that looked a lot like need.

If she was acting, she deserved an award.

"I might be by for a late dinner," he said as a couple walked behind them. Since small towns usually spread word around and he didn't know the players yet, he added, "Once I get my homework finished."

"Then, I'll see you before my shift is over," she said, throwing him a smile that radiated.

What was he supposed to do with that? There was an innocence and determination in her eyes that he hadn't seen in a long time, not in others and not in himself.

"Bye." He feathered a kiss on her lips before she took off without looking back.

He just stood there for a long moment wondering what in the heck had just happened to him.

Shaking it off, he turned and made his way back to the cabin. Once there, he opened the blinds. There was enough sun outside to light the cabin. Plus, he wanted to snap a couple of pictures as vehicles showed up, start the process of figuring out who the regulars were versus those just driving through town or stopping off specifically to eat there.

Within the hour, the lot was full. Quint snapped a pic of the activity, zeroing in on faces when possible. He needed to get to know the locals and this was the best way. Plus, he could have home base run facial recognition software if he could get a good shot on a suspect.

Curiosity had him pulling Ree's file out of his backpack. He skimmed the contents, noting her marital status as single. He should have asked earlier, telling himself he needed to know for the assignment rather than for personal knowledge. He couldn't deny the relief that washed over him at the realization she wasn't married. Then again, she might have a boyfriend or a significant other. People didn't have to be married to be in a committed relationship. Although, he wouldn't know. After a bad breakup in his early twenties he'd decided not to touch that stove again.

Besides, he'd had all the company and friendship he could want from work, with Tessa as a partner. The two of them had done everything together when she was alive. Dinners? Check. Beer and sports nights? Check. Paintball wars on days off? Check.

They would spark romance rumors from time to time, but anyone who really knew them realized they were best friends and nothing more. Not the kind of romantic best friends that made for a good marriage, either. Just two buddies who got each other and enjoyed hanging out. There were discussions about the need to back off the friendship when one or both of them got involved in a relationship, and they did. Their baseline had always been mutual respect and giving space when needed.

The formula worked and eased the pinch when either one ended a fling. It could be a relief in many cases when a date went south because Quint always knew he could call Tessa and grab a beer. Until Tessa started drinking water out of nowhere, like he wouldn't notice. She covered by complaining about an ulcer. The excuse had bought her a little more time.

Quint stayed lost in thought longer than he'd intended. By the time he shook out of the haze of memories it was time to head next door. Before leaving, he closed the mini blinds and sneaked in a few more shots of the parking lot. He sent those to headquarters, so Agent Grappell could run the plates.

Taking and sending pictures every night would give him a sense of who the regulars were. Now it was time to pack up, hide the files and see what this Charley person looked like in the flesh.

REE HAD KEPT one eye on the door all evening before she caught herself doing it. The night so far had been one big dinner rush. But it was dark outside now and the tables were thinning, while the bar area was starting to hop instead.

Live-music Thursdays would bring a band tomorrow night. She could only imagine what that might do for business considering how lively it had been tonight. And it was only a Wednesday. The specials had looked and smelled amazing all evening. Of course, after working here for a while she would probably get sick of it all.

"Hey, table five is looking ready for their check," Adrian said as she buzzed past.

"Thank you," Ree said to the veteran waitress. Ree had literally gone to the bathroom for five seconds.

She dropped off a check as she heard the door open behind her and a familiar voice call her name.

"Ree Sheppard?" Sarah Combs's voice sent a shock wave down Ree's back.

Ree spun around to face Sarah and Marcus Brown.

"What are you doing here?" Ree stared into the very brown eyes of someone she'd gone to high school with in the small town where she grew up outside of Houston, and her youngest brother's best friend. "And when did you two start going out?"

"Heard the food is top shelf here," Sarah said, then held up her wedding finger. "We've been married five years now. We have two kids who are with my parents this weekend. We're on a road trip and heard about the food here. This is so crazy. What are the odds? We just went out with your brother last weekend. Didn't we, Marcus?"

Marcus nodded.

"I'm Matthews now." Ree could feel the blood rush to her cheeks as she displayed her wedding band. She heard a whoosh sound in her ears. She had to finagle a way out of this before Adrian or Zoey caught on.

"Are you okay?" Sarah asked, twisting her face up.

"Yes. Of course. Just surprised to see y'all. Why don't you guys sit over here in my station where we can catch up in between customers," Ree said, motioning toward a booth along the opposite wall from the bar.

"The crowd is slowing down and I want to hear about the kids."

"Okay, but I'm so confused. How are you a waitress? Your brother just said you worked in—"

Ree shot Sarah a look that could cut through steel. Marcus wrapped his arm around his wife's shoulder and mouthed an apology. He led Sarah to the booth Ree had indicated a few seconds ago.

The hairs on Ree's neck pricked as fear washed over her. She cleared her throat and turned around in time to see Zoey staring. Did she suspect something?

Was Ree's cover blown?

A pair of guys walked in the door. One was tall, bald, and wore a leather biker jacket. The other was short and round-bellied, with a full head of hair and ruddy cheeks. They were an odd pairing and the kind of people trouble usually followed.

"Table for two?" she asked as Zoey lingered at a nearby table.

Ruddy motioned toward the bar.

"Live music is tomorrow. Thursday. Bar closes early on Wednesdays," she informed him. The look she received in return could freeze alcohol.

"Go ahead and take a seat," she urged, motioning toward the bar. "I'll grab Charley."

Ruddy nodded.

Rather than give in to full-scale panic, she grabbed two waters from the back and brought them out to her new table. "Menus are right here." She pointed. "I'll be right back."

Ree needed to find Charley and let him know his "friends" were in the house. She darted to the kitchen. "Has anyone seen Charley?"

Chef was retying his apron. He glanced up. "Cold storage, maybe?"

Ree crossed the room to cold storage and located Charley sitting on a stack of boxes, staring at a tablet. He was most likely doing inventory.

"Hey, Charley. A couple of guys are here. I think they're friends of yours. They're insisting on sitting in the bar area even though I told them it was closed," she said.

A momentary look of fear flashed across Charley's face. His muscles tensed before he took in a breath and looked up from his tablet.

"Should I serve the table?" she asked, noting his reaction.

"I'll handle it," he said in a world-weary voice. "Just see if you can get them anything to drink and tell them I'll be right there."

"Will do," she said before making a hasty exit. Could she still save the situation with Sarah?

As she crossed the kitchen, she saw Adrian whispering to Zoey. What was that all about? This investigation was crumbling right before her eyes. Sarah and Marcus's timing couldn't be worse, and the pair of men in the bar needed watching.

She hurried to Marcus and Sarah's table. He was on the phone in an animated conversation.

"We'll be home shortly, Mom," he said. "Tell the kids to stop crying. We'll be there to tuck them in."

Sarah's face was pinched. She whispered, "We have to go. Sorry."

"Are you sure?" Ree asked, trying to sell the lie they'd just met in case someone was listening. "The food here is top-notch."

"Yeah, no, sorry," Sarah said a little loudly. "It's the kids."

Marcus ended the call as they left the booth. "We'll come back another time."

"Okay," Ree said, her heart racing. "Suit yourself."

As the two left, she glanced toward the bar and saw him. Quint. He sat across the bar from Ruddy and Bald. Her stomach flip-flopped and her breath caught at the sight of her partner. He had the kind of rugged good looks that said he could handle himself in just about any situation, which only added to his sex appeal.

He sat on a barstool, finishing a beer, looking a little too good in his jeans and button-down. Be still, her heart.

It was probably naive to think she could surprise him, considering not much seemed to get past the man. This time seemed no exception as she walked up behind him. He reached back, grabbed her hand and squeezed before letting it go without missing a beat.

Someone would have to be watching to catch what had happened and when she glanced around, she saw Charley staring at them from the mouth of the hallway that led to the restroom, his gaze bouncing from her and Quint to his visitors. His expression could best be described as interested as he seemed to study them. Even from this distance, she could see his frown. Had they crossed a line?

Chapter Five

Rather than guess, she walked right over to Charley with a wide smile. "That's the husband I was telling you about on break earlier."

"Oh, really?" Charley's eyebrows knitted together.

"It's okay if he comes here to eat, right? We can pay for his dinner if that's a—"

Charley shook his head.

"No problem. Family gets the employee discount. Make sure Stevie knows." Charley nodded toward Quint. "I'd keep an eye on your man around here if I were you."

Ree turned around in time to see the female bartender throwing her hair back, laughing, and making conversation with Quint as she closed down the bar. A twinge of jealousy formed a knot in her stomach.

"Didn't realize I would have to," she said, trying to joke. It fell flat.

"No physical contact while you're working. It's bad for business," Charley said before walking away and heading into the kitchen.

Ree stood there for a long moment.

"Don't worry," Adrian said as she walked over. "Charley is all bark and no bite."

"He's serious about the no-touching policy, though. Isn't he?" she asked, not needing to fake disappointment.

"At first, I'd toe the line if I were you. Give it a few weeks and he'll lighten up," Adrian said. "Charley usually takes a shine to the new girls, so he probably doesn't love the fact you're married."

. Ree decided this wasn't the time to mention that she wasn't a "girl." Adrian probably hadn't intentionally been offensive. "Are you saying he has a crush on me?"

"You wouldn't be the first," Adrian said. "He's gone out with several of us."

Ree picked up on the *us* immediately. She didn't need to be a good investigator to realize Adrian had dated Charley. Had Zoey done the same?

"It's all fun and games in the beginning," the other waitress continued wistfully. "He can be quite a charmer when he puts his mind to it."

"And when he doesn't?" Ree asked more out of curiosity than anything else. This information was painting a picture of the man who ran Greenlight, and Ree needed all the information she could get.

"Let's just say it gets real cold in the shadows," Adrian said.

Ree nodded toward Zoey. "What about her? Did they date?"

"I'm not sure what to think about poor Zoey," Adrian said, moving closer and whispering.

"Not cool." Ree figured Charley could go down on at least one charge even if he wasn't responsible for the guns running out of the back of his establishment. At the very least, he needed to learn how to respect women.

Adrian shrugged. "She's young and doesn't talk much. I know she's staying at the motel a couple of blocks from here. It's one of those pay-by-the-week places."

"Any family around?" Ree figured she needed to let it go, so this would be the last question. She didn't need to snap into investigator mode.

"Just the jerk over there at the bar. He used to show up more, yelling at her in the parking lot," Adrian said, making a face.

"Poor kid." Ree shook her head. "She can't be more than twenty."

"Yeah," Adrian agreed. "What's your story?"

Ree gave her the two-minute version before excusing herself to check on an order from the kitchen. Adrian had handed over interesting information about Zoey. When Ree really looked at the other waitress, she thought Adrian might have a point about age. Zoey could pass for twenty but she might barely be eighteen. There were some very physically mature teenagers who looked much older than they were. Puberty could be an interesting mixer. Ree fell into the late bloomer camp and she'd always been told she looked younger than she really was. She figured she'd appreciate it later in life. Not so much after she'd turned twenty-one and was constantly carded while ordering a beer after work or trying to buy a bottle of wine on her way home.

After setting down plates, she made rounds. Table three needed their check, so she handled that. More water for table two, so she fixed that easily enough.

At least they'd made it through a night. Everything hurt after being on her feet all day. Time to close up the restaurant side couldn't come fast enough. The scare with Sarah and Marcus had her nerves on edge.

After filling her last ketchup bottle, she got her handbag out of the locker she'd been assigned in back. The room wasn't much larger than a walk-in pantry with space for no more than three people at one time. The back door was beside it and a small employee bathroom sat directly across. Ree took special note of the layout, and the camera positioned above the back door.

Quint was no longer sitting at the bar by the time she reentered the dining room, but Charley was in deep conversation with Ruddy and Bald. A moment of panic struck as she scanned the room. He probably headed back to the cabin without her. They hadn't exactly come up with a plan for how to handle nights. Still, for reasons she didn't want to examine, it bothered her that he hadn't stayed to walk her home.

Mentally shaking it off, she said good-night to the others and headed out the front door.

Quint was there, sitting, and her heart gave a little flip. He stood up the minute she walked outside.

"Hey," he said, dipping his head down and kissing her before linking their fingers. Heat swirled through her body. Instead of fighting the feeling, she leaned into it.

"How was work?" he asked, giving her hand a little squeeze.

This might just be for show but there was something nice about him being there.

"Good tips tonight but my feet are ready to fall off," she admitted.

"Too bad I have this injury or I'd carry you over the threshold," he said and she couldn't tell if he was serious or joking as they headed home to the cabin. He lowered his voice when he said, "I have information."

Ree's mind immediately snapped to Ruddy and Bald. Then there was Zoey. The young woman was on her mind now and she couldn't shake the feeling of wanting to help.

QUINT LET GO of Ree's hand the minute they were safely inside the cabin. He instantly felt cold where warmth used to be. "Charley's cousin is the sheriff."

"Interesting. I don't remember seeing that intel in the brief." Ree kicked off her boots at the door and walked over to the sofa before plopping down. She started rubbing her feet almost immediately.

"They had different last names and there's a step-family situation, which took the agency a minute to figure out," he stated, walking over to the fridge. "Do you want anything to drink?"

"Water would be nice. I had fifteen minutes to gobble down my dinner, which was the most amazing chicken-fried steak I've ever eaten, and almost no time to stay hydrated." She groaned her pleasure at the mention of the food and it wasn't a sound he needed to have associated with her.

He might have had doubts about being able to work with Ree but he was coming around. She'd held her own on a long shift and, in his estimation, had to do the heavy lifting in the case by working at Greenlight.

Quint poured two glasses of water and brought hers over to the coffee table, setting it down within arm's reach.

"Thank you," she said. "Interesting about the sheriff. Did you get his or her name?"

"Sheriff Welton Rice," Quint supplied.

"I'm sure the agency is doing a deep dive into his background," she said. "Seeing if he has any blemishes on his record."

He nodded. She was on the right track. He dimmed the lights before taking a seat across from her.

"I'm sure you took note of the two men who came in at closing time," she stated.

"The bald guy and the one with the ruddy complexion," he said. "Hard to miss those two."

"And the fact my cover was almost blown by my brother's friends." She gave him a quick rundown. "I don't think anyone caught on but I did see Adrian and Zoey whispering."

"Could have been about anything," he said.

"I know. The timing is terrible, though," she said.

"It's never a good time to run into people from your real world," he stated. "I can feel Stevie out to see if you hit her radar. She keeps tabs on what goes on at the place."

"You definitely hit Charley's radar," she said as a look flashed behind her eyes. If they were a real couple, he'd say it was jealousy. Under the circumstances, it couldn't be.

"What did he say?" he asked.

"No touching. Said it's bad for business," she stated. "You can swing by for dinner. I get the impression he doesn't mind as long as we steer clear of each other inside those glass doors."

"Got it," he said. "The man keeps a close eye."

"He's either very involved at running his business or has something to hide," she said.

He nodded. The two of them were hitting a stride with each other.

"Mind if I ask a personal question?" he asked, trying to capitalize on the comfort they were developing with their partnership.

"Go ahead." She picked up the water and took a sip.

"Why did you get into law enforcement?" he asked. Everyone he'd come across, be it cop, agent or investigator, had a story.

"Um, well…" She seemed a little surprised by the

change in direction. "Let's see, I grew up with four brothers thinking I was one of them, so I was never going to be a prima ballerina, much to my mother's great shock and disappointment."

"Expectations are hard to live up to. I can't imagine what it must have been like to come from such a big family, though," he said. "To be honest, I always wished for siblings."

"Mine are all great in their own ways and they never treated me like I was anything less than an equal," she admitted with a smile. "But I followed in my dad's footsteps going into law enforcement. He was killed in a high-speed chase when I was little, so my grandfather stepped in. He was always my role model and hero." The note of melancholy in her voice said she missed her father very much.

"What made you decide law enforcement was the right career?" he asked.

"Why does anyone follow in anyone else's footsteps. To make them proud, I guess. It's in the blood for me," she admitted. "What about you?"

"Okay," he started. She'd been honest with him, so reciprocating was the least he could do. "You already know that I grew up with a single mother who worked two jobs. We lived in a trailer park on the outskirts of Houston and she was gone most of the time. I got bored. Lonely. So I got into trouble."

She winced before taking another sip. "Must have turned out okay since you're here. What happened?"

"There was a liaison officer at my school who realized I needed a male role model in my life," he said, thinking that he never told this story. "His name was Officer Jazz, so, clearly, we used fake dance behind his back. Jazz hands and all."

She laughed and it was the most musical sound.

"One of the times I got into trouble, he took it upon himself to speak to the office about me. My teachers came forward saying I used to be a good student and they weren't sure what happened. Jazzy, as I used to call him, didn't leave it there. He kept digging and then eventually asked if he could sit with me at lunch one day. Said there was a program and wanted to know if I'd be his little brother," he said. "I balked at first but then I got into really bad trouble. I remember distinctly sitting across the dining room table from my mom and seeing the exhaustion and hurt in her eyes. She could barely stay awake because she'd worked all night at the hospital changing bedpans. It just clicked for me in that moment she deserved better from me."

"Your mom sounds like an amazing person," she said with so much admiration in her voice a place deep down inside him awakened, bringing a peek of light.

"She was," he said, covering the emotion building with the realization he never spoke about his mom to anyone. Not even Tessa.

"I'm so sorry." Ree's expression changed from admiration to sorrow.

"She got sick. It was a long time ago." Those were the mantras he repeated in order to shove his feelings aside.

"It sounds like you two were very close," she observed.

"Yes, and the point of the story is that having someone other than my mother believe in me, having Jazzy, made all the difference in the world. It saved my life," he said in a tone that revealed this conversation was changing directions.

Ree sat there for a long moment, looking lost in thought. "I wonder who Zoey has had in her life."

"The young waitress?" he asked.

"Yes. Adrian mentioned Zoey might be in a bad relationship and living with the guy in a motel down the street," she said.

"Think you can get close to her? Find out her story?" Quint asked, his own anger rising at the thought of a lost young person.

Ree nodded.

"It's just sad. You know?" She lifted those incredible green eyes to meet his. "She is still so young and it doesn't seem like she has anyone to look out for her."

He did know to a point. He'd never doubted his mom's love and it was the other reason he'd wanted to shift gears and be a better person all those years ago. Desire was one thing and a good place to start. Having support taught him how to cross the finish line.

"The boyfriend might be an abusive boyfriend," Ree said.

"We'll do what we can to help her no matter what else happens on this case," he promised, and he had every intention of following through. No young person should be left to their own devices when others could step in and offer a hand up. "Which doesn't mean she'll take it. We can't do anything for her. She has to be ready to leave him if that's the situation."

"We can try. This is good," Ree said, her eyes lighting up. "What's the point of doing this job if we can't make a difference, right?"

Quint couldn't have said it better himself. Up until now, he'd viewed his job as taking bad guys off the streets. He realized how cliché it sounded early on in his career, so he didn't bring it up with other officers, or civilians for that matter. There'd been a few cases involving misguided young folks that had stuck with him. Maybe he and Ree could make a difference in this case.

He glanced at the clock. They'd been talking way too long and Ree needed to get some rest if she was going to do this all again tomorrow. They'd made good progress tonight toward getting to know each other and working together.

"What do you think about turning in for the night?" he asked.

Ree checked the time. "Oh, wow. I really lost track of time here."

She stood.

"I'm a night shower person, so I'll just grab my clothes. This sofa is fine with me for sleeping if you want to throw a blanket and pillow over here," she stated, biting back a yawn as though being reminded of her exhaustion suddenly kicked her body into sleep mode.

"I'll have everything ready for when you're done," he confirmed. There was no way he was letting her take the sofa when he could easily grab a nap during the day if needed.

Ree left the room as he thought about how little he ever spoke about his mom. Tessa had stepped into the role of his only living family and he'd buried childhood memories down deep. Memories of how he and his mother used to have one meal a day together, his breakfast and her dinner. It was the half hour their lives crossed and they spent time talking, checking in with each other. Looking back, he could see those meals started happening after Jazzy came into their lives. Quint's mother had been seventeen when she'd given birth to him and, although he never doubted her love for him, she probably didn't have the necessary parenting skills.

This whole conversation with Ree reminded Quint to catch up with Jazzy, maybe take him out for a beer.

He shifted his thoughts back to the case. He needed to review the video footage from the pencil-sized cameras he'd placed in the windows. The recordings were feeding to his laptop and he needed to watch the footage so he could start getting a sense of routines and behaviors. Since he didn't have unlimited data storage and the Wi-Fi was sketchy out here, he would have to take notes and then erase the recordings on a regular basis. He opened his laptop and fired off an email to Agent Grappell about the sheriff's connection.

For the time being, he would have to mostly rely on intel Ree provided, since he hadn't gotten a toe in the door yet. It was early and these investigations could take weeks, even months when going deep undercover. Considering they already knew weapons were being run out the back, this one should be on the shorter side. Why did the thought hold less appeal now that he was getting to know Ree?

For the first time since this whole case began, he didn't balk at the idea of being with another female partner. Ree had proved she could stand up to him, which was important. She'd more than proved she could handle the job next door. Her waitressing skills looked on point when he was in the room and she'd already scored critical pieces of information and that was just on day one. Charley seemed to have taken a shine to her. As much as Quint didn't like that part, she'd played her hand perfectly with the restaurant owner, proving to be a valuable asset while under pressure.

For the first time since losing Tessa, Quint was

warming up to working with a new partner. Now it was time to check out the camera footage and see what else he could find.

REE FINISHED HER shower in record time, exhaustion having settled in the minute she peeled off her work clothes. She would get two uniforms so she could wear one and wash the other. Thankfully, she'd seen a washer/dryer combo in the hall closet. The embarrassment of her undergarments being hung outside for the world to see wasn't exactly something she could digest at the moment. She didn't exactly want Quint handling her bra and panties, either.

The day had been productive for a first day. Groundwork was being laid. She'd established a few boundaries and Quint had been introduced to the picture. This was all good progress.

Ree toweled off, and dressed in the most innocuous pair of pajamas known to man: lounge pants and an oversize T-shirt. She secured a light robe on top as if the other pieces weren't figure-hiding enough. Besides, she was a tornado when she slept, so she needed coverage. She threw her uniform and day's undergarments into the washer and turned it on.

Walking into the living room, she noticed the sofa bed had been pulled out. She started toward it when Quint practically growled at her to take the bed.

"Why? What changed in the last fifteen minutes since I was in the shower?" she asked.

"You need a good night's sleep." He pointed to the sofa bed. "That thing isn't going to give it to you."

"With all due respect, the same is true for you," she said, standing her ground.

"I can sleep sitting up if needed, and take a nap if I

crash in the daytime. You, on the other hand, have to be on your feet all day again tomorrow. Do you want to do that after sleeping with a rod up your back?" he asked, not looking up from his laptop.

"When you put it that way, no," she admitted. "But I don't need you to make concessions for me because I'm fem—"

"I wasn't," came the growl that practically shook the walls.

"Good," she shot back, forcing herself to be unafraid. She'd seen his gentle side when he spoke about his mom. A good person was behind those steel walls he'd erected. After learning about his background, she understood him better. She also realized her brother Shane was right. She had to be brave if she was ever going to have a chance to break down Quint's barriers. A voice in the back of her head told her that he wasn't the type to share his past easily or with many. The moment that had happened between them was special, and despite initial evidence to the contrary, the two of them might just end up friends.

The same voice picked that moment to remind her that friends didn't cause electricity to pulse through her at the lightest contact or her stomach to free-fall with a glance in her direction.

She shelved those thoughts under the category of *unproductive.*

Quint's reputation said he was one of the best at his job. She intended to use this time to learn from a master because who knew when an opportunity like this would ever come along again? Being paired with an agent like Quint was a dream come true.

"You want me to sleep on the bed? I'll take the bed," she said, throwing her arms up like it didn't matter one way or the other to her. "I don't mind being comfortable and this mattress looks like a dream."

It didn't. But she didn't let that stop her from singing its praises.

Quint didn't respond. After growing up with four brothers, she realized she'd scored a direct hit.

"Bathroom is yours," she said, climbing under the sheets. She checked her cell before going to bed and saw there was a text from Preston. Hey, was all it said. She wasn't touching that one with a ten-foot pole. The last time she responded to one of her ex's texts a six-week fling had kicked off. Granted, the sex had been worth it, but walking away from him a second time had practically gutted her. Plus, she was on an assignment. The rest of the world had to wait. She didn't even contact her brothers when she was undercover.

The lights were dim enough for her to sleep. She'd never been especially picky in that department. All she needed was a bed, covers and AC in order to be good to go for a night's rest. And not even a good bed, which was the reason she'd volunteered to take the couch in the first place. It really didn't matter much to her and his sheer size should dictate he take the larger mattress. But hey, whatever he wanted was fine with her.

"Is Charley still hiring waitresses?" Quint asked.

"Not that I know of," she said. "Why?"

"I was trying to figure out the reason for the double shift and if this was going to be the norm," he said.

"A waitress called in sick. Normally, I'll be working the lunch shift but he needs me for both while she's out," she said.

"At least you'll get to know the players faster that way," he said.

Tomorrow, on her shift, she planned to keep a closer

eye on Zoey as long as she could do it without getting caught. No matter how much her heart went out to Zoey, she couldn't become a distraction to the real assignment. Could she get the young woman to talk? Share her story?

Ree glanced at the clock. She would know in less than twelve hours.

Chapter Six

Sunshine was already peeking through the slats of the mini blinds when Ree's smartwatch buzzed. She sat bolt upright, trying to get her bearings.

"Morning." Quint's whiskey-on-ice voice poured over her and through her.

"Don't you ever sleep?" She squinted through blurry eyes as she yawned.

His chuckle was a low rumble in his chest. He pushed to standing from the chair and headed into the kitchen. A few seconds later, he returned with a coffee mug in hand.

"Thank you," she said, taking the offering and inhaling the smell of fresh brew.

"You're welcome." He reclaimed his seat and stared at his laptop. "I do sleep, by the way."

"Really?" She took a sip, welcoming the burn on her throat. "And this is amazing."

"Yes. Everyone does. Don't believe anyone who tries to convince you otherwise. I just came into this assignment well rested. I'm good for a few nights sleeping in short bursts."

"Gotcha. I'm more of a 'straight eight' type but can get by on six and a half when absolutely necessary. It gets ugly after that," she said with a smile. "Are you a robot?"

"Yes," he said, as serious as a pastor during Sunday morning church service. Then he picked up his own coffee mug and rewarded her with a smile in a show of perfectly straight, perfectly white teeth. Teeth were just the beginning of perfection on this man. Some might have considered the half-inch scar above his right eyebrow and other physical traits as flaws. Ree didn't fall into that camp. Those little things were precisely what set someone apart and made them even more attractive, gave them sex appeal as opposed to just being a beautiful shell. Personality influenced looks. She'd met plenty of beautiful-on-the-outside people whose looks deteriorated in her eyes once they opened their mouths to speak. Intelligence was sexy. A sense of humor...sexy.

"Oh, you actually have a sense of humor," she teased, thinking how nice it was to break some of the tension by joking around. Last night had thrown a lot at her at Greenlight. Based on the stress lines etched into his forehead, he didn't laugh nearly often enough and was as concerned about her going back today as she was. She knew his mother was gone and wondered if there'd been someone else special in his life that he'd lost.

Hold on a minute. It was coming back to her now. Didn't he use to work with someone who'd been killed on the job? Ree made a mental note to research that later. There would be news articles if an agent had been killed on duty. It was a big department but she'd heard about a female agent being killed in a bust after the New Year.

Setting the thought aside, she took another sip of coffee, figuring she needed to milk this morning before her day shifted into high gear.

"What are you studying on that thing?" she asked, hugging her knees into her chest.

"Video footage from the past—" he checked the time "—ten hours or so."

"Are you seeing anything worth talking about?" she asked.

"Not yet. I'm still getting the lay of the land so I can start memorizing routines, regular customers, delivery flow," he admitted. "I snapped a couple of faces to send to Grappell so he can run them through facial recognition software. See if we can get any hits there."

"Looking for patterns," she said. "How much data can that thing store?"

"Yes. And not enough to keep more than twenty-four hours of video on hand," he said.

"Of course, we don't need that much," she surmised.

"Nope. So I'm capturing screenshots of vehicles with their license plates, too. Sending everything to headquarters. There was a liquor delivery at ten o'clock last night that I recorded," he said. "I grabbed pictures of faces in the truck but I got side views and the pictures are grainy when I blow them up. There's enough there to see if the same delivery drivers worked the route but not to ID anyone."

"I'll try to work the back of the house a little more today. A camera is pointed directly at the back door." She grabbed a pen and notepad before drawing out the layout of Greenlight. "To be honest, yesterday was such a whirlwind that I didn't do a great job of getting to know the players in the kitchen," she admitted. "It's been a really long time since I was a waitress and I spent most of the time praying I wouldn't drop a tray while serving customers, and getting introduced to the other waitresses. I put most of my energy toward trying not to get fired my first day on the job. Then, we already know about Sarah and Marcus's visit."

She rolled the coffee mug around in her palms, appreciating the warmth after pushing the notepad toward Quint.

"It's too soon for me to approach Charley about helping out with his computer system," Quint said and she agreed. "This layout is helpful."

"I caught him staring at you from across the room last night," she said. "I meant to mention that before."

"Then I better back off today. Think you'll be okay?" he asked before seeming to catch himself.

"Yes," she said a little too defensively.

"I didn't mean that—"

"You don't have to apologize," she reassured him. "I jumped the gun. I can see that you trust me to get the job done."

"You did great work yesterday. I believe you'll do the same today," he stated, looking over his screen. "How long before your shift?"

"An hour and a half." She issued a sharp sigh. "I should get up and make something to eat."

"On it," he said, setting down his laptop and heading toward the kitchen.

"You're spoiling me," she teased in an attempt to lighten the tension from a few seconds ago when she'd overreacted.

"Anything for my new bride," he quipped in a surprising show of his sense of humor. It had peeked out a few times and she liked that side of him.

"Be careful. I can get used to this," she shot right back, enjoying the lightness of the conversation, realizing her day would end up another whirlwind. It might take a couple of days, but she would eventually get into a groove and, hopefully, the video footage would reveal something soon. Give them a path to follow.

"We should have something back about the sheriff before you head to work. Since I need to avoid the restaurant today, I might go into town and do a little grocery shopping. Check out the local scene," he said as amazing smells emanated from the kitchen.

"What are you cooking?" she asked.

"Eggs," he said. "I called your older brother Shane last night while you were at work and he said you love scrambled eggs, toast and jam for breakfast."

"Wait a minute. How did you get my brother's number?" she asked. "And how do you know his name?"

Quint shrugged his broad shoulders. She forced her gaze away from his muscled back.

"You need to tell me before I get really angry," she said.

"Technically, he called me," he confessed.

"He wouldn't do that," she said. Would he?

On second thought, that was exactly what her older brother would do. As the oldest, Shane had always felt responsible for his siblings. "Was he worried he gave me bad advice?"

"It sounded like he was. He seemed bothered by the fact the two of you didn't have a chance to talk the situation through," he said.

"How did he get your number?" she asked.

"Through the department, but he requested that I not tell you. He said he was afraid you might come on too strong after the two of you spoke on the phone. Everything happened so fast, he said, and then you cut off the conversation," Quint said.

"If he asked you not to tell me, then why are you?"

she asked, curious as to why he would break her brother's trust.

"If we're going to be 'married' we can't have any division between us. No secrets. I thanked your brother for touching base with me and saw how much he cared about you. But I told him I couldn't go behind your back. I didn't tell you last night because we got off topic and you needed rest. I'm telling you now because this was the earliest point that I could bring it up," he said, turning to study her like he was gauging her reaction.

"Sounds like my big brother," she said with a sigh. "Always looking out for me."

Quint set the plate down on the two-top in the kitchen area. "Breakfast is served."

She cocked an eyebrow at him. "Did you make me my favorite breakfast to smooth over the fact you quizzed my brother about me last night?"

"I don't know," he said, feigning being offended. "Would it work?"

More than she wanted to admit. Ree shook her head and smiled.

QUINT WASN'T TRYING to roll her brother under the bus. He also didn't want to hide anything from her. It could show on his face at a critical moment. There could be no secrets between them, especially one like this. He wasn't kidding about that before.

Ree crossed the room, coffee cup in hand. Lounge pants, a T-shirt and robe shouldn't be this sexy on a person. Her sleepy smile tugged at his heart as he pulled her chair back like a server might at a five-star restaurant.

She took a seat and he pushed it in, handing over a napkin.

"If this is what waking up is like, I'll take this treatment every day," she said with a smile that smacked him square in the chest.

"You should be treated like an angel," he said so low he wasn't sure she heard him. Did he want her to?

Good question, he thought, trying to convince himself that he was only stoking the flame of attraction to "sell" their relationship to others when they were in public. He was doing nothing more than method acting. An annoying little voice in the back of his mind said there was more to it, but he wasn't ready to unpack the meaning just yet.

"Are you eating with me?" she asked.

"I'm not missing out on scrambled eggs and toast," he said, appreciating the lightness happening between them. It was a good way to bond and build a partnership—a partnership that could mean the difference between life and death. He needed to work with a sketch artist today while the bald guy and the one with the ruddy complexion were fresh on his mind. He could accomplish that while Ree worked, too.

As he walked over to the stove and plated his food, he flashed back to all the times he'd made breakfast for Tessa. Bagels, cream cheese and jam had been her hands-down favorite. Coffee with milk and two raw sugars had been her go-to before the pregnancy. He'd missed another sign early on because she'd switched over to decaf. Tessa had most definitely never been a decaf person. The only reason he'd caught on to the change was because he surprised her with one of her favorite coffeehouse drinks only to realize she let it sit on her desk. Before, the vanilla mocha would be gone in a heartbeat.

The memories fell into the category of too late and

of no use anymore. He set his plate down on the table so hard there was a noise and eggs got shuffled around on the plate.

Ree gasped. Her gaze darted toward him before dropping to his hand where he fisted his fork. Quint released his grip and the fork tumbled onto the table.

He sat down without making eye contact.

"Anything you want to talk about?" Ree asked, pushing a clump of egg around with her fork.

"No," he said with a finality that should tell her this subject was off-limits. He needed to find a way to get through this assignment without thinking about Tessa every hour. No matter how hard he tried, his mind kept cycling back to how he'd failed her when she'd needed him most.

Ree took in a slow breath that he could hear from across the table. And then another. She didn't immediately move. She didn't speak. She seemed to realize this wasn't the time for words. He wouldn't be able to find the right ones to express his anger, frustration and disappointment at himself anyway. Instead, the two of them sat in the same companionable silence and suddenly Quint felt an intimacy and connection to someone like he'd never known through spoken words.

He couldn't be certain how long they stayed at the table but at some point he picked up his fork and began eating. Ree finished her plate, gathered both once they were empty, and then disappeared into the bathroom.

A short time later, she came back out, kissed him on the cheek and said, "Any word yet about the sheriff? I'm leaving for work now."

"I can check if you have a minute," he said.

She glanced at her cell. "I'd better not hang around. It'll look good if I'm a few minutes early to work and

I might be able to strike up a conversation with one of the other waitresses in the breakroom."

"I'd like to walk you over, at least. It'll familiarize Charley with me. Plus, he'll see that I'm respecting his boundary by stopping at the door." He instinctively reached for her hand, then stood when he found it.

"Okay." Her smile was sunshine after a monsoon. "I'd like that a lot actually."

Ree led the way. He left the cabin door unlocked during the short walk. He stopped at the restaurant door and planted a kiss on his "wife" that caused a tornado of heat to swirl in his chest. When they pulled apart, both were breathless. They opened their eyes at the same time and he saw a deep well of need in her glittery green eyes.

All he could think was...*damn.*

There hadn't been anyone so off-limits and so tempting that he could ever remember. The breakup in his twenties seemed like nothing compared to what would happen if it was Ree instead of Maisy.

For a long moment, he stood at the door after she walked inside. Then he pulled it together and headed home. Halfway across the parking lot he realized he didn't have on his boot. Quint cursed. It wasn't like him to slip and that was a huge one as far as errors went. He could only pray the mistake wouldn't cause unwanted attention or harm the investigation in any way. He cursed again.

As he rounded the corner to the cabin, he saw the unlocked door was open.

Quint glanced around, surveying the area. This cabin was closest to the restaurant and had the least amount of privacy from the road. He took in a deep breath, calming his racing pulse. Going in looking like an officer would risk blowing their cover. After Bald Guy and Ruddy Complexion last night and the fact Ree's cover might have been compromised, Quint's radar was on high alert. Was someone on to them?

Chapter Seven

Back flat against the building, Quint eased toward the opened door. He peeked inside. It took a second for his gaze to adjust to the dark cabin after walking in the bright Texas sun.

No one was in sight in the open living space, but he heard the sound of the hallway door being opened. The washer opened and closed. Then, the dryer. Someone was rooting around in their cabin. Did Charley catch on? Bald Guy? Ruddy Complexion?

With light steps, Quint moved into the main living room. He reached for his ankle holster, and then retrieved his SIG Sauer. Whoever was snooping around was moving through in a hurry. The medicine cabinet in the bathroom opened next.

Quint checked his laptop and saw an unfamiliar thumb drive. There were protocols in place to block any attempt to steal information. But he didn't like this one bit.

Keeping his attention on the bathroom, he moved over to his laptop and pocketed the memory stick. As he moved to the mouth of the hallway, an older woman stepped out of the bathroom.

She let out a yelp as she clutched her heart. "Sorry. You scared me."

She was short, five feet two inches if he had to guess. She had a round middle, timeworn skin and gray eyes. Her hair was piled on top of her head and she looked like the kind of person who would always have candy tucked inside her apron pocket. Not exactly what he expected to come across and definitely not a skilled thief, but she could have been paid to snoop. Based on her reaction, he figured that was the case.

"My wife and I will be staying here for a long time," he started, playing the part of a newlywed and hoping she didn't see the boot he should be wearing that was propped up against the chair in the living room or the weapon he hid behind his leg. If she just got there, he should be fine. "There's no need for cleaning this cabin during our stay."

"I thought this cabin was going to turn over today. Let me see." She put on reading glasses that were on a string around her neck and then pulled a small notepad out of her pocket. Her hands were empty save for her cell. She didn't appear to have taken anything, so she might have been snapping pics. "This is number eight, right?"

"Number three." He took a couple of steps back and then pointed to the open front door, and the number on it.

"Oh, really?" She seemed genuinely shocked, which meant she was a good actress. "I'm new. I must have read the number wrong. Serves me right for not putting on my glasses. I'll just get out of your way." She started scurrying around, gathering the supplies she'd set out on the kitchen counter.

"No rush." He walked over to the chair and sat down. Without being obvious, he scooted the boot out of her sight and out of the line of sight of the door.

While she was distracted, he slipped off his walking boot and tucked his foot inside the apparatus.

"Please don't tell the office about the mix-up, sir." She spun around as he reached for his laptop.

"Honest mistake," he said with a shrug and a smile. "They won't hear it from me."

"Thank you, sir." Her face dropped for just a second when she glanced at the spot where the thumb drive had been.

"Do you mind locking the door on your way out?" he asked, motioning toward his foot, making certain she noted he was injured.

"Oh, no, not at all. I don't mind at all," she stammered as she moved toward the door like a swirling dust cloud. She peeked her head back in before closing the door. "Thank you for understanding, sir."

"Not a problem," he said. "We all make mistakes. You barely set foot inside here. No harm, no foul."

"You're very kind," she said.

"I didn't catch your name," he said.

"Patricia," she said before closing the door and getting out of there as fast as she could.

The snick of a lock came a few seconds later. Quint bolted toward the window and watched as the older woman waddled away. Then, just to be one hundred percent certain, he swept the place for bugs.

Once he was assured the cabin was clear, he retrieved his cell phone and called Agent Grappell, who picked up on the first ring.

"I walked in on a cleaning lady in the cabin who was going through our stuff," Quint said after perfunctory greetings. "She tried to use a thumb drive on my laptop."

"Give me a description and a name," Grappell said,

as the click-click of his fingers on a keyboard came through the line.

"All I got out of her was *Patricia*," Quint said. He made a fresh cup of coffee before returning to his chair. "She exited darn fast once I caught her in the act."

He sent over pictures of several license plates from last night. He'd homed in on lone male drivers. He kept a couple of photos of the parking lot when it was full, for a comparison. In his experience, repeat customers tended to park in the same spot every time if it was available. People who were comfortable at a place had a tendency to repeat their patterns, including ordering the same meal.

Give him a week and he'd have better data. One night wouldn't be enough unless he got lucky, in which case he needed to use that luck to buy a lottery ticket. The front and side parking lots were interesting, but he planned to target most of his attention on what happened in back. The liquor truck from last night interested him, but in his experience criminals weren't usually so obvious. At least, not the good ones. Those would use a meat supplier truck or dairy. Something people wouldn't think twice about if they were pulled alongside it on the roadway, not giving it a second glance.

"I'll do a little digging," Grappell said. "See what I can come up with."

"My gut feeling is someone paid her to do it," he stated. "She was an amateur."

Quint went on to explain the pair from the bar last night. "I'd like to work with Aaron to come up with a sketch of these two if he's available. Run it past Lionel to see if we can get anything out of him."

More clicks came through the line.

"I'll have Aaron call," Grappell said. "Lionel has gotten quiet on us."

"He's scared," Quint said. "Romanian gangs are lethal, and they have long fingers."

"Which is why the boss has requested he be placed in the infirmary until this case is over," Grappell said. "He'll get twenty-four-hour security there."

"We might get more out of him that way," Quint agreed. He also realized this case had bigger implications if the boss employed a tactic like that. "How do you want the thumb drive?"

"Any chance you can overnight it?" Grappell said. "It's too dangerous to risk a drop."

"I can do that. I'm driving into town today anyway under the guise of running errands and meeting people," he said. "It's probably too late to get a print. Patricia had on plastic cleaning gloves."

"Convenient," Grappell said.

"Isn't it," Quint stated, thinking the same thing.

"We'll dust anyway, see what we can find," Grappell said. "I'll run employment records with the rental agency for the cabin to see if we come up with a match."

"Good." Quint figured it couldn't hurt. "What did you find out about Sheriff Rice?"

"I sent an email half an hour ago, but there haven't been any investigations or blemishes. His record is clean so far."

"Maybe he's a good guy after all," Quint said before ending the call. Charley could be the bad seed, running weapons right underneath the nose of his squeaky-clean cousin. *Interesting.* Wouldn't be the first time Quint had witnessed a similar scenario. This news, in many ways, made his and Ree's job easier. Dirty law enforcement officers had been rare in his professional career and the few he'd come across infuriated him. They were usually hard to catch and deadly if they figured an agent out. There was no worse crime than someone who'd sworn to uphold the law turning on the people he or she was supposed to protect.

He had no patience for people who made it harder to do his job or caused the public to lose respect for his profession—a profession he loved even if he could admit the job was losing some of its spark lately. But then, since losing Tessa, he could say the same thing about life.

Rather than go down that path again, he decided to get out of the cabin and do a little digging around in town. In his experience, investigations only took one spark to get off the ground. Quint wanted to get a sense of Charley's reputation while in town.

He also wanted to stop at the hardware store and buy a new lock.

Going in early had been a bust. The second day of work was much like the first, a whirlwind. Lunch came and went in a blur. Ree's feet felt like they might literally fall off by the time the dinner rush started. She'd failed miserably at getting to know the kitchen staff so far, and the earlier text from Preston was a distraction she couldn't afford while she was undercover.

The band was setting up over in one corner of the bar on a small triangle-shaped stage. Ree was busy with her station when she noticed a couple of waitresses she hadn't met yet coming in through the back door.

"Do the white-boot waitresses only work the bar? No food shifts?" Ree looked to Adrian, who rolled her eyes.

"Those are the barmaids," Adrian said. She motioned toward her chest area. "Notice a difference between them and us?"

Before Ree could respond, Adrian added, "Well, maybe not you but definitely me and Zoey. There are a couple other waitresses you haven't met yet who work the dining room and they look more like me in that department."

"Come on, you're beautiful," Ree pointed out.

"I do all right," Adrian said, swatting her hand at Ree. "But those barmaids are stacked." Adrian made eyes at Ree and Ree laughed. "You could be one of them, but you have to work here for at least six months before you can even be considered. Then I hear Charley is the one who asks."

"Sounds like the A-team," Ree said before realizing she might have insulted Adrian. "Not that you aren't."

"I've only been here four months and Zoey has been here a month less than me," Adrian said on a shrug. "Neither of us have put in enough time but I can only imagine the tips they make. They work Thursday through Sunday night, when the bar picks up."

"We do all right," Ree stated. "I've never made more money working at a restaurant."

The best way to describe the trio of waitresses was *extra*. Their lashes had to be fake. Good, but fake. There was no way natural lashes were long enough to see from this distance. Their uniforms had sparkles on them and their white boots had been polished and spit shined. Ree glanced down at her shirt that was in okay shape. She probably should have ironed it after it came out of the dryer. Her brown boots were her own but they didn't nearly stand out in the way the trio's white ones did.

No one on the dining room floor had on expensive boots.

Ree figured there was no way she was going to be here long enough to make six months on the job. She

would never be part of the special group of waitresses
and it might not be a big deal. Could she befriend one?
Get information? Looking at the way they sashayed
their hips after they high-fived and started toward the
dining area, Ree wondered if all they did was waitress.
Grappell had run a list of names of the staff. It appeared
to be outdated considering the head count on waitresses
was off, but then there was probably a lot of turnover in
this industry. She needed to put her head together with
Quint and figure out if these ladies were paid under the
table. It would be an easy way to hide a person.

"Good job today, Red," Chef shouted from behind
the counter dividing his space and hers.

"Thank you," she said, realizing this was the first
time he'd complimented her.

"Fender should have a good report for the boss." Chef
was short, in his late forties, with thick wiry hair that
was slicked back and graying at the temples.

"That's a relief," she said. Fender and Charley met
at the end of the shift outside in the back while Fender
had a cigarette. With the meeting being held behind
the restaurant, there was no guarantee the two only
discussed work. Ree had been told they discussed the
waitstaff, but they could be talking about any number
of things. Speaking of which, Charley's cousin was in
the bar tonight having a social drink with one of his
deputies. It would be nice if Quint was here, too, but
being overly eager could cast suspicion and that would
defeat the whole purpose.

She also wished she could stick around and have a
drink so she could get to know the barmaids better, but
Charley had been clear about leaving when her shift was
done. She'd put in a food order for her "injured" hus-

band a few minutes ago, figuring it would give her an excuse to hang around a bit after her shift.

"My husband got hurt on the job and I need this job while he finishes his certification," she continued, picking up the conversation thread with Chef.

"Oh yeah? Sorry to hear it. What did your husband use to do?" Chef asked, leaning toward her. Another sign he was interested in what she had to say.

She realized a few ears had perked up near where they were standing. No one looked over at them and she figured Chef had all their respect.

"Owned a moving company," she said. "He stopped by yesterday. Sat over there." She motioned toward the counter.

"Oh, right. I remember him. Big guy," he said. "Wore a boot."

"That's the one." She had no idea where this conversation was going. Interesting to note that Chef remembered Quint. Although, to be fair, his stature and good looks made an impression. She didn't want to think about how convenient his physical attributes were when trying to get information from the opposite sex.

"What happened to him? If you don't mind my asking," Chef continued, grabbing the towel off his shoulder before wetting it in the sink.

"I don't." She shrugged. "He hit it on a curb while carrying a piano. It came down hard, he landed funny, and shattered his ankle. We got sued and that's when we found out the partner handling the books let our liability insurance lapse. Basically, we lost everything and that was a month into our marriage. So, here we are."

She threw her hands in the air, praying that she hadn't just given too much detail, the hallmark of a lie.

Chef winced at the part about the piano going down

on Quint's ankle and she figured that was a good sign her story was believable. She needed to update Quint so he wasn't caught off guard with any of these details the next time he showed up here.

"That's too bad," he said, squirting cleaner on the metal prep surface before wiping with the wet towel.

"He's learning how to program computers now, though," she said.

"A desk job." Chef put a hand on his lower back and stretched. "Can't work on your feet for ten to twelve hours a day forever without breaking your back."

"I just hope he can do it," she admitted. "He's used to being active all day. But he says he's not twenty any longer."

"Amen to that," Chef agreed.

"He always liked tinkering around with computers. Said he might as well figure out how to work 'em," she said.

"When he does, maybe he can take a look at the one I have at home." Chef shook his head. "It stopped turning on last week and I have my life on that thing. Can't even pay my bills in two weeks if I can't get it up and running." He put his hands up, wrists together. "It's got me handcuffed."

"I won't make any promises but Quint sure could use the practice," she said, figuring this was a start to gaining her coworker's trust.

"Maybe you could give me his number and I could give him a call," he said.

"Absolutely," she said. "Let me go get my cell. I haven't memorized anyone's number since high school, not even my husband's."

Chef laughed. "I don't know my own mother's number. I just push the contact and, bam, there she is on the line."

"Same." Ree disappeared into the breakroom, grabbed her purse and returned.

Chef stood on her side of the counter with a to-go bag in one hand and his cell in the other. "Dinner is ready. I threw in a few extra rolls and doubled the portion. You barely ate your dinner."

"Thank you. That's really kind of you," she said, holding her phone out with Quint's information.

"I'll give him a call tomorrow," Chef said.

"I hope he can figure it out. The practice sure will be good for him." She hoped this wasn't getting too off track with the investigation. Chef seemed about as honest and hardworking as they came. But then, this job had taught her looks could be deceiving, and everyone was a suspect until ruled out based on fact.

She held up the bag. "Thanks again for this."

Chef nodded but his warm smile touched her. Was it wrong to wish he wasn't involved? It wouldn't change her investigation but she would be disappointed in humanity if he was implicated.

What better cover for an operation than to have genuinely good people in place and a cousin for a sheriff? Ree had a lot to share with Quint and couldn't wait to get home to talk to him.

Chapter Eight

Quint stood outside the restaurant, boot on, waiting for his "wife." He did his level best not to be obvious about checking out the bar scene. The music thumped and it sounded lively in there. He tapped the toe of his good foot to the beat, noticing additional head count.

Ree came into view and his heart fisted. She stepped outside and met his gaze. Time stilled. All he could hear was a whoosh sound in his ears as blood rushed through his body. This was the same effect of an adrenaline rush without the smoking gun aimed at his chest.

Admittedly, he'd thought about Ree more times than he could count today, and spent even more time telling himself it was necessary for the investigation. The annoying voice in the back of his head countered his argument every time.

Right now, though, all he wanted to do was hold her against him and kiss those pink lips of hers. The kiss was for show, so he decided to be convincing. By the time their lips parted, they were both left gasping for air, chests heaving. If anyone watched, they should be convinced the two of them were into each other. Thankfully, he didn't have to fake an attraction to her.

"Sorry about that," he said low and under his breath, still in the mental fog that was Ree.

"About what?" she asked, slowly opening her eyes.

"All the kissing," he said, remembering the stance she'd taken yesterday.

"If it has to be done," she said, still a little breathless. His ego didn't mind the fact she seemed to be just as affected as he was every time they were this close. She cleared her throat and put on a smile. "I mean… it's important. You know?"

"Yes, which probably makes it wrong that I'm enjoying it so much." There. He'd said it. He couldn't stop himself. Plus, it was true.

Ree rewarded him with a smile that could melt ice in a freezer.

"Something smells amazing," he said, redirecting the conversation by taking the doggie bag and then linking their fingers.

"Tonight's special, packed by Chef himself," she said. "Chicken and waffles."

"My mouth is already watering," he said. The restaurant portion of the business was legit and bustling, which could make it easy to hide illegal activity. There was a reason that crimes often occurred in busy places. Folks were distracted. There was lots of mental stimulation, sensory overload.

"Your mouth is very talented," she quipped. Her cheeks turned two shades of crimson and pride swelled in his chest. His pulse kicked up a few notches, too.

"That's good to hear. I was afraid being out of practice would show," he admitted, and then wished he could reel the admission back in. A real attraction was out of the question with a colleague, so he did his best to quash his reaction.

"If being in practice gets better…" she said, the words so low he barely heard them.

Not the time to reply, Quint. Hand in hand, they crossed the parking lot. At the cabin, he opened the door for her. Once inside, he set the food bag on the table.

"Why don't you take a load off?" he asked, nodding toward the table.

She toed off her boots and gave him a quick and dirty rundown of the day's events, starting with the waitress trio. He made a note to check the roster Grappell had provided. "An establishment like Greenlight has a lot of moving parts, so it shouldn't be too surprising there is specialized staff. We can double-check the roster but these things are usually out of date and fluid."

"I sure hope you actually know something about fixing computers," she said with a smile after updating him on Chef's request.

"I'm handy. It's kind of a hobby of mine and the reason it works as cover," he admitted. "I like to know how things work."

"Makes sense you'd use that in our cover story then," she agreed.

He pulled out two plates and filled them with food. The garlic mashed potatoes smelled out of this world and there was just enough spinach on the side to make two meals. He grabbed a Coke from the fridge and poured it into a glass with ice.

"When you do decide to get married, your wife is going to be the luckiest woman on earth," Ree said as she seemed to take in the setup.

"Let's pretend that's not an option," he said, taking his seat. The first couple of bites sold him on Chef's cooking abilities. Hook. Line. And sinker.

"Why not?" She quirked a brow. "Think about ever getting married?"

"Not my particular brand of punishment," he stated.

"You wouldn't be so bad to live with," she shot back before quirking a smile. He could tell she grew up in a house of brothers, based on her sense of humor.

"Funny," he quipped, and she seemed content to leave the discussion alone. It was a closed subject as far as he was concerned.

"I've been serving this dish all night. I wasn't one hundred percent certain I could eat it if I wanted to but it's literally the best thing I've put in my mouth in ages," she said before blushing. "I mean, kissing you is pretty great, too."

"Well, thank you," he said, not minding the compliment.

"I just mean that you're pretty good at it. I can hardly tell you're acting at all," she said before taking a big bite of food, clearly oblivious to the hit he'd just taken to his pride.

Ouch. The offhand remark shouldn't bruise his ego like it did. No one had ever complained about his kissing abilities before. So why was he all of a sudden questioning himself? Rather than give away his true feelings, he laughed it off. "What can I say? I'm good like that."

"A little *too* good, if you ask me. But it's good for the investigation. You almost convinced me you meant it and I should know better." She shrugged as she chowed down, unaware of the fact she'd just delivered a second blow.

"It's good to put on a show in case someone's watching," he said.

"And someone is always watching while on a case," she quipped. "I know I'm new to the restaurant and, therefore, will be under scrutiny until I prove myself, but I can't help the feeling of being constantly watched."

"You're new. Might come with the territory," he said before updating her on Patricia.

"Do you think Bald Guy and Ruddy Complexion were behind the bribe?" she asked point-blank.

"No idea. But I did work with a sketch artist today on that subject." He grabbed his laptop and opened it to show her the sketches filling the screen.

"Those look good," she said, then pointed to Bald Guy. "He had a dark mole near the tip of his nose."

Quint took note.

"And Ruddy Complexion had thicker eyebrows." She examined the sketches for a long moment. "Other than that, these are on point."

Quint made the notations and sent an email to Aaron to make the changes.

"What did you find out in town?" she asked when she'd brought him up to speed on the rest of her day. Her plate was clean and her glass empty.

"Turns out Cricket Creek's Cricket Toss Festival used to use live crickets," he said with a forced smile.

"For real?" She scrunched her nose up and it only served to make her adorable.

"According to the lady who runs the post office, they stopped doing that years ago. Now all the critters are stuffed and no one gets hurt in the festivities." He polished off his meal and water glass in record time. The food at Greenlight was top-shelf. Of course, that could be part of the distraction. If folks showed up for the food and the live band, money flowed, and people had a good time. No one would dig too deep into the financials.

"At least they stopped. That's good," she said.

"You might want to hold off on your relief. They serve cricket pie and fried cricket," he said, unable to imagine a worse taste than either of those two.

Her entire body shook. "Oh, heck, no."

"Not exactly going to make the menu at Greenlight," he quipped.

"What else haven't we covered?" he asked, before remembering to give her the new key for the changed lock.

"I already know where you stand about marriage. Are you in a relationship?" she asked, catching him off guard with this line of questioning.

"Whoa there. I should have specified *work* questions," he said. "Ask away. While we check the footage from the past twenty-four hours."

He rinsed off the plates and then left them in the sink to be dealt with later. He slipped off his boot and brought his laptop over to the couch as he updated her on Lionel's situation.

"Do you mind if I grab a shower real quick? I need to wash the work ick off me," she said.

"Go for it. I'll go ahead and start." This was the tedious work of an investigation. Things didn't work in real life as they were portrayed on television. There was a whole lot of sorting through footage, gathering information, and then waiting. In life, cases weren't neatly wrapped up in less than an hour. He grabbed his laptop and checked the employee roster at Greenlight.

Quint heard the spigot being turned on in the room behind where he was sitting. An image of Ree slipping out of her clothes and into the water assaulted him. He gave himself a mental headshake, trying to erase the image. They didn't lack a spark between them but it was good she didn't seem attracted to him in a greater sense. Seriously. All good.

Running through the recording, Quint snapped a couple of screenshots. There were three repeat custom-

ers from yesterday. He opened a file and typed in the
license plate numbers with a pic of each driver and their
vehicles. He then sent the documents to Grappell. There
was a dairy delivery around back that he took note of.
Wednesday whiskey. Thursday dairy. Chef had come in
both mornings by 7:00 a.m. with his arms full of bags of
fresh ingredients. He made three trips to his sports car
on Wednesday and five this morning, which probably
coincided with anticipated business levels. Naturally,
there'd be more customers on live band night. At least,
that was the working assumption from his experience
surveilling other restaurants.

Chef was in and out within an hour before returning
three and a half hours later, presumably ahead of the
lunch rush hit. No surprises there. Could the man pushing fifty be running weapons in those bags? Granted,
looks could be deceiving, but Chef's short, apple-shaped
body and hair that was graying at the temples made him
come across as innocent. Despite the fact it didn't seem
likely he was guilty, it was too early to cross anyone off
the suspect list. Besides, trucks made the most sense in
terms of moving the kind of volume that would have
caught his agency's attention.

The sound of water shutting off behind him sent his
thoughts back to the place they didn't need to go with
Ree. Shoving them aside proved trickier than he'd have
liked. He'd been distracted by her before and could
have cost them their credibility. Quint refocused on
the screen as he watched a guy go out back and have
a smoke while he waited for someone. And that someone was Charley.

REE TOWELED OFF and dressed in her pajamas, thinking about how awkward she'd become with Quint after

their kiss at the restaurant door. Seeing him standing there, waiting, had thrown her off-kilter. And then she'd tripped all over herself in conversation with the man.

She sighed. What could she do? Pick herself up and move on.

After brushing her teeth, she stood at the door ready to join him in the living area, doing her level best to forget how incredible his lips were when they were pressed against hers. And how right the world felt when she was in his arms. Ree had always relied on herself. Growing up with four brothers had toughened her up, taught her to depend on herself, and given her one wicked sense of humor. So the reaction she was having to Quint caught her off guard.

There was more heat when she was in the same room with him than during all of her past relationships combined. There was something a little unnerving about her attraction to him, an attraction there was no way he possibly reciprocated. He was going all in for show in order to sell them as a couple despite the bits of encouragement she'd received from him. It seemed he was trying to convince her, too. She took her hat off to the man. He was doing a great job of making her believe there might be something special brewing between them.

Ree could admit she'd been in a string of past relationships that didn't do much for her. Except Preston. He'd been different. She could blame her lack of interest in long-term dating on the focus on her career, but that wasn't exactly true. There hadn't been anyone who made her want more than a few dates or a casual fling. There hadn't been anyone who caused her heart to feel like it might explode out of her chest into a thousand flecks of dust if he walked out on her. And there hadn't been anyone who could kiss her so thoroughly that she was probably going to be ruined for every other man for life.

Another sigh and she was ready to face Quint. It was a short walk into the living room, so not a whole lot of time to rid herself of the aftershocks of her realizations. He sat there on the couch, barely glancing up at her as she entered the room. Rightly so. They weren't in public now and he could drop the facade.

He patted the seat next to him without looking up. "Want to see my notes so far?"

"Yes," she responded, hearing the frog sound in her own throat. She took the seat next to him and tucked her phone underneath her leg. Out of the corner of her eye, she saw him wrinkle his nose. It made her want to sniff herself to see if she had body odor but she'd just gotten out of the shower so that was impossible. He might not like her choice in bath products. She needed to get over it all because she'd never been one to get inside her own head about the lavender bodywash she used.

Quint pulled up a document and explained what he'd observed so far. He brought her up to speed on Chef's routine.

"Is it strange the barmaids come through the back door instead of the front?" she asked.

"It might be but I don't think it's unusual considering they enter while customers are already in-house dining. They probably don't want to parade them in front of the tables while people are still eating," he stated before picking up a small device from the coffee table. "This should help us figure out what's going on in the breakroom."

"Right. I meant to ask about a listening device," she said.

"I didn't want this to be anywhere near you for your

first couple of days at Greenlight in case Charley or one of his cohorts suspected something might be up with you," he said. "I do think it's safe now, so you can drop it in the bottom of your handbag so it'll be on-site when you are."

"Of course, we don't have any evidence so far that would convince a judge to give us a warrant so we can listen in," she stated.

"Exactly. I'm planning to place a similar device out back but I need to make certain there are no cameras back there that might bust me. Have you seen anything that might indicate there are?" he asked.

"I haven't been out back yet," she said. Her gut instinct said Charley was a smart character and he would take precautions.

Right now, she wanted to ignore the way her heart pounded in her chest when she breathed in Quint's spicy masculine scent and home in on finding answers.

Chapter Nine

Quint wrinkled his nose again as he breathed in Ree's fresh-from-the-shower, lavender scent. She had an effect on him like no one else. Was his attraction to Ree inconvenient? Yes. Was it getting in the way of his better judgment? If he thought so, he needed to pull himself from this case immediately. The only question that mattered was whether or not he could contain it and continue in a professional manner, because when her mouth was moving against his, all logic flew out the window and he was engulfed in a flame that threatened to turn into a raging wildfire.

He pulled up the document for Ree, noticing the excitement in her voice. Was she on to something?

She inched a little closer as she studied the screen like it was finals week in college. Her tongue darted across her bottom lip, and he tried to ignore the silky trail it left.

"What is it, Ree?"

"Phillip." She pointed toward a blond-haired guy from truck number two. "I'm almost a hundred percent sure I overheard Adrian call him by this name at some point."

Quint took down the information, placing a question mark next to the name.

"He must be a regular if Adrian knows him," she said. "I wish there was a break in between shifts so I could really talk to her. You know, ask for the lay of the land. Find out who is who and some background information on everyone. But that would be difficult to do without sounding like an investigator."

"True. If we're too eager or ask too many questions it could put the spotlight on us," he said, realizing he had to be more careful after the boot incident. It wasn't like him to be sloppy and he sure hoped he was able to cover, but he didn't like making mistakes. She nodded. "We might be in this one for a few weeks, a month." He glanced at her. "Or it could be done in four days. My experience has been all over the map."

"Somehow, I don't think this one will be like that," she said. "But if we're going to be a couple for longer than a few days, we should probably dig a little deeper into each other's lives."

He didn't mind sharing a little bit about his background for the sake of the investigation. Plus, a surprising part of him wanted to talk to her about Tessa.

"Do you know about my former partner?" Quint asked on a sharp sigh, figuring he needed to get that part of his history out of the way. He might have a desire to share but that didn't mean it was going to be easy.

"I think I heard something," she admitted.

"Do you know what happened to her?" he asked.

"I can piece bits of the story together, but I'd like to hear your version," she said, taking in a slow breath.

"She was killed in the line of duty when we were working with another agency," he said. "You know how it is. We don't always have time to get to know each other or rehearse before it's go time."

"Those little things like who likes to come in from

the right get glossed over," she said. "It's one of the easiest ways to be killed on the job."

She did know and it sounded like she had a story to tell. Had her father's high-speed crash resulted from another agency getting involved?

"Tessa." He flashed eyes at Ree. "That was her name. Tessa was more than my partner."

Ree's gaze widened and he realized the implication.

"She was my best friend," he quickly added.

"Were you in love?" she asked before seeming like she tried to quickly reel the question back in.

"I loved her but not in the romantic sense," he admitted. "We had a long history and were basically the same person on the inside."

"Did you ever date?" she asked.

"No, because I think we always knew we were too much alike to be anything more than friends," he said. "Plus, it was much more like brother and sister. I'm sure you can relate to the thought of dating one of your brothers being less than appealing."

The puckered face she made proved it. She fauxgagged in a way that was both endearing and funny.

"That's basically the way I felt about Tessa. I will always love her but dating was always out of the question for both of us. She was pretty but I was never attracted to her in the same way that…" Had he really just almost admitted to an attraction to Ree? "Suffice it to say that we never even tried to go there with each other. We bonded over similar upbringings and had a lot in common, not the least of which was going into law enforcement. We both had someone step in during a critical time in our lives whom we credit with saving us."

"Parallel lives?" she asked.

"You could say that," he said. "Except that she got into a relationship that ended with a pregnancy."

"Ended?"

"The guy bolted the minute he found out Tessa was carrying his child. Said it couldn't be his and accused her of cheating on the relationship." Quint fisted his hands. He flexed and released his fingers a couple of times to work off some of the tension of talking about it. Tessa being treated badly was a sore subject with him.

Ree surprised him by reaching over and touching his hands. "He sounds like a real jerk. Why is it that smart, beautiful women can walk into the trap of falling for a creep?"

Her words were balm to soothe a wounded soul. She brought more of that light to the darkest corners inside his soul.

"This guy doesn't want to ever run into me in a dark alley," he said, realizing that was probably the wrong answer and not caring. Five minutes alone with Mr. Jerk and the guy would think twice about getting a woman pregnant and then accusing her of sleeping around to get out of his responsibilities. Of course, Tessa could have forced a paternity test once the kid was born and gotten child support at the very least. But she hadn't wanted anything to do with a man who could walk away from his own flesh and blood like that. Based on personal experience with his own non-dad, Quint couldn't agree more.

"Or me," Ree added, as indignant as he was. "Or any one of my brothers."

"Sounds like you had the family we all wished for," he said.

"We have our problems and disagreements, believe me, but we love each other to the moon and back," she said. The warmth in her eyes poured more light into the dark.

He'd read as much in Shane's voice during their phone call.

Ree was studying him when he brought his gaze up to meet hers. "What aren't you telling me about the situation?" she asked quietly.

THERE WAS A storm brewing behind Quint's eyes, a storm she recognized from the conversation they'd had at the table right before he'd shut down and walked away earlier.

"About Tessa?" he asked, and she could tell from his tone that he was holding something back.

"Or the situation in general," she clarified. "What exactly happened on the bust?"

"Other than the fact she died?" he asked, his cold words cutting a hole in her chest. He seemed to regret his word choice immediately when he added, "It's all still a little raw and I'm a whole lot of angry. I didn't mean for that to come out the way it sounded or be so blunt."

"You know what? You don't have to apologize to me for being human," she said. Growing up around guys had made her able to read through the lines when something was aimed at her or the world. Quint's anger fell into the latter camp.

He didn't speak for a long moment. But when he did, he said, "Thank you. I can't say that anyone has understood what I meant rather than what I said before. I'm generally the king of miscommunication in relationships."

"You're welcome, Quint. Here's the thing. We might be here for two more days or two months. Neither of us ever really knows what the future is going to bring, especially on a case. So, if we can really talk and do a little good here between us, it'll make the time in between following up on leads or general investigating a whole lot more meaningful." Ree surprised herself with the realization even though she meant every word. Truths like this came from the heart and she couldn't have scripted it any better to get her point across.

Quint rocked his head.

"You're right," he said. "I just don't normally talk to people."

"Ever?"

He shook his head. "Not since Tessa."

"I'd like to be friends, Quint." This whole attraction welling up inside her, gaining steam, wished for something else, something more. But she would settle for friendship.

"She shouldn't have died," he confessed. Saying the words out loud seemed to take a lot of energy. "It was my fault."

"I can't imagine that to be true," she said.

"What makes you say that?" he asked.

"Because you aren't the kind of person who would go back on an assignment if you had been responsible for someone's death. You would punish yourself for years to come and I highly doubt you'd ever do the same job again," she said.

He nodded.

"The reason it's my fault is because I let her convince me to keep quiet about the pregnancy when she should have been on desk duty. Now my godchild is…"

The news Quint was to be a godfather to Tessa's baby caused a half dozen puzzle pieces to click together about the strength of their bond and the amount of guilt

he must be feeling for letting Tessa down, like he believed he had.

Ree highly doubted Tessa would blame Quint for
keeping her secret, but the blow that would cause to a
person like Quint would devastate most others. The bur-
den he'd been carrying around with him at the double
blow would crush a lesser human.

"I'm so sorry," she whispered as she leaned into him.
She had no idea, at that point, if her touch was welcome or not but it was all she had to give in the way of
comfort. There was no way in hell she could sit idly by
and watch him suffer if there was anything she could
do about it.

He wrapped his arms around her, so she scooted
closer. The steady rhythm of his heartbeat against her
body comforted her beyond words and she could only
hope he felt half the same as her in that moment.

"It's not your fault," she said quietly, reassuringly.

"Yeah?" he asked and she could hear his voice break.
"Because it sure as hell feels like it is exactly my fault.
I had the power to stop her from doing something that
caused her to die. I should have been the one to force
the desk duty issue sooner so she would still be here,
dammit."

There was so much pain and anguish in his voice
that her heart nearly cracked in half.

"I know you feel that way and I know it feels like the
truth right now. But you would never have done anything to hurt Tessa or her baby," she said in as calm a
voice as she could muster. She drew on all the compassion she had when she added, "Other people's choices
are not your fault. You did what she asked because you
trusted her to make the right decisions."

"I shouldn't have and then she would still be here

holding her daughter in her arms instead of..." His distress was palpable.

The sound of beer bottles being slammed against a wall broke into the heavy moment. Quint kicked into gear as immediately as Ree did.

"Boot," she reminded as it seemed to dawn on him, too.

He bolted toward it, taking the extra few seconds to strap it on as she flew to the window, listening.

"Two male voices," she whispered before risking a peek. "Charley just came running out the front door with Phillip." She paused a couple of seconds to watch as Quint took off toward the front door. "Oh, goodness."

"What's going on?" Quint's fingers were already wrapped around the door handle.

"They're arguing," she said.

"Is it possible Phillip's drunk?" he asked, pausing at the door.

"From here it looks so. I'll ask about it tomorrow at work and see if I can get anything else. It'll make a nice conversation starter with Adrian," she said as Quint backed away from the door.

"It's getting late and you need rest if you're going back there for the whole day again," he finally said. "I'll grab a shower."

"Quint?" she began.

"Yeah?" He stopped halfway across the room but didn't turn to look at her.

"Thank you for trusting me earlier," she said. "It means more than you could ever know."

"It's a two-way street," he said quietly. There was a stillness to his voice that brought her nerves down a few notches after the excitement. "And I'd appreciate if you kept everything I've said between us."

"I wouldn't tell a soul," she said, hearing the defensiveness in her own voice. Rather than apologize for it, she left it out there.

"There's more to it but that's as far as I can go with it tonight," he said. There was a detached quality to his tone now. So she shifted her focus to Charley and Phillip and the buzz of questions she anticipated at the beginning of tomorrow's shift.

Chapter Ten

Ree arrived fifteen minutes early to work the next day. The minute she walked into the kitchen, Chef greeted her.

"I just called your husband," he said, looking mighty proud of himself. "He sounds like a good guy."

"I'd like to think so," she said with a friendly wink.

The gesture seemed to endear her to the older man's heart.

"He's coming over after I set up for the lunch rush to take a look at my machine," Chef said.

"Thanks for giving him the chance," she said. After the way she and Quint left things last night, it was hard to rally the fun-loving newlywed act. Her heart went out to him for what he'd been through and she wished there was something she could do to ease his pain.

"Here's hoping he can fix the problem," Chef hoisted his glass of water in the air in a mock toast.

"Yep," she said, remembering the listening device she had stashed at the bottom of her purse. She held up her handbag. "I better put this thing away and get ready for my shift."

"Hope the tips are good today," Chef said.

She really hoped he wasn't involved in any way because Chef had wormed his way inside her heart. She also realized she couldn't afford to let anyone but Quint in. It was too risky because she could miss a critical piece of evidence if she had blinders on. And then there was the simple fact that some people who seemed amazing on the outside were hardened criminals. Some people had an ability to compartmentalize their lives like nobody's business.

"I'll be right back," she said, leaving him to put away her handbag. She hoped to get a little more insight into conversations among kitchen staff later. Pele and Craig kept to themselves, and Eddie only ever nodded and smiled. When her shift started rocking and rolling, it would be game time and she barely had a chance to breathe, let alone gain valuable intel. She needed to feel Adrian and Zoey out to see if they were on to her after the Sarah and Marcus debacle. Of course, she realized Quint was working hard behind the scenes. She also figured him getting into Chef's computer was a huge win. At the very least, they might be able to rule him out as a suspect.

Ree walked out of the breakroom to find Chef almost exactly where she'd left him a minute ago. "So, did you hear about what happened last night?"

Chef shook his head. He walked a small square and then said, "This is my domain. What happens outside this area is none of my business."

"Smart," she said, figuring he was loyal to Charley at the very least.

He leaned over the metal counter. "I'll tell you what, though. A guy has been giving Charley a hard time lately. This is the third time this person has shown up in the past few days." Chef threw his hands in the air. "Something about money owed but it must be personal. The guy isn't one of our vendors to my knowledge."

Adrian bolted in last minute, looking in a frenzy and breaking into the conversation.

"Has Charley been around today?" she asked as she scurried past.

"I haven't seen him yet," Ree said, before giving Chef a smile and exiting the kitchen.

Zoey was on her side of the room, checking bottles and saltshaker lids. She didn't speak a whole lot and definitely not to Ree. She figured this might be a good time to strike up a conversation and get a feel for Zoey and her situation. If Adrian's suspicion was correct that Zoey was in some type of trouble, Ree had to intervene before she moved on from the investigation.

"Hey, did you hear what happened around here last night?" Ree asked.

Zoey didn't turn around. "No."

"It was a drunk guy," she continued. "I think his name is Phillip. Do you know him?"

Zoey shrugged. She wasn't much more than skin and bones despite a beautiful face.

The glass door opened.

"Looks like we have our first customer," Ree said to Zoey, trying to build some comradery.

Zoey turned to the side and nodded. There was a fresh-looking bruise on her forearm that she was trying to cover with makeup. Granted, Ree could attest to the bumps and bruises that came with this job, but her warning bells sounded nonetheless.

Holding her tongue for now, Ree headed back to her own station as Adrian returned to the room.

"What a day," Adrian said, wiping down her shirt that was markedly wrinkled. "And it hasn't even gotten started yet."

Adrian rolled her eyes as Zoey took the first customer to her own station.

"What's wrong with her?" Ree asked, feigning frustration.

Adrian shrugged as the second customer came in.
"I try not to get too involved. You know what I mean?
Everyone has to do their own thing and it's best not to
ask too many questions."

"So true," Ree agreed despite this going against everything she believed in and was trained to do. Helping
others was embedded in her DNA. "I shouldn't stick my
nose where it doesn't belong."

"Especially not around here," Adrian said before
seeming to catch herself. She glanced around before retying her blouse. Did she know something? She had to.

Thankfully, more customers started filing in and the
rest of Ree's shift became a blur. She was more than
ready to get home and put her feet up after cashing out
her last table.

The car was gone, as was Quint. A note on the fridge
read: *Out helping Chef. Be back soon. Lunch is in the
fridge. Love, Q.*

Ree spent her break cleaning her boots and munch-
ing down on the sandwich he'd made for her. As much
as she loved to rely on nobody but herself, it was nice
to be able to lean on someone else for a change. It was a
foreign thought to her that she could maintain her independence and still draw strength from someone. Funny
to think this hadn't occurred to her before age thirty-six.

When this investigation was over, she had a lot to
chew on with regard to her views on relationships.
There really had only been one person in her past she
could see herself dating long-term. Preston. Had she
been too hasty to cut off their relationship after their last

fling? The old cliché about absence making the heart grow fonder made her wonder if that was the case here. Because she was starting to miss Preston. Or maybe it was just being in a relationship that she missed. Dating her brother's best friend came with complications. The downside had been Shane knowing too much about her personal life. With four brothers, going out with someone who didn't know her family or wasn't friends with one of them had proved difficult enough. When she'd been in school, there wasn't really a way out of it. Now that she was grown, however, she'd made a promise to separate her dating life from family. There'd been too many times when one of her brothers had intervened on behalf of a friend.

Did she want to deal with that for the rest of her life? And why did her mind snap to wishing she could find a man like Quint out in the real world?

QUINT PULLED UP in front of the cottage-style house in town off Main Street. From the outside, Chef's place could best be described as tidy. There were window boxes filled with fresh flowers and the yard was nicely manicured.

A bright yellow sports car roared up behind Quint. The man Ree had described as Chef came out of the driver's seat. He made a beeline for Quint as he slowly exited his clunker.

"Sorry to keep you waiting. I had to prep for the lunch shift so Pele could take over while I'm needed here and then the requests for help didn't end until most of the customers were gone," Chef said, waving his arms in the air. By the time he reached Quint, the man's cheeks were ruddy.

"I just got here," Quint responded.

Chef offered a firm handshake. Quint could see how easily it would be to like the man. He had a calm demeanor and seemed genuine.

"I can't get the thing to fire up anymore. The screen went black and won't come back no matter what I do," Chef said, motioning toward his home.

"Let's go inside and take a look," Quint stated. "Unless you want me to take it home with me and tinker with it there."

"No. No. I can't imagine trying to pack it up. See if there's anything you can do to save it." Chef headed toward the front door. He turned his head to one side as he put his hand on the knob. "No locks needed here in Cricket Creek." True to his word, he opened the door without a key.

"Nice thing about a small town," Quint agreed. "My wife and I are from the Houston area, so we still keep everything locked. Cars. Cabin door. It's a force of habit."

"Life here is an adjustment," Chef agreed. "I moved here two years ago after owning my own restaurant in Dallas. I got jumped one morning on my way to the farmers market and decided no more. I reached out to a few friends and one connected me with Charley. It's been a quiet life for me ever since. Once I got out of the hospital."

Chef turned around and lifted his sleeve to reveal a four-inch scar.

"Knife?" Quint asked.

"From my own restaurant. One of my bar customers was arrested two days later," he said. "The guy came in every Thursday night for three months. Barely spoke to anyone and ordered the same meal every week.

Seemed nice enough but I guess he was casing the place." Chef shrugged.

"That's a nasty scar," Quint agreed. He lifted one leg of his jeans to reveal a similar mark from a gash on his shin four inches above the boot. "Glass coffee table shattered on a move."

Chef winced in sympathy and the attempt to establish common ground seemed to do its trick. The man's shoulders relaxed as he nodded. "Tough business."

"Especially when a piano fights back," Quint said with a chuckle.

"Ree told me." Chef winced again.

"There's a reason it's for young men," Quint quipped. He motioned toward his boot. "But this one helped me realize how ready I am for a desk job."

"The moving world's loss is my gain," Chef said.

"Let's see what I can do."

The inside of Chef's home looked a lot like the outside. There were vases of fresh flowers on most surfaces and the place could be described as tidy. The decor might be simple and clean, but it had a nice aesthetic.

"The second bedroom is my office," Chef said as he walked down a short hallway. The door was open and the room barely big enough to accommodate a desk, chair and bookshelves along one wall where a closet might have once been.

"I'm guessing this is the offending computer." Quint motioned toward the desktop.

"That she is," Chef stated.

"By the way, the chicken and waffles were the best things I've eaten all year," Quint said with a lot of enthusiasm. He wasn't kidding and it probably showed. He'd learned a long time ago to be as authentic as possible while undercover. It really was the best way to sell himself. Staying as true to himself as he possibly could was key. Otherwise he ran the risk of tripping himself up with a lie.

"Music to my ears." Chef's grin was almost ear to ear.

"Okay, so I'll start with the obvious." Quint made his way around the desk and checked the power outlet to make certain the cord hadn't jiggled loose. His initial thoughts on Chef was that the man was innocent. He had a traumatic experience in a bigger city then chose to move where he could keep his door unlocked. The probability this man was involved in bringing crime to this town was slim. Still, Quint might find something on the man's employer on the computer. "It is plugged in."

"I didn't even think to check," Chef admitted, hovering at the door.

Quint pushed the power button. "It's looking like the system is booting up and the fans are spinning." This was going to be an easier fix than he'd hoped. "Looks like a monitor issue or the graphics card died."

"How will you tell the difference?" Chef asked.

Quint checked to ensure the monitor was plugged in. "Ah, here's the problem. The video cable from the computer to the monitor has become loose."

After he corrected the problem, the screen came alive.

"I think we've solved the mystery," Quint said with a smile. He was hoping to really get inside the system before he found a solution, but this was where it ended.

"Well, that sure turned out to be easy?" Chef chuckled, walking over to stand behind Quint. "Looks like I need to stay in my lane working the kitchen."

"I'll tell you all my computer tricks if you share your batter for those chicken and waffles," Quint joked.

"Not a chance," the slightly older man shot back. "I'd rather throw my computer out and start over than give away one of my family recipes. But my creditors will thank you for me being able to pay my bills now."

Quint stood up and stepped away from the driver's seat. "It's all yours now. Pay away."

"I can't thank you enough for helping me," Chef said.

"It really was nothing," Quint argued. "But let me know if you have any other trouble with it."

"You might live to regret that offer," Chef stated with a laugh. His demeanor was casual as Quint had messed around on the computer. Another sign the man didn't have anything to hide on there.

A quick glance at the screen said the house and yard was where the tidiness ended. The desktop was cluttered with shortcuts to bank accounts, apps and games.

"I better get back home." Quint glanced at his watch. "Online class starts in an hour."

"Take this with you." Chef hurried into the kitchen, urging Quint to follow. "I baked a loaf of sourdough for you and Ree. It'll pair nicely with this minestrone soup." He pulled a decent-sized container from his fridge.

"There's no way I'll refuse food from you, Chef," Quint quipped, taking the offerings.

Then Chef handed over a bottle of wine. "The fruity notes in this chardonnay will be the perfect complement to this meal. Light a candle and voilà." Chef winked. "Insta-date."

"You're sure making my job easier with my wife," Quint said with a smile. "I appreciate this."

"It's the least I can do," Chef said. "And my name is Lorenzo Rocco. Everyone at the restaurant calls me Chef."

"Pleasure to meet you, Lorenzo." Quint glanced

down at his haul. "I'd offer to shake hands but I don't have a free one at the moment."

Lorenzo got a kick out of the comment. "I'll grab the door for you."

"If you know anyone else who might need help, I'd appreciate a referral," Quint said before thanking Lorenzo again.

"You got it," Lorenzo said.

Quint unloaded his gifts into the passenger seat of his vehicle. He glanced at the yellow sports car with a little bit of envy.

The thought of a date night with Ree felt a little better than it should while working together on an investigation. Quint had never been unprofessional a day in his life and had no plans to start now, no matter how interesting and incredible Ree might be. Dating another agent crossed a line he had no intention of violating. He could use a friend, though. It wasn't until he talked to Ree that he'd realized how much of his and Tessa's lives had been entwined. He and Tessa had become inseparable. Losing her had been the equivalent of cutting off his lifeline.

Plus, there was the whole bit about Ree believing none of the passion in his kisses could be real. His second mistake slapped him in the face as he claimed the driver's seat. Was she already in a relationship? She'd asked him before. Why hadn't he done the same? According to her file, she was single. Didn't mean she wasn't in a relationship. He made a mental note to ask the next time they brought up their personal lives. He hadn't wanted to know earlier, thinking the less he knew about her personally the easier it would be to keep her at a distance.

Why did the thought of Ree being committed to someone else feel like a gut punch?

A few reasons came to mind. He'd opened up to her about Tessa. Quint also found that he actually liked talking to Ree.

Shoving the thoughts aside, he focused back on Lorenzo. In Quint's experience, a man who had something to hide locked his doors. Based on Quint's assessment of Lorenzo's openness and general disposition, he moved over to the witness list.

The other person of interest from the kitchen was Fender, the food expeditor. Then there was the mystery men from last night.

Maybe the bug in Ree's purse could turn up a clue.

Chapter Eleven

Ree finished another ache-inducing, foot-breaking shift, deciding she needed to buy some of those boot inserts from Dr. Scholl's. Quint waited at the door, as usual, as she made her exit. Her chest squeezed at seeing him standing there and warmth flooded her body.

This time, when he greeted her, he threw his arm around her neck and walked her to the cabin without a kiss. It was probably for the best. A person shouldn't get used to being kissed so thoroughly by another agent. Plus, they'd successfully sold the lie about being a couple. No one seemed suspicious in the least about their relationship status.

When he unlocked and then opened the door, she gasped.

"Where did you get all this?" she asked. The table was set; candles were lit. There were roses on the table.

"Grappell finished your social media page this afternoon. He pieced together a few pictures but thought we should have recent ones about embarking on our new life," Quint said. "He wants us to take one tonight."

"Good idea," she said, tamping down her disappointment. "I'll just change out of this uniform and throw it in the wash. Be right back." She set her phone on the table. "Why don't you go ahead and set up the shot you want."

This wasn't a real relationship. She and Quint weren't newlyweds. They weren't even friends in real life. He was a veteran agent and she was fortunate enough to get to work with him. Blurring the lines between work and real life wouldn't be good for her. Then again, Ree's mother would be happy to point out that at thirty-six years old, Ree had no life outside of work and no prospects of giving the woman grandchildren.

Ree washed the heavier makeup off her face with a makeup wipe, changed into a sundress and threw in a load of laundry.

"Once we get the picture, we can turn the lights on," Quint said as she joined him in the main living space. "Not much happened on my visit to Lorenzo's house."

She shot him a confused look. Then it seemed to dawn on her who he was actually talking about. "I'm so used to calling him Chef at work."

"Right now, let's get the shot for Grappell," Quint said through gritted teeth.

Ree took in a deep breath and turned on the camera feature on her phone with a swipe, wishing she'd brushed her hair while she was in the bathroom. With the roses, the candles and the bottle of wine that had beads of sweat from being chilled in the fridge and then set on the table, she couldn't help but wish this was reality. The setup was convincing enough.

She snapped a couple of shots of the table by itself so that she could find the best one. Then she took a selfie in front of the table. And then she brought Quint in for the shot.

He stood behind her, his masculine frame dwarfing her. She leaned into his muscled chest and her stomach free-fell. She tried to convince herself it was just the mood that had her wishing this was real. It had been a long time since she'd been on a romantic date like this one. She couldn't remember the last Valentine's Day she'd spent with someone.

Reaching back, she found Quint's hand and brought it around just under her breasts. She held on to him. It took a few seconds for her to realize how tight her grip was. Nerves?

There was no reason for them. This was nothing more than a photo shoot. Try to tell that to her senses every time she breathed in his warm, spicy scent.

"Okay. Hold still," she said, lifting the phone for the couple selfie. She snapped the pic but didn't immediately move. Neither did he. She could, however, feel his heartbeat thumping wildly against her. The frantic rhythm matched her own.

Suddenly, her throat dried up. She tried to swallow but it was basically a desert in there.

Pulling on all her strength, she cleared her throat and took a step forward.

"I got it," she said, and the air in the room suddenly became all kinds of awkward. "Um, should I send the pictures to Grappell or do you want to?"

"They're on your phone," Quint said, turning away from her. He walked over and flipped on the light like it was nothing, but a storm brewed behind those sapphire blues. It was more than a little satisfying that he seemed affected every time they got too close.

"Lorenzo seems innocent," he said, taking a seat at the table before ladling out soup.

"I get the same feeling," she said, taking a chair opposite him after tapping the screen a few times in a flurry. She sent the pictures, so that was good. Time to get her emotions under control and her head back in the game. "Is that sourdough bread?"

"Made fresh for us, apparently," Quint said and his voice came across with the same emotion as someone reading the ingredients on a cereal box. "I have a good impression of the guy." He explained his reasoning.

"This all smells amazing," she said, taking a few seconds to process the shift. "And I do, too."

Quint nodded as he dug into the soup. "Minestrone."

"I could tell," she said. "What about the bug in my purse? Did you get anything there?"

"All I can tell you is that when Charley doesn't want anyone to hear what is being said in the breakroom he turns up music and talks too low to be audible," he said.

"Not exactly the actions of an innocent man," she noted.

"No, they are not," he confirmed.

"But that also tells me you didn't get anything to work with," she stated. "Maybe I can take the trash out and drop a bug outside. There's no way Fender and Charley are only discussing waitresses and how the shift went when they go out there."

"Absolutely not," he said so quickly it almost made her head spin.

"I could—"

"Implicate yourself and give away our whole operation. Do you know how many undercover missions I've had to abort in my career?" he asked.

"No, but I didn't know there'd be a pop quiz, either," she quipped, not appreciating how cold he was suddenly being toward her.

For a split second she saw his jaw muscle tick, and that was not a good sign. Then he shook his head and seemed to laugh to himself. She sure wished he'd let her in on the joke. The temperature around this man could change in a heartbeat.

That wasn't entirely fair but she ran with it anyway. It shouldn't hurt her feelings that he'd snapped back into professional mode.

"The answer is one," Quint said. "It was my rookie year and I made a promise it would never happen again. Because do you know what happens when a cover is blown?"

"The case is abandoned," she said.

"And guilty jerks get to walk free," he added. "They often relocate and it can take years to get anything on them again."

"What about Tessa's case?" she asked without making eye contact.

"We busted the small guys. The lower tier on a crime ring out of Romania," he said.

"Weapons? Trafficking?" she asked.

"Weapons," he said.

"I've heard about a few other Romanian rings. None of it has been good," she admitted.

"This group seemed harder than the others. If one of their own became sick while crossing the border or moving weapons, they literally shot them and dumped the body," he said.

She shivered. "That's ruthless."

"A-12 is the group we spent weeks cracking. And we got in, too. Drugs were involved so DEA showed up on bust day. It quickly became clear there were some political ties to this case, considering the multiagency approach. The governor needed a win against them to counter the fact crime was rising in the state," he explained. "So, yeah, it got complicated."

"Sounds like you arrested A-12," she said, tucking a stray strand of hair behind her ear.

He nodded. "I've always felt like it was the tip of the iceberg, though. One of our informants gave us the name Dumitru before it all went down. Once the dust settled, I checked back. No one arrested went by that name. I've always had a niggling feeling we caught the small fry and missed the big fish. The night of the bust, a motorcycle was parked out front. It was gone by the time the ambulance arrived. A window was open in the middle of January during a cold front, which we all know never happens at night in Texas. Someone else was there and the five guys we arrested seemed worried about going to jail."

"Isn't that normal?" she asked.

He fished his phone out of his pocket and pulled up a file. "Take a look at this."

She studied the information for a long moment.

"Each of the five died in prison within two weeks of each other," she said.

"Two were suspected to have committed suicide. Two were killed. The last guy was put in solitary confinement for his own protection. Guess what happened? He was poisoned. How did they get to him there?" He set the phone down in between them. "No one went to trial."

"So no one could roll over on anyone else," she surmised.

"Exactly. I know I was distracted once Tessa was shot. I can wholeheartedly admit that all my energy went into saving her once the place was secured. But I can't shake the look on the perps' faces when they looked at each other after we arrested them and walked them out," he said. "They seemed resigned to die."

"And that's exactly what happened," she stated. "All very interesting."

He nodded.

"I'm guessing you didn't leave the investigation alone," she said. "What else did you find?"

"Not much," he said. "The trail died with the five guys who were arrested. I shopped the name Dumitru around but have been told by every informant I've ever known that he either doesn't exist or left the country."

"But you don't believe it?" she asked.

"It's a convenient excuse," he said. "Here's the rub. The minute I bring the name up, people get real uncomfortable. Every single time."

"Which means they're scared." She was a quick study.

"Terrified. One of my trustiest guys asked me never to bring that name up around him again. Right after he told me the guy probably went back to Romania," he said.

"I'm sorry," she said. "What happened to the informant who gave you the name Dumitru in the first place?"

"I don't know. No one has seen or heard from him since," he stated.

"Why am I not surprised?" She also realized how much Quint would want to nail this jerk.

Quint stood up and then cleared the dishes from the table. Ree set her phone screen-side down before joining him.

"I got this," he said.

"I'd like to help," she countered. "I feel like I'm getting off too easy around here."

"You're doing all the heavy lifting, remember?" he asked.

"I'm making decent tips," she quipped, retrieving a bankroll from her handbag. She sat down at the table and started counting. "Too bad we don't get to keep any of this."

He smiled.

"Nope. But you can hang on to it for a while until we have to turn it over," he said.

"I'm only working the dinner shift tomorrow, by the way," she said. "The waitress I've been covering for is coming back to work. I figured you and I could run some errands. Grab lunch in town. See if we can meet any more locals."

"Good ideas," he said.

"It's what young couples do who've just relocated to a new area. They make friends," she said.

"Sounds awful," he quipped.

"I'm more of a movie person when I get a night off. Unless there's something to do," she said.

"Like what?"

"I don't know. A concert is nice. I like festivals," she said before adding, "but not ones involving eating or tossing a cricket, cooked or stuffed."

"There's a German beer festival called Wurstfest that's in New Braunfels every year," he said. "Have you been?"

"Are you kidding? Of course, I have. It's one of my grandfather's favorites," she said, practically beaming at the mention of her grandfather. It wasn't hard to realize the two were close. Then again, in a family with four boys and one girl, she was probably his princess. Losing her father must have done a number on the family and had to be the reason for her mother's concerns over Ree's chosen line of work. "Did you know it started out being called Sausage Festival?"

"Glad that name didn't last," he quipped, thinking it was a little too easy to talk to Ree.

Then again, he could use a friend even though the annoying voice in the back of his head tried to tell him the ship had sailed.

"Seriously, though," she said with a laugh that caused his heart to squeeze. When the dishes were done, he turned to find her staring at him. She immediately dropped her gaze.

"So, what about you?" He figured it was now or never. "You asked me if I was in a relationship. Are you?"

Quint suddenly felt beads of sweat form on his forehead as he waited for her answer. It wasn't like he and Ree had a relationship outside of this case. He shook it off, figuring he was just missing his friend a little too much lately. The six-month anniversary of Tessa's death was around the corner.

"No," she said before standing and mumbling something about taking a shower.

Why did his heart hammer against his ribs at the thought of her being available?

Chapter Twelve

Ree finished her shower in record time, trying her best not to think about Quint's question. Why did admitting to him there was no one special in her life stir all kinds of mixed emotions? Rather than focus on something she had no control over, she wished there was something she could do to help Quint get answers on Dumitru. Maybe then he could get closure?

She toweled off, brushed her teeth and then moved her clothes from the washer to the stackable dryer in the hall closet. Thankfully, the cabin had laundry or she would be in a world of hurt trying to handwash her uniform every night.

Her shift had been a real winner. Two tables had stiffed her on a tip despite her giving them amazing service. Adrian had shrugged and said it happened from time to time, but at least Ree was getting Adrian to open up more. She'd said Ree must've drawn the short stick on customers. Even so, Ree earned a wad of cash that she kept balled up with a rubber band. Best not to leave it in her purse, so she tucked it inside a coffee mug and replaced it in the back of the cabinet.

"What should we do tomorrow?" she asked. Quint's gaze was focused on the screen as the sounds of squeaky truck brakes cut across the parking lot. The temptation to run to the window was real. She took in a deep breath and resisted.

Quint's gaze flew to the window.

"Don't worry. The camera will capture the activity," he reassured her, as though he could read her mind. Then again, he was the one with all the experience. Her instincts were good, she realized that right away. But she lacked practice.

"Right," she said, trying not to think about all the mistakes she'd made today alone. Adrian wasn't as chatty after Ree had started asking questions. She'd made a judgment about Chef's innocence and now it was difficult to keep her objectivity with him. At least Quint had the same impression. But she doubted he would let that get in the way of keeping an objective eye on the man. All she wanted to do was keep asking. "I wonder if I should push Adrian for a little more information."

"What do your instincts tell you?" he asked casually.

"To back off. But I want to charge ahead," she said. "There's so much we don't know, and I feel like a sit-down lunch or a reason to have drinks with Adrian could clear up a whole lot."

"Or draw attention to us," he stated.

"There is that," she acquiesced. "I'm also wondering if I should nudge Charley about considering me to be a barmaid since progress is slow with the other waitresses."

"Being too eager might cause Charley to back away from you instead of bring you in closer," he said. He was right and she knew it before he said the words. Still, she wanted to do something more than wait on tables and Charley's 'friends' seemed to like the bar.

"What else did Chef say today?" she asked, tapping her finger on the table.

"I wasn't there for long enough for him to say too much. If it was a test, which I highly doubt, then I seem to have passed," he said. "I couldn't dig into his files since it was a cord issue and not a bigger problem. If I'm honest, I'd hoped to be able to take a look around. But I established trust and that's important."

"Yes, it is," she agreed.

"Looks like I'm up," Quint said, pushing up to standing. "It won't take me long to shower."

Why did those words send warmth swirling low in her belly?

Mentally shaking off her reaction, she cleared her throat. She thought about her last relationship, and was reminded how bad she was at them. There'd been good qualities to her ex. For instance, they'd known each other for a long time, so they were comfortable together. Being away from him reminded her of all the good times they'd shared.

Had Shane been right? Did she keep her running shoes at the door? Was it time to start dating with a different attitude?

Preston was the only person from her past she could see herself going there with. Maybe she should give him a call after this assignment. Or not. The few fights they'd had were over her commitment to work. He'd framed one of them as her lack of commitment to their relationship but he'd been saying the same thing in different ways…he wanted to be her priority over work.

Ree had been up-front with him. She'd explained that she was building her career and that it had to take precedence for now. She'd explained that it wouldn't always be this way, and that once she got established there'd be time for more. Preston had been clear on his stance. He wasn't willing to wait it out.

Curiosity had her wondering what had changed. He had to realize her priorities were still the same. If anything, she was deeper into her work now than before she got her last promotion. Going undercover was an even bigger commitment. Was that the reason she was reaching back for the familiar? She was so outside her comfort zone right now? And had been for the last year?

She didn't know how to grow without pushing herself. Work had to be a priority. There would be plenty of time for a spouse and possibly kids later on down the road. An odd realization struck. Did she even want kids? The honest truth was that she didn't know. She hadn't given much thought to her personal life. It just seemed like she had time.

Had Tessa thought the same thing?

The question struck like stray lightning on a sunny summer day. Didn't everyone take for granted that tomorrow was a given? Despite being in a dangerous line of work, Ree never once questioned that she would come home at the end of the day or assignment. Her mother, on the other hand, reminded Ree far too often how risky the job was.

At least her grandfather had nothing but confidence in her.

Was Ree being naive to think nothing could ever happen to her on the job?

Probably a little, at the very least. Then again, worrying never solved a problem, either. And if she didn't believe with every fiber of her being that she would come home every night she'd probably picked the wrong line of work.

If Preston was reaching out to Shane, did that mean

he'd come to accept her priorities? She could see herself doing long-term with him if he could give her space to develop her career and to figure out if she wanted to have a family or not.

Rather than stew on that any longer when she didn't have any clear answers, she shifted gears. There was something niggling at the back of her mind about this whole investigation, and she had yet to pinpoint exactly what it was. A distraction would be nice. Or maybe she just needed sleep because her thoughts kept circling back to the kisses she'd shared with Quint and the disappointment burning in her chest at the lack of them tonight.

Getting sleep just jumped up a few notches on her priority scale. She settled under the covers, trying her level best not to think about Quint. And mostly succeeded.

As she closed her eyes, he came out of the bathroom. The lights were dim. She pretended to be asleep, figuring this wasn't the time to speak to the man she couldn't seem to shake from her thoughts when she should be thinking about a man she might actually have a shot at a future with.

Rather than beat that dead horse, she rolled onto her side and tried to go to sleep.

Ten minutes ticked by and all she'd done so far was roll from side to side. She heard the occasional click-click-clack of fingers on a keyboard, and wondered what Quint was up to. This was the point in the day when he examined footage.

When she couldn't stand faking being asleep for another second, she sat up. "Find anything yet?"

"Is everything okay?" he asked, not sounding as

caught off guard as she'd suspected he might. "Why aren't you asleep?"

"Can't." She didn't think this was the time to go into the fact she was torn between thinking about her on-again, off-again boyfriend and Quint. She sat up and hugged her knees into her chest. "Are you getting anything?"

"I'm not seeing anything big enough to carry weapons, no matter how hard I'm trying. There's no activity to suggest crates of guns are moving through here," he admitted. "There's something here, though. There has to be. We just haven't found it yet."

"I'm not seeing anything illegal or immoral going on inside, either," she said on a sigh.

"What are we missing?" He tapped his fingers on the sofa's armrest. His cell buzzed and it seemed to catch them both by surprise. He retrieved his phone and checked the screen. "Looks like today was more productive than we thought. Charley is asking if I can come in tomorrow and take a look at his computer. Said Lorenzo couldn't stop talking about what I did for him."

Was this the break they needed?

Chapter Thirteen

Quint figured his strategy of staying away from the restaurant had worked. He was beginning to question whether this establishment was the center for crime the informant had made it out to be, though. The information had come from a credible source, so he was surprised nothing had turned up so far. Then again, his luck might just be about to change.

Coffee in hand, he headed over to the restaurant at 9:00 a.m. as Charley had requested in their text exchange last night before bed. Leaving the cabin while Ree slept had him slipping out the door quietly. The second thing on his mind this morning was her single relationship status. It wasn't any of Quint's business, but he'd asked the question anyway. Then again, maybe that was where she drew the line between work and relationships.

Work was work. Home was home. Quint had a similar philosophy. His went more like he didn't work where he lived. In a job such as theirs, it was easy to blur the lines. Good for her if she'd made the division this early in her career. Becoming best friends with his partner had taken away his objectivity about her. If the two of them hadn't been so personal with each other, Tessa would be holding her baby in her arms right now instead of being buried with her.

The dark thought soured Quint's mood as he opened the front door of Greenlight. He walked inside, shouting a hello. The doors to the kitchen were propped open. Charley appeared, waving Quint back.

"Thank you for coming. Lorenzo is still embarrassed all you had to do was plug in a cord. He did nothing but sing your praises." Charley offered a firm handshake. Quint took note of the man's cold and clammy hand. Was he nervous?

"I don't know about that," Quint stated. "I'm still a work in progress on that front but I'd much rather learn how a computer works than move another one."

Charley laughed at the joke. Good. The trick to working with a creep was to focus on their good qualities and they always had some. Quint had once had to get close to a man who'd murdered his own mother. But the guy loved his fourteen-year-old kid, who was in juvie at the time. So much so, in fact, that the murderer was willing to roll over on a drug operation in exchange for a lenient sentence for his boy. No one was either all good or all bad. Quint had learned to concentrate on the good.

"My books are a mess and my inventory is based on what's in here." He pointed to his head. "I've been told there is a way to automate all this so I'm not doing manual counts. Have you heard of any of this?"

"There are accounting software programs for small businesses that should help with the books," Quint stated. "I hear some even link up to inventory and can place orders for you when stock is down based on what dishes are being sold. But I'm not sure if that is too complicated for what you're looking for."

"I like the idea of help with the books. What about starting there?" Charley asked.

"Fine," Quint said. He was surprised Charley would give access to his books to anyone outside the company, but Lorenzo's endorsement seemed to go a long way.

"How should we go about this?" Charley asked, then said, "First things first, I'd like for you to take a look at how I'm set up now and see what you can improve on."

"Sounds like as good a place as any to start," he said. "I have a ten-thirty class, which gives me an hour or so to get the lay of the land."

Being too available could raise a red flag, Quint knew from experience. Seeming too eager could raise another one. Patience won every time.

Charley's eyes widened for a second in surprise, but then he nodded. "You could come back at any time. Set your own schedule."

"Sounds good. I'll have to do a bit of research to figure out which program would be best. I can also ask one of my professors." Quint added the last part for effect.

Charley kept nodding. He seemed to like what he was hearing.

"I'd like to pay you something for your efforts," Charley said. "Not sure what the going rate is."

"You're keeping my wife employed," Quint countered.

"Still. If you do work for me then you should get paid," Charley said.

"Since I'm still in training, how about you pay me with dinners on the house?" he asked, motioning toward his stool from the other night. "Then, I get to see my bride while I eat."

"Dinner's the least I can do," Charley said. "But we'll start there."

"I've already had a few meals from here. Believe me when I say I'm on the good side of this deal." Quint winked.

The smile on Charley's face said he was proud of his restaurant's reputation for good food. Interesting, though, because while he seemed to care about Greenlight, he was also risking his business by running guns out the back. Or was this being done right underneath his nose? Fender, the expeditor, came to mind. Or it could be a supplier. Or both. Phillip was another mystery.

However, Charley was no saint. The question was whether or not he was involved in other crimes that were feeding into a bigger crime ring.

"Follow me." Charley walked to a small office in front of the breakroom on the left-hand side of the kitchen. It wasn't much bigger than a good-sized closet. A custom-fitted desk with stacks of paperwork on top gave the place a distinctly cluttered feel. There was literally something on every surface, which didn't give him a whole lot of confidence the man's computer desktop was any better.

Quint's house was a complete contrast to this. Some folks might call his decor minimalist, but he didn't collect more than he could use at the time. When he was done with something, he donated it, pitched it, or gave it away.

He cracked his knuckles and looked toward Quint. "No time like the present to get started."

Charley grabbed a piece of paper and tore off a corner. He shuffled a few stacks of papers before locating a pen. "Here are the passwords you'll need." He scribbled a few down and Quint could only hope he could read the handwriting. "Ignore all the curse words. This is what happens when a place keeps kicking back my attempts."

That made Quint laugh.

"I'll be back but you have my phone number if you need anything," Charley said.

"Sounds good. I'll play around in here. See what can be optimized and what can be eliminated," he said. This very well could be a test to see if he could be trusted alone at the restaurant. So Quint would play it cool. In all this clutter, there could be a tiny camera or listening device planted somewhere. Today meant taking a huge step in this case. Cool was the only way to play it. "We can start with the basics."

"Like making sure you have all the right utensils before you start cooking?" Charley surmised.

"Basically, but more like making sure we have a building with a fridge, ovens, etc. before we open our restaurant," Quint explained.

Charley seemed to take to the line of thinking. His grin was wide, and he kept nodding. "I never looked at the computer like that before. It helps me understand its usefulness when you put it like that."

"Score one for technology," Quint said, trying to capitalize on the light mood.

"I'll leave you to it," Charley said. The vibes with this guy were mixed. The intel versus what they were witnessing didn't add up. The expectation he ran a hardcore criminal operation out the back door didn't seem to be panning out.

Quint nodded before taking a seat and grabbing the scrap of paper. The passwords were the best part. There was quite an education in creative cussing built into those.

Maybe he could finally dig around enough to either

find something on this guy or think about moving on from this investigation and calling it a bust. The system booted up fine. Much like the small office Quint was in, the computer's desktop was a cluttered mess. Icons littered the screen. At least the guy had a PC instead of a Mac, so the icons were on a grid. That made it a little bit easier to make sense of them.

First things first: no one needed this much disarray on a desktop. Before Quint could rearrange the icons and clean it up, he needed to figure out which ones were actually being used and also useful for Charley.

Quint made a show of studying the screen. He nodded his head a few times in case there were cameras. Based on what he saw with the desktop, no one around here knew what they were doing with technology.

The first thing he did, though, was uninstall the virus protection software. Next, he built a custom firewall. By the time he finished, his "class" would be starting in fifteen minutes. He located a sticky note pad and a pen, and then jotted down the two changes he'd made before sticking the yellow square on the bottom of the screen. He also opened a new spreadsheet, saved the file to the desktop and recorded the date along with his actions for future reference. He glanced at the payroll versus the schedule and noted the barmaids were paid under the table.

It was too early to install spy software. He needed to get a better lay of the land first. That was okay. This was progress.

And now he needed to get home to update his "wife" on his progress. His heart skipped a couple of beats thinking about her and how beautiful she was with her long silky waves spilled across the pillow.

Quint gave himself a mental headshake to clear the

sexy, sleepy image of Ree as he walked out into the sun and toward the cabin.

REE FIXED A BAGEL. There was cream cheese and jelly, her favorites. She slathered them both on as soon as her bagel popped out of the toaster, and then poured a cup of freshly brewed coffee. She didn't mind doing these things for herself, so it must just be Quint's presence that she missed.

Shaking off the thought, she moved to the table and checked her phone. No messages from Quint.

The door opened, and she was a little happier than she should be that Quint was back. He immediately closed and locked the door before toeing off one boot. He unstrapped himself from the other at the door, leaving them both beside the door.

"Good morning," she said as he turned around to face her.

He took two steps forward before his gaze dropped to her plate. His face momentarily lost all color. "I thought you liked eggs."

"Thought I'd change it up today," she said, unsure why he would care about her breakfast.

"Okay," was all he said before heading over to the coffee machine. He poured a cup as she sat there, dumbfounded.

"Could you explain to me what just happened?" she asked, not ready to let him off the hook.

He shook his head as he turned around and then leaned his hip against the counter. "I had a good meeting with Charley this morning."

Apparently, they were changing the subject.

"What about his computer? Did you get anything to work with there?" she asked.

"Not yet. I'm getting the lay of the land first," he said. "But I do have a sense of how the man works. Disorganized."

"Not when it comes to his restaurant," she said. "The walk-in freezer has to be organized a particular way. Same goes for the fridges."

"Isn't that Lorenzo's domain?" he asked.

"Yes, but I get the impression Charley would have a fit if everything wasn't just so," she said. "He checks everything despite having what appears to be full trust in Chef." She flashed eyes at him. "Lorenzo."

"Charley's office and desktop are the complete opposite," he stated. "So that's interesting. It signals a person who cares about the details of his business. In my experience those folks aren't usually criminals, so it will be interesting to see how this all plays out. Also, the barmaids are not on payroll."

"Oh. Really? Other than dating new-hire waitresses, I agree with everything you've said about Charley, Quint." She picked up the bagel, took a bite and then chewed.

Quint took a sip of his coffee.

"I haven't seen any trucks out back that look like they could be carrying in weapons. We're at square one, but it's still early. I'm gaining trust. I might be able to install spyware tomorrow morning," he said.

"Is that the schedule?" she asked. "Are you going back every morning?"

"That's what we agreed on so far," he said. She couldn't pinpoint the difference but there was a subtle change in Quint. Was this always the case when he went deeper undercover? She wanted to ask but figured this wasn't the time. Not when she was picking up on a strange vibe from him.

"Do you want a bagel?" she offered, trying to find some middle ground.

"No. And I'd prefer if you didn't make yours that way but I can't force you to do anything you don't want to," he said through gritted teeth.

"Do you mind telling me what about my breakfast has offended you to this degree?" Or was it just her in general he seemed offended by?

"You can eat whatever you want. I'd just prefer not to watch." He walked over to the sofa, set down his coffee and grabbed his laptop.

"If you didn't want me to eat this…why did you buy all the ingredients?" she asked, frustration making her unable to let it go.

She should be able to get past it but she couldn't. He studied the screen without looking up at her.

"Are you serious right now?" she asked. "You're not talking to me?"

When Quint brought his gaze up to her it was like all hell came up with him. "If you must know, that was Tessa's favorite breakfast. I bought those ingredients separately, not thinking anyone else ate like her. My bad."

"I had no idea," she said, refusing to feel bad for something she didn't know would be a trigger. This was what it would be like to live with a ghost.

Chapter Fourteen

"It's my fault," Quint said, realizing his mistake. "I shouldn't have snapped at you. To be fair, I didn't want to talk about it at all. I owe you an apology."

"Nope. You sure shouldn't. But I accept," she agreed. Her lips formed a thin line. "I need to get some air." She picked up her plate, and then walked right out the door.

Quint sat there, unsure of his next move. They weren't a couple, and he didn't owe her any explanations on his personal life. So why did he feel like the biggest jerk on earth? Again, he couldn't afford the distraction from the case.

He refocused on his plan. Tomorrow, he could dig around in a couple of apps under the guise of trying to figure out what was needed for the restaurant and what wasn't. If he clicked onto an account he wasn't supposed to, it could be easily explained as housekeeping. In a day or two, he might be able to slip spyware on the system. It was risky and he needed to make absolutely certain he wouldn't be found out.

He wrestled with another thought. Could he bug the office without giving himself away? The clutter would make it easy to hide a listening device around the size of a fly. If it was found, though...

Quint opened his email and wrote a brief account

of their progress to date before sending it over to Lynn Bjorn, the boss. Bjorn was probably in meeting after meeting and wouldn't read the email until around midnight. Quint had learned a long time ago to send anything urgent via text. His boss read emails before she logged off her home computer for the night. This didn't qualify as urgent.

Before he could stand up to check on Ree, he heard male voices outside. Quint raced to secure his "bad" foot in the boot and then slid the other one inside his walking boot. He stopped at the door and listened. There were times to interrupt a fellow agent and times it backfired or caused them to lose momentum in a good conversation.

"I'm not working the lunch shift today, fellas," she said with a voice that bordered on flirty. She might be playing a part but he didn't have to like it. He also had no right to dislike it. Officially.

He couldn't make out a response.

She said, "I doubt my husband would like that."

His chest flared with jealousy. He tried to write it off as being in character.

Ree could hold her own. Clearly. But that didn't stop him from wanting to rip open the door and tell those guys off.

"People have to eat," she said, sounding like she'd rather poke her eyes with needles than be in this conversation. "I'll catch you guys later."

A few seconds later, the door opened, hitting him in the face.

"Oh, sorry," she said when she realized what she'd done.

"No need to apologize. I was just listening to see if you needed your 'husband' to come out and back you up." He made air quotes around the word *husband*. "The door is on me."

"Literally," she said without that trademark sense of humor of hers. However, the spark in her green eyes made him wish he could claim those pink lips again. Part of him had gone into self-preservation mode when it came to Ree. He did what he had to in order to survive.

He couldn't help but smile at her reaction, though. So he didn't try to contain his amusement. "Good one, Ree."

"That's what happens when you grow up with so many brothers. You develop a sharp tongue," she said, sticking hers out at him.

Again, he laughed at the silliness of it. She had a way of breaking through his frustration and making him smile when he probably needed to go to the gym for a couple of hours to work off his tension.

Ree possessed magic like he'd never seen before. All she had to do was make one well-timed wisecrack to break him down. Clearly, his tough-guy skills needed some work.

"All right." He rubbed the spot on his nose that took the worst hit. "Let's talk about work."

"Can't. I have to get ready for my job," she said.

"I thought the plan was to go into town and get to know the locals," he stated.

"It was, until Zoey sent me a text out of the blue asking me to switch shifts with her today." She held up her phone.

"But you just told those guys you weren't working." He must've shot a look because she wiggled her eyebrows at him.

"Did you think I wanted those Neanderthals on my shift?" she asked with a devious grin.

"You really are a force to reckon with," he said.

"Darn right," she quipped. Her smile had a way of shooting straight through a person. No wonder she had a stash of tips bigger than any bootleggers. "And I have to get ready because I don't have a whole lot of time."

"Don't let me stand in your way." He stepped aside and held his arm out like he was presenting a Ferrari at a car show.

"You couldn't. I'd never allow it," she said with more of that spark in her emerald jewels.

"No one would argue that," he said as she passed by him. "Oh, and I updated our boss. Bjorn is up to date on the progress we've made so far."

"Great." Ree disappeared into the bathroom, returning ten minutes later looking ready for her shift. He preferred her in a little more clothing if she was going to leave the cabin, but the uniform couldn't be helped. The white boots uniform showed even more skin, if that was even possible without being a swimsuit.

"You look good," he said.

"Thanks." Her eyes perked up at the compliment.

"We're a newly married couple who has been home far too much since we arrived," he said. "Since we can't have lunch in town, why don't we have dinner out instead?"

"As long as it's not Greenlight, I'll take it," she said. "Don't get me wrong, the food is amazing, but I don't want to spend my night off—"

"Don't worry. I have something much better in mind." If memory served, there was a honky-tonk, boot-scootin' bar that was more tourist attraction than authentic country dive within easy driving distance. As much as he'd rather keep her off her feet, and by that he meant like at the movies, they needed to get out and mingle, just like she'd suggested. Newlyweds rarely stayed in on the weekends.

"Is that right?" She walked over to him and grabbed a fistful of his shirt. She locked gazes and for a split second he saw her confidence falter. She recovered by clearing her throat. "How about walking a lady to work?"

"The pleasure would be mine," he said, not wanting to admit how much he liked their routine.

REE'S SHIFT FLEW by and before she knew it she was refilling ketchup bottles. There should be no surprise there, considering it was Friday. She could only imagine what kind of business the weekends would bring. The money was good. The barmaids had to be bringing in serious cash. Could they be part of the weapons ring? Quint had already confirmed none of them were on payroll.

A man walked in, wearing jeans, boots and a tan shirt with the word *Sheriff* written down one arm. Gaze intent on the kitchen door, he didn't say a word to Ree. His intensity said he was on a mission. Law enforcement officers made her nervous while she was undercover. Officers could generally spot each other half a mile away. Clothes didn't matter. The person need not be in uniform for her to clue in. There was a swagger to their walk and they always held their left arm a little too far from the body, a sign they were used to wearing a holster and accommodating space for a gun. She had to consciously do the opposite in order to untrain some of those habits.

Adrian shot a look and compressed her lips before

shrugging and going back to her duties as she closed out her station. Raised voices could be heard from the back as the kitchen staff came through the dining room and then out the front door. Fender lit a smoke. He walked toward the road and away from the others as he pulled out his cell and made a call.

For a split second, Ree debated following them. Her station was closed out and there was no real reason to stick around. She waved bye to Adrian before heading out and to the cabin.

Chef Lorenzo leaned against the building, thumbing through his cell. He barely glanced up as she passed by.

"See you tomorrow," she said.

He gave her a friendly salute.

At the cabin, Quint was in the middle of a workout session when she walked inside. His shirt was off, and he wore shorts that sat low on his hips. She couldn't tear her gaze away from a bead of sweat that rolled down his chest as he pulled up into another crunch. Muscles rippled with his movement. The man's body was made for sinning. She tried not to calculate out how long it had been since the last time she'd had sex. *Too long*, her body screamed. As tempting as it sounded to have a fling, she'd never been the one-night-stand type. For it to work for her, she had to have an emotional attachment. Different things worked for different people. She had no judgment on how other people conducted their lives. If it wasn't illegal, immoral or didn't hurt puppies, she had a live-and-let-live philosophy.

Despite her convictions, she'd never wanted to have sex with a man more than she wanted to have it with Quint in that moment.

He stood up, picked up the towel he'd been on and mumbled an apology.

"No, don't stop on my account," she said, stumbling over her words like an awkward teenager. "I need to get out of these clothes anyway. You're not going to bother me." The words flew out of her mouth at a surprising pace.

"If you're sure you don't mind," he said with a grin that said he noticed.

"Nope. It's good to keep in shape. Bodies need exercise." Well, hadn't she just handed over all the wisdom? What was she going to say next? The sky is blue? Grass is green?

Before she dug a deeper hole, she fast-walked across the room and to the bathroom where she changed out of her work clothes. She dabbed a little more pink gloss on her lips and blew out her hair. She had no idea what the plans were for tonight or what she needed to wear for them. Rather than interrupt Quint's workout for the second time, she stayed in the bathroom fixing herself up for their date.

When she could stall no longer in front of the mirror, she changed into a cream-colored minidress that she planned to wear her boots with.

Opening the door to the bathroom gave her quite a shock as Quint stood there, leaning against the wall, toweling off sweat before it dripped off his golden, sun-kissed skin. It had been a long time since anyone rattled her nerves the way he did.

She chalked it up to the stress of the mission and moved past him. "All yours."

He thanked her before she heard the door close behind her. No way did she intend to look back. Instead, she marched directly to the fridge for a Coke. The fizzle tickled her throat. Ree retrieved her cell phone and then sat at the dining room table, wishing she could have been a fly on the wall next door before her shift ended.

In the heat of the moment earlier, she'd forgotten to tell Quint about what happened at the restaurant. Could be nothing, she reassured herself. She checked the window. The sheriff's vehicle was gone. Another mistake on her part. She should have stayed focused when she walked through the door instead of getting flustered like a teenager in the same room with a pop star.

Ree checked her cell phone. Shane texted asking if all was well. She suspected her brother was checking up on her since she hadn't responded to Preston. This was exactly the reason she'd separated out her dating life from her family. Her brothers, especially Shane, hovered enough. The last thing she needed was for them to be in her business 24/7 or receiving information about her from another source. When she was ready to talk, she would.

She sighed. As great as Preston was—and he had a whole lot of wonderful qualities—she wasn't sure if she was ready to dive back into that pool. And right now wasn't the time to worry about the man.

Fresh from the shower, Quint emerged from the bathroom. She tried not to stare, or drool, as he pulled a shirt over his head and then shrugged into it.

"I forgot to tell you something when I first got home. The sheriff showed up today at the end of my shift and he didn't look thrilled. He went straight back to the office without making eye contact with anyone. The kitchen staff emptied out and Fender walked away from the others presumably to light a cigarette but he immediately made a phone call," she informed.

"Okay, the activity should be on the recording," he said, moving to the laptop on the coffee table. He took a seat on the couch and raked his fingers through still-wet hair, taming his slight curls. Was he kidding? How on earth could someone be so gorgeous with so little effort?

"I just wish I'd been a fly on the wall when the sheriff confronted his cousin," she said, still beating herself up over not remembering something so important.

"You and me both."

She issued a sharp sigh. It must have been loud because he looked up at her.

"What's wrong?" he asked.

She shook her head, not ready to admit how embarrassed she was about his half-naked body distracting her from her job.

"Whatever it is, let it go," he said.

"Do you?" she shot back.

"No. I can't say that I do. If it made me a better agent, I wouldn't be advising you to do the opposite. Since we seem to be cut from the same cloth, I'll tell you to figure out what works for you and stick to it religiously," he stated. "And if that doesn't work, hit the mat and don't stop working your body until it becomes more tired than your brain."

"Sounds like good advice," she said, wondering if that was exactly what he was doing when she walked in. She also saw how ripped the man was and realized the level of his pain must be as intense.

"Works some days better than others," he quipped, returning his gaze to the screen. Then came, "The sheriff walked inside looking concerned and he left with a scowl on his face. He was inside the restaurant for seven minutes."

"How about Fender?" she asked.

"He stayed outside on his cell phone for another five minutes," he stated. "But it's his body language that interests me. He's waving his free arm in the air. He inhales the cigarette like there's no tomorrow."

"I never have gotten a good vibe from him," she said. "Any chance he's facing the camera?"

"I'll send this part of the video to Grappell for evaluation. See what he can do with it. He can run it through facial recognition. Fender is pacing and when he comes back this way, they might be able to blow this up and read his lips. It's too grainy for us to make anything out," he said. His fingers danced across the keyboard. "There. Now the clip is off." He shifted gears, setting the laptop aside before standing up. "Are you ready to go meet some locals?"

She nodded, hoping they could catch a break while they were out.

Chapter Fifteen

"I feel like I'm missing something here," Quint said as he parked the sedan in a sea of pickup trucks. The legendary country bar on the outskirts of town was large enough to park a fleet of semis in.

"You think?" Ree laughed, and the sound was musical. She'd calmed down considerably on the ride over. "Maybe we should have requested a pickup instead of this ride."

"We would definitely fit in better," he said with a smile.

"Am I about to learn something new about you?" she asked. "As in, you dance?"

"Believe me, I try not to," he said. "And when you see my two-step, you might take those words back."

"I'm sure you're fine at it," she said as he exited the vehicle and then came around to her side to open the door for her.

"At least I have an excuse." He pointed down to his "injured" ankle with the bright white boot strapped on it.

"So do I." She held up her left hand. "I'm pretty sure this gold band is a romance killer for strange men."

"Who knows. It might entice them even more," he

said. He'd seen, heard and encountered all kinds of things during his years as a bachelor.

"That's scary," she admitted, taking the hand he held out to her and using it as leverage to exit the sedan.

"You look beautiful tonight," he said, figuring he needed to slip into the newlywed role before they headed inside. He wasn't kidding, though. She'd taken his breath away when he walked out of the bathroom earlier.

"You're not so bad yourself," she said with a smile and those same sparkly eyes that had him wanting to do things that could get them both in trouble.

Too bad, he thought. Then again, maybe not. Mixing his personal life with work wasn't high on his priority list at the moment. Losing Tessa had hit him on too many fronts. Coworkers needed to be kept at a professional distance.

He put his right arm out for Ree to grab hold of. From the parking lot, he could already hear the music thumping inside. "Shall we?"

"Yes. And I hope they have good food because I could eat my own arm off right now." She took the offering as he broke into a laugh.

"I'm not sure how many newlyweds have the kinds of conversations we do, but it sure would make the idea of getting married a whole lot more tempting," he said, not that he planned to change his single ways any time soon. But no one could argue his point. Being with someone who made him laugh had just made his list of required traits for a serious relationship.

"Laughing is a good thing," she agreed as they walked inside.

It was the dinner hour and the place was already hopping. There was no one on the dance floor just yet but the tables surrounding the sawdust-covered wood flooring were packed. There was no cover charge. A sign near the front door read Seat Yourself.

Quint found a counter-height table on the other side of the dance floor. A couple of plastic menus were sandwiched in between condiments and a container filled with napkins.

Ree wasted no time grabbing two before handing one over to him. "I could probably eat this menu."

He couldn't help but smile. "What looks good?"

"How about we start with the ground beef nachos and then I'll have shrimp tacos," she said after a quick perusal. "And a cold beer."

The waitress turned up by the time Ree finished her sentence. She gave a quick recap.

"All of that sounds good to me. I'll have what she's having and whatever you have on tap," Quint said.

The perky twenty-ish-year-old rattled off a list of options, and he stopped her when she got to his favorite, Guinness.

"Oh, that sounds good to me, too," Ree stated with enough enthusiasm to convince him. "And water, please."

The waitress set down four cardboard squares and he figured she was marking the table to let the rest of the staff know orders had been taken. There seemed to be several waitresses buzzing around, and the casual setting had him thinking there weren't set stations.

"I'll be back with your drinks," she said before disappearing.

Quint reached across the table and took Ree's hand in his, linking their fingers. The move was meant to make a statement to others. The electricity pulsing up his hand gave the whole scenario credibility. He poured on the newlywed loving gaze as much as he could without going overboard. In another circumstance, another situation, another time, he could see himself opening up to someone like her. Ree was special. If he hadn't already done the best-friend-as-partner route and been burned about as hard as someone could be, he could also see himself going there with her.

His heart argued there were quite a few differences between the two. Tessa had been more likely to punch him in the arm or make fun of his anemic dating life. He would be more likely to be her wingman than her date. And he would defend his dating choices and frequency to the grave. So what if Tessa had told him over and over again that he should date women with more... how had she put it?...substance.

He did. There was plenty of interesting conversation. Okay, maybe not so much in the past couple of years, but he'd grown tired of the same get-to-know-each-other conversations. He could admit he'd been going through the motions lately without really putting himself out there.

The truth was that he had Tessa. The person he enjoyed hanging out with the most just happened to be the opposite sex. There were no romantic fantasies with her. Their relationship had been clearly defined from the start and had grown into a deep-seated closeness that rivaled most good marriages. Other agents had joked the two of them were like an old married couple, saying they'd skipped all the fun parts of a relationship and had ended up at the no-sex, best-friend stage of life.

Looking back, he could see they probably weren't too far off base.

"What are you thinking about?" Ree's voice sliced into his heavy thoughts.

He shrugged. "Not much, I guess."

She shot him a look that could have cut through steel. "Don't feed me that line, Quint. I'm not stupid and I have eyes. You were zoned out in thought and I wondered what was running through your mind."

Quint took in a deep breath. "Tessa. I was thinking about her."

His comment really seemed to bring down the mood.

Ree nodded and gave a small, sad smile. "You must have loved her very much."

"It would be the same if something happened to one of your brothers," he admitted. "The pain is unimaginable."

"It's unthinkable to lose someone so young and vibrant," she said. "As much as my brothers can be a pain in the backside, I can't fathom life without any one of them."

"I'm sorry about the mood shift, it's just…"

Ree shook her head. "It's okay. I actually think it's good for you to talk about her. I mean, bottling it all up inside can't be healthy."

"Yeah? I appreciate your concern but we're here for our date night. I don't want to talk about my sister any longer," he said, figuring he needed to provide a cover story in case anyone was listening. There were a dozen tables scattered around. The music was quiet enough to talk over but loud enough to make it difficult to hear anyone who wasn't standing nearby. Try as he might, he couldn't make out what anyone around him was saying unless he tried to read lips.

"Promise me you'll talk to someone about her if not to me." Her serious tone and concerned look made him think twice about what she said. He didn't want to blow her off or pretend he wasn't hurting anymore.

"Okay," he said. "I will. And I'd like the person to be you."

REE SQUEEZED QUINT'S hand in a show of support, trying not to give away the effect his words had on her. One look in his eyes said he would follow through with his promise. She wouldn't mind if he talked to her about Tessa. If he wasn't comfortable enough to do that, all she really cared about was making certain he spoke to someone. No matter what else, Quint had weaved his way inside her heart in the past couple of days of being together 24/7. She cared about what happened to him beyond this assignment.

The waitress showed with drinks. The appetizer soon followed. The music started picking up tempo and volume as the shrimp tacos were served. By the time their bellies were full, a band started setting up on the stage.

"How'd you hear about this place?" she asked Quint after placing her napkin on the table to indicate she was done.

"Are you kidding me?" he shot back and she could tell he was in a much more playful mood by the tone of his voice. "How do you *not* know about Honk-E Tonk? It's one of the most famous bars in Texas after that cowboy movie ten years ago."

"I thought it was called Gillespies," she admitted.

"That was the name in the movie," he confirmed.

She glanced around from side to side, scanning the room for the infamous mechanical bull riding pen. "Where is it?"

"Upstairs." He motioned toward the wooden staircase in the corner that, now that she really looked at it, led to a loft.

"Can we do it later?" she asked before glancing down, remembering he was in a boot.

"You can," he offered. "I'll cheer you on from the sideline."

"Deal." Her heart literally gave a little flip.

"Did you get enough to eat?" he asked, gazing at her with those loving eyes again. This man was a little too good at this undercover thing. Staring into those sapphire blues, she could get lost and trick herself into thinking this was real and not make-believe. Wouldn't do a whole lot of good to fall down that sinkhole.

Her cell buzzed just loud enough to hear over the music. She retrieved it from her purse and then checked the screen. Shane?

"It's my brother," she said to Quint. "I better take this."

He nodded as she stood up, took the call and plugged one of her ears.

"Hello?" she said into the receiver, hoping Shane could hear her over the loud music. Fear gripped her that something might be wrong back home. Shane knew she was on an assignment and wouldn't call unless there was an emergency.

"Hey, sis," Shane began calmly as she got her hand stamped before walking into the parking lot. The sun was descending, creating a bright orange glow in the sky. She thought about Quint and almost texted him to come outside, wondering if this was the exact shade of orange that was his favorite. She imagined it came pretty darn close if it wasn't a perfect match, and she saw the sheer beauty in it.

"Is everything all right?" she asked, bracing herself for bad news. There was no way Shane would interrupt her on an undercover assignment if his world wasn't crumbling.

"I was about to ask you the same question," he stated, sounding a little offended.

"I can't really talk right now but I'm fine if that's what you're asking," she said, confused by how cautious he was being.

"Good to know because Preston called—"

"Hold on right there," she said. "I'm not having this discussion with you, Shane. You're my brother and I love you but this is out of bounds and completely inappropriate under the circumstances."

"Well. I just—"

"Didn't think?" She finished his sentence for him, steaming mad.

One of the kiddos screamed bloody murder in the background.

"You should go take care of that, Shane," she said, leaving no room for doubt as to where she stood on this topic. "Your kids need you more than I do right now."

"Got it," he said. She hoped it was true, because she had no plans to discuss someone she was dating or not dating with her family. If Preston couldn't keep their relationship between the two of them she had no plans to return his texts.

"Bye," she said before ending the call. Her auburn hair had always been blamed for her fiery temper, but her brothers sure knew how to push her buttons. They were probably more to blame for her short fuse than a genetic trait.

Ree took a couple of minutes to walk off her anger before returning to the bar. The minute she stepped inside, she caught sight of the waitress talking to Quint.

The woman twirled her hair around her finger, a sure sign of flirting.

A few calming breaths later, Ree was ready to face her second frustration in fifteen minutes. The way this date night was going she'd be home in bed alone by nine thirty. Okay, the thought made Ree giggle and lightened some of her frustration. She really was going all in emotionally with the fake marriage. Good. She needed to be invested in order to sell the relationship.

"Hey, sorry about that," she said as she walked up to her "husband" and the waitress. She stopped beside Quint and wrapped her arms around his neck before planting a mind-blowing kiss on his lips. "My brother can be dramatic."

"Everything okay with your mom? I was just telling Kelsey about your mom's fall," he said.

"Yes, she's doing much better." She had no idea what he was talking about, so she just went with it.

"I'm still impressed she decided to get on the ladder at her age to clean out gutters," he said, subtly bringing her up to speed.

"My mom is the original DIY lady," she quipped, smiling at Kelsey.

"Are y'all newlyweds?" Kelsey asked.

"How did you know?" Ree asked.

"Shiny bands," she quipped. "Plus, y'all are way too adorable holding hands and cuddling up to each other to be old-timers."

"Guilty," Ree stated.

"How did the two of you meet?" Kelsey continued.

"A pizza place in Austin," she said and then instantly realized that was their first-date story. Her cheeks might have given her away as a red blush crawled up her neck, the glow so bright she could probably land planes if she stood beside a runway. She could only pray the dimly lit room would provide camouflage.

"Actually, that was our first date, honey," Quint said to cover her mistake. "We met at Tony's New Year's Eve party."

"I just totally heard that wrong," Ree stated. "Duh." She made a show of smacking herself on the forehead. "I've literally been working way too many hours lately."

The waitress laughed. She also seemed to know when to make an exit because she excused herself to go check on another table.

"Great job with the jealousy act earlier," Quint whispered into her ear.

"Not so much on the first-date story," she pointed out.

"Don't beat yourself up. We didn't rehearse that one," he said but she couldn't let herself off the hook so easily.

However, with his lips this close, his warm breath on her neck, all kinds of sensations skittered across her skin. Her body became keenly aware of his as he looped an arm around her waist and hauled her against him. He positioned her on his lap and held onto her, resting his hand on her back for a long moment.

If only the jealousy bit was an act. Unfortunately, she wasn't that good an actress.

Her reaction also made her rethink responding to Preston's text. Had she opened a hornet's nest in responding to the first one?

With Quint's arms around her, holding her, all thoughts of another man dissolved. She breathed in his spicy male scent, allowing all that was Quint to fill her senses. It would be so easy to fall for this man hook, line and sinker.

If only they hadn't met on the job, she thought. But

then, that might not matter. He was hurting and leaning into her for support. His emotions were running high and he was channeling them into her right now. The intensity she felt was for his loss and not because he couldn't live without her. The way he made her feel like she was the only woman in the world right now didn't mean there was anything real going on between them. He had to sell the relationship as much as she did. He was clearly doing his part, because a piece of her was starting to believe he'd fallen head over heels in love with her.

How was that for good acting on his part?

The feeling of eyes on her shifted Ree's attention. The hairs on the back of her neck prickled. Was someone watching them?

Chapter Sixteen

"What is it?" Quint asked Ree. He felt her body suddenly stiffen. Every one of her muscles tensed.

She turned enough to whisper in his ear. "Someone's watching us. I can feel it."

"Okay." He feathered a few kisses on her neck, creating an intimate scene for onlookers. Most would redirect their gazes at the public display of affection. Folks became awkward real fast when lovers crossed a line, became too intimate.

With hooded eyes, he scanned as much of the room as he could see from his vantage point. The little moans of pleasure escaping Ree's lips when he shifted in his seat or moved his hands weren't helping him concentrate.

Clearly, he was distracted. He blamed it on the heavy emotions from dredging up the past. There were times when he thought the hole in his heart could never be filled. He certainly didn't deserve to be happy when Tessa couldn't. He didn't deserve to keep doing the job he loved when she couldn't. And he sure as hell didn't deserve to be in love with someone when she couldn't.

How was that for messed-up?

The irony was that he knew, in his heart of hearts, that Tessa would never want him to be unhappy. If she was here, she would be the first one to punch him in the arm and tell him to get over it already. Guilt and shame for letting her down would cloak him for the rest of his life.

Oddly, when he was with Ree, the pain wasn't so great that he couldn't handle it. In fact, it was the first time since the ordeal happened six months ago that he felt a small sense of relief.

"Do you have a visual?" he asked when he couldn't find anyone in the crowd staring at them. The crowd was thickening by the minute as the band kicked off their first song.

"No. It's strange, though, because I could have sworn someone was locked onto us," she admitted, casually casing the room. "Maybe behind us?"

"It's definitely not cool to be caught checking everyone out when we're supposed to only have eyes for each other," he stated. "Don't worry about it. We'll stick around for a while. See if anything comes up."

He could tell she was being too hard on herself when she felt like she missed something, and he respected her for it. It meant she cared a whole helluva lot about what she was doing. Sometimes, the passion could become misguided and a person could become too critical of themselves. Always pushing. Never giving themselves a well-deserved break. Constantly playing out scenarios in their minds when they should be sleeping.

No one operated well under such internal scrutiny. He should know. It was his past.

Was he doing it again? This time with Tessa's death?

He had been over and over the scenario in his mind dozens of times. What could he have done differently? Of course, the most obvious was that he could have stopped her from being there altogether. That was the one his mind kept snapping back to. But on the scene, he should have intervened and stopped her from going inside the building. Of course, that would mean she would have to explain why her partner suddenly didn't think she was fit to go inside like everyone else.

Tessa had given him those eyes that had been so good at communicating to him. They begged him to stop and let her do her job one more time. She'd already said once she became a desk jockey she would always be a desk jockey. Having a kid meant she would change her life. Having the kid on her own meant she needed to insure she would be coming home every night.

Tessa had never stressed about the dangers of the job in the past. She'd been changing before his eyes. He understood, approved even. But dammit, she should have come home that night instead of him.

Before he got too worked up over Tessa, he shifted his focus to Ree.

"I'm going to go sit in my chair now," she said as though she'd been party to the mental discussion he'd just had.

"It'll be good to have us facing opposite directions," he said with very little enthusiasm. The truth was that he liked holding her in his arms. He liked the feel of her heartbeat against his body. And he liked how well she fit him. This seemed like a good time to remind himself they weren't there to bond. He condemned himself once again for losing focus. If he'd been paying closer attention, he might have a description of the person who'd been watching them by now.

Ree moved across the table from him and casually picked up her beer. She glanced around as she started grooving to the beat. Her face was unreadable as to whether or not she was having the same physical reaction to Quint that he was having to her. He needed to know if her judgment was being affected. At least, that was what he told himself.

Setting her beer down, she smiled at Quint. It had the same effect as the sun burning through clouds, warming everything it touched with beams of light.

Quint couldn't help but crack a smile over that one. Since when did he become a poet?

"Did you still want to try the mechanical bull?" he asked when he realized she couldn't find anyone staring at them.

"I'd puke," she said, rubbing her stomach. "I can barely fit any of this beer in."

He had to laugh at her honesty. The beers were mostly for show. Neither would finish theirs.

"I doubt you'll need dessert tonight," he quipped, thinking there were a whole lot of other things he'd like to do instead but couldn't.

She groaned before diverting her gaze, locking onto someone across the room. "It's probably nothing but I've seen one of the guys over there at the restaurant."

"Small towns can be like that," he said.

She pulled lipstick and her phone out of her handbag.

"What are you planning to do with those things?" he asked, curious as to how those items went together.

"Watch and learn," she said with a smirk. She uncapped the lipstick. Held her cell phone up. "Selfie mode turns this guy into a mirror." She applied two coats of a deep red lipstick before pressing her lips together. "We can compare notes later."

It dawned on him that she'd just snapped pictures of the guy in question.

"I know it's still early, but I'm beat from the last few days at work," she said. "Do you want to go home?"

Quint couldn't get to his feet fast enough. There hadn't been anything to see so far, and after watching Kelsey bolt around, he could only imagine how exhausting waiting tables must be for Ree. An iPad that had been attached to the table allowed him to pull up his check and then pay without signaling for the waitress.

Within minutes the two were headed out the door. Quint noticed a male standing near the exit. He had on a red flannel shirt with cutoff sleeves, a pair of jeans and a white Stetson. The man was probably five feet ten inches if Quint had to guess. The reason he wore cutoff sleeves was to show off the arm muscles of a lumberjack. Last time Quint checked, Texas had more cattle ranches than lumberyards. Quint shrugged. The guy looked familiar, though. Maybe going home to look at footage would help place him. Or not. The name came to Quint. The guy was Phillip.

"WHAT WAS PHILLIP doing there?" Ree couldn't stop thinking about the man in the flannel shirt on the way home. There wasn't much in the way of conversation between her and Quint. They were inching along, making progress. Quint now had an in at Greenlight, working on the computer. She was making ground on her relationships with Chef and Adrian. Fender was still a mystery. She hadn't quite figured Charley out yet. And Zoey, that poor young woman, weighed heavily on Ree's mind.

"Your guess is as good as mine," Quint said.

"Are you thinking what I am? He is the one responsible for paying the maid to spy on us?" she asked.

"I'd be lying if I said it didn't cross my mind," he stated.

"Should we turn around and follow him?" She craned her neck around.

"There's no need. He's been behind me for the past three miles," Quint stated. "If we had turned back, we would have played right into his hands. Our cover would have been blown. He looked me dead in the eyes when we walked out." Quint pulled into the parking spot in front of the cabin as the vehicle behind them drove on past. Greenlight seemed to be rockin' and rollin'. Relief washed over her that she didn't have to work tonight. As busy as she'd been over the past few days, she wasn't sure her feet could handle another shift.

A loud voice carried across the parking lot as they exited the sedan. She shot Quint a glance. He nodded. She recognized the voice as Adrian's.

Moving purposefully, they rounded the dark side of the cabin that faced the street. The voice wasn't coming from the parking lot; it came from behind the restaurant. There was a second voice, too. Fender's.

Ree strained to make out the details of what they were saying. She pulled out her cell phone and hit the video button to try to get some kind of recording that could be sent to the lab later. She glanced around, thinking they needed to get closer. Quint was already taking action.

There was a gaggle of trees toward the back of the parking lot, separating the other cabins from Greenlight. The trees also acted as a sound barrier. Quint made eye contact as he eased toward the first tree.

It was a huge risk, but this could be the turning point they so desperately needed in the investigation. Then again, they might end up witnessing nothing more than a lover's quarrel. But Fender and Adrian?

Ree had to really think about that one. A relationship could explain why Adrian had been so secretive and never wanted to talk about anything that went on at Greenlight. It could also explain why she seemed to be so protective of the kitchen. Were there other signs Ree had missed? Would a more experienced agent have seen the signs?

Before she had a chance to work herself up to a point of no return, she followed Quint. Tree by tree, they pushed closer as the pair of voices shot across the lot. It sounded like an argument, from the tone of the exchange. Again, Ree's mind snapped back to the thought they were lovers. Again, she tried to discount the possibility.

Keeping an open mind was the hallmark of a great investigator. It would stop her from missing important details. Removing personal bias out of an investigation could be tricky. Mentally taking a step back to allow the facts to speak for themselves and not locking onto an opinion too early would allow the truth to bubble up to the surface.

She held her phone toward the quarrelers, hoping the sound quality would be good enough for the lab to analyze. This was definitely the time she wished she had a booster with her. They'd had to keep equipment to a minimum in the event Charley had connections to the owners of the cabin. Small towns had their charms and one of them was people tended to know each other. If there was a connection and a favor was called in, the cabin needed to be as clean as possible. Even the laptop's screen saving password was encrypted. The only information someone could get out of "hacking" into his laptop would be exactly what the government agency wanted them to reveal—a fake screen set up by a genius tech agent. The person would be privy to a fake email account set up as Quint's, and a desktop with links to a convincing but fake online computer degree program that appeared to be in process.

Ree strained to hear but couldn't make out the words. Quint's movements were impressive, to say the least. The man was stealth whereas she felt loud. Even his footsteps were silent, not a single crunch. He seemed to feel his way with calm, deliberate steps. She chalked it up to his years of practice and experience.

A door slammed. A curse was shouted. And then the sound of a motorcycle engine roaring to life ripped through the night. Fender took off, spewing gravel underneath his tires. This had all the signs of a lovers' fight.

But Ree decided not to snap to judgment too quickly. She challenged herself to think about what else it might be as Quint linked their fingers and they made their way back to the cabin, careful not to draw attention.

Once safely inside, she huddled up with Quint and played back the video.

"The music is too loud in the background. The way sound carries, I couldn't get a recording that is discernible to the naked ear," she said on a frustrated sigh.

Quint stood there not two feet away from her. His arms were folded over his chest and his head bowed as he listened intently. "No, but I saw you reach for your phone the minute you heard voices. Your instincts are spot-on. It's why I didn't need to reach for mine. I saw what you were doing."

His reassurance helped but her frustration was still high at her mistakes.

"You probably already realized you can send this off to the lab for analysis," he continued when she didn't respond. "And you're right. They have pulled off some miracles. We can upload the video right now and get its place in line for analysis. Grappell can manage the process for us from there."

She gave a slight nod at that.

Quint walked over to his laptop and booted it up. An alert filled the screen after he entered his password.

"Someone has been in the cabin," he said.

Ree couldn't get beside him fast enough. She perched on the edge of the couch, sitting so close their thighs touched. She'd grown accustomed to the electric current that came with contact. Anticipated it. Needed it?

Pushing the thought aside, she stared at the access warning that filled the screen. When someone besides Quint tried to access the computer, a picture was taken.

Quint's fingers danced across the keyboard.

"Zoey?" she said. "What on earth would she be doing here trying to get into the computer?"

Quint seemed to be thinking long and hard. "If the abuse theory holds water, she might have gotten in a fight with her boyfriend or been kicked out of the motel where she was staying."

"We make good tips," Ree countered. "Why wouldn't she have enough money to pay for a place?"

"Her boyfriend could have rented it," he offered. "If he left her high and dry, she might not have another place to go."

"You changed the locks." Ree's eyes widened. She glanced around. There weren't a whole lot of places to hide in this small cabin. She held a finger up before popping to her feet. Not three minutes later, they cleared the place before proceeding. Thankfully, Zoey wasn't there, or she would have overheard too much.

"A good skeleton key would work on what I bought from the hardware store," he supplied.

"Seems like Zoey has many talents. I can't help but

wonder if she's involved with Phillip in some way." Ree moved to the fridge. Opening the door, she instantly noticed food was gone. "Wasn't there some milk left in the carton?"

"There should be. I didn't drink it," he said.

Ree glanced at the trash under the sink. The carton was there.

"The cheese is missing too," she noticed. There were other things gone—a pair of apples, lunch meat and half the lettuce. "Maybe your theory is right after all. She must be hungry, but I wonder what's happening to her money. We both know that I make more than enough to cover food and put a roof over our heads."

"She might have been robbed. A guy she was dating could have taken her money and disappeared. It might have been the reason she wanted to change shifts with you," he offered. "I'm reaching here."

Ree nodded. "I saw a huge bruise on her arm. She's withdrawn, doesn't really speak to Adrian or me."

"It's impossible to know what's going on without digging into her circumstances a little more," he continued. "She might have any number of addiction issues."

Again, she agreed.

"There could be a relative in the background needing the money," he surmised.

"Something is bothering me and I can't quite pinpoint what it is," she admitted.

He nodded. "Hold on to it, because intuition is usually right when backed by training and experience."

She had all kinds of intuition and plenty of training, but not a good handle on Zoey. Confronting her at work tomorrow might get the answers Ree was searching for.

Chapter Seventeen

Quint woke early and checked his email. He realized it was too soon to get analysis back on the images he'd been sending over to Grappell, but he hoped. There was nothing.

He did, however, have an email from his boss. How's the case?

Not yet ready to respond, he drained his coffee cup and closed his laptop. There was a problem with the two of them sleeping in separate beds now that they'd picked up a snoop. He remade the couch and slid his pillow onto Ree's bed.

Her steady, even breathing said she was still in a deep sleep. The urge to climb under the covers next to her and draw her close caught him off guard. He couldn't walk away fast enough. Outside, the temperature was already warm, the sun hot, as he locked the door and crossed the parking lot.

A question from last night bugged him. How did Zoey get inside their cabin? Then again, security wasn't exactly tight here. Thankfully, he'd hid the tackle box behind the washer/dryer combo in the hall closet. His next step would be to find out her last name and have Grappell run a background check. Of course, Zoey might not even be her real first name. So many questions with that one. Could he get a fingerprint and have Grappell run it through the database? It would work if she had a driver's license or even a criminal record.

Moving on from Zoey, he was still chewing on the disagreement between Adrian and Fender last night. Since Quint was coming in mornings, he hadn't had a chance to work the relationship he'd started developing with Stevie the bartender.

Then, there was the fight between Charley and his cousin. Tensions seemed to be running high at Greenlight. Where there was smoke, there usually was fire. There was enough to indicate a forest fire around here. Smoke everywhere. No flame.

The door to the restaurant was unlocked, so Quint walked inside. Rather than call out, he headed to the back and to the small office. No one was around, which was surprising. There was an SUV parked out front alongside Charley's truck. Quint had memorized the license plate. He pulled out his cell and sent the plate information to Grappell.

A loud banging noise caught his attention as he moved the mouse to wake up the desktop computer. Instinct and adrenaline had Quint on his feet in two seconds. He reminded himself about the boot he was wearing so he wouldn't give himself away in the heat of the moment.

More noise came from the opposite hallway leading toward the bathroom.

"Everything okay out there?" he shouted from the office. In times like these, he also had to remind himself that he was supposed to be a regular Joe Schmo, and not a highly trained agent with a black belt in kung fu.

There was a loud grunt, followed by the sound of someone being thrown against the wall. The noise got

Quint moving in its direction. It appeared as if someone was being killed and he couldn't stand by and listen without trying to do something about it.

As he rounded the corner of the hallway, he saw Charley straightening his shirt. The metal side door was closing.

"Everything okay?" Quint asked.

"Me? I'm fine. Just had a skirmish with someone I kicked out last night. He thought he left his wallet here and didn't believe me when I said no one had turned it in." Charley kept his face down but when it turned toward Quint, it was easy to see the man's nose was bleeding.

"Your nose," Quint said, but Charley waved him off.

"It's okay. All over now," Charley said.

"Are you sure about that?" Quint needed to push back a little. "I'm here to help. I can call the deputy or—"

"No. No. Slight misunderstanding is all. No crime has been committed here." Charley gave a forced smile. "Why don't you go on back to the office and finish whatever it is that you were working on. There's no trouble."

"You sure about that?" Quint asked.

"One hundred percent," Charley assured him. "Chef is going to be here in a few minutes. I need to make room for a delivery."

Quint made a show of being reluctant about leaving. Charley made eyes that told Quint to retreat. So he did. The camera back at home would be recording the SUV and driver as they exited. Quint had a plate. Before he could forget any important details and while Charley was still in the hallway, Quint shot a quick note to Grappell with everything he could remember about the exchange and the mystery guest.

Tensions at Greenlight were most definitely a boiling pot on a hot stove.

An hour later, Quint came home and updated Ree on the morning's events before letting her know that he'd planted an app on the desktop that would give him remote access without anyone being the wiser. Before he could get into much else with her, she walked out the door for work.

"I THOUGHT YOU might want to use this next time." Ree walked over to Zoey's station before their shift began and set a key down on the table.

Zoey blanched, her skin paled, and then she quickly covered by clearing her throat. She shrugged, trying to look casual and failing miserably. "I don't know what you're talking about."

"It's okay. I'm not mad and neither is Quint," she said in the same tone of voice she would use if she was talking about picking up the mail. Consistency was key. Calmness was key. Understanding was key.

"Why should you be?" she quipped, finding some of her usual sass.

"I'm not." Ree pulled a piece of paper and pen out of her apron. She set those on the same table, moving the key on top. "In fact, why don't you just write down a few of your favorites from the grocery store so I can make sure they're stocked in the house next time."

"There won't be a next time because there wasn't a first." Zoey's tone was defiant and she came off more than a little embarrassed.

Ree was convinced more than ever that Zoey was in some kind of abusive relationship. Since pushing the issue would be a whole lot like cornering a wounded animal, Ree turned around and walked off. To do otherwise could prove dangerous and naive. Besides, Ree had put it out there. Zoey now knew they were on to her and she had to be wondering how they knew. There'd been no judgment about the incident. Only understanding and a not-so-subtle offer of help.

The other incident from last night could be nothing more than a lovers' fight. In fact, what else could it be?

Besides, how many eligible men and women were there in a small town? It was exactly the reason Ree had dated friends of her brothers growing up, and look where that had gotten her. She'd learned real quickly that her brothers were way too in the know about her personal life when it all became intertwined. Shane's call last night still struck a raw nerve.

Adrian blew through without saying a whole lot. Fine by Ree. She wasn't in the mood to speak to someone who lied to her. Betrayed her? At the very least kept secrets from her.

Adrian and Ree weren't friends in real life. Why did the relationship with Fender rub her the wrong way? Adrian could date anyone she wanted.

Sure, the woman was secretive. She didn't gossip at work. Those were probably signs that she was up to something. The fact she knew Zoey might be young and in a relationship that could hurt her but was unwilling to do anything about it also didn't sit well with Ree.

Then again, maybe she woke up on the wrong side of the bed today. She closed her eyes with her mind churning and woke in the same spin cycle. She still couldn't pinpoint what it was about Adrian and Fender's relationship that bugged her so much. Was it that the relationship was happening right underneath her nose and she hadn't caught onto it? Had she made another critical mistake?

Although with all of Quint's experience, he hadn't caught on to it, either. Then again, he wasn't the one working with Adrian. He probably would have been able to handle waiting tables, working the other wait-staff, the kitchen, all while gathering intel. He would probably be on top of everything.

Ree needed a nap. She was cranky as all get-out. Exhaustion wore her thin after tossing and turning most of the night. She'd finally fallen asleep as the sun came up. Ree needed her sleep, too. Maybe another cup of coffee would do the trick.

She walked into the kitchen as the first customer walked through the front door. From behind her, she heard Zoey greet them and ask if they preferred a table or booth. At least Ree was back to working one shift a day. She could get through a lunch rush.

"What's wrong with you today?" Adrian asked, surprising Ree from behind.

She jumped and clutched at her heart. She should probably be acting at this point but Adrian had actually caught Ree off guard.

"Guy trouble?" Adrian asked, taking a cup from the counter.

"Tired," Ree admitted. At least she could be honest about that one aspect of her life.

"Perk up," Adrian teased with an elbow jab to the rib cage. "It's gonna be a busy one today."

"What about you? Any guy problems lately?" Ree asked Adrian.

"Isn't there always?" Adrian shrugged, trying a little too hard to be nonchalant.

After finishing the first cup of coffee, Ree didn't

have five seconds to catch her breath for the next few hours. The nice part was the day zipped by and she got into a decent rhythm waiting on customers. If this whole law enforcement thing didn't work out, she could waitress for a living. Lack of sleep was really getting to her now. She was making corny jokes. Worse yet, they were to herself.

Zoey passed by Ree and stuffed something in Ree's pocket.

"Don't look at it now," Zoey demanded.

As she was on her way out, one of the barmaids checked in. She was here early. Ree took note of the bleached blonde with a tan and legs for days.

"Hey," Ree said as they passed each other.

The blonde didn't give her the time of day as she rushed past, heading toward the kitchen door where Charley waited with a scowl on his face. Ree thought about Adrian and Fender's argument last night. She made a mental note to watch their interactions over the next couple of days.

Middle of July in Texas meant walking back to the cabin in pavement-melting heat. Quint waited at the door, as usual, and Adrian winked at Ree as she left. What was Adrian so happy about? Based on her fight with Fender last night, she was a screaming mess. Had Ree misjudged the situation? Had Adrian brought him outside to reem Fender out for something work-related? He was the expeditor, after all. It was his job to keep the work flowing and meals delivered fresh and hot.

Ree filed the information in the back of her mind and moved on.

"I need a cool shower and ice packs for my tired feet," Ree stated as she walked in the door. She reached in her apron to empty her pocket when she realized Zoey's note was inside.

Ree walked to the table after toeing off her boots. She smoothed out the crinkled-up piece of paper and read the list: Cap'n Crunch Berries, apples, cheese swirls, bread, lunch meat and milk. The word *lettuce* had been hastily scribbled at the bottom.

A tear welled in Ree's eyes. This wasn't the grocery list of a grown adult. This was the grocery list of a college-age kid.

Quint walked over, stopping beside her. Ree ducked her head, chin to chest, to hide the rogue tear that fell, staining the slip of paper.

He didn't speak. Instead, he wrapped an arm around her. She turned into his muscled chest and cried.

"It's okay," he said, whispering other reassurances in her ear. "We'll get help for her. She's not alone any longer. She has us."

As crazy as Ree's childhood might have been after she lost her father at a young age, Ree wouldn't change a thing except for maybe bringing him back. She had few memories of the man before he died. Her grandfather and brothers had provided more than enough male influences in her life. She couldn't imagine her life without them despite needing breathing room.

Were they annoying at times? Yes. Did they cross boundaries that shouldn't be crossed? Yes. Did they also have hearts of gold and ultimately want what was best for her? Absolutely yes.

She made a mental note to circle back after this case was over and tell Shane that he still needed to stay out of her business, but she loved him anyway.

As for Quint? It was difficult not to start falling for a guy who seemed to know when to pull her into a hug and when to give her space. This assignment, this "act" of being married to this amazing man was getting inside her head. Was that part of what had kept her awake last night?

To be honest, yes. She'd drifted in and out of sleep alternating between thinking about the case, and how incredible it had felt to be in Quint's arms. One thing was clear: she couldn't fall for a coworker. Not only would that be unprofessional, but it could distract her at a critical moment as well. She needed to get her head back in the arena. She needed to face reality. Quint was temporary. Once this assignment was over, the two of them would be saying goodbye.

It was a harsh truth. One she needed to accept in order to move on with her life.

Chapter Eighteen

It was true. A good night of sleep could cure almost anything. Ree stretched her arms out wide and yawned. Quint's bed was made back into a couch. His pillow was on hers. He must still be next door at Greenlight.

She threw off her covers, pushed out of bed and headed toward the coffeepot. It was already brewed. All she could think was that she could get used to this treatment.

At thirty-six, was it time to think about settling down? Ree had no idea where these thoughts were coming from. She'd never been the type to depend on someone else. And yet, sharing this cabin was making her realize there might be more to life than her job.

Gasp.

Was that true? Could she begin to consider a life that didn't involve thinking about work 24/7? She'd worked so hard to get where she was and still had a lot of track left in front of her. The thought of trying to balance both had never really held much appeal. But she could admit that lately she'd felt a certain sense of loneliness about her life. She'd been attributing it to burnout, figuring a good vacation would do the trick and get her back in the game.

She pulled up her fake social media account as she

nursed her cup of coffee. The images of her and Quint from the night before last, looking so happy but also knowing it was so fake, hit her square in the chest. A hot tear rolled down her cheek and a hollow feeling ripped through her chest.

The reaction couldn't be about Quint. She'd only known him less than a week. Although, to be fair, it felt much longer.

Ree wasn't ready to unpack the real reason. Instead, she flattened out the slip of paper from Zoey, careful to straighten out the edges. Ree couldn't always bring justice or right wrongs in her job. More often than not, she was able to lock a bad guy away. But there were times to take a stand, go above and beyond. For the next hour, she researched services for women in abusive relationships.

There was something very right about how this path made her feel. As cliché as it might sound, she'd gotten into law enforcement to make a difference.

Ree made breakfast, finished a second cup of coffee and dressed. Greenlight closed at three o'clock on Sundays after what she'd been told at one point on her shift yesterday would be a legendary brunch.

She clocked in early, passing Quint in the parking lot on the way over.

He hauled her against his chest before whispering, "We have another break in the case. Tell you all about it later."

He pulled his head back, gazed into her eyes and then pressed a kiss to her lips. She brought her hands up to his face, deepening the kiss. He tasted like French roast coffee and bacon. Her new favorite combination.

"See you at home later," he stated with a look that made her think she'd caught him off guard.

"Can't wait to finish this shift," she said. Before heading to the restaurant, she added, "I missed you this morning."

Her comment clearly caught him off guard. He recovered quickly. "Me, too."

"One more thing," she said before she let him go. "I left Zoey's list on the table. Would you mind running to the store and bringing the items with you when you come to walk me home later?"

"I'd be more than happy to," he stated with conviction.

"Thank you." She smiled at him. Really smiled. Not the fake wife smile but one that came from the heart.

Sunday brunch had a different setup than the rest of the week. The whole shebang was arranged as a buffet with various stations, one of which was a Belgian waffle station. The cooks were out, ready to man their stations. Cars started filling the parking lot in anticipation of opening.

"What's going on today?" she asked Adrian.

"The good news is that we're done by three o'clock," Adrian said. "The bad news is if you think we were busy before, you haven't met Sunday brunch."

"Sounds scary." Ree could hardly imagine being busier.

"Basically," Adrian went on, "you won't need to exercise for a week. It's constant running to clear plates, attend to drinks. Charley wants coffee mugs refilled at all times. Word of warning. He doesn't like it when customers have to ask for service."

Ree searched her memory to see if she'd been attentive enough to her customers. She couldn't recall any needing to flag her down, so that had to be a good sign. "Okay. Good to know. Anything else?"

Adrian motioned toward the line already forming at the door. "Strap on your seat belt. You're in for one wild ride."

Within minutes, the room filled with customers, the running started and didn't stop until half past three, when the last of the customers cashed out. Ree took one look at Adrian, who was sitting down, propping up her head with her hands.

"Told you so," was all Adrian said as Ree texted Quint.

"I'm not sure that was adequate warning for what just happened," Ree joked.

"Money's good, though." Adrian rubbed the tips of her fingers together with her thumb.

Fender cut through the dining room and Adrian's smile dropped so hard it could have hit the floor.

"Everything all right between the two of you?" Ree asked.

"Of course. Why do you ask?" Adrian seemed caught off guard by the question.

"I've got eyes," Ree shot back. "And I'm not stupid."

Adrian shot a warning look. "Well, you better keep those eyes closed and your mouth shut if you want to get along."

With that, Adrian stormed off and made it more than clear she was done talking to Ree.

By the time Ree closed out her station, Quint stood at the door. She walked to him and he hauled her to his chest. She was going to miss the intensity of his touch and the way her heart danced every time she saw him. He discreetly handed her a bag of groceries, which she held out behind her as Zoey left the building.

"Thanks," Zoey murmured, taking the offering before heading down the road on foot. She did a great job of hiding the bag in front of her as she disappeared.

Ree remembered what Quint had told her the last time he hugged her in the parking lot. There was a development in the case. In a couple of minutes, she was going to find out if it was the break they needed.

QUINT CLOSED AND locked the door behind them back at the cabin.

"I asked Adrian about Fender," she started.

"And?"

"It didn't go well," Ree said on a sigh.

"What happened here today?" Ree asked as she headed toward the closet. "Please talk away but I have to get out of this uniform."

Did she have to go and put the mental image of her stripping off her clothes in his mind?

Quint performed a mental headshake. "There was someone at Greenlight this morning. He gave Charley a bloody nose by the bathrooms. I went over to check on the commotion and he was gone. I did think to get a license plate on the way in."

"Sounds promising," she shouted from down the hall.

He moved to the fridge and opened a bottle of Coke for her. He set it on the table along with the tray of meats, cheeses and fruits that he'd picked up at the grocery during his store run.

"He kept his face down for the camera, so we didn't get a good image there like I'd hoped to," he explained. "However, Grappell is running the plate through the database to see if he can get a hit."

"That's encouraging," she said, reemerging wearing form-hugging exercise pants and a soft cotton tee. Ree could make a paper bag look sexy. "What did Charley say?"

"That it was no big deal. There certainly has been a lot of activity at Greenlight. I installed spyware on Charley's desktop. Fingers crossed there," he continued.

"Charley doesn't seem like the type to put up with being hit," she stated.

"Not to me, either. Not unless he has to," Quint said.

Ree stopped at the table. "Holy smokes. What is all this?"

"Food. Something to drink. Your feet must be ready to fall off after a week at Greenlight," he teased.

"I don't know how anyone does it. How do they keep running around? I'm ready to drop." She took a seat and started right in. "Thank you for this, by the way."

He waved her off. She didn't need to thank him. It was teamwork as far as he was concerned.

"It is a big deal to me," she said, making eyes at him. "You know, for someone who never wants to get married you sure would make an amazing husband."

He didn't know what to do with that statement, so he let it sit there between them.

"I wasn't suggesting you should get married or anything," she said as if anxious to clarify. "In fact, your marital status is none of my business." The way the words came out in a rush, practically tripping all over each other, he could tell she spoke before she thought.

"Don't worry. I'm not offended," he stated for the record, adding, "Marriage probably works for some people. I don't have anything against the institution in and of itself. It's not for everyone."

"Can I ask you a personal question?" She didn't bring her eyes up to meet his. Instead, she twirled a piece of cheese between her fingers.

"Go for it," he said.

"You're obviously very dedicated to your job. It shows. You probably already know this but you are kind of a legend at the agency," she began.

So far, he didn't see a question.

"Do you ever find yourself in a spot where you're just flat-out lonely? Like, it might be nice to share your day with someone special or feel as if you can take off your gun and badge, and relax with your girl, or in my case, guy?" she asked.

There was a lot to unpack in her statement turned questions.

"Let's see if I understand what you're asking," he started and she slowly brought her gaze up to meet his. "Do I ever get lonely?"

She nodded.

"I didn't used to. Since losing my best friend and partner, the answer is yes. All the time." He surprised himself with the admission. "Does that mean I would change being focused on my career...the answer there is no. I can't imagine doing anything else in life."

His last statement was partially true. After losing Tessa, he had thrown himself deeper into his career. Recently, he'd questioned if there was anything else he might want to do for a living. He'd dabbled with a few thoughts of retiring from the agency and starting a small business like a bait shop where he could live next to a lake.

But that was only recently.

"If you ever wanted to leave this career behind, you could totally start a food truck business," she stated. "You're very good at feeding people."

He chuckled. "I don't know how good I'd be at that, but I'll take the compliment."

"You should consider it once you're done with undercover work," she said with a bright smile. "Oh, actually, with those muscles you could be a trainer."

Her cheeks flamed with the admission.

"I'm pretty sure that's already happening," he quipped with a wink.

"Well, yeah, there is that," she said. "I highly doubt you're going to be stuck with me through another assignment. I'm half surprised you didn't already kick me back after our dicey start."

He shot her a look.

"How many times have you thought about quitting since you started this line of work?" he asked.

"Me?" She looked him square in the eye. "None."

"Then, you might just make it to retirement," he stated.

"The only guy I've dated seriously in years thought I was too focused on work to be in a relationship," she said. "He asked me to reevaluate my priorities."

"What did you do?" he asked, not really wanting to hear about her relationship with another man even though he had no designs on her.

"I did as he asked," she said. "It led me to break up with him."

"And now?" he asked.

"I don't know. Sometimes I question whether or not I've done the right thing by always putting my personal life behind my career. I wonder if I'll end up with a bunch of accolades and no one to share the news with. You know?" She cocked an eyebrow as she tossed a piece of cheese back onto the tray.

"As a matter of fact, I do," he admitted. "The choices I've made are obvious."

"You can't become the best at something if you only give it half your attention," she said.

"That was always my philosophy," he stated. "But then, I also had Tessa to fill in the gap."

"And now?" She turned his question back on him.

"Life can be a real face punch," he said, wishing he could go back for five minutes and tell Tessa how much she meant to him. His cell buzzed, indicating an email had come in. "Grappell might have gotten a hit. I should check this."

Chapter Nineteen

"What is it?" Ree asked, letting his statement about life sit in the back of her mind as she watched him check his phone.

He moved over to the laptop and then brought it over to the table. She cleared off space and then moved her chair beside his, ignoring the heat washing over her body at being so close. "Grappell got a hit on the plate."

Bald Guy. "It's registered to an eighty-year-old female by the name of Betsy Warner. She lives about an hour away from here," he informed. "Grappell attached the address with a map pinpointing the location."

"I'm guessing the agency is sending someone else to follow up on the lead," she said.

He nodded. "No one wants to risk us being seen or made. Grappell said he'd keep us posted on what they find out."

More waiting around. *Great.*

"In the meantime, we can go through last night's footage to see what else we can dig up," he suggested, rubbing his hands together. "It's not the sexiest part of the job but it is where most of the work is done."

"Remind me not to sign up for any more possible long-term undercover gigs unless it's with you," she said in response. "At least your food game is strong."

"I see the SUV parked again on Thursday," he said as he studied the screen with a slight smirk.

"How badly do you want to go check out the house it's registered to?" she asked.

"As much as I want to breathe air," he stated.

"Remind me how wrong it would be for us to take a drive right now," she said.

"And give Grappell an ulcer?" he shot back with a grin that said he could easily be talked into it.

She wiggled her eyebrows. And then the thing that had been niggling at the back of her mind at the bar last night stepped out of the shadows.

"He was at the bar," she said.

"Who?" He arched a dark brow.

"Bald Guy. We were focused on Phillip but Bald Guy was standing next to him. The guy from the sketch. He was there and I'm certain the two of them were together."

She grabbed her phone and located the picture she'd taken.

"Yes. See. He's right here," she said, holding up her cell so he could get a good look.

"That's him," Quint confirmed. "Before we decide to go for a drive, I need to dig around in Charley's files. See what I can come up with."

The minute Quint located evidence, Charley would be arrested, and the assignment would come to a close. The thought shouldn't make her heart hurt. Once arrests were made, she wouldn't be able to show her face and Zoey would continue to be left to her own devices. Without this job, what would she do for money? Would conditions worsen for her?

"Bingo," Quint said. "I'm seeing a lot of money come through here and into a bank that we know is fake. This is tens of thousands of dollars a day. He is breaking up large amounts of money into smaller transactions, shuffling through this fake account and into his business account. From there it's going into untraceable shell companies."

"Does that mean he isn't moving weapons?" she asked.

"It could be where the money is coming from but I'm not seeing any evidence of guns moving out the back door. Let me send a note to Grappell with this new information. He's going to want to give tech a few days to take a deep dive into this and put together the case. I'll update the boss, too. She'll want to identify who the shell accounts belong to so they can bust as many people as possible," he said. "In my experience, this phase will move fast. Do you have a few more days of working the floor of the restaurant in you?"

"I've been hanging in there so far," she said. "Tomorrow is my day off since Mondays are the slowest."

"I'll still have to go in during the morning to clean up the desktop files and keep up my work of finding accounting software for Charley," he said. "He's the only one who accesses the computer as far as I know, so he has to be the one behind the crimes."

"I'm wondering just how much Phillip is pushing the buttons," she stated. "Charley might be a pawn based on what you saw this morning."

"Then he'll most likely get a chance to turn state's witness if he's willing to testify against the others and bring down the whole operation," he stated. "Not a bad haul for your first time out on a big assignment."

She nodded, thinking she wouldn't feel successful at all if she didn't get help for Zoey. Would she push Ree away? How could Ree approach the subject? A confrontation? She quickly dismissed the idea. Zoey could withdraw further. A handwritten note? That might work.

Thunder rumbled in the sky. The air was heavy with humidity. A storm brewed.

QUINT MARKED AS many suspect accounts as he could before sending his findings over to Grappell. He ran over the facts in his head. Charley was involved in moving money. Phillip, Bald Guy and Ruddy Complexion were involved, but it was unclear exactly what their roles were. The money seemed significant. Where were the guns? He wrote the high-level update to the boss, giving a whole lot of the credit for their findings to Ree. She deserved to have accolades in her jacket for her work on this case.

Rain pelted the tin roof of the cabin, the noise so loud they wouldn't be able to talk over it if they tried. He glanced over at her and saw her scribbling away on a piece of paper. He had no doubt that she had a dozen or so good reasons to convince Zoey, if that was her real name, to go to Austin.

"Do you want to talk me through your arguments?" he offered. "I might be a good sounding board."

Ree glanced at the door and froze. "Did you hear that?"

"As a matter of fact, I did," he stated, glancing around the room to ensure there was nothing out in the open that could identify them as law enforcement. He nodded toward the door as he moved to his boot, strapping it on in record time.

"Who is it?" Ree shouted.

"Zoey." The young woman's voice shook. She had to be soaking, standing out in the rain.

Ree gave a quick look at Quint before opening the door. "You're drenched. Come on in."

Zoey stood there, still in her work clothes, with mascara-stained cheeks, looking about as pitiful as a soaked dog who'd escaped the backyard and gotten itself lost.

Zoey's gaze flew to Quint and then back at Ree. She shook her head but didn't budge. The momentary look of fear in her eyes would probably haunt Quint for weeks. Getting her help would be the only way to make it go away.

"It's okay," Ree soothed. She reached both hands out to Zoey, taking her arms and tugging her into the cabin. "Come in so we can close the door and get you out of this storm."

"It's just thunder scares me a little bit," Zoey said as she stood there dripping on the wood flooring.

Quint pushed up to standing and Zoey flinched. He had to force calm over himself because he knew exactly what that meant, and it caused a knot to form in his gut. "I'll just get a towel so she can dry off."

"Come sit down at the table," Ree continued, her voice tranquil as she led the young woman to a chair.

Quint retrieved a towel and brought it back. He walked the long way around whereas Zoey sat in the chair closest to the door. Smart strategy in case she decided to bolt. He handed Ree the towel and then retrieved three Cokes from the fridge. He held one up and Zoey gave a slight nod.

Again, after he opened the drink, he handed it over to Ree to give to Zoey.

"This place is too small for me to go in another room, but I can sit out in the car if the two of you need some privacy," he offered.

Zoey's eyes widened in surprise. She sat still for a long moment before giving a slight headshake.

"Okay, then, I'll just be over here watching a game." He motioned toward the laptop. On his way back to the couch, he snagged a pair of earbuds. He took a seat, tucked in the earbuds and pulled up a random game. He didn't turn on the volume because he wanted to hear the conversation as much as possible through the driving rain.

"My boyfriend and I had a fight," Zoey said quietly. "He kicked me out."

"Do you need a place to stay tonight?" Ree asked.

From the corner of his eye, he saw the young woman's lip quiver. She didn't respond.

"It's okay. You don't have to say. We can sit here and talk if you want. Or not. You can dry off, drink a Coke and chill." Ree set the Coke bottle in front of Zoey before picking up her own and taking a big swig.

Zoey started drying off as she picked up the Coke and took a sip. "Why do you care if I eat?"

"Because you need food," Ree replied casually.

"You shouldn't care," she said. "And I'm not a kid."

"You know what? I don't even like kids. We certainly don't have any and I don't know if I ever will. I have nephews who have so much energy they make me want to walk out of the room every time they zip past," Ree said with that same calm, collected voice.

Zoey rolled her eyes. "Kids, right?"

"They can be such a pain," Ree agreed. "So, as long as we establish that I'm not trying to be your mother, we're good."

Zoey nodded.

"I'd rather be friends anyway," Ree said. "Being new in town is hard on the social life."

"My boyfriend gets in these rages when I do something wrong and, like, takes everything. He's still angry at me for losing my key," she said.

"Losing a key isn't such a terrible thing," Ree said.

Strangely enough, it was probably Quint, rather than Ree, who could relate to Zoey's past. Ree came from a loving family and a solid home. Quint's background was a little more complicated. But at least he'd had his mother and Officer Jazz. Ree had been right earlier. Zoey had no one.

"Do you have family in Texas?" Ree asked.

"Nah, my mom ditched a couple of years ago. She didn't tell my stepdad before she took off. We weren't close to any other family. I'm probably the last person she wants to see again," she said like it was nothing, but there was an undercurrent of hurt in her voice. She was too relaxed when talking about the abandonment, showing too much of a forced, careless attitude.

Quint never crossed a line when it came to investigations because it might risk the operation. He'd learned to detach, focus on the good he was doing. But he couldn't allow this young woman to continue to be treated this way. This time, he had to put himself on the line.

Chapter Twenty

"Have you thought about other options?" Ree asked. She was making progress with Zoey but they were running out of time.

"What options?" Zoey fired back. "Take off by myself? I tried that once. Didn't work out. I'm nineteen. No one wants to rent to me."

"There are places—"

Zoey was already shaking her head. "Like shelters? No, thanks. I had a friend 'saved' by CPS once. She ended up in juvie after fighting off her foster dad."

Ree knew there were bad eggs in every system. People who viewed taking in fosters as money in the bank. Conditions could be harsh in an overburdened system. Those were the cases people talked about. Those were the cases that made headlines. She understood why, but there were so many success stories that didn't get the attention they deserved.

"I had a friend who got in trouble with a relationship. She didn't have family, either, so she found a place. It worked for her," Ree said, making up the story as she went along.

Zoey shot a curious look as she picked up her Coke and took another sip.

"I'm sure there are places that focus on young people," Ree said.

"Maybe," was all Zoey said.

Inch by inch, this was progress.

This was tough because Ree didn't have a whole lot of time to convince Zoey to get help. Come on too strong and Zoey would retreat.

"My friend went to this place in Austin after she got kicked out by her parents. It turned her life around. She got an associate degree and works in a community outreach program." Ree hated lying but she needed to create a composite so Zoey would have someone to relate to. Since her friend's experience in foster care caused her to shy away, Ree had to find a good counter.

"Really?" Zoey shrugged. "I don't know."

The fact she hadn't turned her nose up to the idea meant Ree had found the right approach.

"I could ask her where she went and give you the information if you think you might like to check it out," Ree offered. "Might be nice to be able to keep the money you work for. Save it to go to college or use it to buy a car."

The freedom idea seemed to strike another chord.

"I need a car, right?" Zoey's brown eyes widened. "Willie doesn't think so but I keep telling him that I can't even go to the grocery store by myself."

"Beats walking everywhere," Ree said. She laughed, figuring it would help break up some of the tension. "But my car is only one step up."

"I know, right." Zoey winced, made a face, and then laughed.

"Hey, you were supposed to tell me it's not that bad," Ree quipped.

"But, like, have you seen it?" Zoey fired back. She had a wicked sense of humor. "I'm glad you stuck around."

"Thanks," Ree said. "Me, too."

Since time was running out, Ree decided she had to push a little on the shelter.

"Did you decide about whether or not you'd consider giving Austin a try?" Ree asked. She tried her level best not to give away just how much it meant to her.

"I mean, can't hurt. Right?" she hedged but there wasn't a whole lot of conviction in her voice.

All Ree could do was try.

"I'll reach out to my friend and bring the info to work with me tomorrow," Ree said, resisting the urge to oversell the idea. "So, how about tonight? Do you have a place to stay? We have a sofa bed that's available."

From the corner of her eye, she saw Quint look away from his screen and at her.

"Willie might get mad if I stay away all night," Zoey reasoned.

"You could text him," Ree offered. "Tell him you're with a friend from work."

Zoey folded her arms across her chest and sat a little straighter. It was the moment that caused Ree to realize she'd pushed too far.

"I better head back," Zoey said. "The rain isn't so bad now."

"Do you want a ride?" Ree asked, figuring she needed to take a step back at this point. Plus, giving Zoey a ride had a double benefit. One, Zoey wouldn't be walking in the rain. Two, Ree would find out where Zoey lived.

"Yeah, sure. I guess," Zoey said. She drained her Coke before holding the empty bottle in the air. "There a trash can?"

"Just leave it on the table. I can take care of it later," Ree said like it was no big deal.

"You sure?" Zoey asked.

"Positive." Ree stood up. "Let's get you home."

Zoey stood.

"Leaving so soon?" Quint asked, pretending he hadn't been listening this whole time. He stood up and walked over to Ree, placing a soft hand on her arm before kissing her. "Where are the two of you off to?"

"Driving Zoey home," Ree said. "Do you want to come?"

"Sure, if it's okay with Zoey," he said.

Zoey blushed as she shrugged. She tried to play it off like it was no big deal but her actions said she had a crush on Quint. Seriously, though, who wouldn't?

QUINT GRABBED HIS cell from the table and then held the door for Zoey and Ree. His actions in the past couple of minutes were deliberate. He wanted to demonstrate a healthy relationship to the young woman if only for a few minutes while she was visiting. The little things had made a big impact on his life when he was a kid, especially when they came from someone he respected. It was clear to him Zoey looked up to Ree.

The car ride was short. Ree and Zoey chatted about the brunch crowd and working at Greenlight. As they pulled up to the address Zoey had provided, Ree asked, "How long have Fender and Adrian been together?"

"You noticed that, too?" Zoey asked.

"Hard to miss," Ree said, and he could tell she was hedging her bets.

"I know, right?" Zoey said, rolling her eyes. "They try to be so sneaky about it but it's so obvious."

Zoey was observant. Then again, it was probably a survival skill.

"I didn't catch on right away," Ree said.

"They've been on and off," Zoey admitted. "I think they've been on a break recently."

"Makes sense," Ree said. "Plus, I've been trying to get the lay of the land. Learning that place is like drinking from a fire hose."

Zoey laughed. "Yeah, I can see that."

"I'm getting the hang of it. I think," Ree continued.

"You? You've been great. You should have seen my first week," Zoey said, reaching for the handle. "Thanks for the ride."

"Do you know who Phillip is?" Ree asked.

Zoey's eye widened before she said, "All I know is that when he shows up, Charley gets nervous."

"I'll steer clear of him then," Ree said.

"Good idea," Zoey confirmed.

"Be careful," Ree warned.

"With Willie, I don't exactly have to do anything to get into trouble," she said as she exited the car.

"Be good to yourself," Ree said to Zoey.

The young woman smiled awkwardly but there was a genuine appreciation in her eyes.

"You, too," Zoey stated before shutting the door.

Both were silent until they made it a good distance from the small shack of a home Zoey shared with her boyfriend.

"It took everything inside me to hold back during my conversation with her," Ree admitted.

"You got her thinking. You said just the right amount," he defended.

"Did you see how fast she decided it was time to go when I pushed too far?" she asked.

"Yes. You pushed her buttons and she wasn't quite ready to face what that meant," he said. "Believe me, you did good."

"What will she do when the restaurant is shut down?" Ree asked on a sigh. "I can't seem to let that go. She'll be out of a job with no way to provide for herself. We're going to be hurting her even more."

"Hopefully it won't matter because by then, she'll be in Austin," he said.

Ree fisted her hands, placing them on top of her thighs.

"This is hard," she admitted. "I'm usually so clear on an assignment that I'm doing the right thing. It's obvious. There's a bad guy who is hurting others. I make sure said bad guy is locked away for as long as he deserves. The streets are safer. I sleep easy at night."

"I understand," he said. "This assignment is complicated. Some are."

"The last thing I want to do is hurt an innocent young woman," she said.

"Because you're in this for the right reasons," he reminded her. "This is hard. There are going to be casualties. Good people are going to have to figure out another move. I don't like that any more than you do. However, I will also submit that leaving the status quo can hurt folks even more."

"I'm listening," she said.

"Is Zoey's relationship with her boyfriend healthy?" he asked.

"Absolutely not."

"Is leaving Zoey in her present environment keeping her safe?" he continued.

"No. I don't believe it is."

"Could she end up more at risk if it was too easy to stay right where she is?" he asked.

Ree paused for a long moment.

"Yes," she finally said. "Leaving her in this environment could hurt her even more."

"Forcing a change breaks folks out of their comfort zone," he said. "And that's when growth can happen. Leave her here and who knows what will happen the next time she breaks into someone's home for food."

Ree gasped.

"You're right," she said. "Zoey was lucky it was just the two of us. She could have gotten herself into real trouble."

"What if someone had been home?" he continued.

"Right again," she said before reaching over and touching his arm. "Thanks for talking me off the ledge."

"It's what we do for each other," he said.

"You say that like it's nothing but it means a lot to me," she said quietly. "I've always been in my brothers' shadows. They've always looked out for me but in a smothering way if that makes sense."

"I can see where that might happen," he agreed.

"You are nothing like them, by the way," she quickly added. "And despite my mistakes, I haven't doubted your trust in me."

"We all make mistakes, Ree."

"And beat ourselves up worse for them than anyone else ever could," she pointed out.

He thought about that for a long moment. She was right. He'd been torturing himself over what had happened to Tessa. Maybe it was time to learn how to move forward without her, without the shame, without the guilt.

"Thanks, Ree."

"For what?" she asked.

"Saying something that I needed to hear," he said.

Rather than speak, she leaned over the armrest and rested her head on his shoulder.

The rain was down to a drizzle. Parts of the roads were flooded. He navigated them back to the cabin, figuring it had been a day.

"Seems like the fight we heard last night between Adrian and Fender was nothing more than two lovers hashing it out," she said as he parked.

"Dating a coworker is always a bad idea," he stated. "I did it early in my career and regretted it every time."

Ree shifted to sitting straight up in her seat, breaking off all physical contact. He hadn't meant for that to happen even though it was probably for the best. Quint needed time to move on from his losses.

"Yeah, I can see where it would be a problem after a relationship ran its course," she said. There was a hint of sadness in her voice.

"Even the most promising ones fizzle out. Next thing you know, you're asking to be reassigned to avoid working with certain people," he continued. "It gets messy."

"Sounds awful," she agreed.

"It'll probably happen at some point in your career," he said. "Can't please everyone and this job does tend to attract strong personalities."

"That, I can see," was all she said as he parked in the spot in front of the cabin.

The minute he shut off the engine, she was out of the vehicle and through the front door. As awful as the hollowed-out feeling in his chest was, it would be best for both of them in the long run. This assignment would wrap very soon and the two of them would go their separate ways.

Quint was laying the groundwork for the inevitable.

Chapter Twenty-One

Ree ate, showered and crawled into bed without saying a word. She kept an earbud in and listened to some of her favorite tunes. "Middle of Nowhere" by Vancouver Sleep Clinic was her go-to song. But even that couldn't soothe her heart tonight.

By the next morning, Quint was back at the restaurant and she breathed a sigh of relief. Having him in the room and knowing this temporary situation was about to end sucked the air from her lungs.

She did her best to shake the feeling, reminding herself to breathe. She poured a cup of coffee and threw together enough of a breakfast to keep her from wanting to chew her arm off. The thought produced a melancholy smile. Hadn't she said the same thing to Quint not long after they'd met?

Grabbing her phone, she scrolled through their fake social media page. Bad idea. The two of them appeared so happy and in love. She had to admit, they were both good actors. If this law enforcement gig fell through, they could make money in Hollywood.

Ree scribbled down the name of the shelter in Austin along with its website, tucked the piece of paper in her apron after she dressed for work.

Quint must have gotten sucked in by Charley because he still wasn't home by the time she headed out for work. Granted, she left fifteen minutes early so as not to spend any more time alone in a room with Quint than absolutely necessary. If she'd had a fantasy, even for five minutes, that something special was happening between the two of them he'd quashed any hope last night with a sledgehammer when he'd brought up the fact it was a bad idea to date a coworker.

No one had to tell Ree twice not to go where she wasn't welcome.

Zoey was already at work. There was no sign of Adrian. Ree figured this was a good time to hand over the note. She walked into Zoey's station. Out of the corner of her eye, she could swear she saw the guy from the bar, the one in the flannel shirt. Phillip.

"Hey," Ree said to Zoey's back.

The young woman jumped.

"Sorry." She turned around. There was no amount of makeup in the world that could cover those red, puffy eyes.

"Everything okay?" Ree asked, taking Zoey's hand and discreetly placing the folded-up slip of paper in it.

"Yeah. Sure. I always look like this when I don't sleep," Zoey said, brushing off the seriousness of what seemed to be happening at home.

"Take a look later." Ree nodded toward the paper in Zoey's hand.

The young woman quickly tucked it inside her apron. "I don't want to get yelled at for talking, so…"

"Of course not." Ree turned and walked back to her station, praying the teen didn't just toss the paper in the trash.

Adrian blew in at the last minute, looking frazzled and upset.

"Everything okay?" Ree asked as the woman breezed past.

"Is it ever?" Adrian asked before pushing open the kitchen door. "I need coffee."

"That's not an answer," Ree said, following. "Seriously, are you doing all right?"

"I won't be if I get my butt fired," Adrian said, grabbing a coffee cup. "This job is how I keep a roof over my head and pay my babysitter."

"You have a kid?" Ree asked, realizing how little she knew about Adrian.

"Yes, but please don't tell anyone about him," she whispered. "He's a year old."

Adrian pulled her cell phone from her apron and tapped the screen. "Here he is."

"What a cutie," Ree said and meant it. Was Fender the father?

"Thanks. He is my heart." Adrian practically beamed as she tucked her cell inside her apron and fixed a cup of coffee.

"Do you want me to put your stuff in your locker?" Ree asked.

"Would you?" Adrian asked, handing over her handbag.

"Go to the bathroom and fix your hair before Charley sees you," Ree whispered. Then she held up the bag. "Do you need anything from in here?"

Adrian grabbed a comb and a travel-size bottle of hairspray before rushing out of the room. Ree listened for the sound of keystrokes coming from the office. Click. Click. Clack.

She walked over and knocked on the door before sticking her head in.

"Missed you this morning," she said to Quint.

"Class was canceled, so I decided to stick around and see what I could get done today," he said before stretching out his arms. He pushed to standing, leaned over and kissed her. The minute their lips touched, a familiar jolt of electricity rocketed through Ree.

"I might just stick around for lunch at this point," he said, a little breathless from the kiss.

"I'll see you later, then," Ree said. She rushed to put up Adrian's bag and hurry back to the floor. The doors had already opened, and Zoey waited on the first table as two men walked inside the restaurant. Bald Guy and Ruddy Complexion. Ree's heart hammered her ribs from the inside out.

"Welcome to Greenlight," she said, forcing a smile. "Table for two?"

Bald Guy nodded. There was something decidedly creepy about this man. She'd arrested some dark individuals. There was something truly evil in the eyes of the most hardened criminals. Bald Guy fit into that category more so than Ruddy Complexion.

Ree led them to one of her tables in the middle of the room. She turned around to Bald Guy, who was shaking his head. He motioned toward the bar area.

"Sorry, it's closed," she said.

Bald Guy shot a murderous look at her. He motioned toward the bar area again.

QUINT'S STOMACH GROWLED. He glanced at the clock. Lunch called. He powered down the computer, grabbed his coffee mug and headed to the dining room. He walked around to the counter and took a seat.

One look at Ree, and he knew something was up. She stood at a table talking to a couple, shifting her weight from left to right, and back. She nodded her head a little too enthusiastically. Something was off with her behavior.

He wished he could scan the dining room. This spot gave him a view to the kitchen.

Three cups of coffee kicked in and he had to use the bathroom. He opened the napkin in front of him and took out the knife and fork so someone would realize he was sitting there after setting his coffee cup down.

He took care of business and stood at the sink, washing his hands as the door opened. Bald Guy stepped inside, his gaze intent on Quint. His hand was inside his shirt.

Bald Guy pulled out a Glock, and then pointed the business end directly at Quint. There was a silencer on the end of it, which would keep the shot quiet. At this distance, Bald Guy couldn't miss. "You're a cop."

"No. What are going to do with all the blood?" Quint asked. "Have you thought about that? Because you should. This is a small room and I'm a bleeder."

The question seemed to catch Bald Guy off guard.

"Didn't consider that before you came in here and pulled that thing on me?" Quint goaded.

Bald Guy pulled a cloth bag out of his back pocket. He tossed it at Quint's chest.

"Put it over your head," the man said, his voice vaguely familiar.

"Where do I know you from?" Quint asked.

"Just do what I say," the man demanded.

This wasn't going well. If Quint recognized this person's voice, it was highly likely he'd been involved with another case. Did Bald Guy realize Quint was an agent?

This was bad. Quint took two seconds to evaluate his options. He could possibly fire off a kick in time to knock the weapon out of Bald Guy's hand. But his finger hovered over the trigger as it was, and he could pull it by accident. Of course, he could pull the trigger on purpose and that wouldn't bode well for Quint, either, at this range. The distance between where Quint stood and the door was too far for Quint to make a move.

Just when he was about to place the bag over his head, the door opened, slamming into Bald Guy's back. He threw an elbow to stop the person on the other side from opening the door all the way. But the moment of distraction gave Quint the window he needed. He fired off a roundhouse kick, connecting with Bald Guy's hand, which was knocked hard to the right. The weapon fired soon after Quint's left heel connected. The cold metal slammed against the opposite wall.

A momentary look of panic washed over Bald Guy's face, but he recovered. He lunged toward Quint. This guy had the size and speed of a linebacker going after a quarterback. Quint used it against the guy. As Bald Guy dove toward Quint, he grabbed two fistfuls of Bald Guy's shirt, dropped down on his back, and helped momentum toss Bald Guy into the wall, headfirst.

There was a concussion waiting to happen as Bald Guy's head snapped to one side and his neck took most of the impact. At the same time, the door opened.

"Quint," Ree said, rushing inside and closing the door behind her. She pulled out her cell and immediately called the situation in.

Bald Guy lay crumpled on the tile floor as Quint located the man's Glock and immediately emptied it. Quint patted the guy down to see if he had any other weapons. He didn't. Quint tucked the empty gun in the back of his waistband as he ushered Ree out the door.

Charley was running down the hallway toward them. "What happened?"

Chapter Twenty-Two

"A guy pulled out a gun and tried to shoot me while I was going to the bathroom," Quint said, making it seem like he was trying to catch his breath. "It's your 'associate' from the other morning."

Charley's eyes widened.

"I'm sorry. This is a business deal that's gone bad. I'll take care of it," he promised, waving his arms in the air.

"Take care of it?" Ree asked. She had one question. Was it possible their cover wasn't blown? "I called the sheriff. This guy needs to be arrested. He's dangerous and just tried to shoot my husband for no reason."

She turned her mouth sideways to Quint when she whispered, "He came in with Ruddy Complexion."

"I can handle this, Ree," Charley warned. "Get back in the kitchen."

Those words sliced through Ree with the efficiency of a blade. She stalked toward Charley. As soon as she came within reach, she poked her index finger in his chest.

"Don't you dare ever tell me to, 'get back in the kitchen' again," she practically growled.

"Stop," came the small voice. Zoey's voice.

She came around the corner.

"All this noise and yelling has run off all our customers," she said, her cheeks red with anger.

In the next moment, Ruddy Complexion grabbed her and started dragging her backward toward the front door. She screamed and flailed.

Ree stood there, helpless, flinching at the gun pointed at Zoey's temple.

"No, Willie," she screamed.

"Stop," Ree said.

"I told you not to look at me or say my real name in public," Willie admonished. "And I'll slit your throat before I go back to jail."

"Stop," Ree commanded in unison with Quint.

Charley took a step to the side, looking bewildered and like he couldn't begin to process things as they were happening so fast.

Quint bolted out the side door, setting off the fire alarm. Ree ran toward Zoey, realizing that she needed to create a diversion if Quint was going to succeed in surprising Willie.

QUINT KNEW EXACTLY where Willie was headed, the SUV. So Quint kept a low profile and beat Willie to it. Zoey was struggling, which was a distraction. Ultimately, Quint didn't believe Willie would physically hurt Zoey but he seemed to have no qualms about using her to get away.

But get away where?

The guy's days were numbered because his identity was now known. Then again, if he was involved with the money laundering scheme, he could be connected to a bigger organization that would send him underground for a while until everything cooled off.

Quint could not let Willie, aka Ruddy Complexion, get away with Zoey. Period.

Sirens sounded in the distance. The cavalry was on its way. And yet, if Willie got Zoey in that vehicle, there would be little to celebrate. Quint couldn't allow that to happen. He kept a low profile behind the SUV as Willie forced Zoey around to the driver's side.

"Don't do this, Willie," Ree demanded. Good, she was keeping Willie's attention on her. It would give Quint the element of surprise he needed.

Wait a few more seconds. Let Willie get a little closer.

Willie moved to the back seat, opened the door and started to stuff Zoey inside. Quint made his move. He dove toward the man, tackling him at his knees. Quint heard a snap, and seriously hoped the broken bone was on Willie's body and not Quint's.

He took a hard elbow to the back of the neck as he wrestled Willie to the ground. The glint of metal being raised in the air sent a jolt of adrenaline rocketing through Quint. All he could think was *hell, no.*

Quint spun like an alligator with prey in its jaws. Willie grunted as his extended hand met the gravel pavement. He managed to keep his fingers clasped around the weapon but he took some damage with the move.

Before Willie could get his bearings, Quint pressed his powerful thighs around the man's midsection, squeezing the air from his lungs.

Willie coughed and grunted, trying to shift the balance of power by gouging Quint in the back with his free hand. Quint squeezed harder. He threw a punch that landed with a head snap, and then went for the knife.

It was a mistake to be too eager. Willie managed to free his arm, and jabbed the knife toward Quint's midsection. Quint shifted his weight in time to miss the blade, catching Willie by the wrist.

Squeezing his thighs with every ounce of strength he had left, he wrestled the knife out of Willie's hand as the sheriff's SUV came roaring up. Willie's face was beet red. He made one final attempt to punch Quint, who caught Willie's other wrist and pushed his hands up over his head, easing up on the pressure to the man's midsection.

"Hands high where I can see 'em," the sheriff said.

"No can do, sir," Quint replied. "This man is a danger. You can come take him from me, but I will not release my grip until I know it's safe to do so."

The sheriff didn't lower his weapon as he moved toward the pair of men. He got close enough to cuff Willie despite the fact he struggled the entire time.

"You got him?" Quint asked the sheriff.

"That's affirmative," came the response.

Quint rolled over and let the sheriff take over. He forced Willie to his feet as Quint heaved for air. The back-to-back fights had left him winded. Ree came over to him, and dropped down beside him.

"There's a man in the restroom who tried to shoot me," Quint informed the sheriff. "He probably needs an ambulance."

Charley's cousin secured Willie in the back of his vehicle. Next, he radioed for an ambulance before disappearing into the building.

Zoey sat on the bench seat of the SUV, looking lost and alone. Quint caught Ree's attention. "You can go to her."

"But you're hurt," she said. "I don't want to leave you."

Quint tried to scoot over to lean his back on the SUV.

Two of the fingers on his right hand were jacked up at odd angles. His pointer and middle finger would be getting real close to each other in the coming weeks. And he planned to take some time off work after this case.

"Go on. I'm not going anywhere," he assured her.

Ree went to Zoey, who crumpled into Ree's arms. Ree glanced over at Quint as she patted Zoey's back and held her.

He made the call to let his boss know what had gone down. She in turn made the call to the sheriff personally. Ten minutes later, Charley came outside in handcuffs as a deputy arrived.

This operation was busted.

"Looks like it's moving day," Quint said to Ree as he loaded the last of his suitcases with his good hand.

"Are you sure you don't want to go to the ER to have that thing checked out properly?" she asked.

He lifted his right hand.

"What? This? The EMTs did a bang-up job," he said with a smile.

"Even he said you should go to the hospital," she countered.

"Don't worry about it," he said. "I have a guy back home. He'll fix me right up."

Ree moved to the fridge and opened a Coke.

"Is it weird that I'm sad to leave? We've only been here a few days," she said. "Why do I feel an attachment to this place?"

"I don't know. Cricket Creek has its good side," he offered.

A piece of him wished he was the reason, but that was just silly. They had separate lives to go back to, and despite the feeling they'd become closer than two people should who weren't wearing matching rings, they barely knew each other.

"Zoey agreed to go to Austin," Ree said. "She's on a bus now."

"That's good," he said.

"I'm thinking about doing a little research when I get home," she said.

"What kind?" he asked.

"Puppy adoption," she said. "It's probably crazy. Right?"

"I've heard of worse things," he said. "Just give yourself a day or two before you make any decisions."

"Heat of the moment?"

"It could be," he said. "Somehow, I doubt it with you but a decision as big as that one should breathe for a few days before you make any commitments."

She nodded.

"I thought I'd take it to Zoey when she got her own place. I'd like to stay in touch with her at the very least," she said.

"Good for you, and her," he said. "Having a mentor turned my life around."

"Your story gave me the inspiration," she admitted and his heart took a hit.

His cell buzzed as he closed up the suitcase. He fished it out and checked the screen.

"Grappell," he said to her before answering. "I'm putting you on speaker."

"Hi, Ree," Grappell said.

"Hey, yourself," Ree called out.

"I'm sure you'll have your wrap-up interviews soon but I thought you might want to know what I found out about the case," Grappell said.

"Fire away," Quint said.

"Turns out that Charley is already rolling over. Phillip Mancuso was the one forcing Charley to run weapons through the restaurant but he's been teeing up for greater things at Greenlight. He was getting pushback from Charley."

Quint perked up. "Any chance this guy is—"

"He is. I thought you'd want to know the name that came up and where this investigation is headed once things cool off," Grappell said.

"Can't be," Quint said as Ree's forehead creased with confusion.

"The name that is coming up as being linked in all this is Dumitru," Grappell supplied. "Phillip has ties to A-12."

Hearing that name sucked all the air out of the room. Quint's lips compressed into a frown.

"Is he…?" Ree seemed to catch on.

"Get me on the assignment when this thing happens," Quint demanded.

"It'll never happen," Grappell said. "We both know it."

"Nothing is set in stone," Quint stated. He needed to be the one to investigate the man who caused his best friend to die.

"This will be," Grappell said. "I just thought you should know."

Quint thanked him before ending the call. His mind was already working, figuring a way to get himself on the assignment.

"Can I give you a ride home?" Ree asked as she closed up her suitcase. She finished her Coke and then tossed the empty bottle in the trash.

"I have the motorcycle," he said.

"You can have it towed," she stated. "You can't ride

like that." She motioned toward his hand. "Besides, you have a suitcase."

"I can strap it on the back of my motorcycle like I did on the way here," he said. "Plus, the open air will clear my head."

Ree picked up her suitcase and walked to the door. She stopped, set it down and turned around. Her green eyes sparkled with a mix of need and determination as she made a beeline toward him and into his arms. Against all better judgment, he dipped his head down and claimed those full lips of hers one more time. She parted her lips enough to give him better access before teasing his tongue inside her mouth. Quint's heart fisted as need welled inside him with the force of a rogue wave, intense and all-consuming. He brought his hands up to cup her face as she dug her fingernails into his shoulders. Their breathing quickened and an ache formed in his chest. The need to feel her skin-to-skin crashed into him.

A reminder she wasn't his to explore nailed his gut. He pulled back midkiss before his heart passed the point of no return, and leaned his forehead against hers for a long moment. Trying to slow his pulse to something within reasonably normal range took all the energy he had left.

"I know you're going after him," she finally said before pressing those sweet lips of hers against his one more time. "Watch out for your blind spots."

Walking away from a successful assignment had never hollowed out his chest before. He did his level best to ignore the pain but the ache was taking hold.

"Give me a call if you ever want to go out for a beer sometime," she said, lingering at the door. Her tongue slicked across her bottom lip, leaving a silky trail—a trail he wanted to spend more time exploring.

"I plan to take you up on that." Quint took in a sharp breath and smiled, needing for her to leave before he changed his mind, got all soft and asked her to stick around.

She stood there for a long moment, staring down at her bag. Then she lifted her head up, bit down on her bottom lip and walked away.

* * * * *

COMING SOON!

We really hope you enjoyed reading this book.
If you're looking for more romance, be sure to
head to the shops when new books are
available on

Thursday 12th May

MILLS & BOON

THE HEART OF ROMANCE

A ROMANCE FOR EVERY READER

ODERN
Prepare to be swept off your feet by sophisticated, sexy and seductive heroes, in some of the world's most glamourous and romantic locations, where power and passion collide.

TORICAL
Escape with historical heroes from time gone by. Whether your passion is for wicked Regency Rakes, muscled Vikings or rugged Highlanders, awaken the romance of the past.

EDICAL
Set your pulse racing with dedicated, delectable doctors in the high-pressure world of medicine, where emotions run high and passion, comfort and love are the best medicine.

ue Love
Celebrate true love with tender stories of heartfelt romance, from the rush of falling in love to the joy a new baby can bring, and a focus on the emotional heart of a relationship.

Desire
Indulge in secrets and scandal, intense drama and plenty of sizzling hot action with powerful and passionate heroes who have it all: wealth, status, good looks…everything but the right woman.

ROES
Experience all the excitement of a gripping thriller, with an intense romance at its heart. Resourceful, true-to-life women and strong, fearless men face danger and desire - a killer combination!

To see which titles are coming soon, please visit

millsandboon.co.uk/nextmonth

LET'S TALK

Romance

For exclusive extracts, competitions
and special offers, find us online:

f facebook.com/millsandboon

🐦 @MillsandBoon

📷 @MillsandBoonUK

Get in touch on 01413 063232

For all the latest titles coming soon, visit
millsandboon.co.uk/nextmonth

MILLS & BOON
Desire

Indulge in secrets and scandal, intense drama and plenty of sizzling hot action with powerful and passionate heroes who have it all: wealth, status, good looks…everything but the right woman.

MILLS & BOON

MODERN

Power and Passion

Prepare to be swept off your feet by sophisticated, sexy and seductive heroes, in some of the world's most glamourous and romantic locations, where power and passion collide.

MILLS & BOON
MEDICAL
Pulse-Racing Passion

Set your pulse racing with dedicated, delectable doctors in the high-pressure world of medicine, where emotions run high and passion, comfort and love are the best medicine.